THE ENDING SERIES

BEFORE THE DAWN

LINDSEY POGUE   LINDSEY FAIRLEIGH

Before the Dawn
by Lindsey Fairleigh and Lindsey Pogue

Editing by Sarah Kolb-Williams
www.kolbwilliams.com

Cover Design by Deranged Doctor Designs

L2 Books
101 W American Canyon Rd. Ste. 508 – 262
American Canyon, CA 94503

978-1-949485-04-2

For Dani and Zoe, our poor, tormented heroines—we're sorry for all of the trouble we've caused you and all of the heartbreak we've forced you to endure. We truly couldn't have written this series without you...and we hope you're happy with how it ends.

NOVEMBER 1 AE

PROLOGUE
ANNA

NOVEMBER 23, 1AE

THE COLONY, COLORADO

Anna brushed her son's bangs off his forehead as he settled back in the reclining chair. She would have to trim his hair again soon; it was growing so fast now. "Just close your eyes," she said, ending the softly spoken words with an even softer sigh. She hated the pain Peter had to endure every day simply to stay alive, but such was the cost of a second chance at life. Such was the cost of being a Re-gen. "It'll be over soon."

John, the former coroner who'd been in charge of electrotherapy since the treatment's inception, turned away from the small switchboard controlling the electrical current flowing through Peter just enough to toss Anna a weak smile over his shoulder. "A word outside while his, uh, treatment is going?"

Anna clenched her jaw, closed her eyes, and took a deep breath. Despite his irritatingly hesitant and uncertain demeanor, Dr. John Maxwell was valuable. He was short in stature, shrewd of mind, and as far as Anna was concerned, more knowledgeable about the anatomy and physiology of the human brain than any other living person. She just had to remind herself of that sometimes. If she lost sight of that—of the help he, and as far as she knew, *only* he, could offer her son—she might "slip up" and remove him from her inner circle.

And nobody survived to talk about Anna's inner circle once their membership was revoked. Her life—her child's life—depended on absolute secrecy, and dead men couldn't talk. Unless they were brought back as Re-gens, but still...*they* had limited memories.

Anna shook her head, disgusted with the direction her thoughts had gone. She was thinking like Gregory, something that seemed to be happening to her more and more with each passing day. What would Tom, her first husband—her *true* husband—say if he could see her thoughts now? Nothing good, she imagined, and definitely nothing flattering.

Peter gave his mom's hand a squeeze, drawing her back to the here and now. The heavy glove Anna wore protected her from the worst of the electrical current humming through his body, but she still felt a slight buzz. "It's fine, Mom. Go with Dr. Maxwell." Peter offered her a slightly strained smile. "I'll live, promise."

Anna clenched her jaw harder, then forced herself to relax and release her son's hand. Standing, she removed the rubber-lined glove and tossed it on the wheely chair she'd just vacated. She paused at the door John was holding open and met her son's eyes. If it had been her in the chair, hosting an electrical current as strong as the one flowing through Peter, she would have been seizing, her brain sizzling and turning to relative mush.

But not Peter. Because Peter wasn't like her. Peter wasn't really like anyone...not anymore. How much longer could this go on? How many more experimental treatments could a sixteen-year-old boy's body endure? How much higher could they crank up the electrical current without it harming even someone like Peter?

Peter flashed Anna another tense smile, and her heart twisted.

How long did she have until Gregory lost patience with their son's stop-and-go—mostly stop—recovery?

Holding her breath, Anna left the room and shut the door. "What is it?" she said on her exhale. "You're very"—she scanned John from sneakered toes to balding head—"twitchy, today." Or, at least, twitchier than usual. "What's changed?"

John hunched his shoulders. "You know that Peter is...he's..."

Anna crossed her arms and raised her right eyebrow. "Peter is *what?*"

"He's, uh, different...fr—from the others, I mean." John scuffed his shoe against the linoleum floor. "Because of the chemo and radiation, not to mention all of the experim—treatments we've performed on him and..." He met Anna's eyes and blanched. "Which were very successful. Excellent ideas, all of them. Wouldn't have done any differently myself, had it been my kid who—"

"Cut the bullshit, John." Anna leaned in toward the pointy-featured man, planting a hand on the wall just behind him. He seemed to cringe into himself. There were *some* perks to being Gregory's wife, however unpleasant the drawbacks. It wasn't a fair trade, not even close. But it was something. "Tell me," she demanded gently.

John took a deep breath and held it for several seconds. "He— he's dying."

Anna shut her eyes. Breathed. Again. And again. When she reopened her eyes, she said, "I'm sorry." Deep breath. "I must have misheard you."

"The treatments aren't as effective as they used to be for Peter...and certainly not as effective as they are for the others." John wrung his hands. "The degeneration is progressing more quickly in him...not that it's not to be expected, considering that he's older in Re-gen terms than the few others left after the rebelli—"

John must've caught the dangerous glint in Anna's glare,

because he shrank back even further. "It's as though I can't target the parts of his mind that are breaking down, like his synapses are firing too intensely, um, burning themselves out before I can reset the connection. And the less effective the treatments become, well, the more quickly the degeneration will progress." Quickly, he added, "And I'm sure it's not just him, or at least it won't be. Soon, the others will reach the same point." He nodded frantically. "I'm certain of it."

Anna narrowed her eyes. "I don't care what you have to do. Find. A. Way. To. Save. Him." She eased away from the wall—and the terrified doctor—and carefully straightened her lab coat. Purposefully, Anna raised her gaze to lock on his. "Find a way, or you'll be of no further use to me." And there it was again, disgusting proof that Anna was, deep down, just like Gregory.

John blinked several times. A deer in headlights held nothing on him. "I—I'll see what I can come up with."

Anna nodded and bared her teeth in a self-disgusted smile. "You do that."

Quick footsteps drew Anna's attention to the stretch of hallway behind her, and she turned around to see Howard, one of Gregory's favorite lackeys, approaching. At least, he was one of Gregory's favorites amongst the lackeys he still had after the uprising, and one of the few who'd remained *by choice* in the chaos and instability that had followed. The Re-gens had exacted a high toll with their unexpected rebellion, and it was one her son paid for every day with his increasingly rapid descent into illness. She needed more Re-gens...more subjects to run her tests on...more scientists to brainstorm possible solutions.

She needed Gabriel McLaughlin.

John tipped the scales in terms of intelligence, but he was an inside-the-box thinker. Gabriel, on the other hand, somehow managed to turn scientific experimentation into an art, constantly redefining the concept of "the box" with his intellectual creativity. Where John was an unquestionably smart man, Gabriel was a true scientific savant. If anyone could find a solution to the degeneration plaguing the Re-gens, Gabriel could.

But Anna hadn't had so much as a glimpse of him in her dreams for months. Not that it was his fault. These were dangerous times in the Colony, and only when Anna was feeling exceptionally desperate or bold would she dare to let her guard down, just for a brief window, while she slept, hoping Gabriel might be trying to contact her in her dreams. It had yet to bear fruit. Each time Anna woke from such an attempt, she had only disappointment to warm her bed—disappointment and the megalomaniac who'd long ago claimed her as his property...as his "wife."

Howard stopped just a little too close to Anna. But she was used to his intimidation techniques. Keeping her feet firmly planted, Anna squared her shoulders and met Howard's eyes. "Did you want something?"

"General Herodson needs you." Howard held her gaze, challenged it. "Come with me." And without another word, he turned and strode back up the hallway.

Anna forced herself to unball her fists. After several slow, even breaths, she looked at John, who was still trembling against the wall. "What do you need to increase the effectiveness of the treatments?" She spoke the words low and rushed. Much as she might find pleasure in making Gregory wait, she knew the repercussions; the anger he would take out on her and the pleasure he would gain from her pain would be far from worth it.

"More Re-gens. More assistants." John paused, squinting. "A more intense electrical current."

Anna blew out a breath. "Alright," she said as she turned away from him to follow after Howard. "I'll see what I can do." Gregory would have to see reason, especially when that reason came in the form of releasing the interred rebel Re-gens into her custody so she could use them to hone the treatment process—and, if she and John were able to make enough progress, save Peter's life.

Her spark of hope dwindled when she realized Howard wasn't

LINDSEY POGUE & LINDSEY FAIRLEIGH

leading her to Gregory's office on the other side of the Colony, but to the underground holding cells two buildings away from the electrotherapy lab. Doubt sprouted in her chest, spreading like a noxious weed. Gregory had been keeping his distance from the makeshift prison and its ailing Re-gen occupants. She feared his presence there now could mean only one thing—he'd finally settled on their punishment for rebelling. And when Gregory came to a decision, he acted on it quickly and without mercy. It was one of his few qualities that Anna actually admired. Except for right now.

Anna had no doubt of the severity of the punishment the uncooperative Re-gens would suffer, had no doubt that she was walking toward a mass execution. And she had no doubt that by extinguishing the rebel Re-gens' second lives, Gregory would be all but killing their son.

✦

A livewire of tension and frustration, Anna descended the stairwell leading down to the long, underground hallway and its intermittent holding cells beneath one of the former college buildings. She couldn't allow Gregory to kill the few remaining Re-gens, not when she needed them so badly. Her mind was awhirl with thoughts…possibilities…logic…arguments…excuses…pleas… none of which would be good enough if Gregory's mind was already made up.

The first door on the right, a heavy, metal barrier set in the reinforced cement wall, stood ajar, and Anna could hear Gregory's disinterested voice floating through the doorway.

"—but some mistakes are just too great to make amends for, MT-01. I can no longer trust you. Your words are now meaningless to me."

Howard passed the doorway and took up a guard stance on the far side of the opening. Anna stopped opposite him and hung her

6

head. Now that she knew which Re-gen Gregory was addressing in the cell, she recognized the emotionless quality of his voice for what it really was—a mask to cover the betrayal he felt, to hide his utter heartbreak.

Mikey—MT-01, in Re-gen terms—had been Gregory's favorite. He'd been loyal to "the General" before his death and had trusted Gregory implicitly, to the point of volunteering for the Re-gen program when it was still in the experimental phase. He was the only Re-gen that Gregory didn't address using a Re-gen identifier. Or, rather, he had been...before the uprising.

And while Mikey hadn't actually participated in the rebellion —in the massive slaughter that had taken place during those few, terrifying minutes that the General's people had been immobilized by Camille's metal-controlling Ability—he'd admitted to knowing about it before it happened. How could he not have when the oracle and orchestrator of the rebellion, RV-01—Becca—had been the closest thing he'd had to a best friend?

"Pl—please, Father." Mikey was sobbing, the sound sloppy and gut-wrenching. It was rare for a Re-gen to feel intense emotions, let alone express what they were feeling, and it yanked on the tangled wad of stored-up heartbreak that Anna kept tightly wound inside herself. She couldn't imagine what it would take to summon such an intense emotional response in her own son. "I kn —knew you w—would be safe," Mikey said between gasping breaths. "I—I would have w—warned you if I thought you—"

His words cut off with the sound of flesh hitting flesh, but his sobs continued.

"There are few things I enjoy less than the bitter taste of disappointment," Gregory said quietly, "and I could count on one hand the number of times I've felt such intense disappointment as I do now."

"Pl—please, Father—"

There was another fleshy smack, closely followed by a wet

crunch that brought to mind a sickening image of the Re-gen's skull cracking against the cement wall.

"You were my favorite," Gregory said in the silence that hung in the absence of Mikey's sobs, thick to the point of choking. "I loved you like a son," he whispered.

Anna couldn't bring herself to step through the doorway, to enter the holding cell that she knew now contained only one living thing. At that moment, she refused to think of Gregory as a person —he was so much less.

Anna squeezed her eyes shut. Gregory truly had loved Mikey like a son; she knew it, had seen it with her own eyes. And he'd killed him anyway.

She just hoped he wouldn't inadvertently do the same to his actual flesh and blood.

I

ZOE

NOVEMBER 24, 1AE

THE FARM, CALIFORNIA

Hurrying through the mud and drizzle toward the stable proved detrimental to both staying clean and staying dry. Wet earth squished beneath each footstep, and I couldn't help but wonder why we hadn't moved our excess canning supplies out of the house sooner. Only a few steps from the sliding stable door, my right foot slipped in the mud, and it was all I could do not to face-plant in the muddy gravel with an armful of empty jars. "Shit," I mumbled, letting out my held breath in relief as I regained my balance.

"That's a bad word," Annie observed behind me. "We're not supposed to say bad words."

I glanced back to find her half lost in concentration with each careful step, her little red rain boots spattered with mud. Muddy boots were better than muddy clothes, which Dani had made me promise to keep clean. Sam only shook his head.

"I know, no bad words," I said, straining as I used my foot to slide the stable door open wide enough for the three of us to scramble through and out of the rain. "I'm sorry. I didn't mean to say it." With an oomph, I managed to push the door open, and Annie shuffled inside, Sam and me following behind her.

Although it was chilly inside the stable, it smelled of leather and hay, a pleasant surprise since many of the horses had opted to remain cooped up in their stalls most of the week.

"Why are we bringing the jars in here?" Annie asked, her tiny voice taut as she crept inside. I passed her in search of a place to store our armfuls.

"Over here," I said, using my chin to point at the table stacked with Vanessa's tattered and soiled clothes—the few items she'd allowed us to remove from her to be cleaned and mended. It was the table Chris and Carlos had put in Vanessa's makeshift room during their daily visits to the last stall on the left.

Hearing Annie grunt, I looked down at her and smiled. Each of her steps was strategic and determined as she drew closer to the table, holding the four jars she'd insisted on carrying, like boulders too big for her tiny arms. As always seemed to be the case when I was around cute little *crazy* Annie, my heart melted a little.

"Why are we putting them in here?" she asked again.

"Because," Sam grumbled, "we all have to eat inside again." He set his case of jars on top of mine. "We need the kitchen table for dinner tonight because of the stupid rain."

"It'll stop soon," I said, but I wasn't sure that was true. We'd been mostly indoors for a couple of days, and none of us were sure when the weather would let up or for how long the break would last once it came, not even Tavis.

"But why aren't we putting them in the shed," Annie rattled on, "with the jellies and the pickles and the—"

Sam cut her off. "We're just storing them in here until Jason and Grandpa Tom can fix the roof on the shed," he said, sounding bored. "They have to wait for the rain to stop again."

"Oh, Sam," I said, nudging him with my elbow. "It's just a little rain…okay, maybe a *lot* of rain. But it'll let up soon."

With a grunt, Annie finally stopped in front of the table, squeezing the jars so tightly I could hear glass grinding against glass. I held my breath, waiting for them to crash onto the hay-scattered cement floor but hoping they wouldn't. Vanessa was chatting happily away to herself in her stall, and I didn't want to send her into a spiraling fit.

Naturally, Sam reached out to help Annie unload her jars, but she turned away from him, her wild blonde hair bouncing despite its damp tendrils. "I can do it," she said primly.

Sam's palms flew up, and he stepped away from Annie's accusatory glare. "Sorry."

Carefully, Annie placed one jar on the table, her brow furrowed in concentration. She set down another. "They're all wet and slippery," she grumbled, smearing a water drop on one with her fingertip.

"That's what happens when it's raining," Sam retorted, ever the older brother he'd seemed to become. "I told you I'd carry them." Although Sam often feigned annoyance with Annie, I knew she amused him, and like with the rest of us, she often made him smile despite his grumpy mood. She was contagious that way.

With a derisive sound, Annie scrunched her face. "I don't like the rain anymore," she said, sounding like Sam, but I knew it wasn't necessarily true. Annie didn't like that she had to stay indoors when it rained, but she thoroughly enjoyed the overabundance of puddles that popped up all over the property. More mud meant more fun, at least where Annie was concerned.

Wishing I'd been in less of a hurry and grabbed my jacket, I ignored the visible puff of breath I exhaled as my fingertips felt for the small cubes protruding from my back pocket.

"Tavis should make the rain go away," Annie said, adamant as she placed the last canning jar expertly on the table. She grinned, triumphant.

"Tavis can't send the rain away just because we don't like it, Annie," I tried to explain.

She looked at Sam, scrunched up her face again, then looked at me. Her bright blue eyes narrowed, but she listened without argument.

"Don't you like curling up on the couch, reading your animal stories with Mr. Grayson?" Despite how much Annie groaned about having to stay indoors, I knew she loved story time almost as much as she enjoyed romping around with Cooper and Jack in the dirt. And Mr. Grayson, *old* Bodega Bay's infamous history teacher and captivating orator—or Daniel, as some called him—was the best man for the job.

Annie huffed, an exaggerated, impatient sound. "Yeah, but—"

"But what? We need the water in the wells and to fill the pond, munchkin. And we need it for our winter garden," I explained. As if on cue, the encroaching storm above us worsened. Raindrops fell harder, echoing on the stable roof, and a gale of wind made the structure shudder and groan.

Shadow stirred in his stall a few doors down, and when Annie noticed my hand was in my back pocket, she grinned from ear to ear.

"I thought we weren't supposed to give sugar to the horses," Sam said wryly. Though he was going for disapproving, I knew he enjoyed our clandestine snack times with the horses as much as I did.

I brought my index finger to my lips. "Dani just said in moderation." I walked over to Shadow, deciding he might like the company since he was cooped up indoors like the rest of us. Little pattering feet followed, and Annie giggled.

When Shadow's head bobbed up and he anxiously approached the opened stall window, my grin widened. He looked like an oversized mountain pony with his shaggy, onyx coat, longer from the cool winter weather, and his unruly mane.

"Hey, boy," I said softly as he stuck his head through the

window. Shadow's eyes were opened wide and bright, and I knew that meant he was growing anxious and ready for exercise. "Sorry, buddy, not today." A notion suddenly dawned on me. I looked back at Annie. "He's going to roll in the mud the first chance he gets, isn't he?"

She simply giggled.

"I knew it." Patting the side of his face, I put one of the sugar cubes out on my flattened palm for Shadow's greedy lips to find and gave the rest to Sam and Annie. "It'll be our little secret." I winked and pointed toward the other stalls. "Just be careful of the last one," I said. Annie and Sam both looked at Vanessa's stall. They nodded, familiar with the drill.

Unfazed to have a Crazy living in our stable—one who'd "cared" for Annie to the best of her mentally unstable ability before Dani had stumbled across them back in Tahoe—Annie giggled and pranced from stall to stall as she and Sam visited each of the horses. Just as they were finishing petting Brutus, Sam squinted beyond me, toward the tack room. I knew that look.

I glanced behind me and saw nothing, though I wasn't surprised. I'd grown used to Sam hearing things the rest of us couldn't.

"Kitty!" Annie sang, then she trotted past me to the corner of the stable, where one of the three two-month-old kittens meowed to life and stretched in the doorway of the tack room.

All of us smiled, unable to resist the brown kitten's sweet mewing while she traipsed toward us in want of attention; her brown fur, blue eyes, and bobbed, fluffy tail looked like—to Annie at least—the Mr. Potato Head doll Ky had given her right before *the incident*. "Ky liked Mr. Potato Head, and he would've liked this name," Annie had said when she'd named the little kitten Miss Potato. No one had argued with the determined little fireball, even if it was a painful memory. It didn't matter that Jason had been forced to shoot his best friend in self-defense, to *kill* Ky—the

Monitor the General had placed on him. It was a day we all wished we could forget.

"She's getting bigger," Sam said, smiling as he watched Miss Potato spastically frolicking and squeaking as she played in the straw.

Unlike Sam and Annie, my mind was shadowed by darker times. Thinking of Ky made my heart ache, then burn with guilt and regret as my thoughts jumped to memories of Sarah's suicide. I thought about Biggs and the twins, whom we hadn't seen in almost six months. They were all gone because of me, because of the tangled, messy web of lies my life consisted of.

Annie giggled and gently stroked Miss Potato's tawny belly as the kitten flopped and played at her feet.

"Where are the others?" Sam asked, peering back at the tack room, the cats' secluded safe haven during our coastal storm.

"Bubbles is coming," Annie explained. "But Doodle is getting a bath."

With hands in his front pockets, Sam leaned back on his heels and let out a deep exhale, one that exuded incredulity, like he might never be able to completely wrap his mind around Dani and Annie's animal-speaking Abilities.

"Look who I found crying outside the door," Tavis said, striding into the barn. His dirty blond hair was matted, and water dripped from his nose as he held out a nearly drowned, squeaky black kitten.

"Bubbles!" Annie exclaimed.

Sam chuffed. "I thought you said she was inside?"

Annie ran over to Tavis and the drenched kitten. "No, I said she was coming."

"What was she doing outside?" I asked. I made my way over to Tavis and the kitten. "She could've gotten washed away."

Annie greedily snatched Bubbles from Tavis's hold. He grinned at me and stepped aside to let Annie fawn all over the kitten. "She was exploring, and then it started raining," Annie explained. "She got scared."

"Well, I'm glad Tavis found her then," I said, and crouched down to pet the matted black mess.

I saw a flicker of something in Tavis's mind, a memory of the past that sent a wave of longing through him—not lustful longing, but something lonelier. He glanced at me.

"Zoe," Annie said.

I looked down to find her holding Bubbles close to her chest.

She glanced from the crying kitten to me, a mischievous look on her face. "Your hair is the same as Bubble's is." She smiled widely, a gaping hole where her right front tooth would've been.

"Yeah?" I eyed the kitten's soggy black fur, dabbled with streaks of white and gray. "I hope not *exactly* like hers," I muttered.

I barely heard Sam's amused grunt over the sound of the dinner triangle clanking and ringing outside. Annie jumped up, startling the kittens when she shouted, "Food!"

"I'm going to eat it all before you get there," Tavis taunted with a wink in my direction, then he rushed back out into the rain, egging Annie on in their daily bout of catch-me-if-you-can.

"You better hurry," I goaded her, "or there'll be nothing left for dinner!" With peals of laughter, Annie handed me the kitten and ran out into the rain, toward the farmhouse. "Stay out of the puddles!" I called after them, hoping the amusement in my voice didn't drown out my authoritative tone completely.

I set Bubbles and Miss Potato back in the tack room with Mama and Doodle, then stalked toward the slightly opened stable door, anxious to get out of the cold and back into the warm house.

The moment I stepped outside, rain pelted me mercilessly, or at least it felt that way as it soaked what seemed like every inch of me. Quickly I pulled the sliding door shut, squinting through wet lashes toward the house. Apparently my authoritative tone needed some work, because, as I'd expected, Annie seized every opportunity to jump in the puddles on her way to the porch. Tavis smiled at me, winked, and ushered the kids inside, and all I could do was hope that Dani didn't kill me when she saw how muddy Annie had gotten, despite my best efforts.

After latching the stable door shut, I jogged toward the house. Heavy, quick footsteps squished behind me, and I couldn't help the knowing grin that parted my lips. It was Jake. We were connected on so many levels now; I could sense his presence and his mind better than anyone else's. He was no longer the mystery he'd once been, with walls and armor that kept him distant and apprehensive. Now, he was the warmth to my cold, the strong to my weak. He was the second half of me I had never realized was missing until I'd known what it felt like to lose him—to lose *myself* and become someone who had no memories at all. At least Gabe, genius that he was, was able to help me get my mind back, the memories that made me *me*.

"Evening stroll?" Jake asked as he jogged up beside me, squinting into the rain. He lifted part of his flannel jacket to shield me from the downpour.

"Yeah, it's been such a beautiful day." I wrapped my arm around his waist, and together we hurried to the shelter of the porch. His heat steadied my cold, trembling bones. He'd become a protective cocoon; I would never grow tired of the warmth and vitality he exuded, always making me feel loved…making me feel safe. With him, I could lose my inhibitions and my fears and, on my favorite occasions, let loose my desires.

"What are *you* doing out here?" I asked, letting go of him when we reached the porch steps. The wood creaked beneath our urgent footsteps. I stared down at my dirt-splattered jeans and mud-caked boots. "Shit." Using the edge of the step, I tried to scrape the chunks of mud off the bottom of my right boot. I could picture Annie now, running around the house and rolling all over the furniture, covered in far more mud than I was.

"I was checking the leaks in the shed," Jake said as he shook out his hair. "The tarp's holding well enough for now." A gust of wind picked up, and I shivered. As I scraped the mud from the bottom of my other boot, Jake shrugged off his jacket.

Laughter, dishes clanking, and amiable chatter emanated from inside as everyone no doubt gathered around the dinner table, just as we'd done most nights since the winter weather had worsened. It was a tight fit to have all fifteen of us together—seventeen when Mase and Camille were around, visiting us from the Re-gen homesteads in Hope Valley—but we made it work. We were growing used to it. In the darkening gloom, I could make out bustling silhouettes illuminated behind the thin, drawn curtains.

"Not that meteorologists were right very often," I said, "but it would be nice to know when the rain is coming and how long it's planning to stay. A little preparation time would be appreciated."

"Are you sure the storm wasn't summoned?" Jake muttered.

I ran my fingers through my damp hair, the shorter strands no longer a shock as they'd grown out a little. "What?" I precariously wiped the water from under my eyes. "Why?" I momentarily opened my mind up to his, wondering his meaning and hoping to catch a glimpse, but then he glanced down at my chest, my gaze following his, and I didn't need to know what he was thinking; it was written clearly on his face.

Jake handed me his jacket. The front of my white, long-sleeved shirt was wet, leaving to the imagination only what was hidden behind my peach-colored bra.

I glowered at him as I donned his jacket, my head tilted in a silent scold for insinuating that Tavis had brought the rain. "I'm pretty sure he had nothing to do with it," I said dryly.

Jake's left eyebrow rose, mirroring my expression, and his mouth quirked at the corner. "Lucky me then," he said. He stepped closer, and although I'd planned on a reproachful response, the intensity of the base desire that burned somewhere deep in my belly whenever he was around, prevented the chiding remarks from forming on my tongue.

"I think this is the first time I've gotten you alone all week," he said, his voice quiet while his mind swirled with tantalizing thoughts that made me forget about cold and hunger and our waiting friends inside the house. He wrapped his arms around me, his heat enveloping me, and he pulled me into him. Chills raked through me, making me shiver with pure anticipation.

"What about this morning?" I whispered, vaguely remembering the feel of his lips on my temple when he woke me before the sun was even awake. My eyelids flitted closed as his lips softly brushed against mine. I couldn't remember the last time we'd been together. Everything had been so crazy, and we'd been so exhausted, it had become a rarity when we were able to lie in bed and lose ourselves in each other's arms.

Despite the plip-plop of rain on the porch awning and the cacophony of voices inside, I began to give in to my desperation to be alone with him. *Just for a little while.* His hands were rough but gentle, his lips firm but pliant against mine. His stubble tickled and teased my mouth and cheeks, the sensitive nerve endings tingling to life. A small moan escaped me as his arms tightened around my waist.

"Zo," Dani's voice whispered in my mind. *"Your dad just asked me where you are. Please don't make me tell him you're making out with Jake on the porch...assuming he doesn't already know."*

With a groan, I leaned my forehead against Jake's shoulder. "We'd better get inside," I said and let out a thwarted breath. "Apparently they're waiting for us."

Reticent, I pulled away from him and opened my eyes to find Jake's silhouette washed in a crimson haze. I blinked a few times, encouraging the desirous fog to dissipate, until I could finally refocus. I grinned. He was staring at me with lust-filled eyes, and images of us, upstairs together...alone...filled his mind.

Anxious for what was to come later, I leaned in for a final, promise-filled kiss and entwined my fingers with his before leading him into the house to join the others.

⬡

My bedroom was bright and open, the sunshine pouring through the window illuminating my toy-cluttered floor. Hunger rumbled inside my belly. Setting my doll down on my princess comforter, I climbed off my bed, humming as my tummy rumbled again.

Tugging down the hem of my sundress, I walked into the hall and plodded down the stairs on little legs, heading for the kitchen. The carpet tickled the bottoms of my bare feet, making me smile. I didn't hear the usual clanking of pots and pans that I usually did whenever Daddy was in the kitchen.

"Daddy?" I stopped in the kitchen doorway, expecting to find him fumbling around inside. But he wasn't there. Still humming, I turned and walked into the living room. He wasn't in his recliner in front of the television either. "Daddy?" I wondered if he'd gone to pick up Jason. Fear flittered through me, and I wondered if Daddy left me home all alone.

Then I heard angry voices coming from the back porch.

Noticing that the sliding glass door was slightly open, I walked over and peered outside. My humming ceased, and I froze. Daddy was standing on the porch with a pretty woman. Her hair was long and black, like mine. Her face was pink, and she rushed around like she was scared or upset.

Suddenly, I was standing outside with them. The woman was staring at me and looked like she might cry as she reached for me. "Come here, Zoe," she said.

I tried not to flinch away from her touch, but I couldn't help it. Scared and confused, I looked up at Daddy. He looked sad, too.

"You look so pretty in your dress," the woman said. She tried to smile, and I found myself hesitantly smiling back at her. I liked her eyes. They were special and seemed familiar.

"I knew you'd come back here," a man said. I jumped when I heard his voice, but the woman didn't seem surprised. Her hands flew to her stomach, and I wondered if she was hurt.

I blinked, and then the man was standing next to me, like he appeared out of nowhere. He had a mustache and a smile that didn't seem happy.

Daddy looked angry and afraid. Something didn't feel right, and I wanted to disappear.

"They didn't know I was coming here, Gregory," the woman started to say. "I just needed to—"

But the man with the mustache held up the palm of his hand. "Shhh," he said, staring only at me. I wasn't sure why I felt scared, but I was trying not to cry. "Look how big you've grown," he said and crouched down before me. He smiled a big smile, his slightly crooked teeth evoking a sudden panic that made my throat tighten. "And you're beautiful, just like your mommy." He looked back at the woman gripping the patio table. Her eyes were shimmering, and I noticed her holding Daddy's arm tightly with her other hand, like she was holding him back.

"Don't you dare touch her," Daddy said, and the smile on the man's face fell a little. I saw something in his eyes that unleashed the tears I'd been trying not to shed. Something bad was happening, I could feel it.

"Daddy..." I began to sob. But it wasn't Daddy who picked me up, it was the scary man.

"There, there, little Zoe. It's okay." He patted my leg and smiled at Daddy and the woman. They said something to him, but I was too stunned to listen. For the first time, I noticed men lining the fence of our backyard. They appeared out of nowhere, like the scary man had. There were a lot of them, but only a few had big guns. Their faces were mad and mean.

I cried louder. I wished Jason was home.

"I told you what would happen if you ever left, Anna. Did you think I was bluffing? That I wouldn't notice...again?"

Through a veil of tears, I peered back over at Daddy and the woman. Daddy was frowning, angrier than I'd ever seen him. I called for him again, but the man's grip on me tightened. I shrieked in pain.

"I will kill your son if you hurt her," the woman growled, and she pointed to her tummy. "I will end your legacy."

The man's fingers dug into my leg, and I hit at his hand without thought, trying to get him to let me go. When he finally set me back on the ground, I ran to Daddy.

"You will not harm them, Gregory. Or I won't hesitate to kill this child. I promise you that." *I stared at her belly. I didn't see a baby, but her tummy was big.*

"You won't kill an innocent child, Anna," the man said. "Me, on the other hand..." *He stared at me again and smiled.* "And then there's the boy, too."

"You leave him out of this!" *Daddy shouted, and I could feel his body shaking.*

The scary man's face hardened, and I noticed his body stiffen. "Watch yourself, Sergeant. My compassion only goes so far."

The woman pulled a needle like they used at the doctor's office from behind her. It was the kind that always poked my skin and pinched me, but just for a minute. "So help me God, Gregory. If you hurt my family, I will kill yours."

The scary man looked at all of us, and his voice was angrier than before. "Then there's not much of a reason for me to keep any of you around, is there?"

"I'll come back with you," *the woman said, reaching for him.* "If you'll just leave my family alone."

The man pounded his fist on the patio table. "I'm *your* family!"

"Not if you hurt them," *she said. The woman looked angry, but she still sounded scared.*

Daddy bent down to me. "Go inside, sweetheart." *He leaned in*

21

*for a hug and whispered, "Hide. Until I can make it go
away...hide."*

*I nodded, not understanding what he meant, but wanting to
hide all the same.*

*I didn't know why the scary man wanted to hurt us. I didn't
understand why the woman wanted to kill the baby I couldn't see
either. But I knew the man with the mustache was evil, and I was
afraid that if I looked away, Daddy would be gone, and I would
never see him again.*

*The scary man shook his head. "I thought we agreed last time
that your family was as good as dead if you ever came back. Yet
here you are, again." He clenched his fist. "I trusted you. I thought
your word was worth your freedom. Apparently I was wrong."*

*The sad woman took a step toward him. "I was just scared,
Gregory," she said, rubbing her belly. "You don't understand how
dangerous this is for me. I just needed to see them, needed to say
goodbye." She wiped the tears from her eyes. She didn't look
scared anymore. "I promise, once I leave, I will never come back."*

*The scary man's eyes narrowed, and he glanced from her
swollen cheeks down to her belly. "You have one more chance,
darling. If you even try to leave again, if you do anything to under-
mine me and my mission, or our family..." He glared over at me.*

"Go inside, Zoe!" Daddy yelled.

*I ran toward the house, but stopped inside the door and
listened, waiting. I didn't want to leave Daddy.*

*"Regardless of what you do in the future, measures will be
taken now," the scary man said, and when I peeked around the
doorframe, the woman looked relieved. "Monitors, in fact. And if
you do misstep, even in the most minimal way, I will hurt your children and make Tom, here, watch, and you might never even know
it. That, my dear, is my promise to you."*

*When my eyes met Daddy's, wide and sad, everything suddenly
faded away. I was in my room, crying in his arms. His familiar
eyes were empty as he stared at me. Gently, he brushed a tear from*

my cheek, and then everything changed again. The memory of the scary man faded away. Then the sad woman started to change. Her special eyes disappeared, her features vanishing one by one until she was faceless and frightening...until she was completely gone, too.

There were no men in the backyard, and Daddy wasn't upset. There was no reason I could think of for why I'd been crying or why Daddy would look so sad.

2

DANI

NOVEMBER 25, 1AE

THE FARM, CALIFORNIA

With a grunt, I adjusted my hold on the box I was carrying and attempted to reach for the doorknob on the cottage's front door. The glassware in the box, an amalgam of random glasses, mugs, vases, and bowls I'd collected from the massive—and dusty—storage room in the barn, shifted and clanked in warning.

"Crap," I hissed. *"Jason?"* I called telepathically. Having my Ability firing on all cylinders was useful in so many ways, not the least of which was being able to request aid from pretty much anyone, anywhere, at any time. *"Come get the door?"*

"Give me a second." He was inside the cottage, in what was slowly transforming into our bedroom in the back corner of the small house. I could sense his mind signature there. Stationary. Not rushing toward the door to let me in.

I pressed my lips together and exhaled with a huff. Clearly, being able to request help telepathically and receiving said help were two entirely different matters.

Gritting my teeth, I raised my right leg and used my thigh to shift my increasingly precarious hold on the box once more. It certainly didn't help that the cardboard was damp from the drizzling rain or that, thanks to the chill in the air, I could barely feel my fingers. At least the porch's shallow eave protected me from getting rained on further. *"Unless you want a mountain of broken glass on the stoop, it'd be great if you could come get the door now..."*

I could sense Jason's movement instantaneously, and seconds later, the door swung open and he plucked a box that had been just shy of way too heavy out of my arms with annoying ease. I flexed my fingers, cringing at the uncomfortable mixture of numbness and sharp, stinging pain.

"You shouldn't have tried to carry this in the first place." Jason gave me a reproachful look—eyebrows raised, chiseled jaw flexed, jagged scar intensifying *everything* about him—before turning and heading through the cozy living room with the box. He set it on the single free corner of the rustic farm table that separated the "kitchen" from the rest of the living area. We'd found the table in the storage room—which, in all reality, put most old attics to shame with all the treasures it contained—and had relocated it to the cottage almost a week ago, during our last "moving day."

Days off were rare on our little communal farm, and Jason and I had been setting up the cottage to be our small family's own comfy, compact, and moderately private home for over a month now. I was more than ready to move out of the farmhouse and settle in here with Jason and Annie and my beloved German shepherd, Jack. To have my own space...to not always be stepping on the toes of every other living person I knew...to make a home with Jason...

I sighed, and after scanning the combined living room and kitchen and beautiful river-stone hearth, after taking in the columns of boxes and piles of clutter that still needed to be moved out, arranged, or put away, I felt my shoulders slump. It looked like I wouldn't be settling in to my little piece of domestic paradise on this rainy November day. *Maybe next week...*

"Red." Jason planted himself in front of me and rested his work-roughened hands on my shoulders. "Look at me."

Unable to resist an order from him, especially one delivered in such a low, silky rumble, I raised my gaze to his and fell in love with him just a little bit more. His sapphire eyes were filled with such warmth, such light and heat and wonder, that I couldn't help but lose myself in them. Lose myself to him.

"What did I tell you last night?" he asked, face placid.

My cheeks flushed and my whole body heated as I remembered things whispered in the cover of darkness. Secret things. Things I was almost certain I couldn't repeat while it was daylight or while I was staring into his eyes...or *ever*. "Um..." I drew my bottom lip between my teeth and lowered my eyes and blushed even more. "Well..."

Jason chuckled, his thumbs tracing the underside of my jaw. "While I think it's pretty fucking fantastic that your mind went *there* automatically, I was actually talking about the promise I made about moving. Into the cottage. Today..."

"Oh!" My eyes flashed up to his, and I smiled shyly. My face and neck were still on fire.

"Unless you're planning on spending the rest of the day digging around in that room"—his focus shifted to my hair, and he pulled a clumpy cobweb from my ponytail's unruly curls—"we'll have plenty of time to finish up in here."

I assessed the chaotic space once again and puckered my lips, attempting to imagine everything arranged just so. And failed. "But—"

"The bedrooms are all that really matter, anyway." Jason shrugged a shoulder and looked down the short hallway to both ours and Annie's future bedrooms. "And those are done."

Narrowing my eyes, I scrutinized Jason's face. He hadn't shaved today—not yesterday, either, I'd have wagered—and the slightly unkempt cowboy look made his already minimally expressive features harder to read. "What do you mean 'they're done'?" I tilted my head to the side. I hadn't been in either bedroom for days, having spent all of my time working around the farm and most of the morning "shopping" in the storage room in the barn. "Annie's room still needs furniture, especially a bed, and—"

Jason shook his head. "She doesn't want a bed; you know that."

I frowned. "She's just a kid. Don't you think she needs—"

"Yeah, she's a kid, and about as unusual as they get."

It was my turn to shake my head. "But still...she needs a bed, Jason. Where's she going to sleep—er, drift?" My voice rose in pitch. "With us?"

Again, Jason chuckled. "No way in hell. At night, you belong to me and *only* me."

A splash of my earlier flush returned. "So...?"

Jason smiled, just a little. "Becca's been helping her set up her room." Almost on cue, Annie's pure, crystalline giggle came from her bedroom.

Capturing my hand, Jason led me into the short hallway and toward Annie's room. Another peal of laughter came from within before he opened the door, swinging it inward with a creak.

Jason glanced at the door, then back at me, and mumbled, "I'll have to fix that."

My gaze was pulled away from his and into the bedroom. In the dim late morning light coming in through the room's two small windows, the space resembled a forest clearing as much as a bedroom—a cozy forest clearing, but a forest clearing nonetheless. All four walls were covered with painted trees, some a dark, ashy brown and others fading to smoky gray in the "distance," but each wall was vastly different, as each represented one of the four seasons. There were silhouetted animals in the shrubbery painted near the floor and birds resting on branches here and there.

"What—*how*?" Eyes wide, I stepped into the room and turned

in a slow circle, taking in everything. A rough-hewn wooden chest and matching dresser—both looking almost as though they'd simply grown into their current shape—had been placed against one wall. In one corner, what I could only identify as a nest of pillows and blankets spilled out, filling nearly half of the room. I pointed to the furniture, then to the walls and the nest. "How'd this —I don't understand."

Annie giggled, finally drawing my attention to where she sat with Becca and Jack, nestled in her bed-nest-thing and lazily scratching the dog's side. She threw herself onto her back and pointed to the ceiling.

I held my breath. I'd yet to look up. And when I did, I exhaled a long, slow, "Whoa…" The moon, larger than life and surrounded by a choir of stars, practically glowed overhead.

"Did—did Zo do this?" I couldn't imagine how she could have; she was easily as busy as me with farm work. Everyone was.

Standing behind me, Jason wrapped his arms around my shoulders and pulled me flush against him. His body heat practically seared through my cool, damp clothing. I hadn't realized how deeply the chill had settled in from being out in the barn all morning with only a hooded sweatshirt for warmth.

Slowly, Becca stood and brushed off the front of her jeans. After a moment, she looked at me. "It was not only Zoe," she said in that careful way of hers, her voice as raspy as ever. "I helped her paint the room. She wished to surprise you by doing something special to make your home as perfect as possible, but she didn't have the time to do it all herself."

Eyebrows raised, I stared at Becca. "Zo…and you?"

She clasped her hands together in front of herself and nodded demurely. "My brother tells me I was an artist of a sort, similar to Zoe, but different in that I preferred three-dimensional art. Though I do find the act of painting quite soothing." I frowned as she glanced around at the walls. I hadn't realized she'd been an artist, too. "Zoe is an excellent teacher, wouldn't you say?"

I blew out my breath, once again taking in the masterful work she and Zoe had done. "Yeah. You guys did an amazing job." I looked at her. "It's beautiful." Glancing from her to Annie and back, I gave her a warm smile. "Thank you for doing this."

Becca nodded, eyes downcast, and walked to the dresser. Placing her hand on the surface, she returned my smile. "This and the chest were Tom's work."

I blinked several times, then turned around in Jason's arms. "Your dad made them? But when?"

"He—" Jason took a deep breath, and tension filled him. "His intentions were good, and he swears he only altered perception around him a few times to keep it a surprise for us."

I felt some of Jason's tension seep into me. After everything that had happened at the Colony, I *really* hated the idea of someone —anyone—messing with my mind. Again.

"He showed me the pieces once he was finished making them." Jason paused for a moment. "We got into a big fu—" Catching himself, he glanced at Annie, then returned his focus to me. "A big argument. He won't admit it, but I think it's hard for him to just live—not changing what those around him perceive to fit his needs. He's been doing it for so long now that it's become second nature."

"Still...I don't like it, Jason." I gave him a meaningful look. *"I don't want anyone messing with my mind."*

A low grunt hummed in Jason's throat. *"I know."* He gave my shoulder a gentle squeeze. *"He wasn't fully aware of what the General did to you, but he knows now. He really just wanted to surprise us, that's all, and he's taking every precaution to make sure he doesn't slip back into old habits. It won't happen again."*

Awash with relief, I smiled. *"Well, that's something."* Forcing the smile to remain, I approached the dresser and examined the odd combination of gnarled and elegant decorations carved into its surfaces. "Well, kiddo?" I peeked back at Annie, who was still staring up at the painted moon. "What do you think of your new bedroom?"

Annie flung her arms out akimbo and sighed dramatically. "I love it *so* much. It's the best bedroom ever!"

I grinned at her. "Like, *ever* ever?"

She nodded enthusiastically. "*Ever* ever." Abruptly, she sat up and stared at me, her face serious and her blonde curls a wild tangle. "But I like yours, too."

"You do?" Curious, I turned around to look at Jason. His face was a mask of bland innocence. "You've been busy." As I considered all that had been accomplished right under my nose—without me suspecting a thing—I realized just how much time and effort I'd been putting into working around the farm. Maybe a smidge too much...

Jason stuck his hands into his jeans pockets and shrugged.

I crossed the room to him and smacked him on the arm. "I don't like it when you keep secrets from me," I said with mock severity.

The faintest smirk touched Jason's lips. "But you like my surprises."

"Yeah, but—"

"You can't have it both ways, Red."

I tried to keep my face stern, but I couldn't hold back my eager grin. "Grams used to say that surprises always leave behind a trail of secrets; good or bad, if you look hard enough, you'll find 'em." My grin faded along with the fond memory, but when I once again focused on Jason's face, it returned at full force. "Well, are you going to show me, or what?"

Jason laughed, low and soft, and turned toward the doorway. Annie was up and running before I'd taken my first step to follow. Somehow, the lithe little sprite managed to make it through the doorway before Jason. I watched him follow her out.

"You love him very much," Becca said from right behind me.

I yelped and spun around, my hand pressed against my chest in a vain attempt to slow my suddenly racing heart. "Jesus, Becca. You startled me."

"I'm sorry," she said, her voice barely more than a whisper. Her eyes, however, shone with a feverish intensity. They'd changed since Carlos had started administering electrotherapy on her, as had the eyes of the other Re-gens; they were no longer that dull gray I'd come to expect of their kind, but hers a violet-gray that was somehow both eerie and entrancing. The returning vibrancy to the Re-gens' eyes seemed to mirror their reemerging personalities and emotions, as though their eyes really were windows to their souls.

Quietly, Becca asked, "What is it like to be in love?"

Taking a step backward, I frowned. "Um…it's great. Why?"

"You and Jason love each other very much." She took a step toward me, her focus intent on my face. "But doesn't it scare you?"

I shook my head, taking another step backward. Sometimes Re-gens could be funny with how they treated personal boundaries —or ignored them. "I don't understand."

Becca took a deep breath, and I had the impression she was struggling with how to voice her thoughts. "It makes you happy, that is obvious, but…if one of you was suddenly gone, the other would be devastated. Love like that seems like a terrible gamble, and I just wanted to know if it's worth it."

Unease took root in my stomach. Was Becca curious because she was interested in someone romantically, or was this something else…something more? "Is it worth what, exactly?"

She licked her lips. Her eyes were haunted, but intent on me. "The pain it causes. The potential for unimaginable loss. The possibility that one day it might be gone. There's something…" She shook her head. "I just need to know if the good balances the bad. I need to know if love is worth the fear and the pain." She swallowed roughly. "Even with my visions, tomorrow is never certain. I just need to know if it's worth it."

Unease was quickly morphing into dread…anxiety. This

strange, totally out-of-the-blue behavior was exactly why I never felt completely comfortable around Becca. She was different from the other Re-gens in that she could see the future, or snippets of it, and she was different from the only other person I knew who had a similar Ability—Harper—because she didn't possess a lifetime's worth of practice interacting with people and delivering life-changing, potentially devastating news. It made her really hard to relate to and all but impossible to understand, at least for me.

But part of me could understand her question. We were living in pretty damn uncertain times, even for one with the Ability to see some of what was to come. Whatever she'd seen in her murky view of the future, whatever she'd felt, it seemed to me that she needed reassurance that there was something worth living for, something worth fighting for, something worth hanging onto, no matter what.

"Yeah," I said roughly. "I think it's worth it." Shaking my head, I amended my answer. "It *is* worth it. I mean, just look at Jason and Zo's mom—she's torn the world apart because she loved them too much to let them go. If that's not evidence proving that love is more valuable than almost anything else, I don't know what is."

Slowly, Becca's entire demeanor changed and she was, once again, the slightly withdrawn, awkward Re-gen just trying to find her place in the world. "Thank you for that…for being so honest." Her gaze sank to the floor. "Sometimes it's hard to relate. Sometimes we feel so strongly, like you, but other times it seems more like a memory of a feeling. I just needed to know."

I cleared my throat. "Sure." I wanted to know if she was telling the whole truth. I wanted to know if her questions about love were rooted in a deeper motivation, if they stemmed from some secret vision she'd seen. I wanted to know—and I *never* wanted to find out. Flashing Becca a pathetic excuse for a smile, I added, "Any time."

Annie was suddenly in the room, skipping circles around us. "Dani! Dani! Dani! Dani! Dani! Dan—"

"Alright, little one," Becca said, expertly capturing Annie's tiny arm and stopping her whirlwind progress around us. I was always amazed with her ability to handle my adopted wild child with such ease. "Let's give Dani and Jason some time to explore their new bedroom." Meeting my eyes briefly, she winked.

I gaped at her as she led Annie out of the room. *Becca winked at me? Becca* could *wink?* Moments later, I heard the sound of the front door opening and shutting.

"Red," Jason called from the room opposite Annie's.

Bewildered, I made my way down the short hallway, past the compact bathroom, and through the doorway into our bedroom. I felt like a zombie, as if Becca and her odder-than-usual behavior and our unsettling conversation had drained the life out of me. Until I actually saw the bedroom—Jason's and my bedroom. My mouth fell open.

The bed appeared to be made of repurposed wood, and it was absolutely stunning. But I'd known about it, as well as the matching armoire, dresser, and simple bedside tables. What I hadn't known about was the quilt Jason must have snuck onto the farm after a visit to Grams's house just outside New Bodega's walls. It was the quilt from Grams's guest room, made up of interlocking circles of blues and purples, and though it really was a beautiful quilt, it was the fact that Grams had made it that tugged at my heartstrings.

"Oh, Jason..." I stepped into the bedroom and ran my fingertips over the quilt. Having it in the room made the space smell like Grams's house in the subtlest ways, hinting at candle wax and at herbs used daily to make teas and tinctures.

Tears welled in my eyes, and without thinking, I turned and flung myself into Jason's arms. My mouth sought his, my hands tugging at his clothes to bring him closer to me. And for a little while, I forgot about the knot of anxiety spooling inside me. For a little while, I let Jason remind me why love—our love—was worth it.

I hummed to myself as Jack and I strolled out to the stable to gather the horses' evening snack. They received plenty of sustenance from grazing out in our abundant pastures, but I still enjoyed the special spike of pleasure they felt when they took a nibble of an apple or a carrot from my hand.

"I already told you, talk to Mase or Becca," I heard Carlos say, his voice raised. "If you've got a problem with their system, take it up with them." His voice was filled with frustration, or maybe with exasperation, and when I rounded the corner of the stable and caught my first glimpse of him through the open door, I wasn't surprised by his tense, almost aggressive stance. He was facing two male Re-gens, one shorter and plumper than him, the other taller and thinner.

I recognized them both as residents of the farm just north of ours. With the Re-gens and the Tahoe folks now residing in our little valley, we'd managed to get two more farms up and running and were putting the physical structures of another two through renovations while we began to cultivate the adjacent land. Our short string of self-sufficient homesteads had come to be known as Hope Valley among our people as well as among the residents of New Bodega, and with each passing week, it seemed more and more likely that our hopes for a better, safer, and more stable future would become a reality.

I didn't know the two Re-gens' names, but they'd both seemed kindly enough the previous times I'd crossed paths with them. Now, not so much; now, they were demonstrating just how much the regular electrotherapy sessions had expanded their emotional ranges. The tall one was pointing his finger at Carlos's chest, nearly poking him, and the short one had his fists clenched and held at his sides and was practically vibrating with pent-up aggression.

"Everything okay, guys?" I asked as I approached.

Jack, who'd been walking at my side, trotted forward a few paces, hackles raised and lips retracted. He considered Carlos a part of his pack, and he was more than ready to fight for the teen if and when necessary.

Carlos swatted the taller Re-gen's hand away. "Yeah. They were just leaving." He turned his back to the Re-gens and retreated further into the stable, no doubt heading for his sister's stall at the end.

The Re-gens stared after him but didn't follow.

"You should go," I said as I passed them. When they still showed no signs of leaving, I asked Jack to gently—and none-too-gently, if the kinder approach failed—escort them away.

A slight smile touched my lips as I listened to his warning growls and the snap of his teeth clacking together as he nipped at his temporary charges. When I heard the approaching click-clack-click of dog claws on cement, I peeked over my shoulder. The Re-gens were gone, and Jack was returning to me.

"Thanks, Sweet Boy."

He wagged his tail happily and let out a single yip.

Ahead, Carlos stood before the sliding door to his sister's stall, his forehead resting against the barred-off window, his hands gripping two of the bars tightly. I stopped a few feet away and crossed my arms over my chest. Jack, however, continued forward, sitting as close to Carlos as was physically possible without actually sitting on his feet. Inside the stall, Vanessa, Carlos's eighteen-year-old sister and our resident Crazy, was experiencing a blessed—and rare—moment of quiet.

"So…what was that all about?" I asked.

Carlos exhaled heavily. "They were here because Jimmy, Dan, and Lawrence—" Seeing my blank stare, he clarified, "They're Re-gen sparklers, but they're not as good as me at electrotherapy." I knew *sparklers* was his slang for people who could handle electricity like he could.

I coughed a laugh. "So humble…"

35

Carlos shrugged with minimal effort. "It's true. They're not as good at controlling the currents. And they're weaker…and that makes the electrotherapy they give weaker. Maybe in time, after they've strengthened their own Abilities by electrotherapizing the shit out of each other, they'll be way better than me, but now…?" Again, he shrugged.

"So what? You're like name-brand electrotherapy and the others are knockoffs?" I glanced back up the empty stable aisle. "And not everybody's getting Carlos-brand electrotherapy, are they?" I stuck out my bottom lip, just a little.

Carlos turned his head to look at me, his temple resting against one of the metal bars. "Yeah, and Mase and Becca and Camille have been really cutting down on who I work on—just them and the other sparklers, mostly. Everyone else gets one session with me per month."

I was undeniably grateful to Mase, Camille, and Becca for their innate ability to more or less rule over the other Re-gens, as well as for their foresight where Carlos was concerned. Six months ago, when the Re-gens first arrived en masse, seeking our help to stave off their slow death by degeneration, Carlos had tried to help everyone, which had led to overexertion in less than a day and a period of burnout that had lasted for three full days. And when his Ability came back online, had Mase, Camille, and Becca not stepped up and reined in the Re-gen horde, they'd have begged and whined and pleaded and bullied Carlos into doing it all over again.

"It's raining…it's pourrrrring," Vanessa sang from within her stall. "The old man is snorrrrrring."

I eyed the shadows through the bars, uncomfortably grateful that I couldn't see Carlos's sister in the dimness. The intermittent rain and cloud cover was making all hours of daylight feel like dusk.

"He went to bed," Vanessa continued, "and bumped his head and couldn't get up in the morrrrrning."

I shivered, and without a word, Carlos slipped his leather coat off and tucked it around my shoulders. "You know, soon it'll be too cold for her to stay out here all the time," Carlos said, and I didn't need Zoe's Ability to know that having his sister locked up because she was a danger to herself and others was killing him inside.

We'd loaded Vanessa's space with all sorts of blankets, but without the electric heat the stable had been designed with, I knew he was right. We all did. What we didn't know was what the hell to do with her. Could we get by with letting her stay in the house, simply keeping a guard on her day and night? It was a thought...

"It's raining...it's pourrrrring." Vanessa's voice was growing shriller with each word.

"We'll figure something out," I told Carlos, giving him a side hug.

"The brother thief is snorrrrring..."

I exchanged a look with Carlos. *Brother thief* was Vanessa's name for me, we both knew it. We also both knew that whatever was going to come next in her revised version of the old song wouldn't be overly pleasant.

"You should go," Carlos said quickly.

"You'll go to bed," Vanessa sang. "Rosie'll bash in your head, and you won't ever get up *again*!"

I shivered, and this time it had nothing to do with the damp cold. Deep down, I hoped we never let her out of that stall again.

3

ANNA

NOVEMBER 25, 1AE

THE COLONY, COLORADO

Anna tapped the nail of her index finger on her desk in a quick staccato while John rifled through the papers in the folder on his lap. He was an undeniably brilliant man, but Anna found that such people were usually lacking in some other fairly essential area. In John's case, it was organizational skills. And social skills. And common sense.

"I know it's here." Carefully, he began to skim each sheet of paper before setting it on the floor beside his chair. "I was just looking at it in my office." He glanced up at Anna, his eyes sliding down from her face to her tapping finger, and froze. "Do—do you want me to come back later…when I've found the results?"

Straightening in her chair, Anna clasped her hands together and set them on her lap. "No, John. What I want is for you to get your head out of your ass."

She watched the high-strung man blanch and regretted her words instantly. She needed him, and he wasn't the kind of scientist who thrived under extreme pressure. No, Dr. John Maxwell required careful handling and ideal working conditions. He was almost more trouble than he was worth. Almost.

Anna sighed heavily and allowed herself a long, slow blink. "I'm sorry. That was uncalled for. I know you're doing everything you can for Peter and the others. I just..." Another sigh slipped out of her, sounding far too resigned. "Can you summarize your findings and share the actual details later?"

"Yes!" John bobbed his head enthusiastically. "Yes, of course!" He scooted forward on his chair, the folder held tightly in his hands. "I've examined the bodies of all of the Re-gens General Herodson executed and, well, as it turns out, he might have inadvertently given us the key to stopping degeneration once and for all, reversing the effects even." The thick file folder trembled in his grasp.

Anna licked her lips and leaned forward, her chest rising and falling at an increased rate to match her suddenly racing heartbeat. "Go on..." She placed her hands palm down on the surface of her desk.

John scooted forward in the chair a little more. Any further and he might find himself sitting on the floor with a bruised tailbone. "By having one of the electricity handlers carry out the executions, General Herodson was essentially conducting an informal study on what the *direct* application of that kind of electricity—human-derived electricity—does to a Re-gen's body. And when I examined the bodies of the Re-gens executed yesterday, most signs of degeneration in the neural tissue were gone. Poof." He clapped his hands together and made a fluttering motion as he pulled them apart. "Degeneration, be gone."

Anna couldn't help her look of astonishment. "This was true for all of them?"

"All thirty-eight," John said with a nod.

"And you're absolutely certain of the cause of their miraculous recoveries?"

"Ill-fated," John mumbled, "but I guess you could call their 'recoveries' miraculous."

Anna narrowed her eyes, refusing to let her hopes rise too high. "I see, well..." She was once again tapping her fingernail on the desk, this time in anticipation. "Start trials immediately. Pick the two strongest and most skilled electricity handlers, and use the seven Re-gens Gregory pardoned yesterday as your initial subjects, then work your way through the loyalists." She paused her tap-tap-tapping, then resumed it noticeably faster. "The order doesn't matter, so long as Peter is last." Another pause. "And bring me the results before you try the new treatment on him."

John started gathering the loose papers and documents off the floor, practically bubbling with anticipation. "I'll need an executive order from General Herodson to appropriate some of the electricity handlers for the day. There are so few now..."

Anna nodded once, rolled her chair back, and stood. "Done. I'm on my way to a meeting with him right now. You'll have what you need by midmorning." She rounded the desk and retrieved her knee-length down parka from a hook on the wall beside the door. As she donned her winter armor, she turned around to give John a few final instructions. "If anyone gives you grief for borrowing their assigned Re-gens for the day, tell them they'll be receiving a visit from both Gregory and me. And make it very clear that the visit won't be a pleasant one."

Gloves in hand, Anna opened the door and ushered John out into the hallway. Once she was finally outside in the below-freezing air, she allowed herself a brief moment of relief. Peter's recovery was hardly a sure thing at this point, but his prospects had never looked this good.

She tamped down on her hopeful excitement, pulled her gloves onto her hands, and started off toward the headquarters building at a brisk pace, not wanting to spend a second more than necessary out in the cold. She'd always hated winter.

"You're certain that it's him?" Gregory was up and pacing, and when Gregory was pacing, everyone was on edge.

Sean, Gregory's official spymaster and one of the Colony's two remaining dreamwalkers after Gabriel's flight, nodded. Despite Gabriel being the stronger dreamwalker and flat-out more capable man, Sean had been Gregory's spymaster for nearly a decade, long before Gabriel was even aware of Abilities.

For about the millionth time, Anna missed the young scientist. He was a pain and a flirt, but he was also one of the kindest, most caring people she'd had the pleasure to work with in the Colony. Sean, on the other hand, was a shrewd man of few scruples—a perfect fit for his devious position.

"One of my agents spotted him in the market at New Bodega," Sean explained. "Apparently he's been posing as a trader of rare and luxury goods, including pharmaceuticals."

"How fitting," Gregory said dryly. "So, the elusive Dr. Cole Michaels isn't dead after all." He moved to stand behind his chair and gripped the top rail so tightly that the color drained from his nail beds. "This is unwelcome news, my friends, unwelcome news indeed. What of his twisted companion? Was news of Mandy's demise at Lake Tahoe as inaccurate as the reports of Cole's supposed death?"

It had been an unexpectedly happy day for Anna, as well as for Gregory, when the reports of the dynamic duo's supposedly gory ending had come in, first from Danielle during her short stay, then from others as they looked into the issue. Ever since Cole and Mandy had broken free from Gregory's leash over a decade ago, they'd been thorns in both Anna's and Gregory's sides—dangerous, unpredictable, power-hungry, slippery thorns. And no matter how hard Gregory's people had tried, the combination of Mandy's Ability to inspire unbreakable adoration and Cole's mind control had made it all but impossible to eliminate them.

For years, Anna had felt like she was holding her breath, waiting for Cole and Mandy to discover that Gregory's main leverage over Anna was her family. And she'd had no doubt that the duo would take swift, permanent action to shred Anna's collar and release Gregory's most powerful ally…by killing her children. Anna was, after all, Gregory's main power source, boosting the strength of his Ability a hundredfold, maybe more. Without her strengthening him, Cole and Mandy would have been free to swoop in, dethrone Gregory, and take over the Colony.

And though Gregory was far from an ideal leader, at least he had an inkling of good intentions, an honest desire to make the future better—of course, his version of "better" didn't quite match up with most other people's. Cole, on the other hand, the master-mind who'd twisted what had once been a sweet, innocent young woman into an undeniable monster to function as *his* main ally, was pure, power-hungry evil. He'd pulled Mandy's strings. He'd turned her into the sadistic cult leader she'd become. The people in the Colony deserved better than Gregory, Anna had no doubt of that, but Cole was far, far worse.

And according to Sean, who was almost always right, Cole was in New Bodega, just a handful of miles from Anna's children.

Anna was suddenly so parched she doubted she would be able to speak. She blinked in surprise when someone set a full glass of water on the conference table in front of her, and she couldn't hold in her grateful smile when she glanced up to find Gregory standing behind her. "Thanks," she said, clearing her throat and raising the glass to her lips. She took several hasty sips, then set the glass back down, gripping the glass more tightly. She feared that if she let it go, her hands would be shaking visibly.

"Give us a moment," Gregory said to the others. "I need to speak to my wife." It wasn't an order he gave often, but when he did, nobody ever argued. The room was cleared in a matter of seconds. "Darling…" Gregory pulled out the chair beside hers and sat. "I know how much this news must be troubling you." He gently removed the glass from her hands and gathered them in his cool, firm grip. "Having him so close to your other children…"

Anna's entire body stiffened. She hadn't known that Gregory knew where Jason and Zoe were, not until now. His last Monitor on Zoe had imploded, and from the few communications she'd received from Gabriel after they first settled on their farm—before Gabriel had gone radio silent, which she could only assume was Jason's doing—she'd believed they were safe.

"I may have lost my Monitors, but I've got Sean keeping an eye on them. They make frequent trips to New Bodega." Gregory's grip on her hands tightened painfully, a physical reminder of the punishment she'd received for contacting her other children and triggering the Monitors in the first place. "We'll make sure that no harm comes to them, not from Cole."

Anna was very conscious of Gregory's wording. No harm would come to Jason or Zoe *from Cole*; it was very clear that if harm did come to them, it would be coming from Gregory himself.

"I—" Anna had to clear her throat. "Thank you, Gregory." Her voice was laden with emotion, mainly fear—fear of Cole, and fear of Gregory. "It—it means so much to me that you're looking out for them," she lied. "Truly."

Gregory smiled his double-edged smile. "Always."

4

ZOE

NOVEMBER 27, 1AE

THE FARM, CALIFORNIA

With each side kick, right hook, and jab I landed on Sanchez during our sparring practice, confidence began to overshadow concentration. And for each of Sanchez's strikes that I deflected, my thoughts flitted further and further away to possibilities I wasn't sure I should explore—possibilities that seemed to swarm around one single question: had my disturbing dream been *only* a dream?

After a few days, the dream about my dad and Dr. Wesley—who I sometimes considered my mom, depending on how I was feeling about her—and the General still haunted me. Not just in darkness, when I closed my eyes, but when I watched Jason going about his chores and tasks around the farm, and I wondered if his mind housed veiled shadows of our past. And when I saw my dad, I felt a slight sting of betrayal, though I wasn't sure it was warranted.

It could all have been a dream. Despite the numerous times I'd repeated that to myself, I had a niggling feeling that it wasn't true, it hadn't been *just* a dream. True, it was just one of many bizarre dreams my mind had conjured over the years, but unlike the others, this dream had actually felt real. It hadn't been a nightmare I'd awakened from, shuddering at the memory of the featureless woman whose hands were too bony and whose voice alone could summon pure terror in my sleep. No, this dream had left behind a sinking heap of dread, a sadness and confusion that felt all too real.

Sanchez's foot collided with my stomach, knocking the wind out of me as I flew backward. Although I used my hands to temper the fall, I rolled and cracked the back of my head against the semi-soft ground.

"Shit," I breathed and squeezed my eyes shut. "*That's* going to ruin my day." I tried to catch my breath, blinking a few times in hopes that the ringing and flashing circles behind my eyes would cease. I tried to focus on the farmhouse standing almost teasingly on the other side of the lawn, wavering in and out of focus.

Sanchez crouched above me, her dark eyes and tanned skin cast in shadows against the midmorning sun, radiant above her. "You okay?" she asked, her voice equally skeptical and concerned.

I nodded, feeling the cool damp earth beneath me as I tried to lift myself up, and I instantly regretted it. "Just hit my head harder than I would've liked."

Sanchez proffered her hand as I struggled to sit up.

My head throbbed, making it difficult for me to focus as I reached for her hand. With one determined tug, she pulled me up onto unsteady feet, holding onto me while I reacquainted myself with the world standing upright. "Let's get you to Harper. You might have a concussion."

I rubbed the base of my skull, and with a derisive noise, I moved to brush myself off, slowly to prevent the spinning world from whirling even faster. As the light dancing around Sanchez—a warm brown sugar that made me think of oatmeal—began to fade, I was certain a concussion was exactly what I had.

"Where the hell is your head today, Zoe? It's like you're on autopilot or something."

I tucked a few dark strands of hair behind my ears and let out a recuperative breath. I wasn't in a chatting mood, so I shrugged. "Somewhere else, I guess."

"Yeah? No shit." Sanchez uncapped a thermos of water and handed it to me. "Drink."

Accepting it, I gave her a sheepish grin. "Thanks." The water was cool and refreshing in my parched mouth, so I took a few sips more before I handed the thermos back to her.

"Let's get you looked at," she said, and slowly but surely we made our way into the farmhouse from the overgrown grassy patch beside it. "Harper's probably out in the herb garden with Dani and Grayson," I realized, but Sanchez was already shaking her head.

"Maybe, but he'll be here soon," she said. "I told him you probably have a concussion."

Telepathy, one-sided or not, had proven very handy living on such a sprawling piece of property. I felt bad having Harper rush to the house, especially knowing that I did, in fact, have a concussion and that there was little he could do for me at this point. But if the way Sanchez was eyeing me was any indication of the sort of mood she was in, I wasn't going to argue with her.

"You're making that angry face again," I told her, groaning as we stepped up onto the porch.

"That's because you're being weird," she said flatly. I could always rely on Sanchez to get right to the point. The screen door slammed shut behind us, making my head pound, and I was unable to suppress a cringe as we headed for the stairs. "The last couple of days, you've seemed confused or something."

I grunted. "You could say that." Confused was an adequate word. Had the damn dream been simply that—a dream—or was it a memory? Had the General actually been at my house, in my backyard? Had he really held me in his arms and threatened my life? These were all questions fighting for space in my mind, but the most trumping of all were: *where*, if it was a memory, had it been hiding all this time, and *why* was it resurfacing now?

Although she was clearly curious, Sanchez didn't hound me for more information. She helped me up the stairs, into the master bedroom–turned–infirmary. "The ibuprofen is in the cabinet to your left," I said and climbed up onto the exam bed. I'd spent way too much time working in this room over the past several months. I knew where everything was.

At first I'd helped Harper reorganize and reappropriate things: two tall dressers had been moved together and served as our supply drawers, Jason had made cupboards to fit on top of them to house our most frequented items, and we'd exchanged the queen-sized bed for one of the twins in another room; once it was lifted on cinderblocks, it served as a perfect exam bed for moments like this. But there were other things I knew about too, like where Harper stored our most crucial medications I inventoried on a monthly basis and where he stashed the lollipops to give to Annie when she was a good little patient.

Harper strode into the room as Sanchez opened the cabinet, a wink preceding his serious doctor face when he took in my rumpled appearance. "Get the shit kicked out of you today, Baby Girl?"

"You could say that," I grumbled, accepting the three pills Sanchez placed in the palm of my hand. She uncapped the thermos again, offering me water to wash them down. "Thanks," I murmured and swallowed the pills without a second thought. I was all for the incessant knocking in my head quieting as soon as possible.

"Well," Sanchez said, handing me the cap to the thermos. "I think I've done all the damage I can do for one day." She smirked at me. "I'm sure there's something more productive for me to be doing." She shook her head when she noticed her muddy boot print on the front of my shirt. "Sorry about that, Zoe. Let me know when you're feeling better—I want a rematch. Distraction is a technicality, not a fair win." With a nod, Sanchez headed out the door. "I'll be in that tiny excuse for an armory with Tavis if you need me." The sound of her quick, heavy footsteps down the stairs was all that was left in her wake.

"Rumor *had* it you were turning into a force to be reckoned with on the sparring field. What happened out there today?" Harper teased, shaking his head before leaning forward to shine his god-awful penlight into my retinas.

"I really hate that thing," I muttered, causing Harper's smile to widen.

"You know the drill, Baby Girl," he said, and I trained my gaze on the light that blinded me, like I'd done almost daily during the weeks when my memory had been all but wiped.

"Since we know I have a concussion already," I started, "can't we skip the bright-ass light and call it good?"

Harper chuckled. "Sure. Let me clean up those cuts on your hands, and I'll get some ice for your head."

I glanced down at the abrasions on my palms. I hadn't noticed them at first, but the longer I sat there, the more the raw flesh began to sting. "Wow, I'm more pathetic than I thought."

Again, Harper laughed. "You think this is pathetic? Have you already forgotten what your fighting looked like nine months ago?"

I glared at him. "That's rude."

Harper only winked at me. "You're *supposed* to get the snot kicked out of you every once in a while, Baby Girl. That's how you learn." He walked over to the gauze drawer I'd refilled the day before and pulled out two large, square bandages for my palms. "I'm going to clean and dress your palms for today, but tonight, when you go to bed, take the bandages off so they can breathe."

"Doctor's orders?" I asked, taking in the white coat he rarely wore anymore.

"Damn straight." In true Harper fashion, his eyebrows danced and another generous smile brightened his face. "I figured if I wore my cowboy hat you wouldn't take me seriously."

I laughed. "No, I don't think I could."

He lifted the thermos Sanchez had left for me. "Drink more water and take more anti-inflammatories throughout the day," he recommended. He set the thermos down beside me, then he headed back over to the counter. "If Sanchez's side kick is as spot-on as I remember, you're going to be sore tomorrow...and probably the day after that." Using an antiseptic pad, he cleaned the scrapes on my palm. "I want you to take it easy for a while, but no sleeping, Baby Girl. You do have a little bit of a concussion."

"I know," I droned and let out a deep breath. It wasn't the first time Sanchez—or anyone, for that matter—had kicked my ass during training.

Harper offered me a sympathetic grin as he opened one of the bandage packages. "I remember a time when you couldn't even lift your own body weight, and all you knew how to do was knee a guy in the groin. And even that was a pathetic attempt."

I flashed him an over-the-top grin. "Aww, you know how to make a girl feel so much better, H. You're too sweet."

Harper's head fell back with a burst of laughter. "I know. What can I say?" And with a steadying breath, he adhered a bandage onto one palm and then the other.

We sat in amicable silence until the heavy clomping of boots up the staircase alerted us that someone was coming. It was Jason; I could tell by the nonexistent mind pattern.

"Heard you got your ass kicked," he said from behind me. The bed creaked as I partially turned to face the doorway. A hint of a smile reflected in his jewel-blue eyes, though his expression was his usual stark somberness that rarely gave anything away.

I shook my head. "I'm so happy everyone knows already. It's only been, what..." I peered down at my naked wrist. "Ten minutes?"

"Sanchez is only trying to rile you up for her rematch, Baby

Girl," Harper said as he sauntered into the master bath. I could hear the water splashing around as he washed his hands in the large washing bowl.

"Oh," I said blandly, "I know, and it's working."

Jason stepped into the room, a grin tugging at the corner of his mouth.

"I'll get you some ice," Harper said as he exited the bathroom. "Be right back." Then he disappeared down the stairs.

Jason stepped up in front of me, scrutinizing the mess that was me. He pulled a twig out of my disheveled hair and deposited it in the trash bin behind him. "So, what happened?"

Although Jason had been more of a brother to me in the past six months than he'd been all of my life combined, I knew he wasn't checking on me because I lost a sparring match. I rubbed the back of my head and stared down at the hardwood floor. "Why, what did Sanchez tell you?"

He sat on the edge of the bed beside me, his arms crossed over his chest. "That you've been distracted the last few days. And according to Jake"—I looked up at him—"you've been having nightmares again. What's going on with you?" Jason's gaze didn't waver like it sometimes did. This time, his scrutinizing eyes were fixed on me, determined and waiting.

I'd considered telling Jason and my dad about my dream many times over the past few days, but every time I told myself it couldn't hurt for them to know, I remembered all the reasons why it would. "I've been dreaming about Mom and Dad. And the General…at our house, when I was little."

Jason's jaw clenched, but his eyes gave nothing away. He remained quiet.

"And I'm starting to think it's not a dream, but a memory."

This time his façade weakened, and his eyes narrowed minutely. "Why do you say that?"

I shrugged and stared down at the bandage on my left palm, picking at the corner of the adhesive with my index finger.

"Because it feels real, like I was actually there—a scared little girl being threatened by the General so Mom would go back to the Colony with him." In Jason's silence, I peered up at him. The brilliance of his eyes darkened and his body tensed. But I continued, "She was pregnant in the dream, with Peter, I'm assuming." I tried to pinpoint why it felt so real. "The General said he'd put Monitors on us to make sure she didn't try to leave him again." Jason simply blinked, and I internally squirmed in his silence. "I wasn't sure I should tell you, in case it was nothing more than a dream."

"But you think it's something more."

I stared up at the ceiling and groaned, "I don't know."

With a heavy sigh, Jason rubbed the side of his face. "I'm not sure that makes sense, Zoe. If you were little..." He shook his head, and I could tell he was running through the timeline of events, just like I had done over and over again. "You saw Sarah's memories. She was a teenager—maybe a little older—when he brainwashed her. If he'd turned her when you were a kid, she would've been as old as you in her memories, just a kid." Jason looked at me. "If that's what he was talking about, that wouldn't make any sense."

I let my shoulders drop. "*Unless* she wasn't my first Monitor... But I don't know. That's why I haven't asked Dad about it. I don't want to bring up all of this, making things harder on him—on *us*— if it's just my brain making shit up. Because you know my brain, always, well..." I thought about all of my dreams, all similar in a lot of ways, but still filled with made-up shit.

We were both quiet. I didn't pry into Jason's mind; I was too lost in thoughts of our parents and how fucked up the whole situation was.

Jason finally looked at me. "What else?"

I shrugged. "What do you mean?"

"There's obviously more that's bugging you, Zoe. What are you thinking?"

Since Jason asked, I decided regurgitating all I'd pondered over the past few days was better than holding it all in. "Well, if Sarah *was* my first Monitor, the General could've had a reason to wait to put Monitors on us until we got older, or waited for the next phase of the Virus when he thought Mom might risk coming back for us again." The ideas kept flowing, and my hand gestures could barely keep up. "Or maybe he was too busy having a son of his own to worry much about us after he got her back. I'm sure he knows she'd never leave Peter, she made that very clear." Brushing a clump of mud from Sanchez's footprint off my shirt, I tried to think like the General, but it was futile. "Who the hell knows why he did any of it."

Then I remembered the strangest part of the dream. "There's also the part where the dream starts to go backward and disintegrates until I can't remember why I was so upset."

Jason's brow furrowed, and he crossed his arms over his chest again. He didn't need to bark at me to continue; I did so willingly.

"I went from jumping forward through the dream—or memory, or whatever we're calling it—chronologically, to moving backward, and then Dad said he'd make it go away."

I watched as a play of emotions shadowed Jason's eyes and hardened his features before his gaze shifted from the floor back to me. "You think he altered your memories?"

I leaned forward, my elbows braced on my knees as I rubbed my temples, exasperated and confused. "He could have."

Jason nudged me, stirring my attention back to him. "You've had some pretty fucked-up dreams, Zoe. And now that we know about the Monitors, it makes sense you'd dream about them."

"Yeah, nightmares of a faceless woman trying to communicate with me. Said faceless woman who was actually *Mom*. It's like I really saw who she was this time, like it's starting to make sense. In my dream this time, she went from her to faceless to"—I shrugged and shook my head—"to nothing."

Jason studied me. "How old do you think you were in the dream?"

I scrunched my face as I tried to guess. "Maybe six-ish? You weren't there, so it's hard to tell. I couldn't see myself, I just felt small and young." I shut my eyes, thinking, wondering if there would ever be a time in my life when I didn't feel like I was losing my mind.

When I opened my eyes again, Jason's were boring into me with more intensity than I wanted to explore. I waited with bated breath for him to speak.

He blinked once, considering something, then said, "That's about the time you started having your dreams."

My heartbeat fumbled and slowed, the questions I'd been wracking my brain to answer solidifying into truths. "Really?"

Reluctantly, Jason nodded, his gaze blank and his thoughts clearly elsewhere. "I remember the first night perfectly," he said, his voice distant. He paused a moment, and he frowned. "You were so scared..." Jason didn't continue, even though a part of me wanted him to. When he looked at me, his expression was once again stoic and solidified in place. "Dad's in town with Jake for most of the day; they're getting some tools repaired. You should talk to him when he gets back." When Jason stood, the bed creaked without his added weight. He hesitated to leave, and his lips flattened into a hard line. He looked at me. "If that son of bitch was at our house," he said through gritted teeth. But instead of finishing his sentence, he ran his hands over his face and shook his head. "It's not like it matters much now."

Jason was right. It wouldn't really fix or change anything if it was a memory versus a dream. But then again, it would make me feel better, less crazy and, strangely, a tiny bit more at peace if it were a repressed memory causing the nightmares that had plagued my dreams since childhood, rather than just my twisted mind.

Jason looked at me, and I thought I saw a soft sort of sympathy in his eyes. "It makes me wonder what else we can't remember."

I let out a despondent, somewhat hysterical laugh. "I know, right?"

Harper walked back into the room, and Jason seemed to take that as his cue to leave. "Let me know if you need anything," he said, and then my brother left, his shoulders slumped a little bit more than before, and I hated that it was because of me.

Later that afternoon, while Annie and I were outside, chatting with the goats—my attempt to keep Annie out of trouble since I was on "light duty" and both Dani and Becca were gone for the afternoon, visiting the Re-gen farms—I waited impatiently for my dad and Jake to come home from New Bodega. Now that Jason knew about the dream, it seemed imperative that I get answers from my dad, that we learn the truth about what happened so many years ago and find out if there were *other* truths we should know about.

"Hey, Zoe." I turned around to find Gabe striding toward the fence I was leaning against. "I heard you got your ass—I meant *butt*," he self-corrected.

Annie paused her conversation with Cinnamon, the russet-colored goat, to listen in on our human conversation.

Gabe cleared his throat. "I heard Sanchez knocked the wind out of you. You okay?"

"I'm fine, thanks," I said. "Just taking it easy, doctor's orders."

Gabe smiled. "Good." He braced his elbows against the fence and peered around at the pens and pastures beyond. "Everything's so green here. I'm used to snow right about now."

"Yeah, no snow here." I peered up at the gray haze above us. "It's just gloomy a lot during the winter," I said. "With intermittent sunshine," I finished in my cheesiest weatherman impression.

Gabe smiled. He was a strange mixture of ease and discomfort, as usual. Like the others, I felt the hum of his mood, the distant flicker of his thoughts, and could sense his feelings, though they'd all become easy enough to ignore. But Gabe was more withdrawn than the others, and I found my mind often drifted to his, opening up so I could understand him more.

"Everything okay?" I asked, knowing he'd had a difficult time settling into a new life here, despite having Jake and Becca back. Now he was away from the conveniences of the Colony—the facilities to make scientific advancements, the electricity and running water. He'd left behind the Colony and everything he'd known for the past several years, only to be surrounded by Re-gens all over again. Not being under the General's thumb had to be a major win, but I could tell Gabe was going a little stir-crazy around the farm with no structured schedule or defined purpose. I just wished he felt more at home like, well, family should.

Running his fingers through his blond hair, Gabe nodded. "Yep, everything's fine."

I gazed over the hill peppered with a rainbow of grazing horses, toward the Re-gen settlement in the northern portion of Hope Valley. "How are things going with the Re-gens? Dani told me Carlos is in high demand."

Gabe made a derisive noise, but his gaze remained on the cultivated land around us. "Yeah. Between Becca, Camille, and Mase, we're working it out. But humans—Re-gens or not—aren't so easy to rein in when their lives hang in the balance. Desperation is a tricky thing."

Although degeneration wasn't something I, personally, needed to worry about, I was concerned about Becca and the possibility that she might be taken from Jake again as a result of her new physiology. So much was changing; we still understood so little, regarding both the Re-gens and degeneration, and with the rest of us "normals"—as the Re-gens called us—and our Abilities. It was impossible to ignore just how much our Abilities had changed over the past year, especially my own.

"Do you think we should be concerned about our Abilities?" I asked Gabe. "I mean, not necessarily death-by-Ability-drainage or anything, but do you think they'll ever stop evolving? Ever stop getting stronger?"

Gabe looked at me askance. I knew something ingenious played behind his shrewd, pale blue eyes, thoughts and ideas most of us only ever managed a slight glimpse of. "It's hard to say, but I don't think so. Think of it like a muscle. The more you use it—control it—the stronger it gets…the more fine-tuned and well-honed."

"That's what I'm worried about," I said. I wondered if, like Dani and Annie, who struggled to balance living in the two worlds their minds occupied—animal and human—the rest of us might face a loss of control at some point, a struggle to be *us* instead of *it*.

"Zoe, *you* strengthen your Ability, *you* hone it. I don't think you have to worry about it becoming bigger than you are." Hoping he was right, I nodded and let out a breath.

When I saw Annie pick up a goat poop pellet and eye it carefully, I straightened. "Annie, you're not supposed to touch the goat poop."

"But Cinnamon says he eats Willy's poop all the time." Both goats looked at me and bahed in unison.

"That's because goats will eat anything," I said and pointed to the ground. "Drop it." Annie scrunched her face, disgruntled, but she didn't argue. "Go to the trough and rinse off your hands, please. And remind me to bathe you in bleach before dinner," I muttered.

Gabe laughed. "Please do," he said. "And that's my cue. See you at supper."

"Okay," I said. "Oh, and Gabe?"

He paused mid-turn. "Yeah?"

"We're lucky to have you here. Who doesn't need a scientist in this day and age?" I flashed him a rueful smile, which I hoped was both endearing and also reassuring; he belonged with us, no matter his unease.

He gave me a small quirk of a grin in return and disappeared around the side of the stable.

Annie trudged over to the trough and primly submerged her hands, the act of washing more a routine I wanted her to get used to than an effective way to remove all poop particles from her hands.

I sighed and rumpled her hair. "You sure are crazy cute, Annie."

She beamed up at me with her missing-tooth grin, and I shook my head. "Come on, let's finish our chores."

By the time Annie and I finished feeding and chatting with the goats and had moved on to the chickens, what I could see of the sun shining through the clouds was setting behind the rolling, emerald hills. "It's getting late," I grumbled, anxious for my dad and Jake to return.

And like they'd drifted in on the breeze, I heard crunching gravel and distant, rumbling laughter coming up the drive.

"They're back!" Annie screeched, her pail of chicken feed forgotten as it crashed to the ground. "Presents!" she called and ran toward the stable and the approaching horses. Deciding a little extra feed wouldn't hurt the chickens, I collected the bucket, leaving the spilled contents behind, and followed after Annie.

I set the bucket outside the stable door and looked up at Jake as he and Brutus clomped to a stop at the hitching post. Jake's pene-trating gaze was already fixed on me, making my cheeks burn, and a smile engulfed my face. Leaning against the siding, I watched him and my dad, their stature and demeanor so different, but both a welcome sight all the same. My dad raked his fingers through his slicked-back, ashy-brown hair as he smiled at Annie, who was jumping up and down in the gravel.

Although I'd seen it numerous times over the months, I was still getting used to the sight of my dad and Jake riding side by side —or, rather, of my dad riding beside any of my new friends, given the fact that around this time last year, I'd thought he'd died of the

Virus. Now he wasn't only alive, he was living with all of us: the man I loved, my brother who it had taken me months to find, Dani, and my friends who felt more like family.

Jason strolled over to us from behind the barn. His long sleeves were covered in dirt, but Annie didn't care. She immediately jumped up into his arms and began bouncing with pure enthusiasm in his hold. "Do you think they brought me something?"

"Maybe," Jason said with a small chuckle. "You have to be patient and see." He glanced at Jake and Grandpa Tom. "How'd it go? Any trouble?"

"Without a hitch," my dad said and dismounted his gray horse, Poppy. He moved to untie the small duffel secured behind his saddle.

"Always good news," Jason said, brushing Annie's crazy curls away from his face.

"Did you bring presents?" Annie chirped, twitching with anticipation in Jason's arms. Her eyes were wide and imploring.

My dad gave Annie an exaggerated frown. "I didn't get you anything this time, sweetheart. I'm sorry."

Annie's face instantly fell. "S'okay," she mumbled.

"Wait just a second…" We all pivoted to look at Jake, who was turned in his saddle, searching through his saddlebag. "How did this little guy get in here?" He pulled out a white stuffed wolf.

Annie squealed and slithered out of Jason's arms. She ran up to Brutus, the horse's head bobbing more to keep from getting hit in the face than because Annie's high pitch and flailing movements spooked him.

"It's just like Snowflake!" Annie jumped up and down, dancing in place as she waited for Jake to dismount. After a thud, both of Jake's boots were planted on the ground. He crouched down and offered Annie the stuffed wolf that bore an eerie resemblance to the Tahoe pack's alpha female.

Snatching the wolf from his hands, Annie hugged it against

her, then lifted it to her nose. "It doesn't smell like Snowflake, though."

"That's a good thing," Jason muttered. "What do you say to Jake for your present?" We all liked to spoil Annie, more than we probably should have, but she'd been so deprived before, she'd been through so much, most of us couldn't resist an opportunity to put a smile on her face. Though every now and again we tried to introduce some discipline and instill some manners in the free-spirited little girl.

"Thank you, Jake!" Annie wrapped her arms around his neck and quickly pulled away, skipping off with her new wolf, leaving us all smiling after her.

"Always wanted to see you with kids one day, son," my dad said to Jason, but I didn't need to be a part of that conversation, so I tuned them out.

Jake stepped up beside me and wrapped his arms around my waist. A twinge of pain pulsed in my side, remnants of my failed sparring match, so I leaned into him—carefully.

"Hey," he murmured against my temple.

I peered up at him. "Hey yourself."

"How was your day?" His rich, amber eyes were searching and bright. Juxtaposed with his dark lashes and the week's worth of scruff that shadowed his features, he seemed almost dangerous, in a carnal, alluring sort of way. "Did you kick some butt today in training?"

I shook my head and leaned into his chest, resting my cheek against him as I watched Jason and my dad carry on a stilted conversation. "Not exactly. Let's just say I was demoted to light duty today."

Jake's body tensed. "That doesn't sound good."

"It's fine," I said, growing more lethargic by the minute. His warmth was comforting in the promise of dusk and worsening wind. "Annie and I have been feeding the animals. I've been watching her all afternoon so Dani and Becca could work at the

Re-gen farms with Grayson, Camille, and Mase. They've decided to help them set up their new vegetable garden."

Jake kissed the top of my head, and I felt his lips part into a smile. "I'm not sure Annie qualifies as 'light duty,'" he joked.

I thought about the goat poop and couldn't help smiling myself. "There's definitely never a dull moment around her, but she's fun."

Jake's voice sobered. "Why light duty? What happened?"

I looked up to reassure him. "It's nothing big. I'm sure Sanchez will fill you in. I—"

"Sorry to do this to you, Jake," Jason interrupted, and I pulled free from Jake's arms. Jason took the small duffel from my dad. "Since we have the tools now, I could use your help with something before it gets dark."

"Sure," Jake said and he reached up for Brutus's reins.

Seeing Jason's vague request for what it was—a window of opportunity for me to speak with my dad alone—I ran my hand down Brutus's slick neck. "I'll unsaddle him for you," I said and looked up at Jake.

He flashed me a smile and gave me a peck on the lips. "Thank you—oh, and I was thinking it's about time for another overnight hunting trip. Maybe tomorrow, weather permitting. Care to join?" he asked. I glanced to my dad who was tending to Poppy, oblivious.

"Just you and me?"

Jake's eyebrows lifted ever so slightly, and with a small, yet ecstatic smile, I nodded.

Over the past few months, I'd found a strange solace in taking small hunting trips with Jake and Cooper, and sometimes a few of the others. My bow skills came in handy—quiet and quick compared to the resounding crack of a rifle or shotgun. But as adrenaline-pumping as those trips were, it was the solo time I got to spend with Jake that I looked forward to the most.

Jake turned and followed Jason toward the work shed, and the clanking sound of metal brought me back to the present. My fingers were swift and agile as I began loosening cinches and unbuckled Brutus's bridle, thinking about what exactly I should say to my dad.

"How was your day, sweetheart?" he asked as he removed Poppy's bit and replaced the horse's bridle for a less intrusive halter. When my dad glanced over at me, he paused. "What's that on your shirt? Is that a *footprint?*" His tone was light and full of mirth.

I hated dredging up the past, ruining his mood, but I knew I had to eventually. I tied Brutus's red halter around his neck. "Yep. It's a muddy boot print."

Because Dad was so much like me, I knew he'd sensed something was up. Instead of probing around in my head, he waited. "Sounds like you had an interesting day."

"You could say that. Apparently I'm a shitty fighter when I'm distracted. Go figure."

We bustled around in silence for a few seconds, tending to the horses and remarking on the consistently dreary weather, before my dad finally asked, "What's on your mind, Zoe?"

"Well," I said, "since you asked…" Focusing my full attention on his expression, I turned to face him and leaned against Brutus's shoulder. "Have you ever erased my memories, Dad?" We were an interesting pair, him and I. Because now that I knew the truth about my lineage and my childhood, honesty was the only stable foundation on which we could build our new relationship. And given our Abilities, if my dad lied to me, I would know.

"I can't erase memories, Zoe."

I rolled my eyes. "You know what I mean, Dad. I've met General Herodson before, haven't I?"

His hands froze, clutching the front and back of Poppy's saddle, ready to remove it.

"And I saw Mom that day, too. That's the day the General said he'd put the Monitors on us…and you erased any memory I had of her." My voice was brittle, emotions I hadn't realized I'd been feeling rising to the surface. I swallowed them.

My dad removed the saddle and walked into the stable, no doubt giving him time to think or compose his response. When he returned, his eyes flicked to me, then back to his horse. "Your memories are resurfacing," he said.

"Apparently," I whispered, my eyes roaming the hills beyond the fence line—the white Milkmaids that sprouted through the grasses were almost violet in the dying light. All sunlight had evanesced behind the clouds, and a chill curled up my spine. "What else have you hidden from us?" My voice was hollowed by the realization that there still seemed to be secrets I had yet to unearth.

My dad finally stopped his busywork and stood beside me. He took my chin between his fingers, forcing me to look at him. "Nothing as big as that, Zoe. I promise you." He stared at me for a moment, and I saw a slew of emotions in the steel-blue depths of his eyes, emotions I'd only seen on one other occasion: the day he'd altered my memory. This new dad of mine was someone I felt I barely knew, someone I was still trying to figure out. "I'm so damn sorry I had to do that to you, sweetheart. But you were so young…"

His empty, desolate expression from that day was etched into my mind. "You didn't want to do it."

My dad wrapped his arm around my shoulder and led me over to one of the benches set against the side of the stable. "I wanted you to remember your mom, Zoe. I wanted you both to be able to know her. But I didn't want you to remember her like that. I didn't want you to remember Herodson or how scared you were—how horrible he was. The fewer questions you could ask, the better." My dad was quiet for a moment, then pulled me tighter against him. "And I didn't want your brother to find out. I didn't want to give him another reason to hate me. It was selfish, I know."

My dad let out a ragged, almost reluctant breath. "The day your mom came home was bittersweet." He released me and leaned forward, like he needed to prepare for the surmounting emotions and memories he'd been trying to forget all these years, and rested his elbows on his knees. "I knew she would never come back again, not after how close she'd come to losing everything she'd worked so hard for to keep us all safe. She'd never risk the outcome of disobeying him again. And that night I finally accepted that our family would never be whole again, and I think a part of me was just…gone."

I watched my dad as he gazed around the farm, first at the gravel in front of us, then at the farmhouse and barn and shed, then at our scattered friends, who were cleaning up and putting away their tools for the night. His eyes rested on my brother, laughing with Jake as he shut the door to the shed and headed out, toward the orchard.

"I hid it from you, knowing I'd have to live with the truth for the rest of my life but the two of you would be somewhat free. I assumed that you both thinking you had a dead mother was better than knowing you had one who'd left you, twice."

When my dad looked at me again, his eyes shimmered. "I love you, sweetheart, no matter how shitty of a dad I've been…you're my little girl, and I've always loved you." He kissed the side of my head, and I felt my throat constrict.

I ignored the resentment and frustration I'd felt toward him growing up, the anger I'd carried since learning he'd lied about his death. And I ignored my sorrow for what his life had been. "I love you too, Dad," I said, because remembering the day he'd come back to life, the day he'd shown up in the farm's driveway and how happy it had made me, was all that mattered. We were a family, and we needed each other, no matter what.

A forgotten memory from that day sparked my curiosity. "When you first showed up here and I told you about Peter, you seemed genuinely surprised, like you had no idea."

Slowly, my dad shook his head and he stared down at his

hands. "I never knew what happened to the baby. I didn't know if your mom miscarried, or if the child had actually been born. A part of me hoped something had happened, that a monster like Gregory would never be allowed to bring a child into this world, and I never let myself consider the other possibilities. Definitely not that your mom would raise his child, that she would love it as much as she loved you kids. But I was kidding myself." My dad's eyes were asking and hopeful, willing me to know the truth. "Zoe, your mom isn't the sort of woman to mistreat or deprive a child. And I'm not surprised she loves him so much. What else does she have to live for there, with *him*?"

I'd never really considered how hard it was for my dad not only to lose his wife, but to have her leave him for another man. She'd had no choice, but still; she lived with Herodson, slept in his bed. I found myself staring through my dad, a war waging inside of me—the girl who yearned for the family she'd always wanted and the bitter woman who hated all that her family had done.

"I know you can't ever forgive your mom, Zoe, but—"

I shook my head, a plea for him to stop. It was like my life was an epic battle—two waves crashing together because it's the nature of their existence and they have no other choice. I closed my eyes and tried to articulate some part of what I was feeling. "I want to forgive her, Dad," I said for the first time aloud. "I think about it all the time. I hate her for what she did, but I love her for trying to save us. Then every time I feel someone's mind, their pain and anger, their sadness, or when I think too much about the way life is now, about how my mom is this specter of death and secrets, I get confused all over again." I felt my eyes burn with unshed tears, but I ignored them. "Sometimes, it feels like I'm drowning." I looked at my dad. His eyes had softened as he listened. "I barely remember the person I was a year ago."

I cleared my throat and let out a steadying breath. "Every time I hear one of Vanessa's outbursts or feel Carlos's constant distress, it all goes back to Mom—the doctor. Every stilted word that comes out of a Re-gen, their dulled view of the world…" I stared down at my dirty fingernails. "It's like a bullhorn reminder to never forget who Mom is and why I should hate her."

My dad placed his hand gently on my knee. "Just give it more time, sweetheart. That's all you can do. I don't expect the making of the last twenty-five years to be undone in mere months. I know it's tough to process, but if nothing else, it will make you a stronger person later. It's like any other scar, they're all—"

I smiled. "I know, Dad. They're all reminders of how strong we are."

He nudged my shoulder. "I guess I used that one a lot, huh?"

Squinting, I pinched the air between my thumb and index finger. "Juuuust a little."

My dad chuckled and patted my knee. "Are you going to be okay?"

Strangely, I felt better, so it wasn't a lie when I nodded. "I'll be fine."

After a moment's pause, my dad rose to his feet and stretched his back. "Better get these horses put away before I can't see anymore. I'm getting old, you know. My eyesight isn't what it used to be." It was nice to have my dad teasing me, lightening the mood.

I stood and followed him over to Brutus and Poppy. "Hey, Dad? If you didn't unlock the memory of Mom, then why can I remember it all of a sudden?"

My dad didn't have to think about his answer. "You have two parents with well-honed Abilities, sweetheart. I guess it's not really that surprising that yours is developing into something so strong. It's only been a year or so that your Ability's been active. I wouldn't be surprised if one day it puts mine to shame."

5

DANI

HOPE VALLEY, CALIFORNIA

"Wait, Jason!" I scrambled over a soggy fallen log and swerved around a couple of moss-covered boulders. "Not those ones! They're death caps!" I skidded to a halt, breathing way too hard and heart racing. When it came to deadly poisonous mushrooms, I didn't mess around. Besides, Grayson had made them sound like pretty much the worst thing ever.

Crouched at the base of a sprawling live oak, Jason craned his neck to peer up at me. He looked perfectly baffled. "I thought they were porcinis."

Shaking my head, I looked at the plump, slightly yellow-tinged mushroom caps mere inches from Jason's fingertips, then followed the wide trunk of the oak up from its exposed roots to its sad excuse for foliage. I couldn't talk to trees like I could to animals, but I had the impression that the poor dear was on its way out of this world. Following an inexplicable urge, I leaned forward and patted the oak's rough bark.

66

Jason stood, and I couldn't help but shift my attention to him when he was towering over me and being so, well, towery. He glanced down at the harmless-looking mushrooms. "So...death caps, huh?"

I exhaled heavily and rolled my eyes. "Didn't you pay attention to Grayson's foraging lessons *at all*?"

Jason's broad shoulders rose and fell. "Must've missed that part."

My hands found their way to my hips all on their own, my foraging basket dangling from the crook of my arm a little askew. "This is our livelihood we're talking about here, man, our livelihood!" I said, flinging my free arm out melodramatically. "But seriously"—I relaxed my arm—"it wouldn't hurt you to pay attention when Grayson shares his mountain man wisdom, you know."

Jason settled his Ice King stare on me. It was a look I didn't receive often, and a year ago, it would've intimidated me to the point of taking a step or two backward...then maybe running away. But not anymore. "I've been a little distracted," he said. There was the hint of an eyebrow raise, the suggestion of a head tilt. "Zoe... my mom...the fucking General visiting our house all those years ago..."

And I suddenly felt like an insensitive butthead. My breath escaped me in a whispered, "Your dad messing around with Zo's memories..."

Jason looked away, focusing instead on the live oak's expansive trunk. He stared at the poor, sickly tree like he was plotting the most grisly way to murder it. And considering that Jason's self-prescribed decompression sessions generally resulted in the dismemberment of an innocent tree, well...

I reached for his hand, lacing our fingers together and giving a firm squeeze. "He was doing what he thought was best for Zo." I hesitated, held my breath, then let it out in a rush. "And I think he did the right thing...*that* time." I gave Jason's hand another, harder squeeze.

Jason laughed bitterly. "I know." He tugged me closer and wrapped his arms around me. The hug was a little awkward with the basket hooked over my arm, but we made it work. After planting a kiss on the top of my head, Jason sighed.

His sigh seemed to soak into me, sour my mood, then escape once more, this time from my throat. I pulled back just enough that I could see his face. "I'm sorry. I didn't mean to make us both so grumpy."

I couldn't remember the last time we'd been off the farm, just the two of us, and I just *had* to go and drag us down the nearest doom-and-gloom rabbit hole. So much for our peaceful, relaxing alone time.

Jason pressed a gentle kiss against my forehead. "Tell me about these death caps."

I relaxed against him, resting my cheek on his heavy raincoat. It was the first period of no rain in weeks that had lasted longer than a day, and we'd jumped at the opportunity to spend the morning together, foraging in the mile-long stretch of woods atop the hills to the east of our valley. But we also weren't about to risk being caught in a surprise downpour unprotected.

"Well, death caps look like normal mushrooms, I guess. They're not ugly or anything." I glanced down at the aforementioned mushrooms. "They're kind of nice-looking, actually, don't you think? I mean, as far as mushrooms go…"

Jason held me tight against him with his left arm around my shoulders while his right ventured under my coat, his hand tracing slow, soothing patterns on my lower back. "Sure…"

Smiling, I shivered, just a little. I loved when his voice took on that distracted quality, but only when I was the distraction. "They tend to grow at the base of oaks," I continued, "especially live oaks, and their caps have a brownish-green or yellow tinge…and there's a bulbous bulge at the base that makes them look a bit like, well…a bit phallic."

Jason grunted a laugh. "Somehow I doubt Daniel mentioned that."

I shrugged as best as I could in his hold. "That might've been a personal observation."

With another laugh, this one low and throaty, Jason brought his lips to my ear. "Gutter-brain."

I grinned against his jacket. "Takes one to know one." Thunder rolled in the distance, and I hoped it wasn't an omen of impending rain.

"That it does, Red." Without warning, Jason picked me up and turned in a half circle, earning a surprised squeak from me and sending chanterelles and oyster mushrooms flying out of my basket, and pressed my back against the oak's rough trunk. Beneath our boots, death caps littered the forest floor, scattered and crushed. "That it does." He leaned in, his hand cradling the back of my skull, and I relaxed my arm, letting the basket fall to the ground.

"Wait!" I hissed. Two blips had just appeared on my telepathic radar. I hadn't noticed them until it became obvious that they were moving toward us. "Someone's coming."

A hairsbreadth from my lips, Jason whispered, "Someone we know?"

"I—" Brow furrowed, I shook my head. "There's two of 'em, and there's something familiar about one mind—maybe someone we've crossed paths with in New Bodega?"

"Hmmm…" Jason didn't sound pleased. I couldn't blame him. I didn't feel very pleased, either. In fact, I felt decidedly *dis*pleased. Gaze scanning my face, lingering here and there, Jason tucked a few flyaway curls back into my braid before stepping away and releasing his handgun from his thigh holster. I did the same.

Squinting, I focused more on my telepathic radar than on the pistol in my hand and, once again, shook my head. "Must just be a couple New Bodega people." At least, I hoped that was the case.

69

"What direction?" Jason asked, scanning the spaces between the mossy trees and gnarled, leafless branches.

I pointed to the southwest. "They're close. Should be able to hear them soon."

"I know you're out there," Jason called, his focus on the woods intent. "Either identify yourselves or start moving in another direction. The choice is yours, but you'd better make it now." He glanced at me, his eyes filled with questions.

I could only answer one. I shook my head. "They're still coming." I did a quick scan of the animal minds lingering nearby. There wasn't much in the way of predators, but I requested that the few hawks in the area and the murder of crows looting a patch of overgrown and rotting pumpkins head our way, just in case.

Jason raised his gun, his eyes never straying from the gloomy trees. "Remember, Red—shoot first, feel—"

"Feel bad about it later," I murmured. "I know." Of course, the last time I'd stuck to that survival philosophy, I'd shot a little girl dead. Sure, she'd been a Crazy who just happened to be lunging at Zoe at the time, and sure, I'd been fairly certain that she was the cannibalistic variety of the post-apocalypse's less-than-sane brand of survivors, but still, she'd also been a little girl. And I'd killed her without hesitating. The blood blossoming across her chest... her body landing on the forest floor...Zoe's aghast reaction...that single moment was forever etched into my memory.

"Hello?" a man called ahead. "Who's there? Can you tell us where we are? We seem to be a little lost."

I split my attention between watching the woods for the intruders and studying Jason's face. The skin around his eyes tightened, and his nostrils flared. The man's words hadn't put him at ease in the slightest. If anything, they'd only fanned his apprehension.

A man came into view between one of the few pines in the forest and a robust oak tree, a woman a few paces behind him. The man was tall and slender, with silver hair that nearly reached his chin and a closely trimmed beard, while the woman, younger—in her mid-thirties, I thought—was brunette and broad-shouldered, looking like she could put up one hell of a fight.

When the man caught sight of us, he raised his hands defensively. "Whoa, whoa, friends...no need for guns. We're simply lost and, well, you see, we were looking for mushrooms to trade in town, and—"

"You're a trader," I blurted. "I've seen you before." I tapped the muzzle of my gun against my thigh. "You traded my friend and me a bottle of antidepressants for—"

"Tincture of white willow bark." The man's face lit up, and he continued walking toward us, though the woman hung back, lounging against a tall pine tree. "Yes, yes, I remember. You were with that pleasant young doctor." The trader smiled broadly. "Quite effective, that tincture. I've had very happy customers. You'll have to give me the recipe." He tilted his head to the side, just a little. "Tell me, how did the Sertraline work on the poor dear? A girl, yes—a teenage girl, if I remember correctly?"

"That's close enough," Jason said, his gun lowered but still drawn.

I holstered my own gun, then waved my hand at him. "It's fine, Jason." I looked at the trader. "Unfortunately, the pills didn't seem to make any difference for Vanessa. On to the next, I guess."

It had been Harper's theory to try Vanessa on the same medications that had worked so well to equalize the brain chemistry of people before the Virus. Chris had been skeptical—which was quickly turning into smugness—saying that something was broken inside Vanessa's mind, and it was something that made her brain function so differently from the rest of ours that she doubted anything but a time machine would fix the teenage Crazy. Not that Chris's pessimism stopped her from spending every spare moment studying Vanessa, looking for a way to return her to a state of normalcy. She loved Carlos like he was her own son, and she was bound and determined to give him his sister back. And a determined Chris was a sight to behold.

"Hmmm...well, I have a few other drugs you could try," the trader said. "I'll take whatever's left of the Sertraline back." Not more than a couple dozen feet away, he reached behind himself. "Exchange it for the same amount of—"

In the blink of an eye, a small, black pistol was in his hand, and it was pointed directly at me. I took a step backward and reached for my own sidearm.

Before I could call for help from our rapidly approaching avian reinforcements, before I could do much of anything, Jason leapt in front of me. The earsplitting crack of a gun firing exploded among the trees.

Crows darkened the sky, filling the late morning air with their scratchy caws.

Two more explosive cracks, and the trader dropped to the ground, his companion already fleeing.

Jason grunted, going down to one knee.

"Jason!" I dropped to my knees, trying to hold him upright, but he was too damn heavy. Somehow, I managed to lay him back, against the dying oak. He'd been hit in the leg and the abdomen, and his blood, thick and slippery, stained my hands crimson. Without thought, I yanked off my belt to use as a tourniquet on his leg.

"Got...him," Jason rasped, then coughed. "But the woman—I don't know where..."

Eyes going wide, I tightened and secured the belt, then scanned the woods around us. My fingers, slick with blood, gripped the handle of my gun, my hands possibly the only parts of my body not shaking. The woman wouldn't be hard to find, not when I could sense her mind and when I had an army of crows circling overhead.

Except I *couldn't* sense her mind.

Jason grabbed my wrist, demanding my attention. "Red..." His eyes shifted from mine to the woods behind me, a warning.

I spun on my knees, my gun raised and aimed directly at the chest of the trader's companion. But instead of focusing on her, my stare was glued to the barrel of the sawed-off shotgun she was aiming at my head.

"You won't shoot me, and you won't use your Ability," she said, her voice softer than I'd expected. "I'm sorry. This was never what I wanted."

"I will kill you," I swore through gritted teeth. Hot tears burned a path down my cheeks, and my heart pounded a primal, vengeful rhythm, but I couldn't bring myself to fire at her. I wanted to shoot her, desperately. But it was as though I didn't have control of my finger; I couldn't pull the trigger.

Dread slithered around in my chest, cold and unyielding. It was her, doing this, stopping me; it had to be. She was like the General. *She* was in my mind. She was controlling me.

The woman shook her head. "I'm going to go now." She smiled at me, her eyes sad, and I hated her for pretending she cared at all. "You'll find that your telepathy won't work for a while. I'm sorry about that, too, but it's the only way." She started backing away, her gun still locked on me. "I, um—" Her eyes flicked to Jason. "Good luck."

I tried to tell the crows to take her down as she retreated, I tried to call out to the hawks who should have reached us by now, I tried to reach out to *any* creature that might help us...but I couldn't sense anything. I couldn't even sense Jason.

"Red..." Jason touched my leg. "Dani, you have to go."

Tearing my gaze away from the section of forest where the woman had disappeared, I shook my head, refusing to look into his eyes, and reached for the zipper of his coat.

"It's no good," he said. "We need Harper. You need to run back to the farm and—"

"No!" I shouted, but my hands fell away from his coat, shaking uncontrollably as I scanned his body. There was far too much blood. "No, Jason. I can't leave you. Just—just *no*." The final word came out as a sob.

There Jason was, his blood smeared and smattered on the poisonous mushrooms and the oak tree and my jeans, and I felt like I was the one who was bleeding out, my desire to keep fighting, to survive, draining away. My life was tied to his so intrinsically. He was a part of me. I couldn't do this again, couldn't keep going.

"Dani…"

My eyes flashed up, finally meeting his, and for an infinitesimal eternity, it felt like I was drowning. I couldn't breathe. I was suffocating. There was no more oxygen left in the world…no more air at all.

"Dani!"

I blinked, tears streaming down my cheeks. "What do I do?" My voice was barely audible.

"Get help," Jason whispered.

Nodding, I yanked the dish towel out from the bottom of my foraging basket and pressed it gingerly against the wound under his coat. "Keep pressure on this, okay?"

"Dani, if I'm gone when you—"

"Okay?" I said, my voice too high, too loud. I refused to accept the possibility that he'd be anything other than here, alive, when I returned with help. The alternative was abhorrent to my mind. Logic and reality shifted, making him dying an impossibility.

Jason's hand replaced mine on the towel. "Okay."

"Okay." I leaned in, careful not to touch any part of his injured body, and kissed him gently. His lips tasted salty and metallic. They tasted like blood. "Hold on," I demanded. "I'll be right back."

And then I stood, and I ran.

6

ZOE

NOVEMBER 28, 1AE

THE FARM, CALIFORNIA

For three hours, I'd been sitting at the dining room table, my sketchpad washed in the baleful color of late morning that shone through the narrow windows, overlooking what appeared to be a deserted farm. Everyone was hiding indoors, dehydrating food, wrenching, painting, and—in Annie's case—playing with kitties, all sheltered from the sudden downpour.

Hearing the creak of the front door opening, I looked up. Tavis stepped inside, rain dripping off his coat as he leaned forward and peered into the dining room at me, his feet planted firmly on the welcome mat.

"Hey," I said, folding my arms in front of me.

Tavis smiled, his warm, customary greeting. "Morning." But even in his natural, easy air, there was something about the way he looked at me that made even the slightest linger of his gaze and the quickest glance seem like something more. I could've pried, could've peeked and prodded, but I was a little too hesitant to learn the reason.

"You seen our animal whisperer anywhere? We've got a horse

with colic out here. We could use her Ability." Tavis pointed to his head.

His facial expressions always made me laugh, and I couldn't help but smile back at him as I glanced outside. Darker clouds approached quickly from the west. "She's out with Jason," I said, "foraging. Hopefully they'll be home soon."

"Ah, foraging," he said with a wink. "Got it." And then he was out the door, and I watched as he strode back toward the stable.

I took a sip of lukewarm coffee, settling back into work mode, and let out a sigh as I stared down at the start of my second blueprint of the day. I tapped my charcoal pencil on the tabletop and glanced between Jason's hasty, ill-proportioned sketch and my own, hoping I was interpreting his floorplans for the new smokehouse accurately. I'd gotten quite good at looking past his scribbled letters and numbers, relying mostly on the arrows and the drawing itself to help me decipher the rest.

Footsteps creaking overhead and feminine laughter were followed by a muffled "You wish, buddy" that floated down the stairs of the otherwise silent house. No wonder Harper had been so anxious to rearrange the infirmary. Chris laughed again, a sound I'd been hearing more and more frequently over the months. My eyebrow rose of its own accord, and I reached for the mug beside my sketchpad. A contented smile splayed my lips as I appreciated the happy routine we'd all seemed to fall into, gloomy weather or not.

After draining the contents of my mug, I absently set it aside, deciding the beams in the smokehouse roof needed to be closer together if they were going to support the wide—

An ear-piercing cry rolled in with the distant rumble of thunder.

Eyes narrowed and heartbeat thrumming, I jumped to my feet and gazed through the window at the gravel drive. Opening my mind, I felt Dani's desperation and anguish before I even saw her.

"—shot!" With hair matted from the rain and her clothes

drenched, Dani sprinted clumsily up the driveway, her eyes wide with terror. "He's been shot! He's dying! Hurry! Harper!"

"H!" I called, already running out the door, trying to process Dani's hysterics as I sprinted toward her. "Dani!"

Both relief and utter desolation warred in her expression the instant she saw me. She was shaking, soaked, terrified, and out of breath.

"Dani," I breathed, reaching for her. "What the hell happened?" I called over my shoulder again for Harper.

"There were traders," she choked out, her eyes boring into mine. "One shot at me, but—"

Dani stopped short and gulped in a breath. She drew in another and another. I guided her toward the barn's eaves, noting the blood that colored her chest and arms. There was blood all over her hands. My heart twisted and my stomach knotted. *Jason.*

My gaze was torn, darting from her in search of wounds to the direction she'd come from...without my brother. *Why didn't she use her telepathy?* Confusion, dread, and anger made it difficult to focus when I registered he wasn't coming.

"...we were just talking, he pulled a gun!" she screeched and broke off in a sob, gripping my shirt and pulling me forward. "My Ability...it wouldn't—I couldn't...I tried, but the woman made it so I couldn't use it!" She peered around, frantic as her gaze swept the concerned, horrified faces of our companions, who had begun congregating around us. "There was so much blood," she said. "Harper..."

"Harper's coming, Dani." My eyes met Grayson's first. He nodded, then ran toward the house to see where he was, but I already heard Harper shouting as he came running toward us. "I'm coming!"

"Come inside, Dani, out of the rain," I said. She was trembling, and although she struggled against me, she was too weak and distraught to put up a true Dani fight.

Warm bodies followed us as I led her through the open barn

door. Jack whined and circled us anxiously, fretful as Dani screeched and cried, paying him no heed. "He was shot—twice!" she said. "He made me go for help…said if he was gone when I got back…" She began to wobble, her knees giving out, and I reached to catch her. "He's dead, isn't he?" Her gaze became unfocused. "And I just left him, alone and dying."

"He'll be fine," I said, forcing the uncertainty from my voice. There were mutters and movement as everyone stood there, confused and completely horrified. Camille pulled a drying towel that hung on a line strung through the barn and wrapped it around Dani's shoulders.

I tried to will away the thickening panic that was alive and scathing inside me. "He's just hurt, Dani. He can't be dead. We'll go get him. Harper and Jake, they can fix him." *They* have *to fix him.*

"Sam, mate, can you help get the horses?" Tavis asked, his voice all cool calmness, though I doubted he felt so collected.

Within seconds, Harper ran into the barn, donning a raincoat. He had his medical kit in hand and a handgun holstered on his hip. "Where is he, Dani?" he asked calmly. "Where did you leave Jason?"

"We went to the hills to find mushrooms." Dani looked to Grayson. "He almost picked the death caps."

"Dani," I said, bracing her shoulders and forcing her to look into my eyes instead of succumbing to the onslaught of shock. "Where's Jason?"

Jake, Tavis, Chris, and Sanchez ran through the barn door, their weapons strapped to their backs and holstered at their sides.

Jake looked at me. "Where are we going?"

"He's in the woods on the eastern hills, by a dying oak," I said, quickly gleaning what I could from Dani's memory. "Somewhere by the rotting log. And the woman might be out there somewhere —mid-thirties, brown hair, muscular. She's dangerous…has some form of mind control." I stared at Dani, unable to remove my gaze from her face, feverish from the cold and crying. I'd never seen her such a wreck. It terrified me more than anything I could remember —more than wondering if my family had died from the Virus, more than assuming they had. There was an emptiness in Dani's emotions, in her eyes, and I feared she might be right.

Jake whistled for Cooper, and they ran in the direction of the stabled horses. Most of the others followed in a rush. I needed to join them; I needed to see my brother, whether he was dead or alive.

"Camille," I said softly. "Please get Dani into the house. Get her warm—"

Dani gripped my arm. "I'm coming with you," she said, a sudden ferocity in her eyes. I was too relieved to see a small spark rekindled within her to argue.

Together we ran for our horses. Mase was already standing with Shadow outside his stall, finishing the buckle on Shadow's bridle. Mase handed me the reins, the only tack he'd had time to dress. Wings was still inside her stall, though the door was open, allowing her to come out.

I glanced at Dani, realizing she still wasn't using her Ability, wasn't communicating with the animals, just like she hadn't communicated with us at all on her race back to the farm. *How long before her Ability comes back?*

Mase must have come to the same conclusion, because he swiftly approached Wings, a bridle in hand. Within seconds he was finished and helping Dani onto her horse, and we joined the others, who were gathering outside.

"Here," Becca said, just as we were all about to leave. She handed those of us without rain gear coats and parkas and hats. Sam was running toward me, a pistol in his hand.

"Show us where he is, Dani," my dad said, peering out at Harper and Jake's diminishing forms as they galloped down the driveway. The dogs loped behind them. "Take me to my son."

Dani nodded numbly, and together they rode after Jake and

Harper, the others—Carlos, Sanchez, Chris, Tavis, and Gabe—nudging their horses into a gallop after them. The chaos around me was a blur as I tried to process that my brother was injured—that he might already be dead—several miles away.

Short of breath, Sam reached me and handed me the gun. "Just in case," he said.

"We'll get the infirmary ready," Grayson said from where he stood by the stable, Annie, Mase, Camille, and Becca alongside him.

The concern and anxiety cast in their eyes was the last thing I registered before Shadow and I took off after the others. My grip on Shadow's reins was so tight that I couldn't feel my fingers, and I ignored the wind and rain against my face as we raced down the road. The gravel turned to pavement, then to wet mud and grass the further away we rode.

Jason will be fine, I told myself. *He* has *to be fine.*

☙

After a couple of hours searching the forest for Jason, we canvassed the verdant hills beyond. And after a few more hours, we'd explored every withered grapevine that lined the forgotten vineyards throughout Hope Valley—around our home that no longer felt safe and comforting. But in the rain, there was no scent for the dogs to pick up, no footprints for us to follow. There was no sign of Jason—of his body...of his blood, save for what was on Dani. There was no sign of the woman or of a struggle at all, not even the trader's body, and the deep-seated fear that had rooted hours earlier was quickly becoming consuming. *Where is he?* Dead or alive, he was nowhere to be found.

I shook the thought from my mind. "He has to be somewhere," I said, standing under a canopy of naked branches and soggy evergreens with the others.

"But where?" Dani sobbed, her wild hair wilted and clinging to the sides of her ashen face. She clutched her stomach, bending over like she might retch out every part of herself even as she tried to control the sobs that wracked her body. She was desperate to find him, we all were, but we were getting nowhere and the sky was darkening, quickly turning the color of soot. "He was *right there*," she howled, pointing at the sickly live oak I'd seen in her memories. After all of our searching, we'd ended up back where we'd started, finding nothing.

"We have to be missing something," my dad said. The disbelief and pain in his voice ripped at my insides. "This isn't making any sense. It had to be the woman. She must've come back and..." But I could feel his uncertainty, his doubt. Why would she have come back and moved Jason and the trader? How would she have done it so quickly? My dad was right; it wasn't making any sense.

We were drenched and exhausted. Our horses were drenched and exhausted. Nowhere seemed the only place left to look. It was like we'd been defeated by an unknown opponent, and all of this was just a cruel, miserable joke.

"I never should've left him alone," Dani said between sobs.

I glanced at her, thinking of her inaccessible Ability, then focused on my dad. "We can have Annie send out some animal search parties, at least until..." My gaze shifted back to Dani.

My dad nodded. "It's a start."

"I'll head to Petaluma proper," Jake said, "see if he's somewhere in the city." Jake was already mounting Brutus. "The outskirts, maybe, hiding." He said it mostly to himself. His voice was almost lost in the incessant rainfall, but I could hear his usual steadfast certainty begin to crack.

I chose to focus on my dad instead. He strode over to Poppy, anxious to head out. Jake didn't stop him, but when Sanchez went to mount her bay mare, Jake shook his head.

"What? You think I'm staying back?" She looked offended.

Jake did a quick scan of our group, huddled beneath the trees.

"I think I'm the only one that won't die of pneumonia, but it's up to you."

The others continued to voice their questions and suggestions, and with the influx of suffocating emotions—of my *own* emotions —I needed a moment to breathe.

I stepped behind the dying oak, using its sturdy trunk to brace myself as I let out a choked sob. None of this was real, it couldn't be. This was a horrible dream, just like the others, and soon I'd wake up. But everyone's distress was insurmountable and felt too real to be false.

Where is he? I wanted to scream. But the more my hands shook and desperation clouded my mind, the more earnest I became. *I have to be strong.* For my dad. For Dani. *We'll find him and Jake will save him—he'll give him blood and everything will be okay.* I had to believe that or I'd crumble and be no use to anyone.

I swallowed thick, nearly immobilizing fear and stepped back out to Dani's side. I wrapped my arms around her. "We should head back," I said, though I wanted to go to Petaluma and continue the search for my brother, too. I didn't want to stop moving long enough to break down again. Jason was so strong, so protective of Dani—of all of us—I couldn't imagine him letting anyone, no matter their numbers and size, get the better of him. He wouldn't have let them win if there'd been any chance that Dani would've been in danger. Not without leaving a bloodbath in his wake. I clung to that hope.

"He's probably disoriented, D," I said, guiding her back to Wings. "He probably wanted to get out of the rain."

Dani's head budged a fraction in agreement, but I knew she felt the hollowness of my reassurances.

"Come on, D. Let's get you back to the farmhouse. Let's get you warm. Jason'll be pissed at me when he gets back if I let you get sick."

"What if they never find him," she whispered, her eyes swollen and red, her mouth and chin trembling. She looked wrung out, unable to cry another tear, but I knew that until Jason was found, until we knew he was alive and safe, there would be more tears and more misery.

"They will."

"How do you know—"

"Because," I said, barely containing my sudden rage, "I refuse to lose another member of my family, and—"

"There was too much blood, Zo. I know what I saw! He's dead."

"You don't know that for sure."

I glared at Dani as she climbed onto Wings's back. I couldn't help the fleeting accusatory thought that had she remained by his side, protected him, he'd still be here. We would've come looking for them by now. We would've found them, and we'd at least have had his body. But now, there were no bodies—absolutely no signs that there'd even been a struggle. We had nothing. Despite having seen Dani's memory, despite knowing that Jason had been losing too much blood to have survived out here without medical attention for this long, I was still angry and upset and uncertain. He had to be here somewhere. He had to be alive, or that woman wouldn't have taken him anywhere.

"Until I see his body," I bit out, "I refuse to believe that Jason is dead." As much as my gut told me something horrible *had* happened, I wouldn't allow myself to give in to fear completely. "He's not dead until we see his body, D," I said more softly. "We'll find him."

Again, Dani agreed absently, but I could feel her mind screaming, could feel the knot of foreboding inside her fraying apart into loose filaments of flailing doubt and despair. I could feel her breaking.

Jake and my dad will find him...they have to.

7

DANI

NOVEMBER 28, 1AE

THE FARM, CALIFORNIA

This feeling.

This lost, sick, desolate, I-don't-understand, why-won't-it-just-stop, I-can't-go-on-like-this feeling was too much.

After losing Cam, I never thought I'd feel like this again. Or, at least, I'd hoped I would never feel like this again. But I'd been an idiot to hope. I was starting to think that in times like these, anybody who hoped for anything at all was an idiot.

What was the point of hoping? Of even trying? The chance to live in a world where we had to fight for everything? A world where every single scrap of food had to be wrestled from the ground or hunted from the last vestiges of our dead civilization or stolen from others who were, like me, just trying to survive? This world, this life...it was sick. Broken. Pointless.

This world had no more room for hope.

I couldn't help but think back to my conversation with Becca just a few days earlier. I couldn't help but think I'd been wrong, that love wasn't worth it. That it wasn't worth *this*. And I couldn't help but hate myself for thinking it.

Did she foresee this? I squeezed my eyes shut and swallowed loudly. *Did she know this was going to happen? Did she let this happen based on my answers? Did I let this happen?* I thought I should've been angry, should've been storming off to confront her. I should've been, but I couldn't seem to muster the strength to do anything.

"You're shivering," Zoe murmured, wrapping the comforter from her bed around us both more tightly. We were in the room she and Jake shared on the second floor of the farmhouse. It was minimal but comfortable, and Zoe's side of the room was cluttered with her clothes, a sight that was strangely soothing. I was glad to be there, or as glad as I could be to be anywhere. Mostly, I was just glad to be out of the cottage, the home Jason and I had made our own. It was unbearable to be surrounded by our things when there was no certainty that it would ever be *our* home again.

"I can go find another blanket," Zoe said and scooted to the edge of the bed. "We have to get you warmed up."

I grabbed her elbow. "Don't go." I didn't want to be alone. I didn't want much at the moment, but being alone was last among a bevy of shitty options—remembering the slick, sticky feel of Jason's blood on my skin and the burn in my muscles and lungs as I ran, replaying what had happened and what I could've done differently, despising myself for being too stupid or panicked or weak-willed to go against Jason's orders and stay with him. Besides finding Jason's body, I'd never wanted anything less than being alone.

Because if we never found his body, there was still a chance that he was alive. At least, in my heart there was, even if my mind disagreed. *There was too much blood...*

Zoe hugged me more tightly, tucking my head under her chin and rubbing her hand up and down my arm. "He's missing, D, that's all."

She sighed. "The only blood we found was on you…" Not even Jack or Cooper had been able to pick up Jason's scent in the woods, not under all the rain, and though the animals who'd been in the vicinity at the time recalled a struggle between two-legs, they'd either scattered during the struggle or hadn't cared enough to pay attention to what happened after. Their memories didn't work like ours, but the fact that none of them could definitively say one way or the other whether there'd been a couple of dead two-legs in the woods after the struggle made a valiant effort at giving me hope. Sickening, poisonous hope.

"Mmphhh." I squeezed my eyes shut, unwilling to give in to the tears again. Because the tears were the all-encompassing kind. I was in full-on, no-holds-barred ugly cry mode, and I was exhausted. My abdomen—my entire torso—ached from the intensity of my sobs, my face was raw and puffy, and my eyes felt like they'd doubled in size. I'd already scared off everyone but Zoe, Annie, and Jack, the latter two being curled up on the foot of the bed.

Zoe inhaled, held her breath for several seconds like she was going to say something, then exhaled. And then she did it again.

"What, Zo?" I didn't bother pulling away to look at her. I knew she could hear the exhaustion in my voice, knew she could already feel everything I was feeling. She didn't need to see my face.

"Well…with Jason gone—"

"Gone?" Was she finally giving in to the inevitable?

"Missing," she amended. "With Jason *missing*, I was just thinking about your drifting. Have you thought about what you're going to do when your Ability returns?"

Let it take me. Give in. Be free. Let go…

"No," I said. I lied. "With everything else, I just…" I sniffled, giving my thoughts a moment to catch up. I just needed a moment. "I forgot about it," I said—lied, again. The possibility of losing myself in the mind and body of another creature was the only thing keeping me from losing it completely. When my Ability finally came back online, I'd be able to escape from myself...from my friends...from my misery, at least for a little while.

Zoe was quiet for a moment. "Maybe we should ask the New Bodega council if they know of anyone else who can null, or maybe if we—"

"There's no need," I said hollowly. "It's not like I can drift right now anyway. Maybe by the time it's a problem, we'll have found him," I added, drawing on her certainty that we'd find him alive rather than mine that we wouldn't. "And if we haven't, I can use it as another way to search for him." *And search for* her, I thought, the desire for vengeance denting the barrier of shock numbing my heart.

I felt more than heard Zoe's breath hitch. "D...it could be days, longer even, before we find him."

And if we don't find him, it won't matter, I didn't say.

Zoe took a deep breath. "Gabe might be able to help, too."

That was Zoe. Always with the plans and definitive action and a goal in mind. Sure, she was creative in ways I would never be and saw the world in colors I couldn't even imagine, but she was also a planner, and a damn determined one. Me, on the other hand...

"I'll make it work."

"D—"

My stomach lurched, and I groaned. "Oh God..." Weakly, I extracted myself from Zoe's embrace. "I think I'm gonna be sick." I stumbled around the foot of the bed, rousing both Annie and Jack, and managed to make it down the hallway and into the bathroom before the actual heaves began. I collapsed onto my knees and sagged against the toilet, my face hanging over the bowl and my eyes closed.

Mere seconds had passed before Zoe's fingers, cool and steady, brushed across my forehead. "You don't feel feverish; just a little clammy." She somehow managed to wrangle my wild mane with her fingers and gather my hair at the base of my skull. "It's probably because you haven't eaten anything. I'll ask Chris to—"

"No." I swallowed repeatedly, hating the metallic taste my suddenly overabundant saliva had taken on. It reminded me too much of the taste of Jason's blood on my lips. I gagged a few more times. "I can't eat. I'll just throw it up, and what's the point in that?" Another gag. I spat into the toilet, then flushed away the acidic liquid that had been all that was in my stomach. "We can't afford to waste food like that."

"Well, we can't afford to lose you, either," Zoe snapped. "And if you starve yourself, that's exactly what'll happen."

I rested my cheek on the cool toilet seat. It was hardly sanitary, but in that moment, I really didn't care. It was cool, and cool felt soothing…like Zoe's fingers. Cool was good…nice…

"D…I'm sorry. I just…" Zoe blew out her breath. "I hate this."

"I know," I said weakly. "Me too."

"Think you've got it all out of you?"

I nodded without raising my head.

"Alright, come on." Taking hold of my elbow with one hand and the side of my waist with the other, Zoe hauled me to my feet. "Let's get you to bed. I'll get you a cool rag, and then sleep's bound to make even this fucked-up situation seem a little brighter."

I nodded, knowing full well that sleep, like food, wasn't on the menu for me. Not today. Not until my Ability returned and drifting was the inevitable result of trying to sleep. I knew what nightmares awaited me in my dreams. I'd fought this battle before, and I had the mental and emotional scars to prove it.

Besides, it wasn't like I'd be able to fall asleep anyway.

DECEMBER 1 AE

8

ZOE
DECEMBER 1, 1AE

THE FARM, CALIFORNIA

Dani's room was washed in what little moonlight shone through the cloud-garnished sky, filling the small cottage bedroom with a murky haze that held so much more than night: anguish—desperation—confusion—disbelief. I was lying on top of Dani's bed, her in my arms and wrapped in Grams's quilt. It was my first night home after a few days of helping to search for Jason. I was supposed to be resting, I wanted to rest, but I couldn't.

As hard as it was to be in her and Jason's room, both of us surrounded by images and memories of them—of Jason—and sleeping in the bed he'd made for her, I knew it had become the only way for her to be close to him—to cope.

We'd been lying there for hours, some of the time in silence, some with ear-splitting sobs filling the room, but not one passing minute was absent the foreboding truth: she saw him dying. His body was gone, at least nowhere we could find, and there was still no sign of the woman.

Dani shivered, not from cold or fatigue, but from raw emptiness. I wrapped my arms more tightly around her. I'd kept my mind open for Jason's for days, and now for all the others' minds too, should something happen while they were away, still searching, still hoping. So, I knew the instant the small search party returned home. And I knew that, like our first outing, they didn't have Jason—dead or alive.

Thankfully, my knowing, silent tears were shrouded in darkness, so Dani couldn't see them. "D," I rasped. I could feel the numbness setting in as she battled the oblivion that had been inching its way in since the moment we'd arrived in the forest, only to find Jason nowhere in sight.

Slowly, I sat up and peered down at her silhouette. She made no sound or movement to indicate that she'd even heard me. "Dani?"

Finally, and ever so minutely, she shifted her head to look at me. *"I know they're back. You should go see them."*

I blinked in surprise. I hadn't realized her Ability had returned. I nodded. "I'll be right back, okay? Keep the blanket around you... stay warm."

Her head inched downward.

"I'll get another blanket from the house, too," I said, which was only half the truth. "Do you need anything?"

Her head inched to the left and then to the right.

I wasn't sure Dani was really registering much of what I was saying. I leaned down and kissed her forehead before tucking the blanket more snugly around her. "I'll be back."

Climbing off her bed, I pulled my long sleeves over my fingers and wrapped my arms around myself. I padded out of the bedroom and toward the creaky front door, where I sensed Jake approaching. Quietly, I opened the door. I was unsurprised to feel his remorse and concern surround me once I stepped outside.

The gnawing wind whipped by us as we stood only inches apart, but my focus was on the light emanating from inside the farmhouse, on rain-soaked buildings and overgrown grasses and the mud-puddled gravel drive nearby…I was focused everywhere but on Jake's solemn expression cast in moon shadows.

"There was no sign of him or the woman in town. I checked Cotati and Rohnert Park," Jake said, defeat radiating from him. In his mind, I saw images of blood-spattered walls in abandoned buildings, of discarded food wrappers blowing around and tire tracks on the roads, but there was nothing specific to Jason, nothing he'd left behind for us to find, and no sighting of a woman who even remotely resembled the picture I'd drawn from Dani's memory. There was nothing even *remotely* promising.

Even though I knew the answer, I had to ask anyway. "The dogs, they didn't find *anything?*"

Jake shook his head and stepped closer, his booted toe touching my slipper. I didn't like the enormity of our mingling emotions. I didn't like what his dulling confidence felt like. I wanted to push him away, to tell him to look harder, that Jason *had* to be some-where and even if the woman had him, they couldn't have traveled so far. But I couldn't push Jake away; I couldn't do anything, but finally let go. And finally, I cried.

When my knees grew too weak and my legs gave out, Jake caught me. I couldn't be strong for Dani and hold back my tears anymore, not when the truth that my brother had been taken from me, from my family, began to finally sink in. "He's dead," I said quietly, hope nothing but ash on my tongue.

"We'll keep looking, Zoe," Jake said as I sat curled and crum-pled in his arms. I gripped his jacket, pressing my face against him to muffle my sobs.

I thought about the day Jason and I had opened the box, the day he'd told me, after so many years, why he had such a hard time looking at me. *You look exactly like her.* That was the day we learned the first, earth-shattering secret about our family.

I thought about the flashes of concern and amusement I'd seen in his eyes when I'd lost my memory, about the way we'd finally found some semblance of family and understanding in one another.

I thought about the stacks of plans he'd drawn up over the months we'd all been settling in, getting too comfortable—too happy—that were sitting on the edge of the dining room table, waiting to be deciphered. We'd become partners in documenting this new life we'd embarked on together—a life that he was no longer a part of.

We've only just become a family again...

I thought about our mom, about our dad. I thought about Dani.

The wind whirled around Jake and me, its taunting howl echoing through my head despite Jake's sheltering embrace. He moved, trying to pick me up, but I didn't want to go inside. "No," I rasped and clung to him more tightly. "Please..." I didn't want Dani to see me like this, couldn't look at my dad...

Thankfully, Jake didn't argue. We sat there on the cottage's stoop, Jake holding me under the awning that barely staved off the drizzling threat of rain. I shut out his emotions and lost myself to my own. Nothing seemed right, nothing made sense. *How could everything have gone so terribly, horribly wrong?*

When my throat was raw from gasping for air and my eyes burned from too many tears, I let out a steadying breath and blinked my eyes open again. The horizon was washed in a pale gray that gave way to ominous black clouds shifting above us. I wasn't sure how long we'd been outside, me wrapped in the warmth and protection of Jake's arms, but I knew that if Dani was still awake, she'd be wondering where I was, why I'd abandoned her. Part of me thought she should know I was no longer hopeful, but then I realized she already did. She had to. Dani already knew he was dead; she'd said so a hundred times, though I didn't want to listen.

It just doesn't make any sense... More often than not, the thought brought me hope, but as the minutes, hours, and days passed, hope became little more than a puff of cold air, too fleeting to hold on to much longer.

I straightened in Jake's arms and let out a deep breath as I wiped the remaining wetness from my raw nose and cheeks. Gently, he brushed the dampened hair from my swollen face. I wished I knew how to make him feel less like he'd failed.

"You've—" I cleared the hoarseness from my voice. "You've done all you can, Jake. More than I could've asked of you. Thank you."

He stared down at me, his eyes filled with a desperation to make everything better...to find his friend.

I cleared my throat again and peered toward the farmhouse. "How's my dad holding up?" I needed to know but feared what I would glean if I let my mind find his.

Jake hesitated. "I'm not sure he's come in from the stable yet," he said, his voice soft and his expression as weary as my own must've been.

My eyes skirted behind Jake, toward the stable. It seemed more dilapidated and imposing than usual. "I should go talk to him," I said with a sniff. "I should make sure he's alright."

Jake nodded.

Then I remembered Dani, alone inside the cottage. "I should check on Dani first. I shouldn't have left her alone for so long. She's been doing a little better with me home."

"Go talk to your dad," Jake said, pulling me into his arms once more. He kissed my forehead. "I'll ask Camille or Mase to check on her."

I peered into the cottage window, uncertain why I'd hoped to see a light on inside. "You should send Chris. She'll help Dani feel better."

Jake's arms loosened and he shook his head.

I frowned.

"She went with Sanchez and Grayson to New Bodega."

"Oh," I said on a sigh. I hadn't heard them leave.

"Chris wanted to check in with the Counsel again, to find out more about the traders, and Grayson thought the townspeople might have seen or heard something the last couple days. They wanted to make a trip before your dad, Harper, and I left again."

"Good idea," I said, exhausted, and I squeezed his hand. "I'll just talk to my dad later. Go get some rest," I said, taking a deep breath as I readied myself to head back inside. "I'll be out in a bit." When Jake nodded, I exhaled, trying to breathe out the tightness in my heart and chest.

The cottage was quiet when I went inside. I hoped, for a brief second, that Dani might've finally found comfort in sleep. But that hope quickly diminished as I realized she was drifting, lost in the auroral morning far away from here.

And she was glowing.

◈

Standing at one of the square, rustic windows in Dani's bedroom, the curtains drawn to the side, I stared out at the farm that was finally less dreary. It was almost bright with afternoon sunshine. I felt a momentary lightness until my dad descended the steps of the farmhouse porch, shoulders slumped as he lumbered toward the barn.

I knew he was heading to the woodshop he and Jason had commandeered at the far end of the structure, where there were cobwebbed windows providing ample light to whittle in, a sturdy old table that passed as a decent workbench, and enough room to store discarded and forgotten pieces of wood that they would inevitably turn into something breathtakingly beautiful. It was a small space of their own that was tucked just far enough out of the way that it felt like it existed in its own manageable little world. It was one of the few remaining connections my dad had to Jason, something I'd only just realized. I watched the increasing urgency in his steps, like he couldn't retreat inside his safe haven, his private world, fast enough.

My eyes began to sting. I ventured a glance at Dani, who was curled up with Annie on the bed, the small child nestled in her arms as they both drifted, searching for Jason in an entirely different way.

Nausea made my stomach clench and roll with unease. Dani was glowing again—a soft champagne-colored halo that illuminated her as she slept. I squeezed my eyes shut. *Pull it together, Zoe.* I probably needed more sleep, but not now, not when every time I closed my eyes I saw the void in my dad's eyes all over again and pictured Jason's childhood room, barren and lonely as I stood inside of it, waiting for him to come home. *Pull it together.*

Knowing I needed to get out of the cottage, out of the confines of Jason's house and away from Dani, I snuck out through the front door and headed outside. Of their own accord, my feet followed my dad's path, and I made my way into the barn.

My dad had barely spoken to me the previous day, when I'd tried to talk to him. He was in complete denial that Jason was anything other than okay, holed up somewhere and waiting for us to find him. At least, that was the façade everyone else saw. But everyone else couldn't sense the truth, not like me. Deep down, my dad wasn't so sure of anything. He knew that whatever had happened, our family would be forever changed—that there would be another irreparable hole inside him he could never fill.

I took my time crossing the driveway, needing to collect myself before we found ourselves standing in silence, both trying to be strong when all we really wanted was to wake up from the nightmare that had become our lives. I wanted him to talk to me; I needed him to. I needed his reassurance that he was going get through this, but I was in no hurry to drum up everything I'd been trying to keep contained over the past seven days, that I'd been trying to keep manageable.

What worried me most was that my dad was supposed to be resting, but when a steady hammering emanated from inside the barn, it was clear rest wasn't something he wanted. Woodworking helped calm him down and let him think beyond his emotions, that much I knew about him. He'd always been that way. Jason, too.

A slight breeze picked up, sending a flood of chills over my skin despite the warmth of the sun. I stepped into the workshop, stopping a couple yards behind my dad in the shadows of the rafters and the hanging tools and contraptions adorning them. I watched as he pounded with more force than was necessary—over and over—on the frame of a large oak cabinet. When he was done with the hammering, he tore off a piece of sandpaper and went to scrubbing the raw wooden surface with even more fervor.

I bit at the inside of my cheek. For some reason, my tethers of strength were shredded at the realization that my dad and Jason were more alike than they'd ever admit.

My dad sanded harder and more furiously, desperation pinching his features into a scowl.

"Dad," I said quietly.

Lost. He was lost and grasping onto what little sanity remained, I could feel his desperation turning into fear and anguish and rage. I called his name again, but he didn't stop or slow. It was like he hadn't registered I was in the room at all. His graying hair fell into his eyes, and sweat beaded on his brow. Purposely or not, he was shutting me out, just like he'd always done.

"Dad," I breathed out shakily, wrapping my arms more tightly around myself. I couldn't ignore the distance that grew between us as I stood only a few feet away from him. I didn't want to lose him too, on top of everything else. I couldn't. "Daddy…"

Finally, he stopped, his chest heaving and his eyes softening as he took in the sight of me. I wiped a straggling tear from my cheek and covered my eyes with my hand, unable to stop the rest of the hot tears I wished would wait just a little while longer. I wanted to disappear.

"It's—" I choked on a sob. "It's happening again, isn't it?" Seeing him so upset, so closed off from me, was more than I could bear. "I'm going to lose you, too." I sniffled, one hand crossed over my stomach, gripping onto my side almost painfully as I tried to keep myself rooted—keep myself standing—the other hand still shielding my tears. I didn't want to upset my dad more than he already was, but I couldn't stop the racking sobs that threatened to drop me to my knees.

"Oh, sweetheart," my dad said, and before I knew it, his arms were around me and he was holding me. "I'm so sorry," he could barely say, emotion choking his words until they were little more than a croak.

I wrapped my arms around him, gripping his jacket as I tried to hold on to the last person I had left in my family. "Why does this keep happening?" I wept, feeling like a little girl in need of her dad all over again. Only this time, he was actually here with me, comforting me.

My dad's arms tightened around me. "I don't know," he said, sounding defeated. He laid his cheek against my forehead. "I don't know." He took a deep breath and then another, though it didn't seem to help him reel in his fear and sadness, his anger and confusion. His tears dampened my hair, and I could feel his chest heaving with each escaped sob.

"I can't lose you again," I whispered, trying to catch my breath. "Not like last time."

"Shhh," he crooned. "You won't lose me again, Zoe. I promise. You won't lose me again." He held my shoulders and stepped back, using his thumbs to wipe the tears from under my eyes. "I need you too, you know?" He made no empty promises or reassurances that everything would be okay, but the fact that he was standing there with me, completely vulnerable, was somehow reassuring enough. He wiped the dampness from under his eyes and offered me a weak smile.

"Hey, Tom, what do you know about the San Rafael area—" Gabe stopped mid-step and glanced back and forth between us. "Oh, uh, sorry. I didn't mean to, uh…"

I stepped back, the blood draining from my face as I looked at him. "No…"

"No what?" Gabe looked confused until his widened eyes narrowed and he frowned. "What is it?"

Like Dani, Gabe was surrounded by color. A light purple haze so soft it was almost gray surrounded him. "You—you're glowing."

Gabe straightened, taken aback. "I beg your pardon, I'm *what?*"

I took another step backward. "I think I'm finally losing my mind." My hands clenched and unclenched at my sides, and I couldn't help what was probably a gaping, horror-stricken expression.

"Come, sit down, sweetheart." My dad led me over to a rusted folding chair. "You're just tired. You need to rest—"

"What do you mean, 'glowing,' Zoe?" Gabe asked, his eyes narrowing as he stepped closer. "What does it look like?"

I let out a slightly strangled laugh and dabbed my damp eyes with my sleeve. Of course Gabe—the mad scientist, so to speak—was curious, not condemning. "It's glowing all around you," I said dryly. "A lavender, pulsating light." I stared at my dad for a moment, seeing no colorful glow surrounding him. "Why does this keep happening to me," I said under my breath. When Gabe's right eyebrow rose, I explained. "Dani was glowing, too."

"Really?" Gabe widened his stance and crossed his arms over his chest. "And when did that start?"

My dad's grip tightened on my shoulder in supportive reassurance.

"A couple days ago—" I hesitated, wondering if that was true. "At least, I think it was a couple days ago. I've been seeing colors around people off and on lately, but I'm not sure this is the same thing. I had a concussion the first time, I think, so I'm not sure that counts." My eyes widened. "Do you think it was more than a

99

concussion? What if I have brain damage?" I knew it wasn't likely, but at the same time, I felt a tad desperate for answers.

Gabe didn't seem convinced. "Not if it's only Dani—and now me—that you've seen these glowing colors around."

I glanced from him to my dad and back, the inside of my cheek raw from pulling it between my teeth. "Do you think I'm losing my mind?" I was beginning to grow seriously concerned.

"You're not losing your mind, sweetheart." My dad let out a soft chuckle and patted my knee.

Thankfully, Gabe shook his head as well, a small smile quirking the side of his mouth, which made me feel a little better. "I don't think it's quite that bad yet, Zoe." He studied my face, like the answers to my puzzling mind were etched someplace only he could see. "There's been a lot going on this past week, and with you experiencing everyone else's emotions…it's more than you're used to. It makes sense that your Ability might be attempting to cope with the onslaught by transforming the emotional input it receives into something you can sense in a more traditional way."

"So it'll probably go away," I prompted.

Gabe shrugged. "There's no way to know for sure. This could be your Ability evolving, or it could just be your mind's way of coping, like I said. Give me some time to study these changes, then I'll have some answers for you…hopefully. Unfortunately," he said, his gaze shifting back and forth between my dad and me, "let's just say that if this has anything to do with the influx of strong emotions, I don't think it'll go away any time soon. Not with everything going on around here."

I felt a small anvil sink to the pit of my stomach. I didn't want to think about how long our world would be turned upside down, inside out, and wrung out and exposed. Clearing my throat, I asked, "But why colors? Why are people glowing? That doesn't even seem connected to emotions…at all."

Gabe started to shake his head, like he wasn't sure. "Could be a form of synesthesia, I suppose…" He paused. "Maybe if we think

100

of your Ability in terms of changing energy levels and intensity—" Gabe stopped, his brow furrowed. "What? Why are you smiling?"

I hadn't realized I was. "I'm just remembering the last time you provided me with the bruised peach analogy, and an hour later my mind was being ripped open and all my monsters were jumping out at me."

Gabe feigned amusement. "Analogies help me process, okay? Besides, I was right, wasn't I?" Crouching down a few feet from me, one arm draped over a knee, Gabe started to draw in the layer of sawdust covering the workshop floor with the other. "Now, if we consider the fact that your Ability is emotion-driven, that it likely picks up on other people's raw energy and brainwaves..." He drew what looked like a prism with wavelengths coming out of it, letters—which I assumed represented colors—in each section he drew. "Energy and light...color..." he muttered to himself.

Gabe squinted up at me. "If we consider the increase in everyone's emotional output—especially the intensity of Dani's," he said, and his voice dropped as the brightness of his eyes slightly dimmed. He took a deep breath. "It could be that you are, in a sense, *seeing* people's emotions now, not just feeling them. Maybe like the intensity—the frequency—is reaching new levels and creating an energy source strong enough that your mind is processing it the only way it knows how...the way the vision centers in our brains process light and color."

"But Dani's color hasn't changed with her emotions," I countered, realizing instantly how strange it was that Dani had "a color" to begin with. "It's been the same since it first appeared."

Gabe ran his fingers through his long, blond hair. "I don't know. It's just a theory. I could be wrong...wouldn't be the first time."

"Or," my dad said, and Gabe and I both looked at him, "maybe it's not necessarily her emotions you're seeing. You've been able to feel people on an intrinsic level since you got your memory back —who they are, what they've done, their fears and passions and everything they don't want you to know about them, all of it in the forefront of your mind if you want it to be." His eyes narrowed. "If Gabe's right, then maybe your Ability is allowing you not only to feel their emotions and who they are, deep down, but to actually *see* who they are now." He pointed down to Gabe's sketch on the floor. "Maybe this visible energy Gabe's talking about isn't for each heightened emotion, but is a manifestation of the basic, raw connection you have with each of them."

"Which would be even more interesting," Gabe piped in. "We're always giving off energy, right? It's what animates our bodies, after all. You've already tapped into our frequencies, so to speak—maybe now you can *see* them."

"You mean, like an aura?" I asked.

"I don't really know. I guess, yeah. I mean, considering the general state of genetic instability the rest of us are in, I wouldn't rule out any possibilities at this point." He shrugged. "It's different for you, being second-generation. Your body didn't mutate spontaneously; you were born this way. Your Ability may have remained dormant until triggered by Wes's clever little genetic stowaway in the Virus, but you *were* born with a body physically and mentally equipped to handle your Ability. Your situation is unique, which makes it extremely difficult for me to diagnose what's happening to you." He scratched the stubble on his jaw. "If this new element of your Ability goes away, I guess we'll have an answer...or, at least, part of one."

"And that would be..." I hedged. I was still struggling to wrap my mind around what exactly they were trying to explain.

"To put it simply, Zoe," Gabe said with an exhale, "you're stressed out—at max capacity—and it's showing through your Ability, for better or worse."

With a grunt, I let out an exhale of my own. My dad's eyes were pensive and waiting. I could tell he anticipated a less-than-ideal reaction from me. But I was almost beyond the ability to react.

Gabe turned his head slightly to the side, also waiting for a response.

After a moment, I threw my hands up. "Well, then I guess that's settled," I said, standing. They both looked at me, expectantly. "I need a drink."

9

DANI

THE FARM, CALIFORNIA

I stabbed my trowel into the soil, taking out my irritation, my anger, on the defenseless earth. I inhaled deeply, the dark, rich smell of damp soil at the peak of fertility filling my nostrils, then huffed, "I *will* find you…whatever your name is." I'd spent every night for the past week using my drifting time to search for Jason and *her*. But despite the keener senses of the animals whose bodies I'd shared, I'd found nothing. Zilch. Nada.

I stabbed the earth once more.

Jack trotted toward me between two rows of raised soil, mud caked in his fur. He shook himself off enthusiastically, then planted himself butt-first well within my personal space. His nose was wet and cool, but his tongue was warm. And slimy.

"Seriously?" I raised my shoulder to wipe my slobbered-on cheek against my hoodie, but his presence was far from unwelcome.

"Mother…upset." Jack's deep mental voice was somber. *"But I am here."* He scooted even closer—though how that was possible, I wasn't sure—and nuzzled my neck, the side of my face, my hair.

He was dead set on making sure that I knew I wasn't alone, that I knew he was with me. The animals had been big on that kind of thing since Jason's disappearance. They'd become my lifeline. Them, and Zoe. But then hadn't that always been the case?

I set a baby spinach plant down in the shallow hole I'd dug and turned to wrap my arms around my dog. "I know, Sweet Boy," I told Jack both aloud and telepathically. "I know. And I love you so much."

He stood partway, the entire back half of his body wiggling with his overenthusiastic tail wag. *"Run with me?"*

I stared into his amber eyes, knowing full well that he didn't want me to throw down my trowel and launch into a sprint alongside him; he wanted me to drift *into* him, to mentally and spiritually run with him. *"Later, Sweet Boy."* Looking away, I reached for another spinach plant with one hand and my trowel with the other. *"I've got work to do right now."*

Without Jason around to null my Ability while I slept, I'd had no choice but to run with Jack—drifting into his mind and that of countless other animals—every night. As a result, restful sleep had become a foreign concept to me once again and nausea a standard facet of daily life, along with fatigue, shaking hands, and an inability to concentrate on much besides when I might be able to drift again.

The animals' minds offered a refuge not only from the concerned stares of my friends but also from the mental, emotional, and physical exhaustion that had become my status quo. I was a wreck, a junkie; I knew it, and I knew that the others were keeping a close eye on me for that very reason. But there really was nothing I could do about it. And considering that it was the most effective way I could assist in the search, there wasn't much I *wanted* to do about it. I wished I knew how Annie managed to survive by only drifting, never sleeping, but I doubted it was anything replicable. Chris and Gabe hypothesized that it had something to do with the fact that Annie's brain was still developing, and because it was still so malleable, it was able to adapt to her Ability. Unlike my developed, unmalleable brain...

Jack whimpered and once again planted himself essentially on my boot.

I sighed. "What is it, Sweet Boy?"

"Angry...sad...scared...lost..." His whine was high-pitched and heartbreaking. *"Don't want to leave you alone."*

I gently buried the little spinach plant's bundle of roots, then leaned my head on Jack's muddy, furry shoulder. "I'm never alone," I whispered. "Not when you're around."

And it was the absolute truth. I'd yet to find an animal I couldn't communicate with, but my connection to some was much stronger than my connection to others. And with Jack and Wings, especially with all of the time I'd spent wholly submerged in their minds lately, it was almost impossible for me to separate myself from either of them completely. We were well and truly tied together. And I didn't mind it one bit.

"Now go help Annie," I said, raising my head and nodding toward the orchard some fifty yards from the vegetable garden. Despite the many things that we shared with our neighboring farm friends—the Re-gens and the Tahoe clan—the orchard and garden were hands-off to anyone who didn't live in the farmhouse or cottage and would hopefully one day produce all of our personal fruits and vegetables, as well as the herbs and other plants Harper and I were growing for medicinal purposes.

I scanned the dormant apple, plum, and cherry trees until I spotted Annie's blonde head. I'd been able to sense her mental signature, but her little forest-green raincoat allowed her to melt right into the background of overgrown companion plants— hyssop, yarrow, and chives, for the most part—as she crawled around on the ground in search of earthworms. She was a small child on a mission, and her focus was commendable.

"Go," I repeated, and Jack obeyed with only the slightest hesitation.

I returned to my work, digging, planting, burying, over and over again. I lost myself in the cathartic motions, finding the ache that settled into my hands a pleasant distraction. I'd opted not to wear gloves, and the sensation of my fingers digging into the cool, damp soil, of the dirt lodging under my fingernails, made me feel connected to the earth...to everything. Even to Jason, wherever he was. Alive or...not.

"Stop it," I said under my breath.

"You shouldn't be out here, D."

I started, nearly tearing the root bundle of a spinach plant in two. It wasn't easy for people to sneak up on me, what with my ability to sense their minds and all, but Zoe'd been making a habit of it lately. Or maybe it was that I'd been making a habit of being more or less oblivious to my surroundings.

"Sorry." Zoe gingerly stepped over the row of freshly planted spinach and knelt in the dirt facing me. "Thought you heard me."

I shrugged, then continued my work. "You're getting your jeans dirty."

She ignored my comment. "Have you eaten anything today?" There was a sharp edge to her voice, an accusatory tone that told me she already knew the answer.

Again, I shrugged.

"I thought we made a deal, D." She sounded exasperated. "Until you're able to keep some food down, you rest inside. What happens if you pass out or get sick while you're out here, *alone*?"

I tucked another baby plant into its earthy cradle. Zoe's long, slender fingers wrapped around my wrist, preventing me from reaching for another plant. "Have you heard a single word I've said?" She squeezed, her nails digging into the inside of my wrist. "Jesus, D, do you even care?"

I breathed in and out. In and out. In and out. And then I raised my gaze to meet hers.

Zoe's tone, her words, the hurt swimming around in her eyes— this was one of those moments that was a surefire trigger to tears.

Or it would have been a week ago, maybe. But now all I felt was emptiness, and a need to push…to work…to do and do and do until all of my muscles ached and my brain wasn't capable of thinking or feeling anymore. Until I was no longer capable of remembering *that day*.

Until I was no longer *in danger* of thinking about that day.

Zoe sighed, and I could tell her patience was thinning. "Why don't we find something for you to do inside at least?" It wasn't really a question. "Come on," Zoe said, her voice somehow both soft and firm. "Let's get you cleaned up." She pulled me up to my feet. I offered no resistance, not that I would've been able to fend her off anyway. With all of her physical training over the past year, she'd become almost as indomitable as Chris and Sanchez.

"Annie…" I glanced back as Zoe led me toward the cottage with an arm around my shoulders and a hand latched onto my elbow. My little wild child had abandoned her hunt for earthworms in favor of a game of tag with Jack and Cooper. And I was pretty sure a pair of ravens had joined the fun.

The ghost of a smile touched my lips.

"Becca made chicken noodle soup and biscuits for lunch," Zoe said as we entered the cottage. We both removed our muddy boots just inside the door. I was quickly escorted to the table, where Zoe all but forced me down into a chair. "Want me to bring you some?" She hustled around the small kitchen taking up one corner of the cottage's front room, filling up a teapot from one of the gallon water jugs on the tile counter and hanging it on one of the iron hooks Jason had affixed to the inside of the hearth in the attached living room.

"I tasted the broth right before I came outside." Zoe knelt in front of the fireplace, taking pieces of firewood from the stack piled high against the wall and arranging them on the embers still burning from the fire I'd started earlier that morning. She glanced over her shoulder, her eyes lingering on me just long enough for me to catch a glimpse of her anguish. "It's really good. You should try it."

"I don't think—" But I cut my refusal short when Zoe bowed her head after setting one final piece of firewood on the burgeoning blaze. "Sure. Soup sounds good."

But despite my acquiescence, Zoe's head remained bowed. "Listen, D...I wanted to talk to you about, well—I think there's something you're forgetting."

I frowned.

"Your memory of what happened that day...of what happened to Jason." Slowly, she turned on her knees, her hands tangled together. "I was talking to my dad and Gabe about Abilities and how the mind works, and it got me thinking—I think that maybe you've blocked something from your mind, something important." She took a deep breath. "Sort of like how my memories shut down to protect my mind from Clara, you know? It seems only natural, given your duress and the circumstances, that your mind might go into protective mode, saving you from something you're not ready to deal with yet, and maybe you don't remember all the details."

She paused, gauging my reaction, but she couldn't see it. My heart clenched, and my stomach twisted.

"But, we need to know, or at least, we need to find out if I'm right, if there really is something you're forgetting or blocking." Her blue-green eyes, brilliant with unshed tears, searched mine. "It could be a way for us to get some answers, and that's something we all desperately need. What if you've forgotten something important—like maybe the woman said something we could use. Maybe Jason wasn't as bad off as you thought, maybe—"

Shaking, I stood and started pacing around the room. I felt trapped, a wild animal caged.

"We can't just keep going like this...not knowing. *I* can't."

I wouldn't do this, wouldn't remember. I *couldn't* remember. We were opposites in this, Zoe and I. She needed certainty; I needed possibility. "No, no, no, no, no, no, no, no," I repeated under my breath.

"D."

"I can't." I wove a chaotic path around the room. My breathing was quick and shallow, and my head was suddenly pounding. My eyes darted here and there, but I couldn't manage to focus on a single thing. Nothing seemed real. Nothing felt tangible. Nothing was worth this desperation…this agony…this dread. "I can't do this. I can't go through it again, even—"

"D!" Zoe stepped in front of me and grabbed my shoulders. "Stop this!" When I shook my head and attempted to break out of her hold, her hands only gripped me more tightly. "You have to stop! You're scaring the shit out of me."

"I *can't!*" I practically shrieked. "I don't want to remember!"

"So you're saying you won't help?" Zoe's words were sharp, pointed, tactical. They cut a path straight to my heart.

My mouth opened and closed several times. I wanted to appease her, wanted to give in. I wanted to do something —*anything*—that would wash the terror clear from her eyes. I wanted to be strong so badly. My shoulders slumped. "I can't do it."

Zoe's face, her entire demeanor, softened. "Because you're afraid of *what* you'll remember?"

I blinked rapidly and stared up at the ceiling. "Yes. No. I don't know." I took a deep breath. "I see him, his blood, every time I close my eyes. Going through it all again, even just in my mind, I just—" I shook my head, desperate for her to understand. "I'm barely hanging on now, Zo…if you're right and I'm repressing something worse, if I actually saw him die…" I inhaled shakily and squeezed my eyes shut. "Knowing he's gone is one thing, but *seeing* it again…" Opening my eyes, I looked at her. "It'll be too much."

Zoe was quiet for a long moment. "But what if you remember

something that'll help us find him?" She paused again. "I could help you remember, if you want."

Slowly, I lowered my gaze, forcing myself to look at her. "I—" My chin trembled. "I'm not ready to find out if..." I took another deep breath. "I'm not ready. Not yet."

"Okay. We'll talk about it later." I could hear the disappointment in her voice, but a high-pitched whistle came from the fireplace, and Zoe released me to retrieve the teapot. "Let's get you cleaned up and something warm in your belly, okay?"

I nodded, unable to look her in the eye. I was too ashamed.

IO

ZOE

DECEMBER 8, 1AE

THE FARM, CALIFORNIA

I was running in a dew-dampened field. The brisk morning air whipped through my hair, across my face. I felt the muscles in my legs growing weary and my lungs pushing and pulling for breath, greedy as my heart pumped. The rolling hills were my solace, the sound of muted thudding a methodic, soothing drum. I felt alive.

But my hair was a mane of white and caramel, my body strong and built for exertion I'd never experienced before; my legs were long and...hooved. I wasn't me. I was Wings.

I was Dani.

"Are you there?" The words were a whisper, not on the breeze that whooshed by my ears, but a voice inside my head, stirring me from an existence so foreign and liberating, I could almost ignore it.

"Can you hear me?" The voice grew louder. "I can feel you..."

. . .

I sat up in bed, disoriented as I registered my surroundings: the raw wood dresser across from me; the matching nightstand to my left, a full glass of water right where I'd left it; my robe in a heap on the floor beside me. I was in the cottage, in Dani's bedroom, the first rays of morning illuminating the room.

I tried to catch my breath. My mind was reeling from the dream, and I was a little shaken by the voice that had punctuated it. *What just happened?* I was certain I'd been drifting, or that I'd experienced *Dani* drifting as she lay beside me. It was an amazing feeling—primal and uninhibited. I could see why she no longer wanted to fight the urge, even if she had little choice.

But the voice...it hadn't been Dani's. It had been a foreign voice, an *unnerving*, haunting voice that seemed too real to be a dream; it was a stranger's whisper.

I scoured the room, my mind seeking a presence in the house. A trail of chills roamed over my skin and a sinking feeling settled in my stomach, but there was no one in the cottage but Dani, Annie, Jack, and me.

Letting out a deep breath, I reached my hand between the mattress and the box spring to retrieve the knife I'd stowed there, just in case. Although I'd never felt unsafe on the farm, I'd learned a long time ago that things could change far too quickly and unexpectedly to allow myself to ever be completely unprepared. Tucking my sheathed knife beneath my pillow for peace of mind, I glanced back down at Dani, lying beside me, and noticed she was glowing again.

My eyes widened at first, then narrowed while I tried to embrace this new skill of mine. Rubbing my eyes, I focused on what looked like two different colors shimmering around her. I was still getting used to seeing *one* aura around her, so trying to comprehend two left me breathless and a little anxious.

Beneath Dani's pale golden glow was a fine, concentrated line of chartreuse, a green so vivid I could almost feel its freshness, its purity. With a sigh, I leaned back against the oak headboard, determined to understand and wrap my mind around the whole aura thing. *Are they really emotions that I'm seeing? Intensifying, changing emotions?* But Dani's aura had never changed until now, and the colors in her aura hadn't changed as much as separated from one color into two. There was no fading or brightening in shade. There were two completely different colors surrounding her.

Dani let out a quiet groan and stirred in her sleep. She rolled over onto her side and pulled her knees in closer to her, hugging herself, almost like she was intuitively trying to keep herself safe. Her dainty hand settled on her stomach, rubbing it ever so slightly.

It felt like a bolt of lightning came out of the sky and struck me where I sat. Some of the scattered pieces composed of the past handful of days began to fall into place—Dani's ongoing nausea and trips to the bathroom, her fatigue and spiraling hormones, her dividing aura...all of it was more than a grief-stricken, broken heart.

With a veil of tears blurring my vision, I reached out, gently shaking Dani back to her body. "D," I said, uncertain whether the tightness in my chest was happiness or sadness, or a mixture of both. "Dani." I shook her more vehemently. I didn't want her waking up to me in hysterics. "Dani, come back."

Like she'd been stirred from sleep instead of from the mind of her equine friend, Dani blinked her eyes open and peered up at me. Her expression quickly pinched with worry. She sat up. "What is it? What's wrong?" Her eyes searched my face in the dim light, quickly filling with dread.

"D..." I breathed, trying to gauge what her reaction would be. I couldn't help my smile or my tears, just as I couldn't stop myself from saying, "I think you're pregnant."

II

DANI

DECEMBER 8, 1AE

THE FARM, CALIFORNIA

" **I** think you're pregnant."

My heart stumbled for a couple beats. I opened my mouth, drew in a breath slowly, then pressed my lips together and frowned. "Zo…what are you talking about?" Yawning, I rubbed my eyes and flopped onto my back, grateful Zoe was just being ridiculous and wasn't waking me up to deliver more bad news. Annie was locked in a snuggle ball with Jack on my right and, trying not to disturb them, I stretched my arms over my head and pointed my toes in as unobtrusive of a stretch as I could manage.

"The nausea flare-ups, your wild emotions, your exhaustion…" Zoe's voice was little more than a whisper.

I squinted up at her; she was hovering over me, her face both flushed and tensed. She looked like she was holding back both tears and laughter simultaneously. "I don't see why any of that means I'm pregnant," I croaked, then cleared my throat. "Harper says it's normal for a grieving person to experience—"

"Your aura," Zoe interrupted, shaking her head adamantly. "It's split. And I heard a voice." She struggled to keep her own voice down.

My eyebrows rose. "My aura—" I studied her face, a mask of contradictions. "My *aura*'s split? And you heard a *voice*?" I couldn't help the thick threads of skepticism laced throughout my words. "Since when are you into metaphysical aura stuff? I thought that was all too woo-woo for you."

Zoe pulled back, propping herself up in a somewhat sitting position with one hand. "I never said that."

I reached over and twirled one of Annie's blonde ringlets around my index finger. "When we were in tenth grade and Grams told you your energy was out of balance and making your aura all whack-a-doo, I believe your exact words were, 'No offense, Grams, but isn't that a little *woo-woo*, even for you?'"

Zoe scoffed. "I did not!"

Pursing my lips, I speared her with my most level Grams-like stare.

Zoe ran her fingers through her disheveled hair and exhaled in exasperation. "Well, I didn't say it like *that*."

I snorted.

"And it's not like I can ignore the fact that you're constantly glowing," Zoe said, her gaze flicking to what I assumed was the glimmer around me. She took a deep breath. "For the past week or so, I've been seeing auras around you guys—or at least some of you." A small, self-effacing smile touched her lips. "Well, it's really only been you and Gabe, and *maybe* Jake and Sanchez, but still…yours was a golden glow—that's all, just a steady, single golden glow—but now there's another color underneath—green. It's still surrounding you, but it's more vibrant and defined. It's just…different."

"That doesn't mean I'm pregnant."

It was Zoe's turn to settle a level stare on me.

"I'm not pregnant!" My shrill denial roused the dog and little girl sleeping beside me, and I tossed them an apologetic smile. "Go on and snuggle up in your room, sweetie."

Jack and Annie groggily crawled off the bed and made their way down the hall.

Lowering my voice and pitch, I looked at Zoe and repeated, "I'm *not* pregnant."

Curling her legs under herself, Zoe turned to face me fully and raised a single eyebrow. "Our cycles have been synced up almost perfectly for the past few months," she said matter-of-factly. It was true and hardly surprising; with the close living and working proximity, the ladies of the farm had all slipped into the same monthly cycle.

"And *my* period started three days ago." Zoe cocked her head to the side. "Did yours?"

My breath caught, and I slowly pushed myself up onto my elbows. "I—" I shook my head. "No." My hands settled on my lower abdomen, the fingers of my right hand twisting the smooth wooden band on my left ring finger. "No, it didn't."

Frantically, my mind started calculating how long it had been since my last period, trying to find some twisted version of the theory of relativity that would stretch out the days for me…that would explain why my period was late, when the other women on the farm were right in the heart of theirs. "It could be the stress," I said numbly. My gaze sought out Zoe's. "And that I haven't been eating much…or sleeping. Maybe all the drifting…and the stress and the lack of food and the—"

"D…" Zoe's voice was soft, kind. She reached out, placing her hand over mine. "When we were sleeping, I picked up on your mind…sort of drifted with you for a while…and then this unfamiliar voice called out to me. It was really weird, actually." She shook her head for about the millionth time. "Look, the point is, I think it might've been the baby." She frowned. "Do you get what I'm saying?"

"Sure," I said, shaking my head.

"D…" Zoe leaned in, squeezing my hand. "Trust me, you're pregnant. I know it."

"I—I don't—" I opened my mouth. Shook my head. Closed my mouth. Shook my head again. "I—"

Tears welled in my eyes as joy, pure and unexpected, became a gathering storm in my chest. Jason had been gone for almost two weeks now, and it was as though I suddenly carried a piece of him —a real, physical, tangible piece of him—inside me. Because if Zoe was right, I *did*.

And deep down, I knew she was right.

Then, panic flared. I'd been spending the days since Jason's disappearance in a state of near-starvation, stressed out to the point of being catatonic. And I'd been drifting every time I fell asleep. I'd been doing everything I shouldn't be doing to support another growing life.

"Zo," I said, lurching to a sitting position. "All the drifting…" I felt instantly ill, my stomach twisting and knotting and my heart beating so quickly it was practically tripping over itself. "That can't be good for it—"

"The baby," Zoe said with a slightly troubled smile.

"And all the not eating." I clutched her hand hard enough that she winced, but I couldn't let go. "I'm starving it! And oh my God, what about the genetic instability and all of that crap that Dr. Wes —your mom wrote about?" The tears streaking down my face that had been born in a moment of unbridled joy were instantly soured by my sudden terror. "Am I going to lose it?" Because according to Dr. Wesley's research, that was the inevitable result of a pregnancy conceived within the first several years of the genetic mutation. I'd seen the charts myself, the data collected from dozens—maybe hundreds—of women and their miscarriages. "Am I going to lose Jason's baby?"

Zoe's smile faltered, then faded completely. "Come on." She pulled me up and off the side of the bed with her. "I'm taking you to Harper. And Gabe. And Chris. And my dad." She practically dragged me out of the room, not pausing when she called to the other bedroom, "Stay here, Annie. I'll send someone out to watch you in a few minutes."

My stomach tossed and turned. "Zo," I said as my best friend pulled me outside. "Zo," I repeated, jogging on shaking limbs to keep up with her long strides down the stone pathway that connected the cottage to the farmhouse. "Zo!" I planted my bare heels on the pathway before we reached the farmhouse's porch steps.

Zoe turned, eyes brilliant and wild in the pale morning light. "What?"

"I need to—"

I pressed my free hand to my stomach as my inner muscles gave an enthusiastic heave. Bending double, I vomited up a liquidy mess of water, bile, and what remained of the few crackers I'd managed to keep down the previous night. I gagged a few more times, coughed, and wiped my mouth with the back of my hand. Slowly, I straightened, feeling like I was about a thousand years old.

"Puke," I finally finished.

And then my knees buckled, and the lights went out.

✿

I lay in the twin bed Harper used as an exam table and shut my eyes while I listened to the others. Zoe reclined beside me on the bed, every few seconds adjusting the cool, damp cloth on my forehead, shifting a strand of my hair, checking the IV needle feeding fluids into my dehydrated body, and generally fussing over me in all of the most comforting ways. My heart clenched; I was so incredibly grateful for her. She really was the greatest best friend I ever could've asked for. I had no clue what I'd done to deserve her, but there was no way I was ever letting her go.

Gabe, Harper, Tom, and Chris were sitting in mismatched

119

chairs arranged in a semicircle around the bed, doing a poor job of keeping calm while they discussed my situation. More like argued about my situation...

"The data couldn't be any clearer," Gabe exclaimed. "So long as one set of contributing DNA is stable, the embryo has a chance to make it over the crucial hurdle to the fetus stage and—"

"The data's *clear*?" Harper cut in. "It was collected from a study done on pregnancies with a one-hundred-percent fail rate—"

"And Sarah." Gabe's retort was a perfect verbal jab.

"Whose gametes had to have been stable for years, according to the letter from Zoe's mom." In my mind's eye, I pictured Harper waving a hand irritably at the letter that Gabe was no doubt brandishing like it was the Rosetta Stone of this new era of human reproduction.

"But Biggs's weren't," Chris said.

There was the sound of chair legs scratching on hardwood, then quick, heavy footsteps as someone—Harper, I thought likely—started pacing around the room. I cracked my eyes open a smidge to confirm. "Yeah," he said. "But Biggs wasn't the one carrying the child. It was Sarah—the *genetically stable* of the two."

Gabe scoffed; it was a rough, ugly sound. "How many times, in how many different ways, do I have to explain to you that *that* doesn't matter? As long as either the egg or the sperm is genetically stable—"

"And how many different times do *I* have to remind you that you're *hypothesizing*?" I'd never heard laid-back Harper so worked up. I knew that he and Gabe tended to rub each other the wrong way and, as a result, didn't spend much time together, but I hadn't realized just how combative their relationship had become. "Jesus, man, you're not even a medical doctor; you're a geneticist!"

"And you're a *medic*." Gabe's four simply stated words filled the infirmary with silence.

"Would you both knock it off? Here—*now*—isn't the time for this discussion," Zoe said, her voice cool and level. It reminded me painfully of the tone her brother's voice took on when his patience had run out and the time for unquestionable commands had arrived.

Someone cleared a throat. Someone else coughed. The tension grew, becoming thick and choking. My interest in remaining in the room was quickly waning, though I doubted that either Harper or Gabe—or any of the others, for that matter—would be willing to let me leave. No, I was stuck in that room until all five of my nurses and doctors were satisfied that I was in tip-top baby-growing shape.

Or, at least, my body was stuck in that room. My mind, on the other hand…

I sought out Jack's mind and found him herding Annie around the beehives while Carlos tended to our fuzzy, buzzing little friends. I searched for Wings's mind next, thinking we might resume our carefree run through the pasture, but she was happily grazing, and I didn't want to disturb her. I'd been avoiding creating too close of a connection with birds since Ray's death, but the idea of flying, the feeling of the crisp winter air streaming all around me and of breaking the chains of gravity, at least for a little while, was immensely appealing.

So I started scanning the avian minds nearby, searching for a bird of prey. A huntress. That sounded like exactly what I needed at the moment. To feel free and powerful, not vulnerable. Not weak. Not pathetic. Plus, I had the mother of all prey to hunt for—*her*.

"Excuse me." Becca's voice pulled me back to my body, and I opened my eyes to find her standing in the doorway. Every time I saw her, I was reminded of our conversation about love—about the costs and benefits, about its worth—and every time, I chickened out and *didn't* ask her if she'd known what would happen that day. I didn't think I was ready to handle the repercussions if she'd really had a vision. The blame I would place on her would be brutal, the blame I'd place on myself unbearable.

I glanced around the infirmary. The others stared at Becca, owllike and apprehensive—exactly how I felt.

Finally, after doing a long, slow scan of the room and all of the faces within it, Becca's eyes met mine. A small smile curved her lips. "You will not lose the baby."

A collective exhale filled the room.

But Becca wasn't done. "So long as you stay on this farm until the baby is born, it will live."

"Wait, what?" I blurted. "Why? What'll happen to the baby if I leave?" I couldn't wrap my brain around how this geographical location could be so important to the livelihood of my—of mine and Jason's—child.

"An unborn child cannot be safe and healthy if its mother is not safe and healthy," she said as though her words made any sense at all.

"Becca," Zoe said, drawing the young Re-gen's name out, "what are you saying?"

Becca turned violet-gray eyes on Zoe. "If Dani stays on the farm until the child is born, both will be fine." Her eyes shifted to me. "But if you don't, you will most likely die."

✦

I was a seagull. I swooped and climbed and dove, riding the swirling air currents gleefully while I searched for an area of stability to glide with ease.

She-who-flew-with-me wished to search the coastline for the one she called mate-killer, a female two-leg she'd been hunting for days. I would aid in her search, gladly. The only thing better than a good hunt was a good, long fly, and the search for mate-killer afforded me both.

Mate-killer was a danger to her young, she-who-flew-with-me told me. Mate-killer couldn't be allowed to roam free. A danger to one's young must always be eliminated. It is known. It is the way of things.

"Dani?"

I felt she-who-flew-with-me pull away enough that her thoughts were no longer an extension of mine. I willed her to stay with me. The hunt was far from over.

"Dani?"

She-who-flew-with-me pulled away further, until I could sense little more than her gratitude and her farewell. And then, between one flap of my wings and the next, she was gone.

"Mase?" I knew it was him sitting beside the infirmary's twin bed before I'd even opened my eyes, so familiar was his steadfast presence. Re-gens' minds felt different than those of us still living our first—and hopefully *only*—lives, but like the rest of us, each Re-gen mind was unique and, if I'd spent enough time with them, easily recognizable.

I opened my eyes, taking in Mase's troubled features barely a foot from mine. I shifted my head away on the pillow, just a smidge. "Everything okay?"

Mase straightened in the chair he'd situated beside the bed. "Sorry. I thought maybe you'd actually fallen asleep, and I didn't want to wake you if you were getting good rest."

I offered him a relieved smile and shook my head. He was such a considerate, kind soul; a valuable reminder that one should never judge a book by its cover, so to speak. He might've looked big and mean and scary with all of his bulky muscles and tattoos, not to mention that his resting expression was essentially a scowl, but he was the gentlest of giants. At least, he was when he didn't fear for the lives of those he cared about.

"I was just drifting," I told him, "so don't worry about it."

He returned my smile with a grateful one of his own.

I did a quick scan of the room. "Where's Camille?" I knew he wouldn't take the question as me being underwhelmed by his solo visit—the two were always together, with Mase literally functioning as the petite Re-gen's voice whenever necessary.

Mase's smile wilted. "She's with Becca." He shifted in his chair, leaning forward a little and resting his elbows on his knees. "She believes Becca has been hiding things, and while I was skeptical at first, I now believe Cami might be correct."

My gut told me she was right, too, but I didn't voice that opinion just yet. Instead, I worried my bottom lip with my teeth while I thought of how to respond. "What changed your mind?"

Mase took a deep breath, then let it out slowly. "Cami was with her before she came up here to deliver the prophecy about the baby." He glanced at the open doorway to the hallway, then leaned in a few inches more. "I wasn't sure whether I should tell anyone else—I didn't want to make you all mistrust her, because I *know* her, and I have never known her to do something malicious, so I feel certain that her intentions are good—so I thought I should ask you. You always know what the right thing to do is."

I snorted my disagreement with that statement. "If you say so."

"You do," Mase said earnestly. "You helped us find a way out of the Colony—away from Father—and helped us find a home." He paused. "You helped us find a way to be together. We owe you everything."

I smiled and broke eye contact, more than a little uncomfortable with his praise. "It was nothing," I said, barely a murmur.

"It was everything," Mase said, his words filled with so much conviction that I couldn't *not* meet his stare. "And you must know that Cami and I would do anything to keep you safe." He smiled a slightly shy, slightly eager smile. "You and your baby. We'll be here, no matter what."

Tears welled in my eyes more quickly than I could've imagined. When they spilled over the brim, I didn't even bother to swipe them away because they were happy tears, the result of a suddenly overflowing heart. While the thought of bearing Jason's child was comforting simply because he or she would be *his*, it was also the most terrifying thing in the world. *Now* was a horrible time to raise a child, this world a terrible place filled with dangers and struggle and the always-present possibility of starving or falling victim to a Crazy or a cruel or greedy survivor. But to realize that Mase and Camille would be there, not to mention the rest of my companions on the farm, two-legged, furred, or feathered...it was more comforting than words could ever express.

"Thank you, Mase," I said, my voice husky and my smile wobbly. "*That* means everything."

He grinned. "You are a sister to me. I'll always be here when you need me. Cami and me, both."

My smile faltered as my thoughts returned to Camille and the reason for her absence. "What happened with Becca?" I asked gently. "What made you doubt her?"

Mase's expression grew serious, and if I hadn't known him better, I would've thought it was a scowl. "Before she left Cami and came up here, Cami overheard Becca say to herself, 'It is time.'"

I stared at him, frowning. "I'm not quite following you..."

"She *knew*," Mase said. "She knew of the pregnancy and that you would need to remain on the farm but didn't say anything. She knew, but said nothing until it was 'time.'" He scowled in earnest. "It makes me wonder what else she knows but doesn't say."

Anger was suddenly an inferno burning in my chest. I couldn't avoid the possible truth any longer. "Do you think she knew what would happen to Jason?"

Mase blinked once and straightened in his chair. "I—I don't know." He narrowed his eyes. "Do you?"

"I'm not sure."

"But you suspect it." He cocked his head to the side. "Why?"

"It was a conversation we had a few days before Jason—before *that day*." My eyebrows drew together as I thought back on what Becca had actually said, not on what I'd been twisting her words into in the darkest recesses of my mind. "She was asking about love, about whether it was worth the potential pain and loss." I shook my head, finding that my memory of her actual words wasn't nearly as damning as I'd made it out to be. "She said that even with her visions, tomorrow is never certain, and that she needed to know if the good balanced the bad where love was concerned, because as a Re-gen, she doesn't always feel things so strongly...she can't always relate."

Mase nodded as I recounted what I remembered, his eyes squinted thoughtfully. When I was finished, he remained silent for several more long, deep breaths. "I can see why her words have troubled you." He paused, his stare distant. A moment later, his eyes refocused on mine. "But I think it's just a coincidence...or maybe, if what she said relates to her visions, it has to do with something else. Becca never does anything without purpose, and I do not see what effect those words could have had on the outcome of *that day*," he said, emphasizing the final two words just as I had.

I frowned. "I suppose..."

"You and Jason were already in love, had been for some time. I think it is more likely that she sought your opinion to determine whether or not she should interfere in the yet-to-be-formed relationship of another pair...or maybe she was asking for more personal reasons?"

I rolled his words around in my head, testing their weight, measuring their merit. His points were valid, his logic sound, echoing things I'd wondered myself. Relief blossomed in my chest, and I smiled broadly. "You know what, Mase?"

His eyebrows rose.

"I think you're right." I laughed softly. It felt like it had been ages since I'd laughed, but it died quickly. "I think I've been seeing monsters where there are none." I reached out and took hold of his hand, finding further amusement in the extreme way that it dwarfed mine. "And I think you and Camille should give Becca the benefit of the doubt too...for now."

Mase glanced at the doorway sidelong. "Well, it's a little late for that. Cami's talking to her right now."

"I know." I gave his hand a squeeze. "But maybe don't blow the whistle on her just yet."

Mase looked at me quizzically.

Smiling to myself, I shook my head. There was nothing like having a Re-gen around to remind me just how confusing our language could be. "Don't tell the others just yet. Like you said"— I shrugged one shoulder—"she's never shown anything but the best of intentions."

I forced another smile, ignoring the four little words that whispered through my mind.

The road to hell...

12

ZOE

DECEMBER 9, 1AE

THE FARM, CALIFORNIA

K neeling in the damp earth, in a row of overgrown herbs, I reveled in the sunshine beating down on my face, heating my clothes like on a warm summer day and causing me to sweat despite the brisk breeze. I wasn't sure how I'd survived on the east coast for so long. The wind and rain storms in California were nothing like the harsh, snowy winters in Massachusetts, but I'd needed the sun on my skin all the same—to refuel the depleted parts of myself that had resulted from endless hours indoors.

Although working with Dani in the herb garden she and Harper had been tending since summer wasn't one of my usual activities around the farm, it was the perfect task today. I was able to bask in the bone-thawing sunshine while keeping an eye on my pregnant, emotionally wrought best friend. Although the search for Jason's body or the woman trader hadn't been officially called off, it wasn't lost upon me that after this long we likely wouldn't find them, and I knew we needed to keep busy if Dani was going to be able to take care of her baby the way she needed to. Besides, it was nice to do something with my hands that didn't result in calluses, splinters, or cramping from holding a pencil for too long, though it had been a while since I'd done any of that even.

I wiped the perspiration from my forehead with the back of my hand and ventured a quick glance at Dani, who was weeding a few rows ahead of me. She was covered in soil and dead, leafy debris, like me. And she was humming, a sound I hadn't heard from her since Jason disappeared. This was good...the pregnancy was *good*. I allowed myself to smile.

In the last twenty-four hours, I'd worried a lot that Dani might struggle with the idea of having and raising a baby without Jason by her side, but I'd had it backwards. This baby—this piece of Jason—seemed to be the one thing bringing Dani back to life.

Almost happily, I plucked off a few dead leaves and put them in my nearly full bucket. We'd been at it for a couple hours—crouched in the soil—picking and pruning and focusing on the rotted or burned greens that didn't look like they belonged in the numerous teas that Dani often made to remedy my cramps or help me sleep. And after I collected the mulchy decay that gathered around the base of one plant's stalk, I sidestepped and knelt by the next. It felt good to start working again. We needed to busy ourselves, Dani and I, to refuel and find some form of normalcy while Jake and my dad were still out, tirelessly searching for Jason's body. They wouldn't let go. Part of me hated myself for trying, and my lingering smile faltered.

Harper's chuckle as he exited the farmhouse and trekked toward us drifted over on the slight breeze. After wiping my brow again, I squinted up at the sun. It was directly above us, perking everything up that was soggy from foggy days and lack of sunshine.

"Hey, D?" I said loudly, so she'd hear above her humming.

She looked up from her yarrow plant—one of the only plants I could easily recognize, since it was a wildflower that grew all along the coast. "What's up, Zo?" She wiped the sweat from her own brow as she turned and squinted at me.

My eyes flicked to the sun and back. "It's getting pretty warm. Maybe you should take a break…get some lunch or something to drink."

Dani frowned and glanced from Harper, headed toward us, to me.

I knew that look. "You're not hungry, are you," I said, feeling a prick of disappointment. She'd been trying to eat more, but it didn't seem to be getting any easier for her to keep much down.

With an audible breath, her hand instinctively went to her belly. "I'll find something. Maybe some crackers or—"

"Hey, ladies!" Harper called as he strode closer.

I pivoted around to face him. His smile was wide, but didn't exude its usual charm. "Hey, H. How was New Bodega? Did you find some nutrition drinks for Dani?"

His smile faltered a bit, and his brows pinched together, like he wasn't sure he should say.

"What is it?" I asked. "Nobody had any?" I wasn't sure what we would do if her nausea kept acting up.

"No, I traded a few of my tinctures—the alcoholic kind"—he winked—"for a case of them. I even threw in a few of Dani's herbal remedies so I could get an assortment of flavors." He flashed his Harper-smile at Dani. "I hope you like strawberry and chocolate. He only gave me one vanilla."

Dani let a small smile play on her lips, and she gave him a thumbs-up. "Sounds good. Thanks for doing that for me."

"Of course. Besides, it gave me a guinea pig to test my new concoctions out on." Harper's eyebrows danced, and I appreciated his attempt to keep the mood light.

I snorted. "Great, I can see it now. You'll be a big-time boot-legger in no time." I stood up, wiping my hands on my jeans.

Harper winked again, though like before, his smile didn't quite touch his eyes. He was exhausted and worry creased the skin around his eyes, though he tried to hide it. "You know I like to ruffle feathers, Baby Girl."

"Oh, don't I know it," I grumbled and turned to Dani, who was now standing beside me. "How does a nutrition shake sound?" I asked, hopeful. "Think you can keep it down?"

"I guess we'll see." Both of us shrugged, though we were far from indifferent about it, and Dani started toward the house.

"I'll be right behind you, D."

Dani and I exchanged glances, and she offered me a sympathetic smile, her gaze sliding to Harper a moment. "It's okay, Zo. I think I might lie down after my snack."

"Okay," I said, distracted as I saw Biggs prominent in Harper's mind. "How is he?" I asked, my gaze leveling on Harper. "I mean, him and the twins. Are they, you know, okay?" I'd been thinking about them a lot, especially since finding out Dani was pregnant.

"He seems a little frazzled, but yeah, I think they're doing okay."

"Yeah?" The knot in my chest loosened but didn't disappear. "Well, that's good." I missed them like crazy, and the fact that Biggs and the kids weren't around because of me made the sting of their absence feel like a yawning emptiness, no matter the months that had passed since Biggs had stormed out of here.

Harper's eyes brightened. "He actually helped me find the guy to trade with for Dani's shakes. Seemed pretty concerned about her situation."

"That's good," I said a little too weakly. There'd been a lingering, burning question I'd had for him since his heated argument with Gabe in the clinic. "Hey, H," I finally said. "I saw a flash of your vision yesterday morning." I turned back to the scraggly plant at my feet. I didn't want to see that look of sympathy on Harper's face as he remembered it, just like I didn't want to bother him with more questions he either didn't want to or couldn't answer, but I had to. "It was about Dani and the baby, wasn't it?" I said quietly, nervous to know about the vision in its entirety. I busied myself with pruning, waiting for his response.

"You saw that, huh?"

I nodded. "What was it, H?" I felt it, his concern for Dani, more than I saw anything telling in his mind.

"Just a glimpse of Dani, struggling—a lot—nothing that we haven't already seen, but enough to know that there's little hope of finding—"

"I know," I whispered. "I figured as much." I pulled what was left of the dying leaves off with more fervor than was probably necessary as I busied myself. The whole thing looked more like a weed than a medicinal component anyway, but what did I know?

As I tore the last leaf off, I paused. "H, what's that smell?" I scanned the area around me. Reluctantly, I brought my fingers to my nose and cringed. "What the hell is this plant?" I pivoted back to Harper, who simply stood there, watching me with a shit-eating grin on his face. My face scrunched as I brought my hand back to my nose, trying to figure out how something so ordinary-looking could smell so pungent. "It smells like...curdled milk." I tried to shake the scent away, hoping it hadn't seeped into my fingertips or singed into my nose.

Harper chuckled. "It's Valerian. The root's an anxiety suppressor."

"Really? As much as it disgusts me to think of ingesting this, I could probably use a shot of this stuff." Interest piqued, I made the stupid decision to smell it again, then wiped my fingers off on my pants. "Nope, never mind. It's not worth it."

"Here," Harper said, and he tossed me his flask. "Why don't you take a shot of this instead?"

My eyes widened with delight. "Doctor," I said, mouth agape and muddy hand against my chest, "I'm not sure whether I should be elated or think you completely distasteful and unprofessional."

Harper shoved his hands into his pockets, his smile once again weak, but present, as always. "Lucky I'm not really a doctor then," he said. Even with his island-dark skin, I could see the shadows beneath his eyes and the exhaustion that filled their green depths.

I twisted off the cap and followed him over to a fallen log that stretched out beneath one of the nearby oak trees. When I brought the cool metal of the flask to my mouth, I wasn't surprised to taste the bite of rum, but the aftertaste was more acerbic than I'd expected. "Delightful," I lied, blowing out the fumes. "Made this all by yourself, did you?" But for all the shit I gave him, his special concoction did just the trick, both enlivening and steadying every one of my senses as it coated my insides.

I plopped down beside him and let out a deep breath. "So, how long is Dani's whole morning sickness, can't-hold-anything-down period supposed to last?"

Harper closed his eyes and leaned his head back against the trunk of the oak whose severed limb we were resting on. "If it's just baby morning sickness, it should end soon…I hope. But if it's stress and nerves and Jason sickness, I'm not sure. And then there's the drifting…"

I'd had a feeling he would say that.

I took another swig of Harper's home brew and handed him back his flask. "I haven't had a shot of anything in a while." My eyes began to water, just a little. "Too bad Dani can't have a drink. She could use one," I muttered.

"How's she holding up?" he asked, taking a swig and staring down at the small metal canister.

I nudged his shoulder. "Strangely, I think she's doing a little better now. It's like she has more to live for, you know?"

"Makes sense," Harper said. He sighed and crossed his arms over his chest. His eyes closed, and I sensed his thoughts as he considered his multiple conversations with Gabe—what Gabe knew about all the failed pregnancies—in addition to how dangerous carrying a child through the first trimester would normally be, and added to that the heap of extra stress that Dani had been under lately.

"Hey, H," I said after a moment. "I know you don't agree with Gabe so much, but do you really think Dani's in danger?"

His eyelids cracked open, and he stared blankly ahead. "I think that it doesn't matter what Dr. Wesley wrote or what happened with Sarah or what Becca says. The truth is, we have no idea what Dani's in for, especially given your family's bloodline, and without the machines and conveniences that would help us find out, it's a waiting game. We can hope and prepare all we want, but there's never any certainty with childbirth, and that scares the shit out of me."

"Too bad you can't choose your visions," I said wistfully. "That would sure be helpful right about now."

Harper nodded. Sarah had been pregnant for about five months before she had the twins. I couldn't help wondering how we were going to get through the next four months—Dani without Jason and me without a healthy Dani, without my brother, and possibly without Jake. He'd been gone so much, searching and frustrated and confused, I was beginning to feel more alone than I'd felt in a long time.

"But you have the rest of us to help, H. Despite your differences with Gabe, he's a really good person to have around. And you have me, too. I'll watch the little one's aura; it's already getting stronger. And to be honest, it's the only one I see now consistently. Hopefully it *keeps* getting stronger." I smiled, hoping my reassurances would put that real, true Harper smile back into his eyes. "That's got to be a good sign."

Then, I realized something. "We're really lucky you stayed behind this last search. I don't think Dani would've gotten through it without having you here." I leaned back, my shoulder brushing his. I replayed her collapsing just before we'd reached the house.

"Yes she would've. She's got you, Baby Girl."

I rested my head on Harper's shoulder. "Thanks, H." I thought about all that Dani and I had been through in the last year, and it seemed that the coming months would be the most grueling yet.

"Did you know," I said, thinking about how painfully amazing it was that Dani was pregnant with my brother's child, "Dani's been in love with Jason since the first day she met him, back when we were in elementary school?" I sat up to gauge Harper's reaction.

"Really?" He raised an eyebrow, and amusement lifted some of the gloom from his voice.

"Yep. And no matter what he says, I think he always saw something special in her, too." I thought back to our freshman year of high school, when Jason found me and Dani down on the beach, having a bonfire with a group of guys from school. He'd been beyond livid. Until that night, he'd never scolded me and Dani both for anything.

"You shouldn't be hanging around these assholes," he'd said. "You shouldn't be down here to begin with. It's dangerous. What were you two thinking?" But Jason had always known that Dani and I had gone down to the beach at night hundreds of times before. We'd watched stars and gotten drunk and camped out when we just needed to get away. He'd known all of that and had never cared. But suddenly, because two of the most popular, hottest guys in our class were with us—one of them rumored to have a huge crush on Dani—Jason had suddenly felt protective.

"Just when I think I remember the moment my brother started looking at her a little differently," I added, "I find another hidden jewel of a memory. I actually wonder if there was ever a time when he *didn't* love Dani in some way." And it was true. As difficult as it had been to digest the fact that they were sleeping together in the beginning, now it wasn't surprising to me at all. "Just goes to show you that whatever is supposed to happen *will* happen, I guess. No matter the circumstances along the way." But then I regretted my words. It was hard to stomach the reality that Dani was having Jason's child and he was gone. Was *that* supposed to have happened? Thinking about it brought the ebbing unease crashing back over me.

Memories were terrible that way, complex and filled with

ravines that swallowed you up and threatened to drown you. They always seemed to surface in your strongest moments, knocking you back down to a pathetic heap of despondency.

"Zoe!" Sam's voice echoed across the garden, rousing me.

I sat up and peered over leafy herbs at his small form, his bow draped over his shoulder and my crossbow in his hand.

"Archery practice this afternoon or what?" he called.

"Better get moving, Baby Girl," Harper said, winking at me as I stood. "I hear Sam is still kicking your ass during practice. Seems to be the norm lately."

"Oh, is that what you heard?" I sneered. "Well, it's true," I admitted. I actually wasn't sure if I would be any good today either; too many distractions, though the two shots of moonshine or whatever it was were kicking in. It was good feeling a little less tense.

Harper smiled and stretched as he stood. "I'll finish up here. Sam's too excited to deny this go-around, and you two deserve a little bit of fun."

"Thanks, H." I raised up on my tiptoes and kissed his cheek. "You're the best."

"Don't forget you said that," he called behind me as I maneuvered through the rows of herbs, heading toward Sam.

Sam's face brightened as I drew closer. I figured today was as good a day as any to have my ass handed to me *again*. Sure, I could hit a target, but never with the hairsbreadth precision that Sam could—though it was fun to try.

But the second I smiled at that, I felt like a horrible person. *Is it too soon?*

"Here," Sam said, and he handed me my crossbow.

"Thanks, Sam," I said, and grabbing hold of the grip that was heavier than I remembered, I followed after him.

When we reached the shooting range on the other side of the pond, I eyed the painted, human-shaped target that was marred with numerous bullet and arrow holes. Pausing for a moment, I couldn't help but wonder if Jason had been scared when the trader had shot him or if he'd been too worried about Dani to care.

I pivoted to another target, to the outline of a buck grazing behind a tree.

"You sure you want to do this, Zoe?" Sam asked, concern softening his voice. "I mean, you don't have to if you don't want to. I'll understand. It's just practice."

I offered him a false smile and nodded toward the targets. "Of course I want to," I said. "You know me. I'm always up for a challenge." Leaning my crossbow against my leg, I tucked the loose strands of hair behind my ears and readied myself to get schooled by a ten-going-on-eleven-year-old.

Sam smiled. I could tell he was anxious for things to get back to a semblance of normal. Although he and Jason hadn't been extremely close, Jason had still been a prominent part of all of our lives, and his absence was acute to everyone.

I took a deep breath and then another, determined to give Sam a run for his money. With my crossbow loaded, I released the safety and found my shooting stance. Deciding on a lung shot, I zeroed in on my target, aligning it perfectly in my sights. Just as I was about to press the release, a strange sensation filled me, making my fingers and toes tingle.

"Why are you so sad?" A voice whispered in my ear.

The arrow was long gone by the time I realized I'd even pressed the release. In a second, I was turned around, my heart racing as my gaze darted around the targets, the trees. Sam was five feet away, and he had a sheepish grin on his face.

"You missed it by a mile," he gloated.

"Why did you do that?" I asked.

He frowned. "Do what?"

"Distract me like that. That's low, even for you, Sam."

Sam was shaking his head, even before he opened his mouth to say anything. "I didn't do anything."

137

I pivoted right, glancing around the house, down the drive, unable to shake the unsettled feeling that lingered.

"I'm not a cheater, Zoe."

I registered the hurt on Sam's face. "I know, Sam. I'm sorry. I just…I thought you whispered something to distract me. It was probably just the wind."

Letting out a deep breath, I squinted downrange, unable to even find my arrow. I truly had missed my mark by a handful of feet, at least.

"Are you sure you're okay?" Sam asked. When I looked at him, his head was tilted in concern.

I winked, rallying myself to ignore the surge of goose bumps that now covered my skin. "I think your skill is just too intimidating for me, Sam."

His grin turned into a laugh, but I couldn't help glancing around the yard one last time, just to be sure there was no one watching.

13

DANI

THE FARM, CALIFORNIA

Lying on my back on my bed, the dim afternoon light filtering in through the curtains, I traced the stitching of Grams's quilt with the fingertips of one hand. My other hand was resting on my belly, where it usually seemed to be lately. It wasn't that I could feel any bump or movement—it was too soon for that kind of thing, even with the accelerated pregnancies we had to look forward to these days—but rather that I could sense something. A presence. My child. *Jason's* child.

The thought was bittersweet, as usual. And though the sweetness had a tendency to outweigh the bitterness, I seemed to be in a bit of a funk. This time, the bitterness was winning.

I glanced at my afternoon snack, a strawberry nutrition shake sitting, half-consumed, on the bedside table. It was settling in my stomach just fine—for once—but no matter how many pep talks I gave myself, no matter how worried I was about getting sufficient nutrition, I couldn't bring myself to finish the drink. I had no appetite *at all.*

And to make matters worse, I could feel the minds of my

LINDSEY POGUE & LINDSEY FAIRLEIGH

favorite drifting companions tugging at me. It was like they were unintentionally begging me to come play with them, run with them, hunt with them...*become* them, just for a little while. It was beyond tempting, but the longer I struggled with my lack of appetite, the more I started to suspect that it was linked not only to my Jason-related stress and grief and to my pregnancy, but to my inability to sleep for even a few minutes without my subconscious opting to hitchhike a ride with one of my animal companions.

I closed my eyes and tried my hardest to block the lure of the animal minds while simultaneously fighting off the bone-deep exhaustion turning my mind into barely set Jell-O. *Make it stop. I just want to sleep. Make it stop. I just want to sleep. Make it stop. I just want to sleep.* Those two thoughts swirled around and around in my mind. *I really, really, really just want to sleep. I need to sleep...*

And then, in the moment between one breath and the next, between one heartbeat and the next, the minds—human and animal alike—vanished from my telepathic senses. Absolutely and completely. My telepathic senses themselves seemed to turn off. Just like when Jason was nulling me.

My eyes popped open, and I sat up like I'd been electrocuted. I had no doubt; I was being nulled. I was being *nulled*—as in, *affected by Jason's Ability*. Which meant he had to be alive. And he had to be okay.

And he had to be nearby.

The cottage's front door creaked open, and my head snapped to the left. I stared at the bedroom doorway so hard, willing Jason to appear in the rectangular opening. My heart was racing so fast that it kept tripping over itself. "Jason!" I scooted to the edge of the bed, and when a shadowed figure stepped into the doorway, I froze, my heart drooping. It definitely wasn't Jason.

"D?" Zoe stepped into the room, her cheeks flushed and her blue-green eyes bright. And I could sense her mind. I could sense all of the minds around me. I wasn't being nulled.

140

I'd imagined it. Or I'd fallen asleep for a few minutes, and it had been a dream. Or it had been a hallucination or anything but reality, so it really didn't matter, other than the fact that it hadn't been real. Jason hadn't returned. The harsh reality stared at me, defiant and cruel and absolutely unwavering.

Jason wasn't going to return.

I couldn't help it; I burst into sudden, uncontrollable tears. Something buried deep inside me bent, strained, trembled, and, with so very, very much resistance, snapped.

He was gone. *Gone.*

He was gone, and it was time for me to discover what had happened that day that had been so awful my mind had repressed it. It was time for me to let Zoe mine my memories, to let her help me remember everything.

"Oh, D..." Zoe sat on the edge of the bed and wrapped her arms around me, pulling me close. "What is it? What happened?"

I shook my head against her shoulder, my sobs too violent to allow for coherent speech yet. But I knew that Zoe could sense the storm of emotions raging within me, knew that she could feel them almost as intensely as if they were her own. And I knew that my memory of the last couple minutes—of my hope and elation turning to miserable disappointment—was likely filtering through her mind in fast-forward at this exact moment.

"Oh, D," she repeated, squeezing me tightly. "I'll do whatever you want. I'll try to help you remember. Just say the word..."

This time, I didn't refuse. I nodded against her shoulder. "Now," I managed to say. "I'm ready now...or as ready as I'll ever be."

There was a long stretch of silence, filled only by the sounds of my gentling sobs, Zoe's steady breaths, and the soft shush of her fingers combing through my wild curls. "After you finish your shake," she finally said.

"Zo..."

"D..."

"But—"

She pulled back, pushing me away by the shoulders, and met my eyes. Her expression couldn't have been clearer. Or more obstinate.

"I—" I searched her aquamarine eyes, bathing in their cool warmth and familiarity, then took a deep breath and nodded. "Okay." I clenched my jaw, took another deep breath, and reached for the unappetizing shake. "Let's do this."

❦

I was sitting in one of the chairs surrounding the kitchen table, counting the cups and dishes stacked on the exposed shelves on the far wall. It was the third day in a row that we'd tried to unlock whatever it was that Zoe was certain I was repressing—that I was moderately sure I was repressing—with zero success.

"I'm sorry, D." Zoe slouched back in the kitchen chair, her knees on either side of mine, and let out a heavy sigh. A fire crackled in the hearth, just a handful of yards away. "I just—I can sense that something's off, or *missing*, but I can't figure out what— or how or why or *anything*." She shrugged weakly.

I worried my bottom lip, disappointment a lump twisting around in my stomach. I tasted sour chocolate from my latest shake, thick on the back of my tongue.

Zoe exhaled heavily, exasperation pinching her features. "It doesn't make any sense. I mean, you've got to be repressing something. With what we have—and *haven't*—found out there, it only makes sense." Squeezing her eyes shut, she rubbed her temples. "This memory-spelunking thing is far from an exact science, you know?" Her shoulders, which had slowly worked their way higher while she spoke, gave way under the heavy defeat lacing her voice.

My chest rose and fell as air whooshed in and out of my lungs. I rested my head back against the top rail of the chair and sighed. "I honestly can't tell the difference between what does and doesn't make sense anymore." Out of nowhere, my mouth opened and I gave in to a jaw-cracking yawn.

"Sleep—or drift or whatever it is you do for rest," Zoe said. "Doctor's apprentice's orders."

I laughed, groaning as I stood, and rested my hand on her arm. "I love you, Zo."

Smiling, she crossed her arms. "Love you too, D."

The man came into view between the trees, the woman not far behind him. He was tall and slender, and when he caught sight of us, he raised his hands up defensively. "Whoa, whoa, friends...no need for guns. We're simply lost and, well, you see, we were looking for mushrooms to trade in town, and—"

I recognized him. "You're a trader. I've seen you before. You traded my friend and me a bottle of antidepressants for—"

Flicker.

A man and a woman stand directly in front of me.

Flicker.

"Tincture of white willow bark." The trader grinned. "Yes, yes, I remember. Quite effective, that tincture. I've had very happy customers. You'll have to give me the recipe. How did the Sertraline work on the poor dear?"

"That's close enough," Jason said, his voice full of command.

Flicker.

I'm holding a gun to my head. I'm terrified that I'll pull the trigger.

Flicker.

My gun is holstered once again. "It's fine, Jason." I looked at the trader. "Unfortunately, those drugs didn't seem to make any difference. On to the next, I guess."

"Hmmm...well, I have a few others you could try. I'll take

whatever's left of the Sertraline back." The trader reached behind himself. "Exchange it for the same amount of—"

In the blink of an eye, a small, black pistol was in his hand, and it was pointed directly at me. I took several steps backward, stunned.

Flicker.

The woman is drawing the blade of a pocketknife along the back of her forearm. She smears the blood on my hands, on the front of my jacket, on my face.

Flicker.

Jason leapt in front of me just as the earsplitting crack of a gun firing exploded among the trees. Seconds later, he was down on one knee and bleeding.

I dropped to my knees before him, holding onto him to help keep him upright.

Flicker.

I'm suddenly back on my feet, and Jason is standing in front of me. "You need to remember!"

Flicker.

A gun is pressed to my head. I'm holding it.

Flicker.

"Remember!" Jason screams.

14

ZOE

THE FARM, CALIFORNIA

I thought I'd fallen asleep in the sweltering warmth of Jake's arms, both of us cozy beneath the soft goose-down comforter on our bed, but the space beside me was cold. Cooper wasn't in his bed on the floor. I was alone. It was Jake's first night home in days, and he wasn't even sleeping.

I peered around the moonlit room and wondered how long I'd been asleep. A few minutes? Hours? Regardless of how long my mind had been resting, it was clear that Jake's wasn't, and I knew exactly where I'd find him. Something was strange about Jason's death, and Jake couldn't let it go, which meant he was downstairs, planning the next search.

Sitting up, I threw the blankets back. The cool air pricked my exposed arms and toes until I found my slippers and donned my purple fleece robe. And, with a groan, I opened the bedroom door and headed down the landing to the staircase. My head was pounding from lack of sleep and drawn-out days, and although I knew I needed rest, I knew Jake needed it more.

With the exception of hushed voices coming from Chris and

145

Harper's room—another overdue reunion in the house—and the wood floors creaking beneath my sluggish footsteps, the house was quiet.

I descended the stairs and wasn't surprised when I saw the glow of the dining room lanterns. Jake stood in front of the wall of maps he, Chris, Sanchez, and my dad had been consulting throughout their tireless pursuits to find Jason, Cooper sprawled out on the rug beside him. Although my heart ached at the reminder that my brother's body had seemed to vanish, I tried to ignore it.

"How long have you been up?" I asked, stirring Jake from his fixed, pensive stare.

He glanced my way, looking surprised to see me, then turned his attention back to the wall of aerial depictions—the mountain-tops, highways, lakes, and coastlines that spanned a hundred-mile radius around us. "A while," he muttered.

I moved to stand beside him. The maps were barely readable anymore, marred with so many notes and lines and Xs I wasn't really sure what I was even looking at. "You need sleep," I said, my gaze shifting slowly to him, hoping more than assuming he would concede and return to bed with me.

He ran his hand over his head, then his face, and let out a frustrated breath.

"Jake…" I whispered. "Let's—"

"It doesn't make any sense," he bit out, his fist meeting the table as he spun around.

I jumped.

"We've found nothing, not in Sonoma or Napa or Marin…" Jake shook his head, his voice nearly boiling over with an anger that was different from anything I'd ever felt in him before. "If he's dead, why haven't we found him by now?" The table creaked as he pushed away from it. "We've combed this valley dozens of times. People, dead or alive, don't just vanish." Jake glared at the maps again.

I agreed. Wholeheartedly. But I also knew the burning emptiness in my chest—the detachment that was beginning to fester inside Dani and my dad, even me—would ruin us all if we let it. Though I hated to say the words, they seemed to jump from my lips, needing to be said regardless of how painful they were. "Maybe it's time you took a break, Jake. I know none of this makes any sense, but maybe it's time we considered what needs to be done in Jason's absence."

One breath passed. Two. And on my third exhale, Jake turned to me, staring, like he couldn't fathom my meaning.

"I can't. Not when someone took—"

"His body?" I shrugged, my head shaking as I tried to grab hold of my waning patience. "I know, but who? The woman? Her friends? Crazies?" I lowered my voice, hating the thought of anyone with my brother's body, and took a placating step toward him. "I want to find him, too, but…" I scanned the stacks of documents that needed to be transcribed, thought about the trips to New Bodega that needed to be made to barter for food and supplies, about the chores around the farm that needed upkeep and decisions that needed to be made—I thought about all the things that had been neglected in the havoc since Jason's death.

I pointed to the kitchen, keeping my voice calm and steady as I tried to explain. "There are fruits and vegetables that need to be canned. There are projects that need to be finished so we have a better crop this year. People depend on us, Jake. We can't neglect everything we've worked for, let it all fall by the wayside. Jason wouldn't want that."

"And if he's still out there somewhere and we just give up?"

"Even if he is out there somewhere, there needs to be some measure of structure *here* if we're going to keep this place going, if we're going to stay sane." All I could think about was trying to keep Dani busy—trying to keep *myself* busy—trying to get her into a routine so she would think about something else, something besides the child she was having without Jason.

Jake stared at me, impassive, like he wasn't listening to a single word.

"Jesus, at some point we have to accept the fact that Jason's gone, no matter how painful, and even if it doesn't make any sense," I said, more urgently this time. "Unless he walks through that door, we might never find him. We have *no* clues. What are you going to do, keep looking forever? Leave the rest of us behind? Leave me? Because I can't keep doing this." It didn't matter the hour and that people were sleeping. I was desperate to make him understand what *I'd* been trying to since Dani came running home, covered in blood. I was exhausted from hoping and holding on to something that might never come to pass.

"I don't want him to be gone," I said, my voice breaking. "I want to be able to say goodbye, to bury my brother's body, and not have to see the emptiness in my dad all over again, every day for the rest of his life." I wiped the dampness from my eyes. I couldn't go on like this. I couldn't cope if Jake was going to keep searching, keep offering me hope, but delivering only disappointment. "When will it be enough for you?"

"Not until it makes sense," he ground out, but then he let out a heavy, exhausted breath, like he knew that day would never come.

Taking a step toward him, I made no effort to control the tremble of my chin. I saw the plans Jake still had, the possible hiding places he wanted to check, the towns unexplored, all of it thrashing around in his mind.

"Please, take a break. Rest. You can't search the entire state, and you can't possibly scour every single town, every forest and county on horseback and expect to be here, too."

Jake sat in the chair at the head of the table, bracing his elbows on the dark wood surface. He held his head in his hands like he was so exhausted his neck needed the extra support.

"My dad's barely even here, you've both been gone for days. Even when he is here, he never comes in the house anymore, unless it's to plan. Dani's barely eating, and she's got a baby to think about now. She can't live like this. We need you both here, with us."

Jake peered up at me, a look so pointed it stopped any train of thought I had. Dark circles shadowed eyes that used to be soft and affectionate, but were now hardened. "I'm trying to bring her closure, to bring everyone closure," he growled. His face was an expressionless mask like my brother's had so often been, save for his eyes boring into me. It was like Jason was haunting me as I stood there, forced to choose between taking care of my best friend and searching for my brother's body for God only knew how much longer.

I knew Jason would want me to choose Dani.

I pulled the chair to Jake's right out from the table and sat down. I reached for his hand, big and strong in mine as I held it on the tabletop and rested my forehead against it.

"I know you're trying," I whispered, and my eyes squeezed shut. Turning so my cheek rested against the back of his hand, I stared up at him. "This can't be our lives. Jason wouldn't want this to ruin all that we've worked for."

Jake's eyes finally softened. "And if there's something out there that we've missed?" he prompted. His eyes shimmered, like he couldn't simply let go but knew that at some point, he would have to.

I took a deep breath and kissed Jake's hand, wiping the silent tears from my cheeks. "And if there's not?" I stood and gazed out the only window unobscured by maps and lists. There was little moonlight now, and I could hear the wind picking up outside. "What if it's not supposed to, if it never makes sense?"

He looked at me, and I didn't need to read his mind to know that he couldn't let it rest, not after everything he'd seen—what he'd lived through. He needed answers, which is what frightened me most.

Jake slowly stood from his chair, his flannel pajama pants and thermal shirt making my heart ache even more. I'd stared at his perfectly folded nightclothes on his side table for a handful of nights, wishing he were home to scold me for leaving my clothes strewn around the room or to wake me up at midnight with a kiss on my nose and caress of my cheek. And now he was home, but it felt like there were still miles, valleys, and counties between us.

Jake scratched the side of his bearded face before he reached for my hand. Though I knew he wasn't going to stop searching, not yet, he laced his fingers with mine. "Let's go back to bed," he said.

Relieved, I nodded, knowing I'd at least won this small battle. I followed him up the stairs and into our bedroom, Cooper padding up behind us. I was so tired, so drained my body threatened to give out on me with every step. Once inside our room, Jake closed the door quietly behind me. We were in darkness, and I wanted it to swallow me away.

I felt Jake's hands at my waist, moving around to untie my robe for me. Like his mere presence could chase away both the tension and what was left of my strength, I nearly crumbled as his arms wrapped around me and peeled off my robe. After he draped it over the foot of the bed, he pulled the covers back enough for me to crawl under.

I peered up at him, seeing only the shadowed contours of his face. Slowly, I climbed into bed. Jake tucked the comforter tight around me before walking to his side of the bed. He crawled in beside me, the mattress protesting beneath his weight more than it had mine.

And as he exhaled, I felt the weight of his mind not lift, but shift as he pushed his troublesome thoughts and fears, his frustration and anger away, and pulled me into him. His chest rose and fell against my back, and his arms enveloped me like he would never let me go. He was comforting me and apologizing, promising that everything would be okay, even though it was something both of us knew wasn't true.

"I'm sorry," I whispered, shutting my eyes as I felt his heat and strength soaking into my body, into my bones.

He kissed the back of my neck. "For what?" he asked softly.

"For making this more difficult on you. You've done so much, tried so hard…I just don't want to lose you to this, chasing something you may never find."

Jake squeezed his arms around me more tightly and inhaled deeply before I felt his warm breath caress the back of my neck and ear. "I'm just not ready to give up yet," he admitted.

It was quiet for a few breaths until, finally, I nodded because it was all I could do. Tears dampened my pillow, and I moved to wipe them from my face, but the rough pad of Jake's thumb brushed against my cheek before I could.

"You won't lose me to this," he promised.

I stared into the darkness, wishing that were true. "When are you leaving again?" I asked, trying not to be angry.

"In the morning," he whispered. I assumed my dad was leaving too, and for who knew how long this time.

Jake shifted behind me, and I could feel his chest against my arm and shoulder as he braced himself and leaned over me. His hand gently cupped my cheek, turning my head so I would look at him. After kissing his palm, I rolled onto my back and gazed up at his blurred outline without a scrap of pride left. I let more tears fall.

I closed my eyes as Jake brushed the back of his finger over my mostly silent tears. He leaned down and trailed soft kisses across my brow, then his nose nudged the side of my face, and he let out a deep breath. "I'm sorry," he breathed. He was torn, ripping apart inside, like me.

When I opened my eyes to face him, a crimson glow pulsed around him. I hadn't told Jake about the auras I'd been seeing. There'd barely been time since he returned.

He lowered his mouth to mine. His lips were firm but soft, better than I remembered, and they burned against mine, searing in the feel of him, searing in his love so I would never forget it. His kisses were slow and mesmerizing, so comforting and soft that I wasn't sure how I'd gone so long without them.

"I love you," I said, staring up at his beautiful face hidden beneath shadow. I needed him to know, to remember that. I embraced the scarlet light that danced around him, memorizing it in contrast with the inky darkness so I could keep it with me in his absence.

His thumb stroked the side of my face.

"Just don't forget about me," I halfheartedly teased.

And without a word, Jake's mouth was on mine, promising me that he never would.

⬡

I stared into a white room, and pain filled my head as I tried to focus. There was so much light—blinding, humming light—and when my vision finally adjusted, I whimpered. "Jason?"

He was standing in the doorway of what looked like some deranged exam room filled with large machines with straps and harnesses, making them seem all the more terrifying. For experiments? Torture?

But even as the dread infected my mind, my gaze was transfixed on my brother, standing no more than ten feet in front of me. I was too confused and awestruck to be distracted.

"Jason," I said almost giddily. "You're alive!" I waved to get his attention, but he didn't acknowledge me. "Jason!" I shouted, my body shaking. "Jason! Look at me!" I tried to step forward, but I couldn't. I was cemented in place, merely an observer in this twisted place. "God damn it, look at me!" I knew he wouldn't. He couldn't hear me, but I was desperate for him to see me standing in front of him as he stood there, indifferent and frozen.

A tall, dark-haired woman with a short bob walked between us. She stopped to stand in front of Jason, partially blocking him from my view. I could tell by her slim build and the long, elegant fingers she extended toward him that this was our mom...this was Dr. Wesley. She reached for him with the same reserve, the same uncertainty as she always had in my dreams.

Although I worried Jason would strike her or shout, he stood emotionless...simply staring. Like always, his features were fixed—his jaw clenched and his eyes hard and empty.

After our mom touched his face, his stance and expression unwavering, she turned away from him. Her eyes were shimmering, her cheeks wet with overflowing tears. Whatever she was doing, she was miserable despite her stoic expression. Shaking hands were all the alert I needed to know that whatever she was drawing into the syringe that was suddenly in her hand wasn't good.

"Jason!" I shouted. "Please, look at me!" But there was nothing I could do. I was frozen in place. A fixed feature in the wall with no voice, unable to move. All I could do was scream. "Please don't kill him," I begged, willing Dr. Wesley to hear me. Because this woman wasn't our mom, and I knew killing him was exactly what she was going to do.

She turned to face him. He didn't even look at her, but beyond. He didn't flinch or tense. I couldn't watch my mom kill my brother. I refused to. Squeezing my eyes shut, I begged and sobbed.

"It'll be alright..."

I sat up in bed, my body trembling and my mind reeling. "Jason," I said, my voice reedy.

The sun filtered through the white linen curtains as I tried to gather my bearings. I peered around the bedroom, determined to catch my breath, to calm down. I stared up at the ceiling. Feeling coolness on my cheek, I brought my hand up to find the damp remnants of silent tears.

I dropped my hand onto the empty space beside me. Once again, I was alone.

Feeling strangely uneasy, I peered around the room. *That felt like more than a dream.* That voice had been there again—a strange, garbled whisper. It had come and gone, leaving me with yet another ominous sense of urgency. One that I couldn't ignore this time. It wasn't a child's voice; it wasn't Dani's unborn baby, I knew that now, somehow. *Was it Jason?*

Flinging the blankets off me, I jumped out of bed, struggling to pull on a pair of sweatpants and a wadded-up T-shirt from the floor. Jake was leaving this morning, I just hoped he'd gotten a late start. I needed to tell him that Jason might be alive, that he might be at the Colony.

I tried not to let the horror of that thought paralyze me as I galloped down the stairs. I didn't have time to prepare myself for the fact that the dream might not even be real. It *felt* real, and that was all the spurring my dwindling hope needed to get me moving.

"Jake!" I called. My bare feet pounded against the wood floor as I ran through the house.

All the rooms were empty, except for the kitchen, where I found Grayson, Sam, and Tavis, having a morning snack.

"Where's Jake?" I barked. "Did he leave?"

"Zoe," Becca said from behind me. I twirled around to find her still in her pajamas, her shoulder-length hair unkempt and her wide, pale violet-gray eyes staring back at me.

"Becca, I had a dream about Jason at—"

She was nodding before I could finish. "I had a vision of him. I believe he was dying." In spite of the general lack of emotional expression afforded her by her Re-gen nature, Becca looked remorseful. "I am sorry you had to see that, Zoe."

"No, it's a good thing." I smiled, unable to help myself. "It's only a possible future, right? And he can only die if he's not already dead, which means he's alive and we can still save him!" My hope quickly dwindled. "How long ago did Jake and my dad leave?"

"They're outside, saddling the horses," Sam said through a

mouthful of cereal. I was already running out the front door, the screen flinging open then slamming shut behind me.

"Jake! Dad!" I called, barely registering the sound of the screen door opening and closing again behind me or the muffled chatter.

Jake turned to me and frowned. "What is it?" he asked, and though the sun had barely risen, he squinted as he scanned me from head to toe.

Cooper trotted up to me, and I absently pet him as he licked my hands, my eyes too busy searching for Dani.

"Where are your shoes?" I heard someone ask.

Chris brushed her hands off on her pants, taking in my disheveled appearance. "Long night?" she teased.

"I had a dream," I said, a little out of breath. "Where's my dad? Where's Dani?" I glanced back and forth between her and Jake, unconcerned with the others forming a circle around us.

Jake and Chris exchanged skeptical looks.

"A dream about Jason. He was alive—at the Colony."

Chris looked from Jake to me. "Zoe, it was only a dre—"

"Becca had a vision—saw a possible future." It was difficult to stomach, let alone say, the next part. "My mom was going to do something to him. I think she was going to kill him. But it means he's alive, that he's not dead yet." When everyone stood there in silence, I continued. "There was a voice, a voice I've been hearing a lot lately, and—"

"You've been hearing voices?" Sanchez asked as she came up beside me. "Tom tells us you've been seeing auras, and now you're hearing voices, too? Why didn't you tell us this before?"

Jake's eyes leveled on me, but what could I do? "You've been home for what, ten hours? There's a lot that's happened since you guys have been gone. I guess I thought Dani being pregnant was the most important update." I shook my head. "Look, what matters is that I know, deep down in my gut, that Jason's alive. He's at the Colony, or he will be, and if we don't get to him soon, he *will* be dead."

"With no sign of a struggle?" Sanchez said and looked across the group at my dad. "There's no way Jason would let someone take him, injured or not."

"And what about the woman?" Chris said.

"This is the Colony we're talking about. They can do whatever the hell they want." I was growing impatient with their lack of urgency. Everyone looked at me, half doubtful, just like I would've looked had I not experienced the vision firsthand.

"You really think he's in Colorado, sweetheart?" my dad asked as he stepped toward me.

My eyes met his and then settled on Jake, his hope holding at a low simmer, along with the rest of them. "I know what I saw. Isn't it at least worth it to go there and see?"

Everyone remained silent, watching me and wondering if this was an act of desperation, if I was only seeing what I'd wanted to see. They all wanted to believe me but barely dared to hope.

I felt my face fall. "Becca saw it, too," I said defensively. "I'm not delusional."

"We know you're not, Zoe," Sanchez said. Her voice was skeptical, but not unkind. "But the Colony is a whole different ball game. If he's there—and that's a big *if*—we can't just walk in and ask if we can schedule a play date."

"Well, we have to try," I snapped. "What if he's alive at this moment, but in danger, and we stay here? They'll kill him, Becca and I have already seen that outcome. Nothing has made sense from the first moment he disappeared. Whatever Dani thinks she saw is wrong." I peered around, frantic. "Don't you see? That voice—it could be Jason in my head. I don't know how, but it's the *only* thing that makes any sense in all this craziness. So, if we're searching *anywhere*, it needs to be in Colorado."

"*We?*" my dad said, a frown narrowing his expression.

"What if he tries to contact me again? I'm going," I said. There was no room for negotiation.

Tentative footsteps on the gravel grabbed my attention, and

Grayson and Sam slowly stepped aside to make room for Dani, Carlos, and Annie. Hesitantly, Dani stepped into the throng of people surrounding me. Although her eyes were bloodshot and her golden aura dim, the baby's chartreuse halo was still vibrant and defined. "Can I talk to you alone? I think I—"

"I had a dream, D," I blurted, too frantic to consider her reaction to my theory about what the vision meant. "It's about Jason."

Dani peered around at the wide-eyed faces surrounding us and took a step closer to me. "Wh—what do you mean?"

"I gleaned it from Becca—a vision. But Jason was in it. He spoke to me." I took a deep breath. "I think he's alive, D."

I watched the tears flood her celadon pools of pain and grief as she registered my words. Though hope soared inside her, she was already bracing herself to be let down, again.

"I think he's at the Colony," I said, my certainty gaining strength. "With my mom."

15

DANI

DECEMBER 12, 1AE

THE FARM, CALIFORNIA

I left the others in a flurry of skeptical, almost reluctant excitement, making the excuse that I felt weak and needed to lie down. Considering that weak and needing rest were two facets of my usual state of being lately, not to mention the huge bomb Zoe had just dropped on us all, on top of my own unexpected and disturbing dream, nobody questioned my claim or even tried to stop me. It helped that I really did feel weak and needed to lie down. I also felt overwhelmed and ecstatic and terrified and a little bit like I was losing my mind. Desperation flooded me, eager and hopeful, but at the same time, I braced myself for the biggest letdown yet. Disappointment was inevitable; if I'd learned anything over the past few weeks, it was that.

I wasn't strong enough to do this again—to steady myself for dashed hopes, for shattered dreams—not anymore. And then there was *my* dream, my confusing, haunting dream, not to mention the fact that I'd actually managed to sleep. With everything going on, I felt like I was unraveling. More than ever before, I needed to escape.

By the time I slipped through the cottage's front door, I was already searching the animal minds around me for a drifting companion. I yelped when I noticed Gabe squatting on the hardwood floor in front of the fireplace.

He glanced at me over his shoulder, but almost immediately returned to staring at the copper teakettle warming over the flames. His hair had grown so long that I doubted he'd trimmed it since we'd left the Colony so many months ago. Pulled back into a low ponytail as it was and combined with his several inches of facial hair, he more closely resembled a member of a motorcycle club than the elite geneticist he'd been.

"Sorry," he said softly. "Didn't mean to startle you."

Feet glued to the floor, I wrapped my arms around my middle. "It's okay." For several seconds, I stood in the entryway, watching him and saying nothing. "I thought you were outside...with the others."

"Hey Gabe, nice to see you," he said with fake enthusiasm. "Thanks for stopping by." Again, he looked back at me, this time wearing a wry, tight-lipped smile. "Now get the hell out of my house, or I'll sic a pack of rabid squirrels on you..."

My pent-up nerves escaped in the form of an explosive, tooloud laugh. I slapped my hand over my mouth, my eyes wide. "Sorry," I mumbled. "I'm being rude." I moved to one of the recliners Jason and I had arranged close to the fireplace and practically fell backward into it. I settled my arms on the armrests, letting my hands dangle over the ends. "It *is* nice to see you, and thank you for stopping by." I offered Gabe the most genuine smile I could muster at the moment, which probably fell short...by quite a bit. "And I'm not going to kick you out."

He reached into the hearth for the teapot's handle with a folded-over dish towel. "You say that now..."

I groaned. "C'mon Gabe, just spit it out." I rolled my eyes. "The anticipation is killing me."

He laughed as he stood. "I'm sure." He set the teapot on a thick wooden trivet on the small table by the fireplace, then pointed to a glass jar filled with dried leaves next to it. "Raspberry leaf tea."

I raised my eyebrows, impressed. "You've been reading up on your herbal remedies." I nodded to the jar. "Grams swore by raspberry leaf tea." And she really had; it was well known for easing the less pleasant symptoms of pregnancy. Like, in my case, near-constant nausea. I'd never actually tried it before, but then, I'd never had a reason to. I leaned forward. "Where'd you find it?" While growing raspberries was on my never-ending list of to-dos, I'd yet to actually get around to hunting down some raspberry bushes.

Gabe shrugged. "A tea shop in Windsor."

"Oh." I leaned back in my chair, my desire to speak extinguished. The one and only time Gabe had left the farm on an overnight excursion had been several days ago, and he, Jake, Chris, and Tom had headed up to Windsor to search for Jason…who *might* be alive, who *might* be in the Colony, who *might* escape or be rescued only to fall victim to any of the myriad of dangers that lie between there and here.

"The Teahouse of Windsor," I said, trying to sound conversational. Trying not to sound like I was desperate for Gabe to leave so I could be alone to figure out what the hell I was feeling— ecstatic or terrified or some nauseating combination of the two. The path to earth-shattering disappointment was paved with polished bricks of hope. Shoddy craftsmanship meant those bricks could crumble at any moment, leaving me standing in the mud, alone. "I bet it's lovely."

Gabe nodded as he prepared the tea, placing a hearty pinch of the dried raspberry leaves into one of the mesh tea balls I'd "inherited" from Grams and setting the infuser in an oversized earthenware mug. Carefully, he poured in steaming water from the kettle. "I'd have given it to you sooner, but I wanted to make sure it was safe." He looked at me. "Sugar?"

"Honey," I said, pointing to the small blue and taupe glazed honey pot I'd freed from an abandoned farm nearby.

"So, listen..." Gabe trailed off as he drizzled honey into the mug. The slow-moving, syrupy string seemed to hypnotize him.

After several seconds with no sign that he was going to continue, I said, "I'm all ears... listening away..."

Gabe flashed me a cautious smile. "Without Jason—" He stopped himself and looked down at the mug, then took a deep breath and stood, setting it on the round end table beside my chair. "Your mind's not blocked from me anymore." He took what seemed to be a fortifying breath. "I know that the first real sleep you've had in weeks was last night, and that it was filled with a twisted dream of what happened in the woods that day..." He settled in my recliner's mate, his eyes steady on my face. "I could help with that. Suppress the dream so you can get however much restful sleep you can fit in before you drift away."

I held my breath, ignoring the disapproval threaded throughout his final words and forcing myself not to feel affronted or grow defensive. "It's fine. I'm dealing with it. Zo's helping me, you know, by digging around for the truth—her way of psychoanalyzing me, I suppose." I forced another smile and, wanting to take the focus off of me and my *issue*, said, "Did you hear? Zo had a vision."

Gabe cocked his head to the side.

I waved my hand to dismiss his confused expression. "*Becca* had a vision. Zo just witnessed it, I guess." I took a deep breath, letting it out slowly. "What she saw—it made her think Jason's alive...and at the Colony." *I will not freak out. I will not freak out. I will not freak out.* But I really, really, *really* wanted to lose it right about now. I clenched my jaw, stiffened my neck, and hardened my heart.

Gabe leaned forward, elbows on his knees.

"With Dr. Wesley," I added.

"Jesus fucking Christ," Gabe said softly, head drooping so he could smooth back his already-smoothed-back hair.

I started fidgeting with the hem of my zip-up hoodie, my bottom lip unconsciously drawn between my teeth. Inexplicably, I felt tears well in my eyes, and I bit down a little too hard on my lip to hold them back. I couldn't, however, prevent my chin from trembling.

"I—" Gabe stood abruptly. "I should see if I can find out anything from my old contacts back at the Colony. Excuse me." I watched him stride to the front door, his long legs eating up the hardwood in a mere handful of steps, and then he was gone.

For several seconds, I stared at the door, my eyes tracing the outline of the six small panes of glass inset into the wood but not really seeing. For several minutes after that, I stared at the cup of tea steaming on the end table, then at the low flames dancing in the hearth.

I thought I should pick up the mug of tea, or possibly tend to the fire, or sort and clean up one of the myriad of bunches of herbs hanging to dry from the hooks Jason had screwed into the cottage's low, exposed crossbeams throughout the front room, or do anything else besides sit in that chair doing nothing. But nothing was all I seemed capable of at the moment. I could sit there and do nothing while confusion crept in and the thin veil of numbness shielding me from hope and excitement and all-encompassing joy and fear grew thinner and thinner.

I jumped when someone knocked on the front door. When the door didn't immediately open, I turned my head and stared, hard, but my angle was wrong and I couldn't see through the small windows to tell who was on the other side. Why wasn't the visitor simply letting themselves in?

Again, someone knocked on the door, louder this time. "Dani? It's Tom. Can I come in?" There was no question of whether or not I was within; with his Ability, he could sense me easily enough.

So, with a sigh, I hoisted myself up out of the armchair,

trudged to the entryway, and opened the door. "Come on in," I said, holding my arm out in wilted invitation.

Tom stood in the doorway, hands in the pockets of his worn leather coat, somehow looking both sturdy and rickety at the same time. Though Jason was larger than Tom, he had definitely inherited his father's prominent stature. And for the first time while looking at Tom, I wondered if I might be catching a glimpse several decades into the future. I had to stop myself from studying his weathered features too closely, from seeking every little hint of his son, every little undefinable reminder of Jason.

Ducking his head in greeting, Tom stepped through the doorway. My heart clenched and my stomach twisted. There was so much of Jason in that single motion, and I felt instantly grateful that Tom hadn't visited me in the cottage until now. A week ago, I wouldn't have been able to handle such a raw reminder of what was gone, or even yesterday. But today, everything was different. No matter how hard I tried to quell the hope that Becca's vision had stirred, I couldn't ignore it completely. I couldn't prevent at least a small part of myself from believing that Jason truly was alive.

I shut the door and turned around to find Tom standing behind one of the chairs at the kitchen table. His hands gripped the top rail, seeming to steady him. "Please, sit," he said, pulling out the chair.

Frowning, I crossed the short distance between us, the wood floor creaking under my boots, and sat in the offered chair. My stomach was still far from settled, and I glanced at the mug on the end table indecisively, but before I could stand again to retrieve it, Tom was already moving toward it.

"Here you go," he said, setting the mug on the farm table before me and taking the adjacent chair.

I looked at him, then at the mug for several long seconds, before I finally lifted my stare back up to his troubled blue eyes.

He smiled sheepishly. "Yes, I did just glean that from your

mind, and I'm sorry." He bowed his head, just a little. "I know how much you value the privacy of your own thoughts, and I really do try to keep to myself."

Raising my eyebrows, I picked up the mug and brought it up to my lips. For whatever reason, I'd expected it to taste like bitter raspberries despite the honey, but I was pleasantly surprised by something that tasted quite a bit like black tea.

"Anna enjoyed it as well," Tom said softly, and when my eyes met his, he offered me that same, quiet smile. "The kids never knew about it, but we lost our first baby. It was the stress, after leaving Gregory, or the fear, I guess you could say." His fond expression melted, and I found myself sitting next to the same lost man I'd known as Zoe's dad for most of my life. He cleared his throat. "Your grandmother was a great help during the pregnancy...and after."

My mouth felt suddenly parched, so I took another sip and licked my lips. "I'm so sorry."

Tom nodded slowly. "Thank you." He sighed. "But I'm not here to dig up old losses. I know you think you might be repressing something in your memory of that day, and that Zoe's been trying to help you uncover whatever that may be...and I also know about the dream you had last night."

"How—"

"I picked up on it out there," he said, nodding toward the door. He studied my face for a moment. "I know you both think her efforts have been unsuccessful, but I think you're wrong, and I think your dream is evidence of that. I think she's nudged the truth —uncovered the tip of the iceberg, if you will."

I took another sip of tea, holding the warm liquid in my mouth, waiting.

"The fact of the matter is, Zoe's dead set on going to search for Jason, but I'm not willing to let my one remaining child risk her life on a manhunt unless I know for sure that he's out there."

I swallowed the tea in one big gulp and winced. And coughed. "So what are you saying exactly?"

"Zoe's Ability is strong." Tom's gaze met mine, his eyes blue pools of determination. "Mine is stronger."

"So you want to dig through my memories," I said flatly. It wasn't that it was a bad idea; on the contrary, it was a great one. It was just that it was such a violation of *me*. When Zoe did it, I had no control of what she did or didn't see, or of how long she rifled around in my mind. It was hard enough handing over that control to someone I trusted implicitly. And now Tom was asking me to do the same with him.

But if it helps us find Jason...

I pressed my lips together and nodded resolutely. "Alright. But can Zoe come along for the ride? Is that even possible?"

Tom's shoulders sagged in relief. "I was just about to suggest that myself."

⬡

I relaxed in one of the comfy chairs near the fireplace, footrest extended and chairback reclined. Zoe was perched on a stool to the right of the recliner, and her dad sat on my left. Each held one of my hands; Tom claimed physical contact would only increase the connection, making the memory-excavating process both quicker and easier. Both sounded good to me, especially considering what memory I would be reliving during the process, fully conscious and aware.

"Alright," Tom said, giving my hand a squeeze. "We're going to go through the memory once, as is." When I looked at him, I found his attention on Zoe. "This will allow us to look for any seams—places where a 'patch' might have been placed, however unintentionally, over a memory. Do you know what I'm talking about?"

Zoe nodded. "I think so. Everyone has them…all over the place."

Tom, too, was nodding. "There's no such thing as a perfect memory."

Much as I was a fan of a good learning opportunity, my anxiety and nerves were building to a slow crescendo. "So…" I couldn't help the slight tremble in my voice.

This time, it was Zoe who gave my hand a reassuring squeeze. "Just relax and close your eyes, D." When she smiled, I did as she directed. "You won't see us, but we'll be there with you."

I inhaled deeply, then let it out slowly.

I was in the woods, Jason by my side and one of the traders from New Bodega approaching. His hands were raised defensively, his benign words making me complacent. Only a few moments later, those same hands brandished a pistol. The crack-crack-crack of gunfire was deafening. The sight of Jason, bleeding and on the ground, heartbreaking. The feel of the soft earth under my boots and the damp air whooshing in and out of my lungs barely regis-tered as I ran for help. Jason…

"Ughhh…" Zoe dropped my hand, clearly frustrated. "I've been over it dozens of times, and it's always the same. I can't sense any sort of 'seam' or anything like that." She ran her fingers through her hair roughly, almost like she was trying to pull her frustration out through her scalp. "Either we're wrong and the dream was just a dream, or the whole damn thing is a fucking 'patch' or whatev-er." Yep, Zoe was *really* frustrated.

I smiled weakly. "Sorry…"

Zoe huffed out a breath and met my eyes. "It's not your fault, D."

"No," Tom said. "It's not." His voice was tight, his tone flat. It sent goose bumps crawling up and down my skin.

Zoe and I exchanged a wary look, then shifted our attention to Tom. "What do you mean?" she asked.

"It's a plant." Tom lurched to his feet, his stance rigid. "It's a goddamn plant!" He took several steps away, then turned to face us. His hands flexed at his sides. "They're good, I'll give 'em that. They're really damn good." He shook his head, looking angrier than I'd ever seen him.

"Dad..." Zoe stood slowly. "What do you mean, a 'plant'?"

Tom rushed back to his chair, sitting and leaning toward me so abruptly that I shrank away. "Someone planted the entire memory in her mind." Narrowing his eyes, he cocked his head first to one side, then the other, like I was a specimen to be studied. "That's why there are no seams...no holes to be patched up." He reached out, gently brushing a stray curl out of my face. "The memory is too perfect, because none of what she remembers is real."

"*She's* right here," I said, a teensy bit terrified.

Tom blinked, and his hand fell away. "I'm sorry." His eyes slipped to Zoe as she reclaimed her stool and my hand, then fixed once again on my face. "I'm so sorry, Dani." He shook his head. "It's just that I've never seen an example of another's work that was so, well, perfect." He narrowed his eyes, thinking. "Maybe not thought through completely, but I think it would be almost impossible to blend such a huge false memory into someone's mind without knowing them well. This is impressive—"

"Dad!" Zoe said, sounding more than a little exasperated. "Focus. Can we get rid of the whole thing somehow? I'm pretty sure D doesn't want some stranger's implanted memory in her mind any longer than necessary."

I shook my head vehemently. "Nope, not even a little bit." The realization that yet *another* person had been inside my head frustrated me to the point of tears. "I want it gone." And beyond that, more than anything, I wanted to know what hid beneath the false memory. We all did. Somehow, it had to explain what had happened to Jason, dead or alive. *Please be alive. Please be alive. Please, please,* please *be alive!*

"We need to go back to a time earlier in the day," Tom said, "way before they would've started the false memory. And when we find the beginning, we should be able to peel it away, revealing what's beneath." His eyes were bright, and when he took my hand in his, I could feel him shaking, just a little.

I glanced from his face down to his hand and back.

He gave me a small smile and clenched his trembling hand into a fist. "We're about to find out who's responsible for my son's disappearance. We're one giant step closer to finding him."

"Let's not get our hopes up just yet," Zoe said. But when I looked at her, when I saw the brightness in her eyes, I knew that she was just as excited. I *felt* just as excited.

"Alright, Dani," Tom said. "This is just like before, but think of sometime an hour or two earlier in the day."

I quirked my mouth to the side and searched my recollection of the time before *the incident*. It was filled with small, but not insignificant moments that I'd avoided until now. Moments with Jason that were painful in their sweetness, or at least they had been when I'd felt certain I would never experience another such moment with him again.

I settled on the final few minutes before Jason and I left the farm on foot, our foraging baskets on the gravel driveway. We'd both been kneeling on the ground in front of Annie, trying to coax her out of near hysterics at the prospect of being left behind.

"Good," Tom said. "That'll work just fine. Now just relax and close your eyes and let us do the heavy lifting."

Exhaling a sigh and repressing tears, I closed my eyes.

I was having the best day I'd had in months. Jason and I were alone —we had been for hours—and in the woods, surrounded by leafy trees and the pleasant smell of damp earth and decaying foliage. It was like we were in our own, private fairy land. And as we trampled death caps beneath our boots in our eagerness to get closer to one another, I hoped that this day, this moment where we had zero responsibilities, where we were allowed to just be us, *would last forever.*

But as Jason leaned in to kiss me once more, I sensed two minds approaching. I quickly told Jason about them, adding, "One feels a little more familiar than the other, but..." I shook my head. "Must just be New Bodega people."

"Which direction?" Jason asked.

I pointed to the southwest. "They're close. Should be able to hear them soon."

"I can hear you out there," Jason called. "Either identify yourselves or start moving in another direction. The choice is yours, but you'd better make it now." He glanced at me.

I shook my head. "Still coming."

Jason raised his gun. "Remember, Red—shoot first, feel—"

"Feel bad about it later," I murmured. "I know."

"Hello?" a man called ahead. "Who's there? Can you tell me where we are? We seem to be lost." Moments later, a man came into view between one of the few pines in the forest and a robust oak tree, a woman a few steps behind him.

Flicker.

A woman comes into view between one of the few pines in the forest and a robust oak tree.

Flicker.

A man and a woman came into view between one of the few pines in the forest and a robust oak tree.

Flicker.

A woman comes into view between one of the few pines in the forest and a robust, old oak tree. She's brunette, tall, and broad shouldered. And then there's the sawed-off shotgun she has propped almost lazily on one shoulder and the wary gaze she throws our way.

Jason takes several steps forward, blocking my view of the stranger even as he aims his gun at her. "Don't fucking move."

The woman laughs, a rich throaty sound. "Whatever you say, sugar. I'm good right here."

"Why are you here?" Jason's voice is flat, cold, dangerous. "What do you want?"

"Oh, this and that..."

Their back-and-forth continues, but I'm too distracted by the hard press of what I can only assume is a gun nozzle between my shoulder blades.

"Don't make a sound," a man whispers near my ear, his hand curling around my neck. "Don't move or make a sound unless I tell you to. And do not use your Ability." He removes the gun from my back, but I'm still so scared that I can barely force my lungs to draw breath. "Now, I want you to raise your gun and press it against the side of your head."

Tears are leaking out of my eyes, streaking down my cheeks. I don't want to do it. Every fiber of my being is screaming, crying, thrashing. But it does no good. My entire body is trembling as I raise my pistol and press the nozzle against my temple.

"Very good," my unseen, mind-controlling attacker says. "Now, my associate has been...let's call it 'clouding' your companion's perception of reality for the past minute or so. He doesn't know that I'm here, but she's going to stop just as soon as I tell her to. When she does, if your companion makes a move—any move— to harm me or my associate, or if he doesn't do as I say, you are going to pull the trigger and your brain is going to be all over the forest floor." His hand tightens on my neck, and I can feel his breath hot against my ear. "For your sake, I hope he cares enough about you to make this as painless as possible."

He releases me, and all I can do is stand there, silently shaking and crying while on the verge of ending my own life.

"You can drop the illusion now, Larissa," the man says from

behind me. A few seconds later, he says, "Hello, Jason. It's nice to see you again."

Jason spins around, his second pistol drawn and aimed at the man behind me—and at me. His icy mask falters when he sees me, when the gun I have pressed against my skull registers. "Dani, what are you—"

"Tell him, child."

I bristle instantly, though I know it's stupid to find offense from a belittling name, especially now, when so much more is at stake. After a shaky, deep breath, I manage to say, "He's compelled me, Jason. If you try to hurt him—either of them—I have to..." I stifle a sob. "I'll pull the trigger if you try to hurt them. Or if you don't do what he tells you to do." My chin is trembling, and one lone sob escapes. "I don't want to die."

I can see Jason's Adam's apple move as he swallows. Jaw clenched, he clears his throat. "You're not going to die. I promise you, Red, you're not going to die."

"Good, good," the man says as he steps out from behind me, and I get my first real look at him. I'm shocked to find that I recognize him—I've traded with him in New Bodega a time or two. "Now, Jason," he says, "it's very important that you understand how my Ability works. I can compel others to do as I wish, but I must be touching them for the compulsion to work. Once it has set in, it can last days or weeks or even months, depending on the person. Unless, of course, I release the compulsion."

Part of me expects some smart-ass response from Jason, but he remains silent, a statue of barely-restrained menace, of promised death.

"I'm going to touch your hand," the trader says as he approaches Jason. "You can lower your guns; you won't be needing them." He reaches out, taking hold of Jason's wrist once it's at hip level. "I'm going to compel you. Don't attempt to nullify my Ability, or the girl will die. Do you understand?"

"Yes." The single word is harsh on Jason's lips.

"Good, good." I can hear the smile in the trader's voice. *"Now, you will always obey me, you will never harm me, and you will constantly amplify my Ability, starting immediately."* After a brief pause, the trader sighs. *"Oh God, the power,"* he groans. *"Together, Mandy and I were a force to be reckoned with, but you, Larissa, and I—we're going to be unstoppable. That bastard won't know what hit him."*

With the mention of that name—Mandy—memories click together in my mind, and I realize that the marketplace in New Bodega isn't the first place I've seen this man. He was with the cult in Tahoe, one of the many controlled by Mandy's Ability...or so we'd believed. Now, it's becoming clear that he'd had a much more active role. Because he'd controlled Mandy? Or because he'd controlled them all? *Just her,* I think remotely, considering that most of the Tahoe people were now residents of Hope Valley, not under his mind control.

"I find it quite fitting that you're the one who will help me get what I want," Cole tells Jason, *"considering that you're the one who took it away from me to begin with. When you killed Mandy—"*

"Cole," the woman—Larissa—says as she moves around Jason and toward me. *"Care to order your new pet to give me a little boost while I take care of the girl's memory?"*

"I could do that..." Cole moves to join Larissa, and both stop within an arm's reach of me. *"Or I could order him to kill her."*

Horror flashes across Larissa's bold features, but it's quickly masked behind bland amusement. *"You could..."* She makes a subtle pouty face. *"But then I wouldn't be able to practice, and you know how much better I get at creating memories after each attempt, especially when they contain such strong emotions."* She pauses and glances at me, panic alighting in her eyes, then quickly disappearing before she returns her gaze to Cole. *"And how excited the emotions make me..."*

Cole chuckles. *"You're such a greedy succubus."* He leans in *toward her, his hand coming up to grasp her neck. He pauses just short of his lips touching hers. "Do as you wish, but make sure there are no loose ends. You cannot possibly imagine the things I will make you do to yourself if you fuck this up for me." He kisses her, hard, then releases her and walks away to rejoin Jason.*

Larissa exhales heavily, relief transforming her face. "Now don't you worry, sugar," she says, moving closer to me. She cuts her forearm with a pocketknife, then smears the blood on my hands, clothing, and face, even as I fight the urge to cringe. "For legitimacy, sugar. Trust me." Finally, she places her hands on either side of my head and leans in to stare deeply into my eyes. "I'm going to make this all go away, so you can go home and live a good long life with your friends, just you wait and see."

❦

"Cole," Tom said, slouching in his chair. "Of course it's Cole."

"Cole?" Zoe's face was filled with confusion.

"He was one of the cult leaders with Mandy," I told her. *And holy shit, Jason's really alive!* I wanted to laugh out loud. I wanted to cry. I did a little bit of both, slapping my hands over my mouth almost as soon as the confused sound bubbled up from my throat. "Sorry," I said after I'd collected myself. "I just can't believe it's really true." I cleared my throat. "Jason's really out there, *alive.*" I shook my head, tears welling in my eyes. "I thought it was impossible…thought there was no chance…"

"Don't worry, D." Zoe gave my hand a squeeze, her own eyes shimmering with unshed tears. "We get it, trust me." She exchanged a look with her dad, who nodded.

I smiled weakly, then cleared my throat again. "Oh, but about Cole—we thought he was just another victim of Mandy's. But…" I shrugged. "This explains how he knew what Jason could do." I felt like kicking myself for not having recognized him sooner, but I

173

had only met him the one time in Tahoe, and he'd looked so different then...

"If there's one thing Cole's never been," Tom said, standing and stretching stiffly, "it's a victim."

"You knew him"—I shook my head—"*know* him?"

Slowly, Tom started pacing back and forth between the kitchen table and his chair. "A long time ago. He worked with Anna when Gregor—I mean, when Herodson's plan was still in the developmental phase, then he became the leader of one of the satellite compounds where Herodson conducted research and slowly built his army of people with Abilities. Anna was far better acquainted with him; she even met Mandy before she became..." Tom took a deep breath. "*Cole* is the one who twisted Mandy into the monster she was when you met her in Tahoe, Dani."

"Okay," Zoe drew the word out slowly. "So, Cole wants Jason for—"

"Power," Tom said without hesitation. "He's going after Herodson. Cole's going to try to get rid of him and take everything that he's built." I didn't think it sounded so bad.

"Maybe we should let him," Zoe said, voicing my thoughts. "Then Mom would be free..."

Tom shook his head. "Herodson's a power-hungry bastard, but he at least tries to use his power to make the world better." He held his hand up, cutting off both my and Zoe's sputtered protestations. "Cole is much, *much* worse. He's a psychopath. He just wants power so he can rule...so he can play with people's lives...so he can create and destroy at will." Tom closed his eyes and took several long, slow breaths. "I can't believe I'm about to say this." He opened his eyes and looked at us. "We have to go after them... to stop them."

"And save Jason," I said, adrenaline spiking in my bloodstream.

Tom nodded and closed his eyes, his features tensing. "*And* Herodson."

16

ZOE

DECEMBER 12, 1AE

NEW BODEGA, CALIFORNIA

My dad and I stepped into what used to be the old Tide's Wharf Restaurant, the building and surrounding parking lot now serving as the Transportation and Planning Department in New Bodega. Before, when New Bodega had simply been Bodega Bay and all of us were living our lives blissfully unaware, I'd eaten at the restaurant many times—soups and sandwiches on weekends or during summer breaks with Dani. I was still getting used to the fact that my hometown, which had once been sprawling, was now contained behind a wall dividing "out there" and "in here."

We walked toward the receptionist, needing an "okay" from the manager to use one of New Bodega's vehicles for our pressing trip to Colorado to save Jason...and, much to my displeasure, General Herodson. My shoulders tensed, and my hands clenched at my sides as I, for the millionth time, considered how ludicrous our situation was.

"My friend Lance said there was a pretty lady in charge of all exchanges and rentals—said that I should talk to Cynthia," my dad said, flashing the cherub-faced woman a heart-stopping smile. Growing up, I'd seen that same smile make all the ladies in Bodega Bay blush. I thought back to his flirting with our neighbor, Charlene, and how he'd refused to let that budding relationship turn into anything more than a neighborly friendship. Knowing what I knew now, that he was wrecked and ruined in the wake of my mom's leaving, I began to understand why.

The woman's full cheeks flushed, and her pouty lips curved into a small smile. "*I'm* Cynthia," she said. She straightened her shoulders.

He's still got it. I pursed my lips to keep from smiling and turned away. Moving off to the side to let my dad work his magic, I stared out one of the numerous picture windows that lined the west side of the building.

The pampas grass and wild wheat layering the hillsides in the distance bent to the wind's will, their surrender a plea to the hiding sun. The gulls fought unyielding gusts above the choppy, gloom-colored waves. I remembered a time when all of it—the majesty of nature and the changing of the seasons—had been less ominous, when it had been beautiful. But now everything seemed antagonistic. And considering everything that had happened here—my mom's escape with my dad, Herodson coming back for her, Cole taking my brother, Larissa messing with Dani's head—this place I once thought was comfortable and safe was nothing but an illusion. Up until a year ago, my *entire life* had been an illusion.

I turned away from the window. I needed to stay focused. Peering up at the wood-planked ceiling, I took in the scent of the musty room—the brine and moisture in the air that fused to every fiber and settled into every woodgrain. It was the smell of what used to be home, of a life I barely remembered; it was almost stifling now.

But, in spite of my mind's unwanted meanderings, watching the comings and goings of New Bodega citizens made me feel bizarrely normal. It was like I was waiting in line at the post office in the old days, with people hustling around, going about their lives completely oblivious to everyone else's.

What were people's lives like now that they didn't have to sit in traffic or be on conference calls? Were they worried about the amount of food in their pantries? About clean water? And as far as I knew, no one—save for the exploration, trading, and scavenging teams—ever needed to leave the protection of the New Bodega community. Everyone had probably already forgotten what was out there, hidden in the abandoned alleyways and dark corners of the country. I wasn't sure which was worse, remembering or not remembering. But given the easy, carefree steps of citizens wandering in and out of the building, it seemed they hadn't a care in the world.

Curious, I allowed my cerebral tentacles to survey the surrounding minds. An older man sat in a chair against the far wall, waiting for a young, red-haired woman in the front of the Housing Commission line, decades of smoking causing his shallow, somewhat labored breathing. A bold-lettered sign drawn in black, heavy ink that read *We Are Survivors* hung above him. His companion was flirting with the clerk behind the conference table that served as the counter.

The old man's mind was filled with acutely tangible memories of happiness and pain. His name was Winston. He'd lost his wife seven years back to bone cancer. And when she passed, his life became listless and empty—that was, until the Ending, when he decided that simply breathing in the desolate, dangerous world was no longer worth the effort.

I studied the lines on Winston's face, my heart filling with heaviness as I witnessed memories of him and his wife over the years, memories that had made living without her pure torture for him. He'd been working up the courage to end his misery with a 12-gauge shotgun the day he'd heard a woman screaming outside his apartment building.

The woman speaking with the clerk in front of him was

Debbie, and she wasn't flirting with the mousey man behind the table, not really. Although Winston was some thirty years older than her, he and Debbie were connected in a way they never would've been before the world turned to shit. Winston had saved her life, had shot the crazed man attacking her, likely saving her from certain death or something far worse. Debbie's gratitude and smile had given Winston a reason to live again, and in return, she'd gained a bristly old man to happily care for when she'd felt the most alone.

"Are you sure there's no way we can hurry the paperwork along?" Debbie asked, her eyes wide and pleading as she worried her bottom lip. She leaned down, closer to the clerk, and whispered, "He's my grandpa, the only person I have left. I'm not sure how much longer he has before..."

The clerk's face instantly softened, and he glanced past her to the old man, who'd fallen into a coughing fit.

Feeling unexpected admiration for the woman, I let them be and scanned the rest of the people in the long line behind Debbie.

A girl, about twelve years old, was standing patiently with her father. He wasn't her real father, but the man who had saved her and taken her in when he and his brother had found her in Arizona, seven months back. The girl was chatting telepathically with a terrier named Fritz, who sat obediently outside the window, like Annie and Dani regularly did with their flock of farm animals.

That's when I saw Biggs. His blue eyes and boy-next-door smile flashed kindness and interest at the elderly woman he was speaking with outside, just on the other side of the glass door. *"Stay away from my children,"* he'd said. The sting of his last words to me had haunted me since the day he left. I'd wanted to speak to him, to apologize over and over for the pain of losing Sarah, for the lies. But Biggs hadn't come back to us.

A man with a scar over his right eye and hair hanging in his face walked through the door, momentarily blocking my view of Biggs. Our eyes met for the briefest moment, the stranger's narrowing before he turned and walked away. Frowning, I continued to stare through the glass door, trying to deduce Biggs's state of mind, but I couldn't sense anything from him. Then I noticed that the woman he'd been speaking with was walking away, leaving him standing there, alone.

My feet were carrying me toward the door before I knew what I was doing. My hand gripped the door handle, hesitation and relief warring as I tried to decide whether or not to make myself known.

"Excuse us," Debbie said from behind me, and I flattened against the entry wall to let her and Winston pass. Just as I did, Biggs noticed me, and his relaxed features hardened, just a little.

Winston held the door open for me, a cantankerous look pinching his face as he waited for me to exit.

"Sorry," I said and stepped outside. "Thank you." The wind whipped my hair around my face, but all I could focus on were my sweating palms and my thrumming heartbeat...and Biggs, standing just a few yards away.

"Zoe," Biggs said, straightening. His eyes were opened wide, and I could only hope that, as he wiped his palms on his pants like he was uncomfortable, he wouldn't walk away from me.

Tentatively, I took a step toward him, an uncertain smile on my face. "Hey, Biggs."

Biggs pursed his lips and offered me a nod as he shoved his hands into his pockets. We stood in silence for a few seconds. The sound of dock workers behind us and seagull cries from above filled the space left by all that was unsaid between us. This one time, when all I wanted was to read him, I couldn't. I couldn't remember the last time I'd felt so inept and vulnerable—so normal.

"Biggs, I'm so sorry. I know—"

Biggs held up his hand. "Please, Zoe, don't." His voice was quiet, pained. "There's no need."

I bit the inside of my cheek, wondering if that was a good *no need* or an I'll-never-forgive-you *no need*. I tried to shake my hindering nerves away and hoped for the best. "Well, you...you look well," I said, gesturing to his cargo pants and long sleeves. He did look well—a little tired, perhaps, but well.

Biggs exhaled and rubbed the side of his head. "So do you, Zoe." He cleared his throat. "How are things at the farm?" He gestured to the bench bolted into the sidewalk.

Relief bloomed inside me, and I followed him, clinging to a grain of hope that we might be able to repair our broken friendship.

The bench creaked beneath us as we sat down, and Biggs leaned forward, his elbows on his knees. "Harper said everything is going well."

His obliviousness was surprising. I knew Harper had been to town since Jason's disappearance, so I wondered why he hadn't mentioned it to Biggs. "Things have been better," I said. "We're here securing a vehicle for an unexpected trip back to the Colony."

Biggs stiffened and frowned. "What?" I could only imagine the resurfacing memories of our time there—of what the General had done to Sarah and her suicide plaguing his mind. "Why?"

"Jason's been missing for a couple weeks, and we just found out that's where he is." I crossed my arms over my chest and leaned back, gazing out at the green hills set against the coal-colored sky. "And Dani's pregnant." I granted myself a sidelong glance at Biggs.

"I heard about that," he said, his voice distant. I could see that concern filled his baby-blue eyes, even if I couldn't feel it, which was peculiar. "Is she okay?" I could only assume he meant both emotionally *and* physically, given the circumstances.

I pulled my bomber jacket tighter around me, attempting to stave off the sudden chill. "She will be," I said firmly. "Once we get Jason back."

Biggs eyed me.

I was about to change the subject to something less grim—to the twins—when I heard the door open and shut behind me. I expected to see my dad when I turned around, but it was the man with the scar over his eyebrow. I turned back around to Biggs.

"You know for a fact he's at Peterson?"

"Pretty sure," I said. "Where exactly, well...I guess we'll have to figure that out when we get there." Though I had a pretty good idea I'd find him with my mom.

"Well, you'll be able to feel his mind, right? Or maybe see his memories as you get closer?" Biggs said, offering me more hope.

With a curt nod, I said, "Yep." Though, truthfully, I didn't want to think about the alternative—him nulling everyone—or that fact that we might get there too late.

"Will you stop along the way? Maybe the Tahoe folks can help you. Or have they all moved out here already?"

I finally realized why Harper might have withheld our situation from Biggs. He was growing more anxious by the minute, and our problems weren't something he needed to worry about, not when he had two babies at home. "There are still a dozen or so survivors in Zephyr Cove. The plan is to stop there to regroup, then continue to Colorado, nonstop, if possible."

"You're leaving once you get a car?"

I tucked my wayward hair behind my ear. "As soon as we can get a vehicle big enough for the six of us going." But I didn't want to think about what the next few days had in store for us. "So, how are the babies?" I asked, unable to keep from smiling. I glanced around automatically. "Where are they?"

Biggs was about to answer when my dad's voice boomed behind us. "We got a van," he called. "Let's get back to the farm so we can finish packing and get on the road." He nodded to Biggs. "Hi there. How are you?" My dad extended his hand to Biggs. "I'm Tom."

"Dad," I said, pointing to Biggs as he shook my dad's hand. "This is my..."

"Friend," Biggs finished for me.

I could barely contain my grin. "He's the other member of Harper and Sanchez's Army outfit I was telling you about."

"Hello, sir," Biggs said.

181

"I'm sorry to rush you, sweetheart, but we've got to get on the road." My dad glanced at Biggs and then me. As much as I wanted to stay and talk, for hours if Biggs would let me, I knew we needed to get back home. Every second wasted was another hour, another day, added to our long journey to reach Jason.

"It was good to see you, Biggs. Please, don't be a stranger." I hesitated, then said, "We all miss you."

Biggs gave me a tight-lipped smile and took a step back. "Safe journey," he said, and I felt his eyes on us as we walked away.

17

ANNA
DECEMBER 12, 1AE

THE COLONY, COLORADO

Tap tap tap. Tap. Tap tap tap. Tap. Tap tap tap.

Through the doorway to the back offices, Gregory glanced Anna's way, and her index finger paused just shy of her nail clicking against the windowsill of the gatehouse's broad window. She raised her left eyebrow just a touch, tilted her head just a little, and narrowed her eyes just enough that he would notice. Just enough to let him know that she was displeased. He was wasting her time, after all.

They'd been in the cramped gatehouse, breathing the same stuffy air, for nearly fifteen minutes—fourteen minutes longer than was necessary, as far as Anna was concerned. But ever since Gregory received the news that Cole was still a living, breathing parasite, wandering around, no doubt attaching himself to bigger, stronger allies, he'd been keeping Anna close. He hadn't voiced it out loud, but Anna could tell that Gregory was afraid. What did he think would happen if Cole showed up and she wasn't nearby, using her Ability to boost his to the max? She could only imagine.

And if she was being honest with herself, she was more than a little afraid of Cole, too.

Gregory frowned at Anna, then turned his attention back to the guard, reaching out to push the office door closed enough that Anna was blocked from his view. He'd had enough of her distractions, it seemed. "Whatever the means," he said, his voice floating through the crack in the doorway, "make sure that nobody enters without first being cleared by me. You don't let anyone in—not *anyone*; they can wait outside until I'm here for the morning or afternoon inspection." His voice was soft, calm—dangerous—and it vibrated with a stifling amount of mind-controlling power. "Do you understand, Simmons?"

Gregory was using his Ability so strongly on the lanky, graying guard that the poor man didn't stand a chance of disobeying.

"Very good," Gregory said. "Now, *if* someone does try to enter..." Gregory continued to give the guard commands, but Anna's attention was drawn to the trio approaching the tall, electrified chain-link gate blocking the west entrance to the Colony. Backed as they were by the sinking sun, all Anna could tell about them was that two were male and one was female.

When one of the four other guards on duty at the west gate started sliding it open, she glanced at the mostly closed door to the office, where Gregory was still giving commands. They shouldn't have been opening the gate. Anna frowned. They shouldn't have even been *able* to open the gate—Gregory had already given them all Ability-laden commands not to.

Confused and curious, Anna moved toward the open doorway to get a better view. She considered alerting Gregory to the fact that the exact thing he was currently outlawing was taking place— very obviously—at that very moment. The gate was now halfway open, despite Gregory's orders.

She hesitated, utterly baffled by what was going on. Finally, she gave in and called Gregory's name.

He opened the door a few inches and peered out at Anna, and it would've been impossible for him to miss what was happening at the gate right behind her. Except Gregory's gaze slid right past the telltale view through the window, settling firmly on Anna. "Apologies, my dear. I know today hasn't been a good day for Peter. We'll be done here soon, and you can get back to his bedside."

Anna held his gaze for several drawn-out seconds, at a loss for words—it was suddenly very clear to her that something Ability-related was going on—then forced a small, genuine-looking smile. It was a skill she'd become quite adept at over the years. "Soon it won't matter. The new treatment is proving universally beneficial on Re-gens." Her smile became shaky with relief and the pent-up potential for grief. "By morning, our son should be on the mend."

Gregory bowed his head. "All thanks to you."

He'd always been sparing with compliments, and every time he offered one up, it knocked Anna off balance. "Yes, well…" She looked down at her shoes, then out at the gate that was now wide open. A fact to which Gregory was still absolutely oblivious. So oblivious that he mumbled, "I'll just be another minute," and shut the office door, blocking not just Anna this time, but also the unmistakable view of the open gate.

Anna felt intrigue and a strange combination of hope and dread. It was clear to her that one of the trio approaching the gate could alter the perception of those around him or her, and only Anna's nulling Ability, which she was constantly exercising in an effort to keep Gregory's mind control at bay, was preventing her mind from being swept into whatever delusion the newcomer was weaving around the others' minds. And she'd only ever met one person whose perception-altering Ability was strong enough to pull off such a large and effective illusion—Tom.

Holding her breath, Anna squinted at the trio of newcomers, wishing Tom's lanky silhouette was among them. Praying it wasn't. If he were discovered here, it would mean his death.

The woman was walking a little ahead of the men, who appeared to be carrying on a fairly intense conversation, if their sharp gestures were anything to go by. One of the men was a little taller and more sturdily built than the other, far too muscular to be her abandoned husband. The other, though—he was still tall and of the right, wiry build. Anna focused on him as he and his companions drew closer to the gate. They were a dozen paces out...ten... seven...five.

A bird coasted low overhead, blocking the glare from the sun for a fraction of a second, just long enough for Anna to catch the briefest glimpse of the man's face. Just long enough for her to recognize his aristocratic features, his ever-present, haughty sneer. Just long enough for Anna to feel her heart lurch as adrenaline flooded her system.

Cole.

Cole was walking into the Colony like he owned the place... and, given enough time, a well-planned strategy, and the right allies, he just might.

Sucking in a breath, Anna slipped to the side and flattened herself against the wall beside the broad window, hoping Cole hadn't noticed her. She desperately wanted to alert Gregory, knowing full well that doing so was an impossibility, unless she wanted to also let him in on the single biggest secret she'd been keeping from him—the multifaceted nature of her Ability. Sure, Gregory was well acquainted with her Ability-boosting power, but thanks to her meticulous caution and on-and-off use of the neutralizer, he was still unaware that she could render any other person's Ability useless. If Gregory found out she'd managed to lie to him for all those years...

Anna shuddered. What would be worse—what Cole would do to the citizens of the Colony if he somehow wrested away Gregory's power, or what Gregory would do to Anna if he learned of her years of severe disobedience?

Pressing her lips together, Anna straightened her back and

drew in a long, deep breath. Neither option was acceptable. Which meant she'd have to take matters into her own hands. It would hardly be the first time she'd gone behind Gregory's back to alter the course of events at the Colony—after all, she'd been knee-deep in the Re-gen rebellion, helping guide RV-01 and Camille in the "right" direction. She would have to work quickly—and cautiously, of course—but she had no doubt that snuffing out this latest fire was up to her.

If only Peter weren't in such a critical stage of degeneration, and with his treatment—the cure—at her fingertips. It had reached the point where his mind and his unique, chameleonlike Ability were affected by the rapid degeneration of his neural tissue, and some of his organs were showing signs of failing. His initial round of human-sourced electrotherapy was scheduled for first thing in the morning, and based on the trials Anna and John had conducted on the other remaining Re-gens, Peter's recovery should begin almost instantaneously.

Anna could hear the scuffle of weary footsteps through the gatehouse's open door as Cole and his companions drew nearer. She held her breath and squeezed her eyes shut, willing herself to remain as inconspicuous as possible. The last thing she wanted was to let them know she could see them.

The slimmer man and the woman passed first, and Anna risked a peek through the doorway. For several seconds, she watched their backs as they strolled away from the gatehouse. The broader man followed a half dozen paces behind them, his eyes scanning the way ahead and to either side. Those eyes...they were unmistakable.

Heart leaping, Anna retreated back into the building before his keen survey of his surroundings made him aware of her. She clutched her chest and gasped in shaky breaths, battling elation and anxiety and all-out terror.

Jason—it was him, her son. He was in the Colony.

What was he doing there? What about Zoe? And Danielle?

What about their farm near the coast? Her mind reeled, thoughts lashing about as she tried to understand and failed miserably. She kept coming back to the same disturbing facts, the only two things she knew with any certainty, and both terrified her.

Jason was in the Colony. And for whatever reason, he was working with Cole.

18

ZOE

THE FARM, CALIFORNIA

S tanding in our small, heavily equipped outbuilding-turned-armory behind the stable, I collected my crossbow and quiver, a handgun I preferred never to use, and a few clips, just in case. Jake was just as focused as he swiftly readied weapons behind me: a few pistols, some knives, and whatever else he deemed essential for Jason's breakout.

All I could think about was getting to the Colony. We knew we had to rescue him from Cole, but after the dream I'd had, I wasn't sure if we needed to save him from my mom as well. She'd helped me that night in the golf course, when I'd lost the essence of who I was and had awoken in a dark, foreign world. She'd saved me. I liked to think she would save Jason too, if she could.

And then there was Herodson. I found it hard to believe saving him was our only option. We'd spent months putting mountains and rivers, forests and deserts between the General and us, and now, we were going back. The Colony was terrifying, the one place where civilization was more threatening than the unkempt hillsides and cities where Crazies lurked. But we were desperate,

189

and no matter how unimaginable our situation was, I was ready and willing to do whatever was necessary to bring my brother home, even if that meant shelving the retribution I felt all too entitled to.

"Here," Tavis said, startling me. He set extra fletching, tips, and a few bundles of metal bolts for my crossbow down on the bench in front of me.

"I thought you all said the crossbow would only slow us down, that we'd be using guns?"

Tavis nodded to my own horde of bolts—or *arrows*, as I still liked to call them. "And?"

I shrugged. "You never know, we might run out of ammo."

"Exactly, you never know. And arrows are quiet, in case we need to sneak up on someone. We might as well take what we've got." It looked like Tavis had cleaned out our entire stock.

"You and Sam should keep some—"

Tavis gave me a curt nod, giving me pause. "And Sam will. He has his supply. These are what's left. We'll need all of this more than he will."

I gaped at him and glanced at Jake, whose back was to us while he filled a duffel bag. He was aware Tavis was in the armory with us, but it didn't faze him. I glared back at Tavis. "*We?* You're not coming."

His blue eyes widened, and he took an abrupt step backward. "Excuse me?" He grinned.

I shook my head and tried not to smile. "I mean, you can't. Sam needs you here. What if something happens to us—to you?"

Jake left us alone in the shed-like building, giving Tavis and me some space, and Tavis instantly leaned closer, his expression soft. "Zoe, I want to help. You may be a good aim these days, but you're not better than I am, no matter what Sam says. And I'm not too shabby with a gun, either. Let's face it, we have no idea what that place is like now, and you'll need all the help you can get."

I stared at Tavis, into his blue eyes that always held a smile but were different now. They seemed pained and earnest, something I'd never seen in them before. Although I hated to admit it, Tavis was right. This mission might not end well for Jake, my dad, Becca, Sanchez, Gabe, and me. But Tavis coming with us? I didn't want him to go. I didn't want him risking his life for my family—for me—when he had Sam to think about.

"Look," Tavis said, reaching out to me, but he stopped himself just before his fingers could brush against my arm, and we stood in momentary silence. The vacuum of space between us was thick, making it impossible to think or speak, like this moment meant something for him that I couldn't quite comprehend. Tavis's hand fell back to his side. "Zoe…" He let out a breath that seemed to hold the meaning of a thousand unspoken words. "I know there's been some weirdness between us in the past, but you know that I still care about you," he said easily. He pointed to my head. "Which means you also know that *I* know nothing will ever happen between us and this isn't about that. So don't make this into something it's not, okay? I'm going on this trip because I want to help. You need me. Jason, Dani, your dad…everyone needs this to work, and you have a better chance if I'm there with you."

My mouth was so dry I could barely swallow. He was right, I did know this wasn't just about me, and not just because I could feel his intent. Tavis and Sam were part of our family. "Okay, but," I said on a sigh. I shut my eyes, feeling grateful and selfish and strangely at ease that he would be with us. "I don't *expect* you to come." I opened my eyes again, and his cocky grin returned, gloating, like always.

He shrugged. "I could use a little adventure. In fact, that last six months have been rather dull, don't you think?"

I snorted. "Speak for yourself."

Tavis chuckled and nudged me with his elbow.

"Sam's not going to like this," I grumbled.

"Agreed," Tavis said. "But you need me right now more than he does. He'll understand that."

I nodded, if a little guiltily, and Tavis scooted the additional arrow parts closer to me. "Bag 'em up. I'll go talk to the kid."

"Good luck." I cringed, and with a wink, Tavis disappeared outside.

I shoved my gear into a duffel of my own, and when I finished, I headed out to the van Cynthia had generously loaned us for as long as we needed it, including fuel to get us to our first stopping point in Tahoe. All my dad had to agree to was dinner with her upon his return.

I tossed my bag into the back of the van, where some of our gear was already loaded, then headed toward the farmhouse. The others were still packing, so I went through a mental checklist of anything else we might need.

A change of clothes. Check.

Plenty of weapons and ammo. Check.

Clothes for Jason on the ride back. Check.

Water, and Becca was packing us some food for the road. Check. Check.

First aid supplies packed and loaded. Check.

Then, deciding I should bring the schematic of the Colony Gabe had helped me draw for reference, I reached for the handle to the screen door.

I paused when Sam's high-pitched, urgent voice reached my ears. He and Tavis were arguing in the entryway.

"...and I'm a better aim than you. I should come, too," Sam's voice strained.

"You're a great aim, but I need you to stay here with Dani and help her around the farm."

"I don't want to."

I heard the floorboards creak and held my breath, expecting them to step outside and find me eavesdropping. But Tavis must've knelt down. His voice was softer when he spoke again.

"Sam, I need you to stay here, mate. It's going to be very dangerous, and if anything happens to us, I need you to help keep everyone here safe. You have your bow, and you can help them sense danger. Plus, Annie would have a fit if you left." Tavis chuckled, and I smiled sadly, thinking that Tavis was such a wonderful man and amazing stand-in father for Sam. "You know it's true."

"Yeah, I guess you're right," Sam replied, and my hand flew to my mouth to stifle a laugh.

There was a pause. "I hear you out there, Zoe," Sam said, a little indignant.

Clearing my throat and attempting to put on a straight face, I stepped up to the screen door. "Sorry, I just need to grab a few things."

Tavis looked from me to Sam and rumpled the kid's hair. "We're in agreement then? You stay here with Dani and Annie and protect them?" he asked.

"Okay." Sam groaned and looked over at me, his hair so long it swept over his eyes. I knew he thought of Annie as a little sister, like the one that had been taken away from him last year. He would go to the ends of the earth for Annie if it meant keeping her safe.

"I'll look out for him, Sam," I said and offered the kid a sympathetic smile. "I'll keep him out of trouble."

With a slight quirk of his lips, Sam plodded past me and out the front door, determined to be strong and grown-up. My hand flew to my heart, and I flashed Tavis a piteous look, pouting my bottom lip. "Heartbreaking."

With a nod and relieved sigh, Tavis scratched the top of his head and walked out the front door. "I better make myself useful" were his last words as the screen door swung shut behind him.

I made my way into the dining-slash-archive-room to search through stacks of diagrams and instructions I'd created over the months, looking for schematics of the Colony and surrounding area.

Gabe and Becca hurried down the stairs, their bags packed and hanging over their shoulders. "We're ready," Becca said as they headed for the door. "The food is already loaded."

"Thanks," I breathed, contemplating. "Hey, Becca…"

She paused and looked over her shoulder at me, her eyes holding a fierce glint that hadn't been there mere months ago. "Anything new?" I asked, wondering if she'd had any more visions.

Becca shook her head apologetically. "No. Sorry, Zoe. Nothing."

With a quick nod, I refocused on my messily stacked documents. I riffled around a moment longer before finding what I'd been searching for. "Aha!" With a triumphant exhale, I straightened and peered around the house that had become our home.

Living with twelve people—fourteen when Camille and Mase were staying here—had become something reassuring and expected in my life. The noise, the support, the love and comfort—it had all become constant and reliable. I imagined how weird it would be for those staying behind, how empty the farm would feel, and how disconnected and lonely *we* would feel being away from them.

The screen door flung open again, and this time Dani walked into the house. The look on her face made my insides wad and crumple with sadness and longing and hope, as hers were. There was no way Dani could go with us, not now that she was pregnant, and definitely not after the prophecy Becca had shared about Dani staying at the farm if we wanted the baby to live.

Dani planted herself in front of me, her bright, gleaming eyes searching mine. "You'll bring him back to me, Zo?"

My eyes clouded with tears, and I blinked slowly in hopes of making the pesky things go away. I cleared my throat. "I promise you, D. I'll do everything I can to bring Jason home."

Dani nodded, and she scanned the room like she was lost in a place that should've been familiar. She pursed her lips, and the way she rubbed her belly told me she was petrified—too scared of the unknown to be hopeful. "Just make sure you come back, too," she said, her voice small.

In one quick step, I was wrapping my arms around her. I tried to ignore the tickle of her wild red hair in my nostrils. "I love you, D." I squeezed her tighter, wishing I could take away the sorrow and worry that prevented her from smiling anymore. "I made Harper promise to keep a special eye on you while I'm gone. And everyone here wants to help you. Let them, okay? And keep drinking your shakes."

Dani's head bobbed minutely, and she sniffled as she stepped out of my arms. "I will." She hesitated.

I wanted to probe, to make sure she really was going to be okay, but I restrained myself. *Dani is strong.* She'd already survived so much, and she could survive the next few weeks with Chris, Harper, and Carlos at her side. She'd have Mase and Camille, Annie and Sam, and the animals, too. Dani wouldn't be alone. "You have to be strong for Annie," I said, helping her to refocus. "I don't think she understands—"

"I know, Zo." Dani smiled weakly. "Don't worry about me. I'll be fine, I promise."

With a single nod, I let out an unsteady breath, wanting to believe her. "We'll be back before you know it," I lied, certain that the next week or so would feel like years. "I love you, D."

Dani wrapped her arms around me again, her emotions flaring against her will. "I love you, Zo. Please be careful." A gut-wrenching sound stuck in her throat. "I can't lose you both."

I gave her a squeeze. "See you in a couple weeks," I said quickly. With that, I hurried out of the house. I needed to focus on the Colony and Jason if we were going to have any chance of bringing him back...alive.

19

DANI

DECEMBER 12, 1AE

THE FARM, CALIFORNIA

S howers these days weren't all they'd once been. For us, they'd become a stop-and-go outdoors affair, consisting of our jerry-rigged version of a rather large solar shower out back behind the farmhouse and cottage. We might've had running water indoors to a small degree, but taking a full-on shower would've been far too taxing on our plumbing, and we were still working on our gray water distribution system. And though Jason and Tom had constructed a wooden fence that spiraled around our outdoor shower, giving any bather the illusion of privacy, I still preferred to wear a swimsuit—specifically, the purple- and white-striped bikini I'd lifted on our last trip through Tahoe.

I glanced down at the loose nylon, trying and failing not to notice how defined my ribs were beneath the bikini top or how clearly my hip bones jutted out. My abdomen still showed no visible sign of the rapidly growing life within, which seemed so strange, because since finding out I was pregnant four days past, the knowledge of it—of him or her—had become an ever-present element of *me*. I was hyperaware of the child I was carrying, and it was becoming extremely frustrating to me that there was no obvious physical evidence of said child's existence, aside from the extra aura only Zoe could see glowing around me. Harper claimed it was still too soon, even with the accelerated rate of gestation since the Virus, but still...

Shoulders hunched, I folded my arms over my middle. No wonder Zoe's eyebrows were always drawn together, her forehead always creased, her mouth always pinched with worry. She had a big enough crap storm to deal with without me adding to it. But add to it I did.

I tugged on the dangling handle that triggered the water release and couldn't hold back a shudder as the chilly water rained down on me. Already present goose bumps multiplied with a vengeance, and I combatted them with memories of my last warm bath. Zoe'd taken the enormous time and effort to draw it for me a few days ago, no doubt hoping a little external comfort would soothe my frayed nerves and settle my uneasy stomach. It had done neither, and it had been an unnecessary luxury, but I'd still appreciated the hell out of it—out of her.

And now she was gone. Maybe she'd only been gone a few hours, but she was gone nonetheless.

Jack bounded into the circular washing alcove before the stream cut off overhead and ran a full circuit around me, his wagging tail spraying me with less-than-clean water from seemingly all sides. I couldn't help but squeal. "Jack! What are you doing, you crazy monster!"

He paused just long enough to stare up at me with innocent puppy-dog eyes.

"At least he got you to smile," Chris said dryly.

I spun around to the shower's entrance, where the spiraling fence overlapped a few feet to allow some privacy without requiring a gate—easier maintenance, according to the handier members of our scattered family. Chris stood in the opening, Annie on her hip despite being a smidge too big to be carried around. She gave my body a quick, assessing scan before looking at the brighter portion of twilit sky above the hills to the west.

"You're sad," Annie said, sticking out her bottom lip for emphasis. *"You're not as sad when Jack's around,"* she continued telepathically. *"I told him to make you happy again."*

Jack sat crookedly at my feet—practically *on* my feet—and stared up at me, tongue lolling, and the dark markings over his eyes nudged higher. *"Mother, run?"* He scooted even closer and whined almost imperceptibly.

Chris cleared her throat. "You shouldn't be out here so late. It's too cold," she said, disapproval evident in her voice. "Come inside. There's hot chili. And biscuits."

I looked at her, then glanced away, choosing instead to focus on the bar of soap still resting on the ground a few feet away in its purple plastic traveling case.

"The others are just sitting down to eat," Chris added.

I thought about the others—Carlos, Harper, Grayson, Sam, and Camille and Mase—then took the two steps required to reach the soap and gingerly squatted to retrieve it. Getting back up required the assistance of my hand on the fence and a tired groan. If I went inside with Chris, I wouldn't only be surrounded by the remaining members of our group, I'd be surrounded by the absence of so many others. And though we'd had people coming and going on search parties for a couple weeks now, this was different. We were missing more of our beloved friends than ever before, and the likelihood of them returning soon was low; the likelihood of them never returning at all, far too high.

"So you're ignoring me," Chris said. "Real mature."

I pursed my lips but didn't look at her. Honestly, I was too ashamed to look at her. Because she was sort of right; I was being an enormous baby, wallowing alone instead of facing my issues with my family. Instead, I glanced down at Jack while I lathered the bar of soap between my hands. *"You've got to give me a little space, Sweet Boy. Just for a minute."*

Jack did as I asked, scooting away a few inches and whining all the while. Well, if he was going to insist on remaining so close to me, I wasn't above using him as an impromptu soap dish.

"Hold this, please," I said, setting the bar of soap on top of his furry head, silently promising an abundance of treats later.

Jack became statue-still.

I smiled at him, showering him with telepathic praises while I worked the lathered soap through my unruly hair. It felt exceptionally grimy and greasy, not to mention tangly, and I became all too aware that my last bathing experience had actually been the bath Zoe'd drawn for me days ago. Too long when I spent a good part of my days out in the dirt, clearly.

"So this must be what it's like to have a teenager…" Out of the corner of my eye, I watched Chris set Annie down and angle the little girl back toward the farmhouse. "Go help Daniel set the table."

"But—"

"Now," Chris said, breaking out her famed mom voice.

Annie scampered away without further hesitation as I retrieved the bar of soap to get to work on the rest of my body.

"Alright, Dani, here's the deal." Apparently, it was my turn to be the recipient of the mom voice. "Your obstinacy and flat-out refusal to take good care of yourself isn't only hurting you, it's hurting the baby."

"I—"

She held up a hand, cutting me off. "And I'm not just talking about this kind of thing," she said, waving her hand at me and the shower. "You need rest and food and to get a grip on all this drifting, but you also need to take better care of yourself mentally and emotionally." She planted her fists on her hips. "With Zoe gone for the time being, you've got two options: either you start talking to me, or I'm going to start fiddling around in your head."

"Chris!" I looked at her, aghast. She knew how deeply I'd

grown to despise having people violate my mental and emotional privacy. "You wouldn't!"

She crossed her arms and shrugged. *Maybe she would?* "Either way, we're going to get to the bottom of what you're feeling—and why—it's just a matter of *how* we get there." She leaned against the wooden slats, not a care in the world. "Your call, hon."

Fuming, I turned my back to her and pulled the lever to trigger the shower. I didn't even flinch when the stream of near-freezing water hit my skin. When I was all rinsed off, I looked back. Chris was gone.

Dinner was a tense affair—or, rather, filled with the kind of tension that builds when everyone is pretending things are normal, forcing conversation and laughter that in the end only makes the tension worse. It was exactly the kind of tension that Ky had always known just how to diffuse. I missed him, all the time, but this particular dinner was one of those times when the missing became a physical ache in my chest.

Heart heavy, I sat at the kitchen table and watched Carlos scrub the dishes in a basin at the other end of the table. It was supposed to be my night to do the dishes, but the moment I'd started heating up water to fill the basin, Carlos had stepped in. It was becoming all too clear that Chris had enlisted the others in her efforts to bend me to her will.

"You don't have to do this," I told him, again, and crossed my arms over my chest. "I *can* wash dishes, you know. I won't overexert myself."

Carlos paused mid-scrub and sent an unamused look to my end of the table. "Seriously, Dani, if you say that one more time…"

Sighing, I set my elbows on the table and rested my chin on my palms.

Carlos's brow furrowed and he leaned forward, his lips pursing as he scrubbed what seemed to be a particularly stubborn dish. "There's not that many dishes to do anyway," he said, pausing once more, closing his eyes, and making a pained expression as soon as the words were out of his mouth. "Sorry," he said, meeting my eyes and looking just as lost as me. We all missed Zoe and the others.

"I know," I said. "It's fine. Don't worry about it."

Carlos opened his mouth, and I could practically see the words perched on the tip of his tongue.

"Decision time," Chris said from the hallway opening. Her hawkish gaze was locked on me. "What's it going to be, hon? Traditional therapy or *my* brand?"

I sighed heavily, missing Zoe even more. "If you promise to stay away from my brain chemistry, I promise to spill my guts to you." Under my breath, I added, "Not that I think it'll do any good."

Chris held up her hands defensively. "Whoa, whoa, don't get so worked up. Your enthusiasm is overwhelming."

"So is your sarcasm," I muttered.

"Touché," Chris said, touching her finger to the side of her nose.

Harper squeezed past Chris, but not without landing a decent smack on her backside. She squawked, and he winked at me as he passed by the kitchen table and slipped into the mudroom. Seconds later, he poked his head back into the kitchen. "Hey, Dani, I'd like to get a quick checkup in tomorrow morning—before breakfast. Think you could swing by the infirmary first thing?"

I nodded, and he flashed me a smile before retreating back into the mudroom. Chris followed him, only to reemerge with two fleece-lined raincoats over her arm. She tossed one to me.

I caught it, more out of defense than any sort of practiced hand-eye coordination. Those kinds of sports had never been my thing. "Wha—"

"It's time for your first therapy session." She shrugged into her

201

coat. "Zee doctor vill see you now," she said in a terrible, unrecognizable accent.

"Um, okay…" Slowly, I stood and put on my coat, never taking my eyes off of her. I could only imagine how confused I looked. "But outside?"

"Well, you didn't think I'd rearrange my whole schedule just because you're emotionally constipated, did you?" Chris fumbled around in her pockets, then smiled victoriously. "Ah, thought I had a couple more." She proudly pulled two sticks of chewing gum out of her right coat pocket, unwrapped one and popped it into her mouth, and offered the second to me. "Helps me concentrate," she said as she chewed.

I closed the distance between us and took the proffered stick of gum. "Thanks." As I unfolded the foil wrapper, I peered at her. My stomach was becoming even more unsettled than usual as I deciphered her meaning. "You don't mean we're going to do this out in the stable while you work on Vanessa, do you?"

Chris continued to chew her gum, her only response a flat smile.

"But, Chris…she can't stand me!"

Chris waved one hand dismissively. "Pshhh…"

My eyebrows rose. "She *hates* me."

"She doesn't hate you." Chris made her way toward the mudroom door. "She's jealous of you—of how close you and Carlos are."

I glanced at Carlos, but he was studiously focused on scrubbing the hell out of the final bowl.

"Come on." Chris trudged back into the kitchen, draped her arm over my shoulders, and led me into the mudroom, then outside.

"For the record, I think this is an awful idea," I said as we hastily made our way across the lawn. The rain was starting up again, the sky rumbling with far-off thunder. The squish of wet, overgrown grass soon gave way to the crunch of gravel, until finally Chris was sliding open the stable door.

"It's a wonderful idea," Chris said. She linked her arm with mine. "The only way I can make sure I don't accidentally fiddle with your inner mental workings is to be actively entrenched in someone else's. Consider it an insurance policy." She gave my arm a squeeze. "Just in case."

"Fine," I said, giving in begrudgingly. After all, it wasn't like she was offering me much of a choice, and I preferred to be out there under the pretense of having had some say in the matter—however miniscule. I was, only now, coming to fully appreciate how much of a buffer Zoe had been for me since Jason was taken. Chris, it seemed, had a very different philosophy when it came to taking care of distraught mothers-to-be.

As we approached Vanessa's stall at the end of the stable aisle, I held my breath. The outburst would come as soon as she realized that Chris had a guest tonight. Though the type of outburst varied from taunting songs to outright screams of murderous intentions, the fact that there would be an outburst was just that—a fact.

I closed my eyes when we reached the stall and waited for it. And waited…

And waited…

And waited…

"Vanessa?" Chris said. "Everything okay?"

My eyes snapped open, and I stared through the barred-off top half of the stall door, certain I would find the space empty…certain I would find Vanessa *missing*. Except she wasn't missing. Rather, Vanessa's face was barely two feet from mine, on just the other side of the bars. And she wasn't yelling or snarling or even cackling, like she so often did during her imaginary conversations with her hallucinations.

She was smiling, almost peacefully. At me.

20

ZOE
DECEMBER 12, 1AE

NORTHERN CALIFORNIA INTERSTATE

I-80 was wet, the asphalt reflecting the dying, golden light as the sun sank behind the Sierra Mountains. The rainstorm we'd been driving through for the past couple hours had finally let up, but as we neared our exit toward Tahoe, we were all too aware that any impending rainfall would likely turn to snow. I hated snow.

I thought about the outbreak back in Salem, when all of this began, about Sarah and our journey with Dave. I thought about how cold it would be once the snow started to fall and how hidden everything would become—how much more dangerous everything would be.

Jake drove carefully—too slowly for the urgency that kept my mind hopping and my body fidgeting. I tried not to nag him as he maneuvered the potholes and abandoned cars scattered along the slick interstate.

At first, it was easy; I was distracted. My eyes were glued to the vehicles on the road, like a string of freak show exhibits I couldn't look away from. All of them were gruesome and sad.

Each vehicle housed more than death; they embodied heart-pricking reminders of the past. *Proud Parent of an Honor Student,* humorous, and political stickers covered rusted and cobwebbed bumpers and back windows. Bodies—animal and human, both skeletal and still decaying—filled most of them, some windows and doors open, the rest shut. Babies and children were wrapped in blankets, still grasping their toys and stuffed animals in their eternal slumber.

It was unnerving, the poignancy of driving through a graveyard depicting the past; it was a reminder of what could've been and how lucky we were to have gotten this far despite the uncertainty of what lay ahead.

Eventually, dwelling on what could have been became too morose, and I made myself look away. I focused on the last rays of light splaying up from beyond the untended rice fields in the distance, making the world glow. Then, I watched the citrus and walnut orchards that were no longer pruned or harvested pass by the window. The scattered billboards were tattered and sun-bleached, and the sporadic dealerships and restaurants that we passed were all eerily dark and, not surprisingly, abandoned. A year had passed since the outbreak, and had I not known any better, it would've seemed as if we were the only people left in the world.

Noisily, my dad wrestled with a map in the front passenger seat. He'd been scouring it since we'd been on the road, searching for a quicker, safer route. I knew there was none, as did he, though he couldn't stop examining the map crinkling in his hands long enough to accept it.

I glanced up to the front of the van, my eyes locking with Jake's as they flicked to the rearview mirror.

"Do we know if our Tahoe friends are expecting us tonight?" Gabe asked from his slouched position in the seat in front of me. His voice was hoarse from drifting in and out of sleep.

My dad twisted in his seat and peered at us, scanning the five faces staring back at him, all waiting for an answer. "Lance said he'd keep working on the communication." My dad's eyes settled on Gabe. "As soon as you can find a sleeping mind, we'll know for sure." He looked at Sanchez. "Otherwise, we'll have to rely on you when we get closer."

"There are still a dozen of them there," Sanchez said, stretching as she stirred from her half-sleep. "It shouldn't be too hard to contact them."

I balled up my leather jacket as a pillow and leaned back, looking out the window. "I just can't handle the silent waiting," I mumbled.

"You've never been a patient girl, Zoe," my dad said. Had it been under different circumstances, he might've laughed. At least, I imagined he would have. Instead, he sighed.

Wondering what my dad could possibly have to hold over me —the one who'd reminded *him* to go grocery shopping and did it myself whenever he forgot, who did the laundry and made sure he'd paid the bills on time—I looked at him. "Well I'm not *im*patient."

"You couldn't *wait* for the newest Disney movie to come out," he explained, "even though you swore you didn't care about the princesses at all." He faced the front again, watching the scenery whip by, and I rolled my eyes. "And you couldn't *wait* until you turned ten so you could collect your allowance, and you couldn't *wait* until you were sixteen and old enough to drive...you couldn't even wait for the laundry to dry before you pulled it out of the dryer, grabbing whatever it was you were waiting for and claiming the rest would 'air dry.'"

Tavis chuckled from the seat beside me.

Involuntarily, I smiled and stared out the window. I'd forgotten about things like that. "This is a little different, I think."

"True," my dad said, more than a hint of amusement in his voice. "But patience has never been your strong suit."

When my dad didn't get another rise out of me, he continued, "Zoe, you don't need to worry. Jason's still alive, I promise you."

I resisted the urge to shake my head again. "How can you be so sure?"

"Because they took him alive for a reason. Cole could've done whatever he wanted to your brother, but he clearly needed him alive." He paused for a moment, waiting for my eyes to meet his in the dimming light. "He needs Jason so badly that he was willing to risk everything by showing up in New Bodega to get him."

For some inexplicable reason, it helped knowing that Jason had chosen to let Cole into his mind in order to save Dani, and that Jason had made a choice he could live with knowing the potential consequences. But the thought of my brother—someone I loved and whose Ability was so strong—being brainwashed and under the influence of someone like Cole was still incredibly disturbing. A small part of me worried about what we would do if, for whatever reason, we couldn't convince Jason to come back with us. What if we couldn't find a way to break Cole's hold on his mind?

"Cole's mind control is a little different than Herodson's," my dad said, responding to my train of thought. "It's unbreakable while it's active, so far as I've ever seen, but it requires skin-to-skin contact to work, and it wears off in time, as we saw with Dani and her Ability."

I let out a tired breath, recalling the memories I'd seen of Dani and Jason's dealings with the cult, with Mandy and Cole at the helm, Carlos and so many others at their mercy. But I shoved the memories away, instead watching the newly formed moon shadows play across the window as we drove, though our speed wasn't nearly fast enough. Although it had felt like the longest day of my life—waking after my dream about Jason, Dani's unearthed memory, a hurried trip into and out of New Bodega, and now our journey to Colorado—I was too wound up to relax or sleep, even if I knew I'd regret it later.

Tavis nudged me. "Uh, want to play a game or something?"

I stifled a laugh and shook my head. I appreciated his attempt to keep my thoughts in check. But then, as much as I wanted to say no thanks, I felt compelled say yes, to think about something that wasn't morbid and so sinister. "Okay, sure," I said and turned to face him. "What did you have in mind?"

Tavis's eyes turned round and questioning, and with a sheepish grin he shrugged. He hadn't expected me to say yes. I smiled as he smirked and scratched the side of his face. "I don't know any car games, actually."

"You don't know any car games? What about the license plate game or I Spy?"

Tavis frowned. "I think it's a bit dark for either of those, and our options are somewhat"—he peered around at the darkened scenery—"limited."

"You could always play truth or dare," Sanchez piped in with a soft snort from her seat in front of Tavis.

"That would be entertaining." Gabe chuckled beside her.

"Only if you play, Sanchez," Tavis teased in return, flashing a half grin.

"Ha. No."

I knew Sanchez wasn't likely to partake in any games, and to be honest, I wasn't quite up to playing one myself, but the idea of asking Tavis something, *anything*, in a game of truth or, well, truth was very appealing. He'd always been more of an open book than the others, something I liked about Tavis. But I'd never asked him the fun, interesting questions. I'd never probed his mind or searched for answers to all my curiosities, even when things had occasionally felt uncomfortable or curious. As with everyone else, it seemed important that I let his past remain buried. But now, needing a bit of intrigue to keep my mind off of Jason, I went for it.

"I have a question, actually," I said, turning in my seat to face him properly.

Tavis chuckled. "Okay, shoot."

"You're clearly not from here, originally, anyway, and I know you rescued Sam from Crazies." I narrowed my gaze at him. "But what was your life like before the Ending? What did you do?" I tried to picture Tavis's occupation and how he might've lived. Had he always been a simple, laid-back kind of guy? Had he left Australia for work?

Tavis let out a brusque laugh, not light and amused as usual. "Umm, back home I was a defense lawyer," he said, shocking the hell out of me. He laughed again as he took in my surprise.

I shut my gaping mouth. "You don't really give off the whole you-can't-handle-the-truth, attorney-at-law sort of vibe."

"Yeah, well, get me in front of a jury and I can persuade them with my charm and skill." Tavis's grim smile faded to nothing, and he stared out the window. "Throw me into this world and I'm a fish out of water, so to speak."

I glanced over at Becca, who was gazing, unblinking, out her window. I wondered if she already knew this about him, like she seemed to know so many other things about all of us.

"So," I continued, "you practiced law here, in the states? Is it a family thing?"

Even in the darkness, I could see that Tavis's expression remained blank—a look that seemed familiar, like the strange longing I sometimes noticed in his gaze. I wasn't sure if it was the memories of an old life that haunted him or something else.

"Sorry," I said, more quietly. "You don't have to answer."

Tavis shrugged, deflated, and finally pulled his gaze from the window. "It's fine." He cleared his throat. "It wasn't a family thing. My family were country folks, had sheep and cattle. That wasn't what I wanted." He paused a moment, considering something. "I was here on holiday with my girlfriend, Alice. We were here as a sort of a last-ditch effort to make things work between us. Alice claimed I worked too much and didn't appreciate what I had, even though it was right in front of me...she said nothing was ever good enough and she couldn't live like that anymore."

I could see the harsh reality of her words—the memories—swirling through his mind as I opened my senses up to him, for some reason needing to understand the sudden dullness of his eyes, the defeat in his tone. The pained expression I'd seen earlier in the armory returned.

"She said that if we couldn't have a nice holiday together, without me working, our relationship was over."

Moments from Tavis's life flashed in my mind. I saw the pain- and regret-filled days that followed the outbreak of the Virus, the night Alice had died in his arms, leaving him to hate the man he'd become and wander the decomposing world without her.

"You loved her," I whispered. Even if he hadn't known how to show her at the time, he loved her very much, more than he'd ever loved anyone. I realized my mistake before I could take the words back. I winced. "I didn't mean to pry."

Tavis's eyes shifted to mine, but his expression was constant.

Unable to stop myself, not really wanting to, I dug deeper. When Tavis had found Sam a week later, he knew that the boy needed his help, needed someone to take care of him, like Alice had needed in her final moments. More than anything, Tavis had wanted to prove to himself that he could become someone other than the misguided man he'd turned out to be. He had to prove his life was worth living, that he could be someone else, someone capable of caring for another person and worth the second chance he'd been given.

Then my breath hitched. I saw an image of me in Tavis's mind, and I finally understood the look that sometimes flashed in his eyes, why he felt a connection to me the moment he'd seen me. I didn't look like Alice, not really. Her hair had been long and blonde, and her eyes had been a deep brown that radiated her every emotion. But like me, freckles had dotted her nose, and she'd been, at times, strong-willed and outspoken. She'd been determined to fight for them, for what she'd wanted, and Tavis felt the need to help me—he needed to be the man he'd been unable to be for Alice, in any way that he could.

"You can't blame yourself," I whispered. Between Tavis's emotions and my own, I couldn't look him in the eye. "We were all different before."

When he said nothing, I ventured a glance at him. His grave but apologetic gaze met mine, and I felt insurmountable sorrow radiating from him for the first time in all the months that I'd known him.

"That doesn't change the past," he said, his voice clipped.

Our game had quickly turned into a torturous revisiting of our lives before, and we were both left sitting in a van with five other people, extremely uncomfortable. We exchanged one more disquieted glance before my mind went blank, like had happened in New Bodega. In place of Tavis's emotions, of the white noise of all of my companions' thoughts and emotions I'd grown used to ignoring, was a void, nothingness…

"Something's wrong—" There was a bump in the road before I could finish, causing all of us to grab ahold of whatever we could to hang on.

Jake cursed, and the van swerved. Tires skidded on the wet pavement as the van spun. I could hear my dad's voice. He was shouting for everyone to hold on.

Metal grinded against metal. I could hear the sound of breaking glass and someone's scream, but all I could think about was the pain in my head, and something was cutting into my bicep as we flipped over and over.

Then everything went black.

⊛

I had no idea how much time had passed before I opened my eyes again, but the gray-blue night stretched out above me, and my back burned like hell. Body too weak and mind too fuzzy to concentrate, I let my head loll to the side. Nighttime came in and out of focus. Tavis was cringing beside me, tugging on me—on my arm? We were on asphalt. He was dragging me. His mouth was moving; he was saying something. But a ringing echoed in my ears…I couldn't make out what he was saying. I didn't understand.

There was a crack off in the distance. Then two more.

Tavis froze, eyes wide as he looked down at me, meeting my incoherent gaze for the first time. I tried to read his thoughts, to see into his mind—to understand. But his mind wasn't there.

I blinked rapidly as I tried to focus. Color drained from Tavis's face, and the pain and tension in his features relaxed. He stared at me like I wasn't even there. A moment later, his eyes rolled back in his head.

"Tavis," I rasped, panic quickly taking hold of my semiconsciousness, the looming impression that I'd never see him again making it impossible to think. I tried to reach for him, but my arm was too heavy. "Tavis," I repeated.

I could hear voices around me, but they were distant and unfamiliar. "Jake," I tried to shout as I attempted to reach for Tavis, for anyone, but my arm screamed in pain. I couldn't lift it.

No. None of it made sense. Slowly I blinked, staring up at the naked, withered branches that seemed to be reaching for me from the trees above.

I blinked again…and again…until I could barely keep my eyes open.

Through my lashes, I saw a man loom over me, a scar over his right eye and brown, stringy hair hanging around his sunken face. *I don't understand.* "Tavis," I mumbled, but it was becoming harder and harder to keep my eyes open, to think.

The man knelt down.

Before the darkness of unconsciousness consumed me, I managed to whisper, "Please…"

21

ANNA
DECEMBER 13, 1AE

THE COLONY, COLORADO

Anna stared at the white porcelain mug sitting on the kitchen counter in front of her, eyes heavy and mind awhirl. Her rear end was numb from sitting on the stool for so long—long enough for her tea to cool to that unpleasant tepid temperature that made it more or less undrinkable. Her dangling feet were rapidly approaching a painful state beyond numbness, a deep-seated ache that seemed to resonate from her bones.

She stared at the blinking clock on the microwave; the green numbers read 2:10. It hadn't been blinking when she'd first sat down with her cup of tea just after midnight. Realizing that the power had gone out again, Anna made a mental note to check with Gregory's infrastructure advisor. Things weren't going well around the Colony, not when there were only 752 people to keep the place running—755, if the new stowaways were being counted—a dramatic drop from the Colony's population before the Re-gen rebellion.

Groaning, Anna scooted off the stool and lumbered around the kitchen island to the stove, glancing at her watch along the way. Setting the clock was becoming automatic, and she did it quickly, without a second thought about the significance of the task. Unreliable electricity was a trifling matter compared to the two that weighed heavy on her mind.

Peter was going to be okay, if his body's initial response to his first treatment was anything to go by. The new, human-derived electrotherapy was nothing short of miraculous, not just for Peter, but for all of the Re-gens still residing in the Colony. Anna should have been overjoyed…should have been filled with so much relief that she *should* have been making up for her weeks and weeks of lost sleep at that very moment. For the first time in a long time, Peter's prospects for a long, healthy future were promising.

But Jason's weren't.

Placing her palms on the counter, Anna hung her head. She could only think of one other time she'd felt so torn, so lost, so defeated. So utterly desperate. She was sick to her stomach with worry.

Leaving her family behind in Bodega Bay over two decades ago had been the hardest thing she'd ever done. It had ripped her apart, destroying parts of her soul with such devastation that the woman she'd become by the time she and Gregory reached Peterson Air Force Base—as the Colony had been called in those days—was hardly recognizable as the wife and mother she'd been just days before.

And now Jason was in the Colony. He'd strolled right into the lion's den, alongside the only man Anna had ever had more negative feelings toward than Gregory. She wasn't sure where they'd gone, but she desperately hoped Jason was being led by an invisible leash, because the possibility that he was a willing accomplice to whatever form Cole's latest aspirational madness had taken was too terrifying a prospect. Her stomach twisted. She refused to believe that her own flesh and blood would *choose* to help Cole, and at the same time, she feared what might drive him to make that choice. Had something happened to Zoe and Tom? To Danielle? The prospects and possibilities were more disturbing than reality ever could be—at least, Anna hoped that was true.

She needed to track Jason down. Anna nodded to herself. Regardless of his reasons for being in the Colony, she needed to find him, somehow convince him to abandon whatever agreement he'd made with Cole—or dose him with the neutralizer, if he wasn't assisting Cole by choice—and get him as far away from the Colony as quickly as possible. Because if Gregory discovered that Jason was there before Anna could find him…

"Anna?"

Startled, Anna clutched the gaping lapels of her robe and spun around.

"Darling, what are you—" Cutting himself off, Gregory raised his hands to waist height and made his way into the kitchen. "I'm sorry. I didn't mean to startle you."

Anna shook her head and forced an anxious laugh. She was suddenly wide awake, so alert she was shaking. "It's fine, Gregory. I'm fine." And she needed him to believe that. The worst possible thing that could happen for Jason right now was for Gregory to learn of his presence in the Colony, and of his apparent alliance with Cole. "Though," she added shakily, "it wouldn't hurt if you made some noise *before* you attempted to startle me half to death."

"Apologies, darling." Gregory closed the distance between them and wrapped his arms around her, holding her in an oddly comforting embrace. "I merely missed you and wondered what was keeping you up."

Anna couldn't resist. She relaxed into him.

"You've been working so hard lately." He stroked her hair. "You must be tired."

Anna exhaled shakily. "I'm exhausted."

"I'm not surprised. You've spending so much time and energy on Peter's situation"—Anna stiffened at the thin film of bitterness coating his words—"you've hardly been able to focus on your other duties." He kissed the top of her head, then pushed her back enough that he could look down at her. Though Gregory was only a few inches taller than Anna, he had this way of looking at her that made her feel like she was staring up at a giant about to crush her, body, heart, and soul. Maybe it was because he had already succeeded in crushing two out of three.

"I—" Anna licked her lips. "I've just been—"

"No matter." Gregory smiled, a wolf in broadcloth pajamas. "But I'll need my science advisor operating at full capacity tomorrow, which shouldn't be a problem now that this Peter business is out of the way. Assuming you get some rest..."

Anna had to fight the sudden urge to scream. *This Peter business?* Was he kidding? Their son had practically been on his death bed—for the *second* time in his short life. What parent wouldn't do everything in their power, wouldn't commit every moment of their time and energy to finding a way to save their dying son? Gregory, it seemed.

Anna swallowed a bitter laugh and offered what she knew would appear to be a warm, loving smile instead. "Go back to bed." She gave his arms a squeeze. "I'll join you in a few minutes, after I've cleaned up."

Gregory glanced at her untouched cup of tea. "Of course, my dear."

Anna gritted her teeth, hating his placating tone. She needed a few more minutes alone to collect herself before climbing into bed with him. As Gregory walked out of the kitchen, she swallowed her rage and forced her face to remain placid, despite the grimace trying so hard to contort her features.

Quickly and quietly, Anna disposed of her tea and made her way upstairs, but she didn't head straight to the bedroom she shared with Gregory. She stopped in the hallway just outside Peter's room and eased the door open, poking her head inside. She fully expected to find Peter curled into a ball on his side, sound asleep. He'd always been a good sleeper, even when he was a baby…even near the end of his first life, a little over a year ago, when the leukemia and chemo had taken nearly all of his strength.

Though Peter *was* curled up in a ball on his side, he wasn't asleep. Moonlight glinted off his eyes. The moon was full, or near to full, and it provided plenty of silvery light to make out his puffy eyes and tearstained cheeks.

Anna stepped inside, quickly but quietly shutting the door before crossing to Peter's bed. She sat on the edge and reached out, combing her fingers through his short, brown hair. "What's wrong, sweetheart?"

For a long time, she sat on the edge of his bed, holding one of his hands and combing her fingers through his hair while he wept silently. She could hardly bear to see him in so much emotional pain, but she could do little to help him when she had no idea what was upsetting him.

"Peter?" She gave his hand a squeeze. "Please, sweetheart, tell me what's wrong."

"I—" He sniffed wetly, then cleared his throat. "That song you were just humming—you used to sing it when I was little."

Anna froze. She hadn't realized she'd been humming—it was the same song she'd sung to both Jason and Peter when they'd had nightmares—but beyond that, Peter shouldn't have been able to remember the song, let alone her singing it to him when he was younger. Like all Re-gens, his memory of his first life was extremely vague and spotty, and contained little in the way of specifics. Or so she'd thought. "You remember that?"

"No, Mom," Peter said, sniffling again. He sat up and wiped his face on the sleeves of the navy blue PAFB sweatshirt he always slept in. "But you do…"

Anna eyed him, baffled.

"I met someone today, or"—he shook his head—"I guess I didn't actually meet her, but I saw her walk down the hallway outside the electrotherapy lab. She could read and feel around in people's minds." He sniveled. "Now I can, too."

Swallowing, Anna fought the urge to interrogate her son. He'd always been freer with his words when they came to him naturally, and he tended to clam up when nudged, however gently.

"I can't believe how much I don't remember. I had no idea..." Peter wiped his cheeks with a fresh part of his sleeve. "Like the sad girl. Remember her?"

Anna nodded, unsure where this was going.

"I used to dream about her, didn't I?" Peter's brow furrowed. "A lot...and it frightened you."

Again, Anna nodded.

"I—I still see her," Peter said softly. "She's older now, but she's still *her.*"

For a long time, Anna could only stare at her son.

Even before he'd become a Re-gen, Peter's Ability had been unique, and to this day, Anna didn't fully understand it. Maybe it was because he was second-generation, one of the few born with an Ability—like Jason and Zoe, but lacking the genetic block Anna had planted in her two older children to keep their Abilities from manifesting before they were old enough to understand how to hide them. Peter had grown up with his Ability. It was a part of him, always had been and always would be.

He'd always been able to sense the Ability of another person; all he required was a clear line of sight. But this had changed, or rather *evolved*, when he'd been going through the arduous chemotherapy and radiation treatments that had failed to send his leukemia into remission, allowing him to absorb pieces of other people's Abilities for short periods of time. And after becoming a Re-gen, the daily electrotherapy treatments had only strengthened his Ability.

And then there were his "friends." When Peter had been little, he'd exhibited strange quirks that Anna had chalked up to an over-active imagination—quirks that now, for the first time, Anna suspected might have been Ability-related. His dreams had been filled with the same cast of characters, people he'd spoken of as though they were real. But the one he'd spoken of the most, the one he'd claimed to dream about almost every night, had been the sad girl.

Anna hadn't realized Peter was still seeing the sad girl in his dreams. "You never told me that you still dream about her." Anna shook her head slowly, her eyes narrowed in thought. "Or that you remembered seeing her from before."

Peter frowned. "I thought I was just imagining her, until now." His eyes opened wide, and he smiled. "I mean, she seemed like a real person to me, someone with her own life and everything, but I thought it was just a Re-gen thing, like maybe I was just remembering someone I knew before…but after today, I get it. I *know*."

It was Anna's turn to frown. "Know what?" She tilted her head, trying to process the emotions filling his shadowed eyes. He seemed sad, confused, and scared, but also a bit excited. "What happened today that changed things, Peter—was it the new treatment? Or the woman you saw at the electrotherapy lab?"

Dread pooled in Anna's chest. She was starting to suspect it was the latter, and that the woman was none other than the one who'd been with Jason and Cole at the west gate, who'd altered perception so she and her companions could enter the Colony seemingly undetected. If Anna's suspicions were right and that woman had an Ability similar to Tom's, allowing her not only to alter what people believed to be reality but to see inside their heads, to uncover their most private memories…

"The woman I saw—her name's Larissa—but her Ability…it's like I can remember now," Peter said, but he shook his head. "I mean, *I* can't remember, but I can see *your* memories."

Anna's heart sank. *Her memories?* So she'd been right about the woman with Cole and her Ability. And now, for a little while, this Larissa's perception-altering and mind-reading skills would be integrated into Peter's Ability, too. Anna had tried so hard to protect him from what she'd done, had done everything she could to keep this one, special person in her life from seeing her as a monster.

Peter nodded. "I've seen your memories of me. It's *like* I remember, without actually remembering. But now I know that the woman I keep dreaming about is real...she's the sad girl, all grown up. She has to be."

"I see." Anna swallowed roughly. She'd made so many impossible choices, done so many horrible things. She'd helped tear the world apart...destroyed billions of lives. "What—what else do you know now?"

"I know what you've done, Mom." Peter's eyes darkened, and Anna took a deep breath, preparing herself for the worst, waiting for the same look of disgust and betrayal she'd seen in Zoe's eyes the one and only time her daughter had visited in a dream. "And what *he's* done." Peter turned his head to sneer at the bedroom door. "He's horrible. I hate him."

Nausea churned in Anna's stomach. Closing her eyes, she breathed in and out through her nose several times. She looked at her son. "And me? Do you hate me, too?"

For a long moment, Peter was quiet, his expression considering. Finally, he shook his head. "You...you make me feel sad." His gray eyes, so much like his father's, filled with an earnest openness Gregory's had never held. "Like Zoe."

Anna's breath caught. "Wha—what?"

Peter flashed her an uncertain smile, then looked away. "She's, um—she's the sad girl...and she's why I was so upset." He sniffled. "Mom, she's in trouble."

22

ZOE

LOCATION UNKNOWN

Tap. Tap. Tap.

Silence.

Tap. Tap.

Noise and a light so bright I was near blinded before I even opened my eyes woke me from what felt like the dead. I peeled my eyelids open, a feat akin to opening a window nailed shut. I blinked and squinted. My head was throbbing, and my body ached beyond discomfort. I blinked again, trying to focus past a blur of shapes and shadows as my fuzzy mind stirred.

I was in a bedroom. There was a pink accented wall across from me with empty picture frames hanging haphazardly along it. I blinked again. A white dresser sat a little to my left, a stack of folded clothes on top—what looked like *my* folded clothes—and a half-empty bottle of cheap vodka beside them. I peered down at my attire—a woman's worn white T-shirt and gray sweatpants that felt a little too short. A prick of uncertainty registered as I wondered whose they were and how I'd come to be wearing them.

Tap. Tap. Tap.

With great effort, I turned toward the noise, half expecting to see a woodpecker on the wall. I held my breath.

A tallish, unfamiliar man with dark hair hanging loosely at the nape of his neck stood in front of a boarded-up window. With dark-stained hands, he braced either side of the window frame and stared out a small gap between two nearly rotted two-by-fours. He was wearing thick brown cargo pants, exposed steel-toed boots, and a dirty, tan long-sleeved shirt, like he'd just gone to work.

Tap. Tap. Tap. His index finger rapped against the wall like he was sending Morse code to someone on the other side. Remotely, I wondered if he was nervous or anxious, or maybe a little bit of both. I tried not to panic as I put the distorted pieces of what little I remembered back together. After a moment, my pulse quickened and realization began to set in.

And like he had a sixth sense to know that I'd awakened, the man at the window slowly turned to face me. Instantly, I noticed the scar above his right eye, and dread—too overwhelming to subdue—crashed over me.

I bolted upward, trying to sit up, to run, to flee, but the metal headboard clanked against the wall in my weak attempt, and I was jerked back down onto the mattress. My back was on fire, my left arm screaming in pain, and all I could do was gulp for air. I was restrained, unable to move beyond the wiggle of my fingers, and the asphyxiating cords of fear wrapped around my throat, squeezing.

I fought to breathe. I *needed* to breathe—to clear my mind so I could think. I barely registered my burning wrists as swirling images of Jones and Taylor, of Taylor's hands on me, of the gleam in his eyes in the woods at Fort Knox, spun around and around in my mind. Pure horror and sheer doom were like overturned buckets above my head, washing over me until I was soaking in them.

"What—" I choked, and tried to swallow away the dryness of my throat, the heaviness of my tongue. "What do you want?" I rasped.

The scarred-faced man didn't say anything, his gaze vacant as he seemed to stare straight through me. I couldn't read his mind, couldn't feel his intentions.

"Why did you bring me here?"

His long, black hair was tucked behind his ears, his sunken, sickly face covered in what looked like weeks of patchy scruff. A layer of sweat glistened on his brow and around the black holes of his eyes.

My rapid breaths faltered, my eyes widened, and my body flooded with ice. I remembered him. Realizing I'd seen him in New Bodega made my dread and the million horrific possibilities of what he wanted from me a living monster clawing inside me. I did my best to tamp it down, to make it stop.

Peering up at my restraints, I loosened my clenched fist and tried to maneuver my wrists out of the rope tied around them. But it was to no avail. I couldn't allow myself to appear weak, no matter how innate my desire was to panic, to beg to be let go, to scream. *Why was he following us?*

"Please," I whispered. "Tell me what you want from me." The possibilities circled through my mind, and despite my will to stay calm, a small whimper escaped.

The man's vacant eyes enlivened, and he straightened, his gaze boring into me for a fleeting moment before it softened. He took two measured steps closer and slowly reached for me...reached past me...and grabbed a white cloth from the bedside table. I exhaled in relief.

When his eyes met mine again, they were asking and uncertain, but he only hesitated a moment before he extended the cloth toward my face. His gaze shifted to my quivering lips, then back to my eyes, which were frantically searching his drawn features for answers. The cloth was damp against my skin as he wiped the beading sweat from my temple and forehead. His eyes followed his every action, but he avoided looking into my eyes again. I wasn't sure which I felt more, terror or relief. What was he thinking?

"You're still healing," he said in a gruff but quiet tone. The sharp scent of alcohol and a hint of soap wafted off him. "You need more rest."

"Healing? What—" But then I registered the incessant pain in my shoulder and the burning in my left arm. I looked up at it tied above me. My bicep was wrapped in a blood-spotted bandage. I remembered hitting my head against the window as the van spun and tumbled and turned. I remembered the screaming pain in my arm as something sliced through it and the sound of metal scraping against asphalt. I remembered the sound of gunshots and the way Tavis's face fell and the life faded from his eyes.

My dad...Jake... My vision blurred as my tongue moved too fast and the words tumbled from my lips. "Where's my family? What did you do? Why did you do this?" *What about Sanchez? And Gabe and Becca?* My captor looked away from me, dropping the cloth back onto the side table before stepping over to the vodka bottle on the dresser. He fumbled to unscrew the cap and took one deep pull. Then another.

"Are they all dead?" I asked. There was too much anger and sadness to comprehend anything but the cool wash of blood draining from my face. I wasn't sure that even Jake could sustain a gunshot wound, not if it had been to his head.

The man took another drink, ignoring the hysteria lacing my voice.

"Are they *dead*?" I screeched. "Did you kill them?"

With the back of his hand, the man wiped his mouth and stared at me. His eyes filled with sadness and regret so poignant that I didn't need my Ability to feel it deep in my soul.

"Oh my God," I whispered. *They're dead.* His look said it all.

Tears welled and fell, rolling down my cheeks, and I suddenly couldn't breathe. "Why?" I choked out, rage blooming too intense to keep inside me. I pulled against the ropes, tugging and screaming louder than the pain ever could. "Why? What the fuck do you want from me? What do you want? Tell me what you want!" I sobbed, wondering if it even mattered anymore.

In an instant, the man's hand clamped over my mouth. I could taste the salt on his skin, and his nose was so close it was almost touching mine.

"Shut up," he said, though I barely heard him through my muffled whimpering. "If you know what's good for you, you'll *shut up.*" His tone was level and deliberate. An obvious warning.

I squeezed my eyes shut and sobbed against his hand, not caring what his intentions were as I thought about my companions —about my dad, about Jake—probably still lying out in the middle of the road somewhere.

I turned away from the man, away from his tight grip on my mouth, and cried into someone else's pillow. "Why did you have to kill them?" I croaked. "You could've just taken me. You didn't have to kill them."

"I didn't," he said, his breath cloying and moist against my cheek.

Swallowing mid-whimper, I reluctantly shifted my gaze to his. I didn't care that our noses were touching or that I could see into his eyes, filled with an emptiness so haunting it made me sick with dread. But still, I dared to hope... "They're not dead?"

The man sat up, the mattress squeaking beneath the sudden movement. "Not all of them. We only killed who we had to," he said with what sounded like remorse.

I didn't understand. I tried to stifle the sobs bubbling up. "Who's...*we*?" I felt my lips quivering. "Who did you kill?" I asked more softly. The tears multiplied, knowing his answer would ruin me, regardless of who it was.

"The driver and the man with you. They were the only ones conscious."

My heart squeezed and twisted, hope and sadness sparring inside for control. All I could do was pray that they'd shot Jake in the chest and not in the head. And Tavis... I sniffled. I'd already known he was gone. I'd watched the color drain from his face and the light dull in his eyes.

He was trying to save me.

I tried not to think about the others, doing all I could to convince myself that they'd survived the crash and that Jake, at least, would come for me.

Suddenly, my anguish turned to hope and my sadness to hate and rage and determination. Sooner or later, someone would find me, or I would get away. I just had to be strong, to hold on and figure out how to tell them where I was.

I glared at my captor, teeth clenched as I silently promised him horrible things to come.

But his murky brown eyes held no fear or amusement. In fact, they were devoid of much emotion, save for what I thought might be apathy and compliance. Given his lackluster emotions, it seemed primal lust and physical dominance weren't among the reasons I'd been taken, and I felt my anxiety lessen just a little.

"Why did you do this?" I asked, more steadily this time, though tears still streamed down my cheeks—tears for Tavis and my unknown future, for the rest of my friends and family, who I prayed were still alive. "Why did you have to kill them?"

The man stiffened and stood, the floorboards creaking beneath each footstep as he walked back over to the boarded-up window. I wondered what he kept looking at.

Furtively, I glanced around the room. With the pinks and whites and purples accenting the bed and walls, it looked like a little girl's bedroom. His daughter's room, maybe. I assumed she was dead, whoever she'd been, but I needed to learn more, to figure out what *they* wanted, how many *they* were, and where, exactly, I was. I needed to find a way out.

It would be too naive to think I'd been brought back to New

Bodega, where I'd first seen the scarred-faced man—that I'd be so close to home. There was no salt scent in the air, and I could hear no ocean breeze outside like I could at home, either. "Answer me, please," I pleaded. "You followed us—why? What do you want with me?"

This time, the man glared over his shoulder, an angry glint brightening his deadened eyes. But he didn't answer, and it worried me that I still couldn't sense his mind. There was a wall, an obscurity that only strengthened the harder I tried. Or was it all in my head? Was my Ability now nonexistent? I couldn't tell as a sharp pain shot through my head like a Taser keeping an unwanted perpetrator away.

"What do you want?" I shouted, too impatient to play his game.

He frowned, his eyes hardening. "If you keep screaming, Randall's going to come in here and you're going to regret it, just like the others. I guarantee you that."

My anger fizzled. *The others?*

He turned back to the gap in the boards. "I told you to rest." As if he couldn't stand to be in the room with me a moment longer, or perhaps didn't trust himself, the man clomped past the bed without a glance in my direction. He snatched the vodka bottle off the dresser and flung open the door, exposing a hallway. I saw a chair and shotgun propped up against the wall before he slammed the door shut again behind him.

Alone, tied to a bed—a hostage in a house with people who wanted me for God only knew what—I let out a faint whimper. It took every ounce of willpower I had to keep myself from succumbing to hysteria. I focused on thinking clearly, calmly.

I needed to burn every detail of my surroundings into my mind for later. The wheelchair in the corner to my right. The way the door had popped open a millisecond before the man pulled it shut again, like the latch might be broken. The gap in the window that I needed to pass in hopes of getting a glimpse outside.

Most of all, I needed to keep my mind busy, so I didn't dwell on the fact that my Ability was apparently gone, and with it all sense of security and hope. I didn't know when or if my Ability would come back, and it had been so long since I'd been without it I wasn't sure how I would survive if it never did.

I needed to come up with a plan.

23

DANI

DECEMBER 14, 1AE

THE FARM, CALIFORNIA

*U*nhooking a hanger from a circular clothes rack, I held the tank top hanging from it up against my chest. It was super soft cotton, slightly loose and flowy, and the color fell somewhere in the spectrum between green and yellow. "What do you think, Zo? Too yellow?" Green I could do—it was my favorite clothing color—but yellow, not so much.

Zoe paused from flipping through hanger after hanger of leather jackets to look over her shoulder at me. "It's cute. A little too girly for me, but very you, D." She scrunched her nose. "But..."

I straightened and glanced down at the tank top. "What?"

"It doesn't really go with your guns."

Reflexively, I adjusted the cross-body strap of my automatic rifle, then glanced at the three men standing side by side with their backs to a wall of bladed weapons that wouldn't have been out of place in a medieval armory. "What do you guys think?"

Gabe, tallest of all and looking angelic with his golden hair and crisp white button-down shirt, shrugged.

Cam, with his soulful eyes and wistful smile, sighed and nodded. "I like it, D."

And Jason, standing in the middle and somehow dominating the space with his powerful stance and expressionless, scarred face, tilted his head to the side ever so slightly. "Not very practical, is it? Not good for farming...not good for scavenging..."

I pulled my bottom lip between my teeth. "Oh, well..." I blinked, and the three men standing nearby changed horribly. Their clothes were torn and stained with browns and reds, their skin was sunken, sallow, and seemed to be slipping off of them, and their eyes were dull and milky. "Oh God, no!" I shrieked, lurching toward them, then freezing in place.

In the next blink, Jason, Cam, and Gabe returned to normal.

"So it's this again?"

I spun around to find another version of Gabe, this one standing beside Zoe and her rack of leather jackets. Blinking several times, I shook my head in confusion. "What? Huh?"

Gabe made his way around the clothes rack to his dreamtime duplicate, who was now flashing back and forth between living and walking dead with every heartbeat. He stared at it a moment, then sighed. "And here I'd thought it was such a good thing that you're sleeping again."

"I don't—" I shook my head, dispelling cobwebs of confusion. "You're really you, aren't you?" I glanced around in wonder at the shop's now odd-seeming combination of girly and badass clothing options and antique weapons collection. It had seemed so normal before... "I'm really dreaming?" I'd had the one dream of that day, when I'd somehow, seemingly by sheer force of will, managed to get some sleep. But that had been a couple nights ago, and I hadn't been able to duplicate whatever I'd done, no matter how hard I'd tried. Until now, it seemed.

Gabe nodded. "Congrats. And welcome back." He wound his

way back around the clothing racks until he was standing before me. "How are you doing?" He glanced down at my middle. "And how's the little one?" His pale blue eyes returned to mine; part of me expected his to flash to a milky white like his dream doppelgänger.

I shut my eyes and shook my head. Opening them again, I said, "We're good. Progressing full-speed ahead, as expected. Harper said he'd place me at around twelve weeks if he didn't know otherwise, but we're really only at five or so." Which meant my child was developing about twice as fast as a normal human child...and about on par with Sarah's twins. I flashed him a shy smile and placed my hand on my abdomen. "Chris says that means it's about as big as a lime...and that I should start showing soon."

Gabe's lips spread into a smile, but I could tell that his heart wasn't in it.

"What?" I reached for him, gripping his forearm. "What is it? Why are you here? And why hasn't Sanchez checked in?"

He met my eyes, then looked away. "There's been an accident. The van..." He exhaled heavily and ran his fingers through his shoulder-length hair. "Tavis...he didn't make it."

An accident? Tavis didn't make it? My thoughts swirled as I tried to understand.

"Sanchez couldn't contact you guys because she's been mostly unconscious since the crash," Gabe continued. "And Jake's been shot, so he's out of it, at least for now." Gabe's eyes met mine, and he hesitated before saying, "We're holed up in a hotel just outside of Sacramento until they've recovered a little. Becca, Tom, and I have made a few trips out, gathering what food and weapons we can carry back from the van—"

I swallowed roughly, my heart beating too quickly. "And —and Zo?"

Gabe looked at me with such intensity it was like he was looking into my soul. "We don't know. She wasn't anywhere to be found when Tom came to, and he was the first, so..."

I looked at dream-Zoe, standing placidly by, still holding that leather jacket, and shook my head. "Well, she wouldn't have just wandered off."

"We know."

"So you think someone took her?"

"That's exactly what we think."

"My God..." I squeezed my eyes shut, wishing doing so would block out the truth of what had happened. "Alright, tell me everything."

I woke up feeling ancient. And worried. And absolutely sick and tired of others stealing whatever precious time my people—my family—had left to spend with one another. It barely even registered that I'd been dreaming, that I'd actually slept through the whole night.

I sat up, for once without the familiar twist of nausea, and rolled my neck, using the almost painful stretch as a chance to piece together what I remembered from the dream with Gabe. Of course, only one thing mattered—or four things, really—they'd crashed the van, Tavis was dead, Jake had been shot, and Zoe was missing.

"Chris," I said hoarsely and shook the pregnancy cobwebs from my brain. *Where's Chris?* I fumbled for the watch on my nightstand. *What time is it?*

Almost six in the morning, it turned out. I glanced at the heavy green curtains pulled across the bedroom's two small windows. The sky would start to lighten soon, though the sun wouldn't rise for another hour. At this time of the morning, I knew exactly where I would find Chris. Which was just as well, because I needed to fill Harper in, too.

Zo's missing...

I hastily scooted to the edge of the bed and slid my feet into wool-lined moccasins, then retrieved my down coat off one of the hooks behind the door. I could feel Annie in her room, her mind a gentle hum rather than the bright beacon it was when she was conscious. Over the long months, I'd come to recognize this as meaning she was drifting. Unlike my other companions, Annie's mind never faded from my radar completely, because unlike the others, Annie never actually slept. She rested, true—her mind had adapted to her Ability in ways it seemed that mine never would— but she never actually slept, not anymore.

"*Jack,*" I said telepathically to my dog, who was gazing up at me from his curled position on the bed. "*Stay with Annie and bring her to me in the big house if she wakes up.*"

With a stretch, he made his way off the bed, and the click of nails on hardwood marked his path out of my bedroom and down the short hallway to Annie's door. He yawned dramatically, then settled on his belly and rested his head on his crossed paws.

"*Thank you, Sweet Boy.*"

His ears perked forward, and the small dark patches above his eyes that I always thought of as his doggy eyebrows rose. As I turned to leave, I could feel a deep sense of contentment and affection coming from him through our bond.

"Love you too, Jack," I said as I rushed to the front door as quietly as possible. The fire I'd built up in the fireplace the previous night was nothing but half-dead embers now, but it still produced a small amount of heat. A fact that was made more evident by the burst of chilly, almost freezing air that greeted me when I opened the door.

Zo's missing...Zo's missing...Zo's missing...

I left the cottage and practically ran along the slippery path to the farmhouse. Once inside, Chris and Harper's bedroom was only a short trip up the creaky stairs to the first room on the right side of the hallway. I knocked on their door quietly. There was no response, so I repeated the knock, but with more gusto. One more time...

I could hear lazy footsteps on the other side of the door. This house was so old that it reflected every movement with a unique, usually complaintive sound of its own. "Is that you, Sam?" Chris's voice was hoarse with sleep. "Did you have another bad dr—" She was clearly surprised to find me standing in the hallway instead. "Dani?"

My chin started trembling, my eyes stinging.

Zo's missing...

"What is it? What happened?" She scanned me from head to toe. "Is Annie alright?"

I nodded even as my chest started convulsing with my mounting distress. Shock had worn off, and reality was setting in. First Jason had been abducted, now Zoe. And the others were all either injured or—or...poor Tavis. "The van," I said. "There was an—an accident." It was all I managed to get out before grief took over.

"Alright, shhh," Chris said as she draped an arm over my shoulders and guided me into the bedroom. "Take your time." I heard the door shut. "And when you're ready, tell us what happened."

I found myself sitting in the antique, floral upholstered armchair that had been in this room when we'd arrived, Chris squatting on the floor at my feet. She gripped my hands tightly. I could feel her Ability calming me from within, but it didn't bother me, not this time.

In minutes, I was back to a relatively coherent state. I sniffed and wiped my nose on my sleeve. Clearing my throat, I looked first at Chris, then at Harper, who was sitting on the foot of the bed. "Gabe came to me in a dream."

Chris's eyebrows rose. "So you were sleeping? Really sleeping?"

I nodded. "Up until Gabe pulled me out of the dream. My first full drift-free night since Jason..."

Chris blew out a breath. "Well that's something, at least."

I sniffed again. "Gabe told me they crashed the van. Said they were all knocked out for a while, and when they came to, Zo was gone and Tavis—" I breathed in shakily, the echo of my heaving sobs fresh in my chest. "Tavis is dead."

"Shit," Chris groaned.

Harper scrubbed his face with one hand. "Zoe might've been disoriented and wandered off. If it just happened last night—"

I shook my head. "It was the night before last. They got as far as Sacramento."

Harper's hand clenched into a fist, which he slowly lowered to the bed. He pressed his fist into the mattress so hard that his arm was shaking. "Then why didn't they contact us sooner?"

I shrugged. "I guess Sanchez was knocked unconscious during the crash, and she's been having a hard time with her Ability since then, and Gabe's been sort of busy trying to salvage what they could from the crash and Jake's in one of his healing trances...so they've got a lot going on. And with everything, I guess they decided to wait to contact us until they had some concrete information to give us." I looked at Harper and took a deep breath. "Zoe didn't wander off. It wasn't the crash that killed Tavis." My voice rose in pitch. "It was a gun. And Jake—" After several more deep breaths, I regained some of my unraveling composure. "They shot Jake, too, but...you know."

"Poor Sam," Chris murmured. I met her eyes and gave her hands a squeeze. We all liked Tavis, but he'd become something of a father to the ten-year-old. Sam would be devastated.

Hesitantly, almost like he was afraid to ask, Harper said, "How do we know Zoe's just missing and not...?"

"She's not dead," I said. "Gabe sensed her dreaming mind a couple times. Just quick blips, but enough to know she's alive and nearby, just not exactly where."

Chris nodded slowly, eyes narrowed as she considered what I'd told them.

Harper was gripping the edge of the bed now, and I had the

impression that he was physically restraining himself. "We should go to them, tend their injuries and—"

Chris stood and held out her palm to Harper. "Just hold on there, buddy." She pointed back at me. "You heard Becca; Dani can't go anywhere if she wants to keep herself and the baby safe."

Harper stood as well, facing off with Chris. "Exactly, Dani's staying here."

"You two go," I said, desperate for someone to do *something*. "Gabe said they're in a hotel, just outside of Sacramento. We'll be alright here without you for a few days, and Becca said I'd be fine so long as I stayed here, so I'm sure the baby'll be okay. You should go," I urged. Hell, I was getting close to flat-out begging.

Uncertainty flashed across Chris's face, looking completely out of place. "It'd be a several-day ride just to get there."

"But only a couple hours in a car," Harper countered.

"True," Chris said, drawing out the word. "We could ask the council to lend us another vehicle."

"And if they say no?" I asked quietly. It seemed more than likely that they would refuse, considering we'd just ruined the last one they let us borrow.

"Then we'll leave on horseback first thing tomorrow morning," Harper said.

I bit my lip, considering our options. "You should take Grayson to New Bodega, Chris. He gets along with the council the best."

Chris nodded and started for the door. "I'll wake him up and fill him in." She glanced back at me. "Will you get our horses ready?"

"Of course."

"I'll help," Harper said.

The three of us left the bedroom in a line, worried and filled with uncertainty over what the day would bring. But at least we had a plan.

24

ANNA

DECEMBER 14, 1AE

THE COLONY, COLORADO

With one hand covering her mouth and the other gripping her side, Anna paced in her office, striding from the shut door to the desk, over and over and over again. Her eyes felt grittier with each successive blink, and she kept thinking she was seeing things on the edge of her vision— going nearly two full nights without sleep tended to do that to a person. But in other ways, she'd felt like she'd never been more alert.

Jason was inside the Colony. He'd been there for two days now. She'd been unable to track him down so far, and she had no clue what he, Cole, and Larissa, the perception-altering woman, were up to. Casing the base, likely—learning how it worked, who did what, and who they'd have to remove in order for their takeover to be successful, assuming that's why they were in the Colony in the first place. But it was the only explanation that made any sense at all.

Anna squeezed her eyes shut, just for a moment. How was any of this happening? She *had* to find Jason and get him out of there. She just didn't know *how* to find him, not to mention how to approach him without Cole or Gregory noticing...without getting herself, and probably Jason, killed.

Hand covering her mouth, Anna shook her head and continued to pace. And then there was Zoe; according to Peter, something had happened to her. He'd been able to sense that she was distressed and in pain. Peter's connection with his half-sister was so strong and went so far beyond anything Anna could have imagined. She was astonished by how much he knew about Zoe—far more than Anna herself knew about her only daughter.

But despite *knowing* all of this, Anna was a sitting duck. She'd mulled everything she knew about each situation over and over, all to no avail. She couldn't see any pathway that led to her helping either Jason or Zoe, not this time, not with her current lack of substantial information.

Anna had her hand on the doorknob before she realized she'd made the decision to head home to check in with Peter. It was midafternoon, and he was bound to be up by now, teenager or not, healing or not. She knew she should let him rest after the extreme stress of the new form of electrotherapy. But still, she was so very tempted to run home, wake him if he was still asleep, and beg him to tell her whatever else he might know about Zoe's current status or see if he knew Jason's exact location in the Colony.

Sighing, Anna hung her head and released the doorknob. She both wanted to utilize her son's current Ability and was utterly terrified of being in the same room as him. She didn't want him to see any more of her memories than he already had, not that she had the slightest inkling of how much he'd already seen. She'd considered nulling him but hadn't been able to bring herself to actually do it. After all, he was her son...her little boy. He was her second chance, her do-over.

238

Anna resumed pacing. To the desk. To the door. To the desk. To the door. Her mind was spinning uselessly. She couldn't help Zoe or Jason, and she couldn't help but be scared for Peter...and be a little scared *of* him, if she was being honest with herself.

"Mom..."

Startled, Anna froze, her eyes darting around the office. She held her breath. Had she imagined Peter's voice?

"Mom?"

"Peter?" Anna continued to stare around the room. Apparently he'd recently come into contact with a telepath and had absorbed that Ability for the time being, as well.

"Will you come home, Mom? It's Zoe...I'm scared."

Heart in her throat, Anna inhaled sharply and opened her mouth to demand more information, despite being fairly certain that Peter's version of telepathy only worked one way.

Anna's office door opened, and she spun around to face the intruder. "What the hell do you think you're—" Her question cut off abruptly, and she clutched the front of her lab coat and stumbled backward a few steps until the backs of her thighs hit the edge of her desk.

The intruder shut the door quickly and quietly, then snicked the deadbolt locked and turned to face Anna. "Mom," Jason said as he crossed his arms and leaned back against the door. His face was cold, expressionless, his features twisted on one side by a grisly scar that swept almost from hairline to jaw. But his eyes—they were brilliant and focused. They were accusing. "Been a while," he said, his tone as expressionless as his face.

Anna stared at her eldest son and ever so slowly shook her head, at an utter loss for words.

"Were you at the gatehouse when we came in?"

Anna blinked several times, having difficulty believing that Jason was really there, in her office with her. "I—" She blinked several more times, then nodded. Why was she being such a dumbstruck moron? This was what she'd been waiting for. This was her chance to convince him to leave. This was it...but she could only manage to stare at Jason, eyes wide and tongue tied. She hadn't seen him since he was five years old. She'd seen photos in Gregory's files, sure, but it wasn't the same. She'd left him a little boy, and now he'd returned to her a grown man.

"I thought that was you, but I wasn't sure." He pushed off the door and started moving around the room, eyes roaming everywhere. "Cole didn't notice you, in case you were worried." Jason stood in front of the meticulously organized bookcase to the left of her desk and glanced back at Anna. "With how much he talks about you and Herodson...he would've mentioned it." Jason's attention returned to the fourth shelf of the bookcase, which was filled with neatly labeled binders documenting Anna's research on both the gene therapy and the modified strain of influenza she'd used to spread it.

Anna swallowed, a useless action considering how dry her mouth had become in the last minute.

"His plan is simple, really." Jason continued to browse through the labels on the spines of the binders, apparently not a care in the world. "When he's done scoping out the place, he's going to kill Herodson and take over as leader here...and I'm perfectly fine with that." Seeming to grow bored with the binders, Jason turned away from the bookcase and made his way behind the desk. Slowly, he eased himself down into Anna's chair.

Anna faced him. When had her little boy grown so large? How? It didn't seem possible. "Why are you working with him?" Anna forced herself to ask, even though she feared the answer.

"I didn't have a choice." Again, Jason crossed his arms. "He's planning on killing you, too." He speared her with a stare. "Which means it's time for you to finally leave this place. We're just lucky that Cole's been a little too free with his commands lately. He's managed to get a fair number of your people under his control, but he's drained his Ability too much, even with me boosting him. He renews my commands every morning." Jason smiled grimly, the effect only emphasized by his scar. "But *this* morning he was a little, well, impotent."

"That's how you're here, talking to me?"

Jason nodded. "He's resting right now, and Larissa's scouting the northwestern sector. He'll never know I was gone."

Anna studied his face, searching for hints of the kind, gentle boy she'd left in Bodega Bay so many years ago. "So you came here to warn me that Cole wants me dead?"

Again, Jason nodded. "You need to get out of here, and soon. Herodson and Cole can battle it out." He shrugged one shoulder. "I couldn't care less who's in charge of this place." He looked around the office like he could see the rest of the Colony through the walls. "Looks like it's barely hanging on by a thread anyway." Jason refocused on Anna, his eyes on fire with challenge. "I say we run and don't look back. I say we let it fall apart."

Feeling defeated, Anna collapsed into the thinly padded chair across from her son. She laughed wanly. "Before you showed up, I was in here trying to figure out how to find you and tell *you* that you needed to leave the Colony for *your* safety. It never even crossed my mind that you'd tell me the same thing."

Jason studied her, tilting his head to the side, just a bit, and narrowing his eyes. "This place—it's a goddamn illusion, anyway; it won't last, so what's the point of drawing out the inevitable?"

Anna sighed and raised her shoulders. After a moment, she let them fall and hunched her back. "I can't leave."

"You'll die if you stay," Jason said, frozen in place and voice coated in ice.

Anna shook her head. "That may be, but you don't understand. I *have* to stay here...for Peter." Now that she'd managed to get herself speaking, Anna felt as though she would never shut up. "He's sick, and he needs to be here for his treatments." She shook her head more emphatically. "Don't you see? I don't care what happens to me so long as he's okay."

"Always playing the goddamn martyr," Jason muttered. He held up a hand to keep her from rambling further. "What's wrong with him—with Peter?"

"He—he's—"

There was the clicking sound of the door being unlocked, and Anna's entire body stiffened. There were only two keys that would grant access to her office—hers and Gregory's. And if Gregory was on the other side of the door, Anna had no doubt that this would be the last time she would ever see Jason again. Ever.

"It's just me," Peter said in her mind, right before he slipped into the office and relocked the door.

"Peter?" she said, staring at him wide-eyed. Out of the corner of her eye, she saw Jason freeze, halfway out of the chair. She glanced at the lock on the door, then back at her younger son. "But, how…?"

"Camille's Ability." Meaning, he hadn't needed a key at all. *"From before she left…"* Which meant he'd had her Ability to control metal for more than eight months. It was the longest he'd ever retained an Ability, no doubt a result of his increased electrotherapy sessions.

Anna exhaled a breath she hadn't realized she'd been holding and all but collapsed in on herself. She couldn't take it anymore—all of the stress, the paranoia, the always looking over her shoulder…always expecting the worst to happen. She felt like she was on the verge of having a heart attack.

Peter placed his hand on hers. "Don't worry, Mom." He gave her a squeeze. "We'll get through this; we always do."

"You must be Peter," Jason said. Anna watched his eyes scan Peter's face as he lowered himself back into the chair.

"And you're Jason…my brother." Peter laughed, but it sounded halfhearted and thready. "Until two days ago, I didn't know I had a brother."

Jason lowered his eyes to Anna, his expression no longer

blank; his features were tensed, his eyes heated. "You told him I was here?"

Anna shook her head. "He just knew. His Ability—he can absorb parts of other people's Abilities."

Jason's attention switched back to Peter, a new interest gleaming in his eyes.

"I sort of met a woman yesterday—one of your companions, Larissa," Peter said. "And now I know things about people...can see their memories and feel some of what they're feeling. She can actually change what people think they see and remember...but I can't do that. It's pretty weird." He paused for a moment. "Like, I know she's like you—she isn't here by choice, and she doesn't want to hurt anyone." He gave Anna's hand another squeeze. "She noticed you when they got here a couple days ago, Mom. She could tell that you weren't affected by her illusion, that you saw them come in, but she didn't say anything to that guy Cole about it. She—she hates him, wants to kill him, but she can't because he's controlling her, like Dad does with everyone, just like Cole's controlling Jason. Right?"

Jason nodded slowly.

Baffled, Anna shook her head, her eyes narrowed. "But how could Cole—why didn't you just null him the first time he tried to use his Ability on you?"

"I couldn't," Jason said, his tone cutting off any further discussion on the hows and whys of his current predicament.

Anna pursed her lips. "I see. Well, I'm sure he's commanded you not to try to leave him, yes?"

Jason leaned forward and nodded.

"And I'm sure you can't hurt him, that's the obvious way to break his hold on you, but..." When Jason confirmed her assumption with another nod, she said, "Then you'll need the neutralizer. It'll take a little while to make, but it's the only way I can see to get you out of here safely."

Jason inhaled to respond, but Peter spoke first. "You have to take us with you."

Jason frowned. "I thought you couldn't leave…"

"Oh, but I can now."

"What?" Anna craned her neck to look up at her youngest son. "The treatment's not a permanent fix, Peter. You'll need—"

"I know, Mom, but they've got people who know how to do electrotherapy on their farm." He smiled broadly. "Did you know that Becca and all the others are there? I can see them in his mind…"

Anna had no words. At the moment, she barely had any thoughts. She was completely and utterly stunned. Peter could *leave* the Colony? *She* could leave? She'd long ago given up hope that the day might ever come, but now…

"You're a Re-gen," Jason said, and Peter nodded. "How'd that happen?"

"I was sick—leukemia. I died. Mom brought me back."

Anna cleared her throat. "He was the driving force behind the Re-gen program in the first place," she said numbly. "I knew he was dying, but I couldn't survive losing another of my children." Anna was aware of how desperate and maniacal her explanation made her sound, but it was the truth.

"You didn't lose us," Jason said, the corner of his mouth lifting just enough to show the hint of a sneer. "You left us."

"She didn't have a choice," Peter snapped. "You'd be dead if Mom hadn't—"

Jason stood abruptly. "Don't you think I know that? But now I'm alive and everyone else is either a fucking corpse or has lost their fucking minds." He bared his teeth in a smile. "Can't say I feel real good about that." He stared at them for several seconds, waiting for either of them to defend Anna's past decisions, or maybe daring them to. "What do you need from me to make the neutralizer?"

Anna licked her lips and sat up a little straighter, grateful that

244

they were back on somewhat familiar ground. "I just need a sample of your blood. If I take it now, I should have the neutralizer ready by morning. Will you be able to wait that long?"

"Have to," Jason said with a nod. "Will you?"

Anna nodded eagerly.

"Well, alright." Jason started rolling up his sleeve. "Let's get started."

25

ZOE

LOCATION UNKNOWN

I thought I'd only closed my eyes to collect my wits for a minute, but I opened them to find the scarred-faced man in the room again. I hadn't heard him enter, which meant I must've fallen asleep. I bit back the questions I had and the pleas that pawed for voice. I took a deep breath, in…and out.

Hoping it was all a nightmare, I squeezed my eyelids shut. But the man was still there when I opened them again, sitting on the floor, his back against the wall across from the bed. He was staring down at the now-empty vodka bottle, which he turned around and around in his hands. It wasn't a dream.

"You're finally awake," he grumbled. His words were a tad slurred, but his tone was stern, different than before. It was worrisome. When he looked up at me, a strand of hair hung in his face, making him seem more worse for wear than he had before. Once again, I tried to use my Ability, to sense something, *anything* about this man and his intentions toward me.

He almost smiled. "You're different than the others. I can tell."

Although I dreaded his meaning, I had to ask. "What's that

supposed to mean?" My voice was a tremulous whisper. Though flashes of me semiconscious and a glass of water against my lips— partial memories I could barely recall—came to mind, my mouth was still dry, so dry it hurt.

He eyed me a moment longer than I liked before answering. "You're stronger, more powerful." He looked at me with an unabashed, entertained grin. "I can feel your mind in mine, poking around." But as quickly as it appeared, his smile faltered and he stared through me once more. His eyes were glazed over, like he was lost in memories, memories I desperately wished I could see.

The fact that he could sense my Ability at all made both my stomach roll with alarm and my heart flutter with hope. Although he had the upper hand, at least my Ability wasn't gone, just subdued. And now I understood. "You're nulling me," I said. "That's why I couldn't sense you in New Bodega...why I couldn't sense anything before the accident." I gazed around the bedroom, only seeing a cage. "It's why I can't feel your mind now."

The man said nothing.

"What were you doing in New Bodega?" I asked, figuring I might get more information out of him since he appeared to be somewhat drunk.

He studied me. "We trade with them sometimes," he said after a moment. I could tell he hadn't wanted to divulge anything, but it seemed that, whether it was the vodka or something else, he decided a partial truth was okay.

"And why did you pick me—"

The bedroom door opened, and a taller, short-haired man with bright blue eyes and a goatee stepped inside. "Is she ready?" His eyes shifted from me back to the scarred man. I assumed this was Randall. "She doesn't *look* ready, Carl. Her food's still in her damn bowl."

I glanced to my right, finding a bowl of oatmeal and a cup of orange juice sitting on the nightstand.

"What the hell've you been doing in here for the past hour?"

247

Though I didn't sense that Carl had any predatory interest in me, my stomach rolled again at the thought of him being in the room with me while I was unconscious.

"She was sleeping," Carl said.

"Well, hurry the hell up. Sandy's ready."

I tried not to outwardly react to the clue that there were at least three people in the house, but I didn't like the odds stacking up against me. Had the world been different, I might've taken comfort in the fact that there was apparently another woman in the house with me, but it almost made me feel worse. It was easier to manipulate a man than it was a woman, especially if they were all Crazies. So far, though, it seemed Randall and Carl were simply survivors with an Ability, like me.

Like it was nothing out of the ordinary to have a helpless woman tied up in a bedroom, Randall turned and left, swinging the door shut behind him. Unlike Carl had done, Randall didn't pull the door closed to make sure it latched.

With a sigh, Carl climbed to his feet. He placed the empty bottle of booze on the dresser once more and walked toward the bed. He didn't look at me, as usual, but through me, and I thought I vaguely registered a misty cloud of guilt in his eyes.

He sat on the edge of the bed, causing my body to slide toward him as the mattress gave way. "Lift up your head," he said, pulling another pillow from beneath the bedframe.

"I'm not hungry," I said, too scared and stubborn to eat whatever else might be mixed in the bowl.

Carl was unconcerned. "You're going to eat because if you don't, you'll die," he said. "It's simple."

My simmering apprehension flared. I lifted my head, and he slid the pillow beneath my neck, propping me up and affording me a clearer view of the room. A roll of duct tape sat on the dresser top, along with a small framed photo of a little girl. She was in the arms of a smiling man and a short woman in a nurse's uniform, who was laughing beside them. The man looked like Randall, so I assumed Sandy might be his wife or his daughter. I was in their home, it seemed, and it made sense, given Randall's apparent authority. But I wasn't sure how Carl fit into the family.

I opened my mouth and let Carl feed me a spoonful of oatmeal. His hands shook a little, and his nailbeds were dirty, stained maybe, like he might have been or might still be a mechanic of sorts. The skin around the tips of his fingers was chewed, but despite his rough appearance, he was unexpectedly gentle as he placed the spoon in my mouth.

The oatmeal was cold and thick and bland, but I ate it willingly, scared of the alternative. "What does Sandy want with me?" I asked, licking my lips.

Carl's eyes shifted to mine. "She doesn't," he said with a brusque edge. His lips pursed.

I took another bite off the proffered spoon. "Then what does he—"

"Stop asking questions," Carl growled. "I'm not going to hurt you unless I have to, but that doesn't make me your damn friend. Just be quiet and eat."

Narrowing my eyes, I wanted to refuse the next bite, but I conceded, surprised to find I was starving, and my concerns of whatever the oatmeal might be laced with became a distant curiosity. "Will you at least tell me how long I've been here?"

"Why does it matter?"

"Why would it hurt to?" I said with a little too much impatience.

Carl's lips pursed. "Watch yourself, woman."

Though I knew withholding my frustration was the smarter route, it seemed attitude was all I had left in my defense. "Whatever you're going to do, just do it already!" I turned my face away from him.

"It's been two days," he finally said and exhaled like he'd spoken against his better judgement. "And trust me, you'll need your strength. You need to eat." He brought the spoon up to my mouth again.

"Trust you?" I said without thought.

"Enough!" Carl shouted and stood up. "If you don't eat this, I'll make you regret it," he promised. My impromptu defiance cracking, I took another bite of oatmeal. Truth be told, it was like I could feel it making me stronger with each bite.

"And drink all of this," he said. "You'll need the sugar."

My panic returned. "Why?"

Carl's deep, brown eyes fixed on mine, but he said nothing as he held the glass of orange juice to my lips. I was incredibly thirsty, but taking a drink somehow felt like I was sealing my fate. I turned my face away again.

"Fine then," he growled and slammed the glass down on the side table. Orange juice splashed all over the place. He yanked the pillow out from under my neck, and my head fell back.

"Ouch!" I cried.

"I'm not the one who will feel like shit after." In an instant, he reached up to my wrists, pausing when he laced his fingers in the rope around my right hand. "Don't even think about trying to get away. I promise you, you'll regret that too."

Carl had downed enough booze, I wasn't convinced he had the wherewithal or reflexes to best me. When he untied my right wrist and reached over for the left, I pulled it from his grasp, prepared to punch him in the nose and then in the groin, but a knife was under my throat as my hand slipped from his. I froze.

"What the fuck did I just say?" His voice held the echo of a beaten and bloodied soul that was so desperate, so impatient it fought to stay in control as a knife I hadn't even seen on him pinched the sensitive skin of my neck.

Holding my breath, I closed my eyes, trying to hold back my tears of frustration.

"Try that again and there'll be blood," he warned.

I nodded slowly. This time, I believed him. His reflexes were better than I'd thought. Though he was clearly intoxicated, he was weathered and well trained in this, that much was obvious. My skin crawled and a thick blanket of sweat coated me as, once again, I considered how many others he'd done this to. *How many others have lain in this bed? Where are they now?* But I was afraid that I already knew the answer.

"You try to kick me," Carl said as he untied my ankle, "I'll cut your leg off. We don't need your leg. You got it?" After a few yanks and some manhandling, my ankles were tied together, just like my wrists.

"All of this attitude, you struggling—you're making all of this more difficult on yourself," he said, double-checking the ropes. "You can't change your fate," he said. "None of us can." His tone was dull, hollow, and I wasn't sure if he was saying these things for my benefit or his own.

Carl lifted me out of the bed, and as he carried me by the window, I caught a glimpse of what looked like a church steeple from the gap in the boards, but Carl moved too quickly for me to see anything else as he carried me over to the wheelchair in the corner of the room. His body was well honed, like most of ours were now that we were survivors. I briefly wondered what exactly Carl *was* capable of. His arms were secure around me, his grip painfully tight.

"Are you going to throw yourself out of the chair and flop around when I wheel you down the hall? Or can I skip tying you to the damn thing?" Carl was panting a bit, out of breath, though I figured it was more from the booze than it was from being out of shape.

I narrowed my eyes at him, not gratifying him with a response.

The corner of his mouth quirked into an ever-so-slight smile, and he set me in the seat. He pulled the chair out, away from the wall, and pushed me to the bedroom door. I couldn't tell if my heart had stopped or sped up. It was like I couldn't breathe as the possibilities of what awaited me outside the relative sanctuary of this room became too horrifying and far too imminent.

Carl opened the door and cool, bleach-scented air caressed my face. It burned the inside of my nose. "Please tell me what you're going to do, Carl. I'll beg if you want me to. Please."

Though I could tell he was trying to ignore me for a few heart-beats, he seemed to change his mind. "We're just drawing blood."

I craned my neck around, eyeing him as he grabbed the handles of the wheelchair. "You want my blood?" That didn't seem so bad —but then again, it probably wasn't for reasons that were very good, or I wouldn't have been kidnapped and tied up.

Carl pushed me out into the hallway, the shotgun against the wall I'd seen before now out of sight, as was the chair. It was still daytime, and light filtered into the hallway. There was a closed door beyond mine to the right, only a bathroom separating them, and everything else appeared to be to the left, the direction we were headed.

Carl rolled me down the hardwood hallway and out onto the second-story landing. We passed through a den with vaulted ceilings, and my eyes scoured the family photos in different-sized frames, most of them cracked and the glass broken; they were barely hanging on, like they'd borne the brunt of someone's anger. The wood floor was covered in dust, save for a fresh pathway of footsteps and what looked like wheelchair tracks leading into the room at the end of the hall.

I whimpered, and my eyes burned. Something told me Carl wasn't simply taking me to get my blood drawn. *What's in the room at the end of the hall?* He wheeled me past an open door, to what appeared to be a personal office. Sunlight shone in through the blinds too brightly to see beyond and illuminating the books and stacked papers littering a desk and the floor around it. Dishes were strewn all over, like someone—probably Randall—spent a lot of time in there, locked away…mad. Unbidden, I thought about the Colony and the horrible things they did to people there.

"Carl," I rasped. "I'm scared."

I wasn't sure why I told him that, perhaps hoping he'd take pity on me and turn me around, but he didn't say anything. There was the sound of footsteps ahead and then Randall was standing in the doorway of the room at the end of the hall. He was wearing a white medical coat, but he looked menacing and severe, nothing like Harper when he was dressed in his doctor attire. I wasn't sure if I should be petrified or reassured that Randall at least looked like he knew what he was doing.

His eyes narrowed on Carl. Like before, it was as if he didn't even see me. "Hurry up, Sandy's prepped. We're wasting fuel."

"Carl," I whispered again, my body shaking. He was the closest thing I had to an ally in all of this. But Carl remained silent and picked up the pace as he wheeled me through the bedroom door.

In front of me, Randall searched through a dresser drawer for something. The scent of bleach was strongest in the room—sterile to the point of burning my eyes and the back of my throat instead of just my nose. Breathing through my mouth, I took in the room around me; it was big—the master bedroom, I assumed—and there was a large picture window, undraped and letting in the afternoon sunlight.

Hope and desperation swelled as I peered through the window, outside to the freedom that was just beyond my reach. I could see the side of a blue house, part of a broken window, and a roof obscured by a tall maple tree. I tucked that information away for later, in case it came in handy.

Then my gaze fixed on her—Sandy—and I paled. A woman with a few thin wisps of graying hair hanging from her head was propped up in a hospital bed. There were IVs in her arms and breathing tubes in her nose. I barely recognized her as the woman from the picture I'd seen with the child and Randall. Her green eyes were dulled, almost deadened as she stared at the wall behind me. She didn't blink, didn't move, though her chest rose and fell rapidly, as if she'd just run a mile. I knew that wasn't possible. She was too frail to even walk, her skin too sallow. Her features were strange, fallen and twisted on one side. She was barely human. Barely alive.

Tears pricked my eyes as I thought about what they'd done to her—and what they were going to do to me.

When Carl stopped the wheelchair at her bedside, my eyes latched onto an open, well-worn and bound notebook with a scribbling of notes and lines connected to a list. My nostrils flared and I shuddered as I scanned what seemed to be a list of one Ability after another. *Electricity, revival, healer*—there were at least a dozen of them. I was trying to understand, to fathom what I'd been brought into, when my eyes clung to the last Ability on the list: *mind reader/finder*. I wrung my hands in my lap, faintly aware of the fiery wound still fresh on my arm. "There are so many," I said under my breath, unable to look away from the piece of paper I assumed was responsible for my fate.

Randall whirled around, glaring at me and then at Carl. "No duct tape? Jesus, you're slipping. You know I don't like to hear them talk." Randall shook his head and reached for Sandy's arm. He tossed the notebook onto the dresser, then checked the tubes that ran from her forearm into an empty IV bag... *Ready for my blood.*

"I can't help her," I said. "You don't even know my blood type —if we're even compatible."

"You're compatible," Randall said with an alarming amount of certainty as he addressed me for the first time. He grabbed my arms, still bound together at my wrists, and stretched them out beside Sandy on the bed. When I saw a few dried-up drops of blood on the sheet beneath my arms, I instinctively shrank away. "No—"

A clammy, powerful palm collided with the side of my face, making my neck crack, my jaw sing, and my head spin so much I almost forgot to breathe.

"Move again, I dare you," Randall snarled. "Actually," he started, then hit me again, this time higher, his knuckle meeting my temple. And for a moment, I could only see blackness. "That one's just in case you forget."

My face was branded with pain, my vision veiled with tears as Randall yanked my arms toward him again. I felt the wound in my arm tear open beneath its bandage and I winced. Randall picked up three additional IV bags and laid them out on the bed beside Sandy, who sat there oblivious as he checked the hoses. He attached the first one, and then the others.

My head was shaking, I couldn't stop it. "Four pints?" I breathed. I knew that was extremely dangerous, borderline deadly. I pulled my arms back into my lap, no longer worried what he might do since I'd likely die anyway.

"This will shut the stupid bitch up," Carl said behind me right before rough terrycloth scraped against my mouth and nose, and a sweet smell carried me into blackness.

26

DANI

THE FARM, CALIFORNIA

"Am I doing this right?" Carlos lowered his pruning shears and backed away from his chosen apple tree, surveying his work. He'd been snipping branches off the dormant tree for the past half hour.

I paused with my own shears primed on a branch of my very own apple tree and studied his. "Hmmm…" I gave the shears a squeeze and—snip—the end of the young branch fell about seven feet to the ground. Carefully, I descended the stepladder I'd been using to reach the higher branches and picked my way through the overgrown ground cover to stand at Carlos's side. My rubber boots squelched in the mud created by the previous night's brief but abundant rain shower.

Carlos crossed his arms over his chest and cocked his head to the side. "It just looks so…"

"Clean?" I offered.

With a soft snort, Carlos shot me a sideways glance. "I was gonna say 'pathetic,' but sure, 'clean' works."

I shrugged. "It looks like the picture in the book, and it does only have five main branches, and I *think* you could describe it as goblet-shaped." My voice slowly rose in pitch, highlighting my absolute lack of certainty.

Carlos snorted. "Maybe if we lived in that painting with the melting clocks by that guy with the crazy mustache."

I laughed; I couldn't help it. I'd been fretting all morning, trying to keep busy around the farm to stave off feeling utterly useless while so many people I loved were in danger, and now that it was well into the afternoon, my nerves were frayed beyond belief. Chris and Grayson should've been back by now.

The laughter died too quickly, and I reached out and gave Carlos's arm a squeeze. "Thanks." I smiled briefly. "I needed that." I narrowed my eyes. "So where'd you learn about Dalí, anyway?"

"Oh, you know...around," Carlos hedged. He moved on to the next tree in our small but abundant orchard—another apple tree, though there were also pears, plums, peaches, apricots, figs, an avocado tree, and a bevy of various citrus, all planted years before we'd arrived. Mase and Camille had returned to the farm the day after Zoe and the others left, and they were slowly working their way through the smaller citrus trees on the other side of the orchard.

I returned to my tree, scooting my stepladder over a couple feet. I was almost done, but my dependency on the damn ladder really slowed me down. "Around, eh?" Snip.

Carlos stood with his back to me, apparently still assessing his new target. "I don't know. Maybe it was in one of those art books Zoe and Sam are always looking at together." I thought I caught just the faintest hint of envy in his voice.

"You know," I said, doing my best to sound nonchalant. "Zo loves talking about all of that art stuff with people—Sam, Becca..." I choked on a swell of panic mixed with terror. *Zo*... Clearing my throat, I continued, "I'm sure she'd jump at the chance to do art lessons with you, too." My voice was noticeably shaky, but I chose to ignore it, just like I chose to ignore the glassy feeling of tears welling in my eyes and the tightness in my chest. And, thankfully, so did Carlos.

"I don't know," he said, snipping his first crooked branch off the tree. Snip. Snip snip. "I guess." So vague; he could be such a teenager sometimes.

I bit my lip, grasping my amusement at his stereotypical reaction with all of my might. I laughed under my breath, when what I really wanted to do was fall to my knees and pound on the soggy earth and scream out my rage at how unfair the world had become. Swallowing roughly, I reached for another off-shooting branch. Snip.

For minutes, the only sounds were those of our shears clipping branches and the faint hum coming from the beehives nearby, along with their roaming brethren. It felt somehow empty outside, now that so many of us were absent. It was too quiet, unsettlingly so.

But if there was one good thing about the lack of hustle and bustle around the farm, it was that sound carried remarkably well.

Clip. Clop clip. Clop clip.

I stood taller on the step stool, peering out at the road beyond the pond. There were trees blocking my view, but I had other senses.

"Hey!" Carlos's head snapped to the right, his eyes searching the trees. "I think I heard—"

I nodded. "It's them. They're back." I scouted out their minds, finding not only Chris, Grayson, and their horses, Cookie and Bernard, but four others, one equine and three human. I lowered my shears and slowly backed down the stepladder, setting the tool on the top rung. "They're not alone."

Carlos glanced at me, frowning. "I don't hear an engine, either. No car."

I shook my head, my right hand finding the pistol resting snugly in my thigh holster, just making sure it was still there.

Touching it made me feel more secure, a new development after Zoe and Tom uncovered my memory about Jason's abduction.

I pulled my hand away from the weapon. I recognized the minds. It had taken me a moment, because it had been so long, and two of them had changed so much, but I had zero doubt. I grinned despite all of my anxiety and fear at what would happen next—tomorrow, or next week, or next month…

"It's Biggs," I said, laughing and tearing up at the same time. "It's Biggs and the twins!"

⬡

"They said no," Chris said, handing me a small, warm bundle of gurgling baby wrapped in pink. She slid down from Cookie's saddle, but I couldn't look away from Ellie's face.

The nearly seven-month-old baby had sticky-outy ears accentuated by a green and purple headband and the most perfect face in the world. She smiled at me, not just with her adorable little mouth, but with her endless blue eyes.

For the briefest moment—the mere blink of an eye—everything made sense. My place in this new, terrifying world. The new, terrifying world itself. Zoe's situation and the crash. Jason's abduction. Everything Dr. Wesley had done…and the General. Cam's death, and Grams's and Callie's…my mom's…my father abandoning me before I'd even been born. For the first time in a long time, I understood. It all made sense, and I felt at peace, completely and utterly.

"Dani!"

Blinking, I looked up at Carlos. He was standing in front of me, both hands on my shoulders, squeezing almost painfully. "Owwww…" I wiggled out of his hold, Ellie squirming in my arms. "Carlos!"

He held up his hands defensively. "Sorry, but you were in, like, a trance or something."

259

"She got baby-whammied, that's all," Chris said as she dug through her saddlebag. "Ellie there got me good, too." She paused in her search and stared up at the cloudy sky, then whistled. "Thought I was seeing the light." She resumed her search. "Can't remember a bit of it now, though, and no matter how hard I looked into her eyes, she wouldn't do it again." Chris shook her head.

"Sorry about that," Biggs said. He strode toward Carlos and me, a second bundle of joy asleep against his chest in a cloth carrier. "She just started doing it a couple weeks ago, and she and Everett are the only babies in New Bodega, so nobody knows what to expect where Abilities are concerned."

I offered him a smile. "It's fine, really. I can't actually remember what happened, just that I felt, I don't know…at peace, I suppose." I stared down at the innocent-looking baby nestled in my arms—which were growing tired. I adjusted her higher up. "You sure are getting big, Ellie-girl." Of course, part of the problem was that I wasn't nearly as strong as I'd been even a month earlier.

Biggs rubbed my arm, and I looked up, meeting his eyes. "How are you doing?" His lips spread into one of those closed-mouthed, gee-this-sucks-but-you-can-do-it smiles. And where such an expression on most people would make me want to punch them, on Biggs, it actually comforted me. Of course, that could've just been Biggs being, well, Biggs.

"Okay, I guess." I glanced down at Ellie, then back up at Biggs. "Did they tell you about—that I'm…" I struggled to form the words with Ellie in my arms.

"Yep," Biggs said, nodding slowly. "I think, well…just know that the twins are the best thing that's ever happened to me." He grinned broadly, his eyes glassy. "They're my everything." His conviction was both wonderful and terrifying.

I cleared my throat, searching for a new topic. *Any* other topic besides children. "So," I said, "what are you guys doing here?"

Biggs smiled again, this time with less conviction. "I'm here to help." He nodded toward Harper, who was walking to the stable with Chris and Cookie. "Looks like I'll be riding up to Sacramento with Harper."

I eyed him skeptically. "What about Chris?"

He looked off at the hillside, and I had the impression that he was avoiding looking at me. "She wants to stay here, and I've been getting restless. And my conscience won't let me do nothing." Everett wiggled gently in his cloth prison, and Biggs started rocking from foot to foot. He smiled at me, hopeful this time. "Besides, I could use a little excitement."

All I could do was shake my head. Because deep down, I could totally relate.

✦

I snorted myself awake, and my head shot upright. I blinked as I looked around the farmhouse's living room from my preferred spot curled up on the sofa. Annie was lying on the floor with Jack, Cooper, and Sam, a board game—*Sorry*, it appeared—set up between the little girl and pre-teen boy. Sam was handling the news about Tavis really well, but I could only assume that was because Chris was keeping close tabs—and an even closer hold— on his mental and emotional states. It was difficult for any of us to deal with the loss of someone we loved, but it had to be so much harder for a kid who had only a few of his friends around for comfort.

Chris couldn't exactly feel others' emotions like Zoe or Tom could, but she could sense the chemicals in a human brain and had become very well accustomed to what was normal and what was abnormal brain activity, not to mention a virtual expert at regu- lating those chemicals to mimic "normal" brain function. In my opinion, it was Grayson who'd described Chris's Ability best, comparing her to a clockmaker, someone who's knack is keeping an eye on a myriad of tiny working parts and making small tweaks here and there when necessary to keep the whole thing working properly.

"Good nap?" Chris asked from her perch beside me on the couch. Her ever-present spiral notebook was resting on her knees, a pen balanced precariously behind her ear. I figured that by now she must've built up a stash of at least a dozen notebooks, all filled with her theories, hypotheses, and "experiments." Though, to her credit, the experiments had taken on a much more methodical nature once Gabe joined our group and became her partner in scientific crime.

Narrowing my eyes, it crossed my mind that Chris and Gabe's close working relationship—if you could even call anything a "working relationship" these days—might be part of what was causing such friction between Gabe and Harper. I dismissed the notion without a second thought. Just because I was prone to jealous fits didn't mean everyone else was.

"Dani?"

"Hmm?" I focused on Chris, who was studying me with a perplexed look on her face. "Yeah?"

"Your nap…you were asleep," she said, though it had the mild lilt of a question. It took me a groggy moment to figure out that she was wondering if I'd been drifting.

I blushed, despite having done nothing wrong. Drifting in the midst of the others had quickly become a faux pas, unless it was an emergency. Understandably, it rubbed my human companions the wrong way if I chose to mentally leave their company in favor of time with my animal friends.

"You were drifting?" Chris's voice took on a disapproving tone.

I shook my head. "No, no, I wasn't. Promise." Arching my back, I stretched my arms over my head and groaned. My spine cracked and popped in several places, and I sighed as I flopped back against the sofa cushions. "I conked out, that's all." I curled my knees up and rested my left hand on my belly. My brow furrowed.

"Don't worry." Chris leaned closer and gave my knee a squeeze. "I didn't start showing until my second trimester, and I had two boys growing in there." Hurt, loss, regret, longing—so many emotions flitted through Chris's eyes, there one second, gone the next. She smiled. "You're doing just fine." She glanced at the kids and dogs playing on the floor, then at Carlos and Grayson, who were sitting side by side at the kitchen table for one of Carlos's nightly interdisciplinary lessons, the twins only a few feet away, fast asleep in their carriers.

We watched the older and younger man discuss the allegory of the cave for several minutes, the splash and clink of Mase and Camille washing the dishes in the kitchen soothing background noise. Carlos and Grayson's discussion of Plato heated, verging on an argument. Chris and I exchanged a fond smile.

"Did you dream?" she finally asked.

I nodded.

"Gabe?"

I nodded again, wrapping my arms around my knees and hugging my legs to my chest.

She shot another glance at Sam and Annie. "Anything new?"

I shook my head. "Just more of the same." Meaning a couple more super brief glimpses of Zoe's sleeping mind, but none that lasted long enough to pinpoint her location. Sure, they were searching Sacramento for her, but the search was akin to the proverbial needle in a haystack. "I told him Harper and Biggs are on their way." They wouldn't make it to the outskirts of Sacramento until the following night at the earliest, even with the change of horses they'd taken with them, including Wings. Sending her had been less about her physical prowess—she was average in terms of speed and strength—and more about my strong connection with her. A side effect of all of the time I'd spent drifting with her, I could find her mind anywhere with barely any effort, just like Jack's. Which meant I'd be able to find Harper's and Biggs's minds almost as easily. It was the next-best thing to actually being able to go with them.

"And Sanchez?"

Again, I shook my head. "Her Ability's still acting wonky." I hesitated, biting my lip, then said, "I could keep trying to find their minds. Then we wouldn't have to rely on Gabe...plus it would give me a better idea of where to focus the nonhuman search for Zo."

It was Chris's turn to shake her head. "I don't want you to wear yourself out any more tonight." She flashed me a lopsided, light-hearted grin. "Why do you think you passed out like that in the first place? Besides, it's enough trying to stay connected with Wings so far away. Searching for their minds is too much when you don't have Jason here to boost you."

I shrugged sheepishly, the mention of Jason's absence not nearly as painful as it had been a week ago. The power of hope...

She patted my knee and stood. "Come on." She nodded toward the mudroom, just through a door in the kitchen. "Let's check on Vanessa."

I eyed Sam meaningfully. "You sure?"

She smiled, but it was coated in sadness. "He'll be okay." Her smile turned mischievous. "With the right motivation, I'm better than the best kinds of drugs."

Rolling my eyes, I shook my head and stood. "Don't I know it." Though I hadn't let her fiddle with my brain chemistry much lately, I'd experienced her brand of pharmaceuticals plenty of times before. Lucky for me, my current emotional crisis was being managed quite well by our nightly talk-it-out therapy sessions, and my healthier state of mind was already reflecting itself in a healthier *me*.

When we were outside and able to speak more freely, minus the presence of young, perceptive ears, I crossed my arms over my chest and shivered within the shelter of my down coat. "What if they don't come back? What if none of them come back?"

Chris wrapped her arm around my waist and pulled me close against her side. We bobbed slightly out of synch as we walked through the grass to the driveway and stable. "Then we go on—you, me, Sam and Annie, Daniel, Carlos, and Mase and Camille." She squeezed me closer. "We're a family, whatever happens."

"But—"

"It's no use worrying about something that hasn't happened yet," she said, cutting me off. "It's wasted energy, and it probably upsets the baby. Besides, I'll believe the others are gone for good when I see their bodies myself, not a second sooner. I think this whole Jason situation has taught us all that much, at least." She gave my shoulders a jiggle. "They're coming back, Dani. Until we learn otherwise, that's what we'll *know*, okay?"

I nodded, not trusting my voice to be steady if I spoke.

Chris released me to slide the stable door open, shooing me away when I tried to help. "You might have your appetite back," she said, reaching through the doorway to retrieve one of the oil lanterns hanging on a hook beside the doorframe, "but you're still weak. Try not to overdo it, okay?" She lit the lantern quickly, and we stepped into the stable, making our way down the aisle toward Vanessa's end stall.

"I hardly think opening the stable door is *overdoing it*," I said dramatically.

Chris snorted.

"No, Rosie!" Vanessa's voice was high-pitched and panicked. "I don't want to! I won't!" There was a moment's pause, no doubt while Vanessa's hallucination of a dead teenage girl took her turn in an argument only Vanessa could hear, and Chris and I exchanged a look. "I mean, I don't know...I guess when you put it like that, it seems like the right thing to do." There was another pause. "I know, I just don't want Annie to get hurt, too."

"Looks like it's a not-so-good day for the kid," Chris said to me under her breath.

I hesitated, lagging behind a few steps, and folded my arms

over my abdomen. "Maybe I should go. The last two nights went fine, but maybe it was just a fluke, and…" I hunched my shoulders as Chris turned around, holding the lantern up to better see my face.

"Are you kidding me?" The lantern light bathed Chris's features in a warm glow. "This is perfect! I was hoping she'd be in one of her moods. I've got a theory to test, and it involves you and her"—she nodded behind her toward Vanessa's stall—"and squirt in there," she finished by pointing at my shielded midsection.

"You do?" I asked, full of skepticism.

Chris nodded and continued on down the stable aisle. She seemed to have no doubt that I would follow. Which I did. "I've got all kinds of theories about that kiddo, especially now that the twins are here and we've seen some of what they're capable of… and they're barely six months old! Imagine what they'll be able to do in a year—or ten years!" Her voice was filled with wonder, whereas my face was no doubt filled with worry. There were so many unknowns, both for the twins and for the child growing inside me.

Chris stopped in front of the door to Vanessa's stall, and the one-sided argument within halted mid-sentence. "How are you doing tonight, Vanessa?" Chris's voice was soft but authoritative. It was the perfect mother voice. I frowned, doubting I'd ever be able to master the mom voice even half as well as her.

I joined Chris just outside the stall door and stared through the bars, searching the moonlight and shadows for our resident Crazy. I found her perched on the edge of her cot, her eyes glassy pools in the relative darkness.

"I—I'm fine," she said with an unusual amount of hesitation. She was often so vociferous and free with her opinions and insults, especially when I was around. Except for the past two nights; she'd been subdued, almost calm, and, to Chris's and my surprise, almost *sane.* Vanessa spoke again, her voice quieter. "I'm glad you came back…both of you."

"Vanessa," Chris said, drawing the teenager's name out, "The past couple nights you've seemed different. Does something change with *them* when Dani's out here?" She held up the lantern, allowing the dim light to shine into the stall.

Vanessa nodded slowly, almost like she was afraid. "I—I don't know why."

"What happens?"

"They—they get quiet." She looked up at us, the lantern light glinting off her dark irises. "They go away."

27

ANNA

DECEMBER 15, 1AE

THE COLONY, COLORADO

"Nice place," Jason said, the words empty. He surveyed the dim entryway, clearly disinterested, then skewered Anna with a bold stare. "You're sure it's safe? Nobody'll look for you here?"

Anna nodded absently, choosing to focus on the small metal medicine case she'd set on the entryway table rather than on her intense son. She opened the case and removed the syringe within, sparing only the briefest glance for the tasteful, yet empty-feeling space. "This was Danielle's home while she was here," she said without thinking and removed the vial of neutralizer specially attuned to Jason.

"It wasn't her home," Jason said quietly.

Anna looked at him. "What are you talking about? Of course it was her—"

"She might've lived here," he said, "but it was never her home."

Anna rolled her eyes. "Semantics, Jason. I hardly think it matters whether—"

"It matters," he said, his voice quieting as his tone hardened.

For a moment, Anna studied Jason's face. She didn't know how to talk to this man, her son. She didn't know how to *be* in his presence, how to show him how much he still meant to her. She felt, just for that moment, that she didn't know a single thing, that she was unwinding, becoming an untethered mass of cells and energy...becoming meaningless.

Anna cleared her throat and continued preparing the injection. "So how long have you two been seeing each other?"

"We're married."

Anna stilled, closed her eyes, and drew in a deep breath. Here was yet another significant milestone in her children's lives that she'd missed. Opening her eyes, she filled the syringe with neutralizer and turned to face Jason. "I see. Well...congratulations. She's a remarkable young woman, and I hope you'll tell her how much I—"

"For fuck's sake, you can tell her yourself when we get out of here."

Anna didn't reprimand Jason for his harsh language, though she felt the instinctive urge to do so. Rather, she arched an eyebrow and gave him a pointed look.

Jason lowered his eyes to the floor, but only for a second. With a determined stare, he held out his arm toward her. "Let's get this over with, then."

Anna set down the syringe and exchanged it for an alcohol swab. Taking hold of his elbow, she jerked Jason closer to her and raised the swab, bypassing his proffered arm and going, quite literally, straight for the jugular. She swiped the alcohol swab over the side of his neck. "Sometimes the neutralizer fails if it's allowed to circulate throughout the entire body before it reaches the brain; it becomes too diluted to be effective."

Jason nodded once, quickly and decisively.

Anna discarded the alcohol swab and, reclaiming the syringe, met his eyes. "This will likely hurt far more than you expect. Free will is often seen as intangible—an idea—but it's not. It's a real, visceral thing. It's the physical manifestation of consciousness, the presence or absence of choice. For some time now, you've been without choice, a prisoner in your own body, and you've grown accustomed to your chains. Breaking them always hurts."

Jason stared at the syringe. "It sounds like you're speaking from experience."

Anna stared past him, at the staircase leading to the house's second floor. "There have been moments in my life when giving up my free will was less painful than holding on to it." She could feel Jason's gaze boring into her.

"If given the chance," Jason said, "I *will* kill him."

With a protracted blink, Anna lowered her chin in assent, her syringe hand drooping. She wouldn't stop him.

Jason moved closer to Anna and rested a hand on her shoulder. "Mom..." His voice was softer than before, almost gentle. "You must've had a thousand chances to get rid of him over the years."

Anna raised her eyes, meeting his.

"Why didn't you?"

"I—I—" Inexplicably, tears welled in Anna's eyes. "I wanted to...so many times, but..." She wanted to look away from Jason's intense stare, from the unexpected compassion mixed with the anger and hurt filling jewel-blue eyes that were nearly a reflection of her own. "I—" She sucked in a shaky breath. "I just—I couldn't," she said, feeling pathetic.

"Why not?"

She said the first thing that came to mind. "I'm not a killer."

Jason scoffed quietly. "Actually, you're the single most prolific killer who's ever lived. That answer's a cop-out. Tell me why. I need to know if I can trust you." After a brief hesitation, he added, "Do you love him? Is that it?"

Anna's chin trembled, and tears spilled over the brim of her eyelids, but she didn't break eye contact with Jason as she shook her head. "You, Jason. You, Zoe, and Peter." Lips trembling, she managed a weak smile. "I think a mother's love might be the greatest, most terrible power on earth. There's nothing—*nothing*—I wouldn't have done to keep you safe."

Jason shook his head minutely, his brow furrowed. "But that doesn't make sense. There must've been a way, a time when you could've gotten rid of him."

Anna raised her hand and pressed it against the scarred side of Jason's face. "At first, I feared what the Monitors would do to you if something happened to Gregory." She smiled bitterly. "He swore they had special orders to punish you and Zoe if he 'met an untimely end'—his words. He didn't like using his Ability on me; he wanted me to be with him by choice, but he didn't understand that I had *no* choice. I couldn't let anything happen to you kids. And then Peter came along, and the cancer..." She shuddered, reliving the tortuous past. "Gregory had the best connections, and staying with him gave Peter a real chance."

"But it didn't matter," Jason said, not unkindly.

"Leukemia's tricky. For years, he fought...but even the best medical care couldn't keep him alive." Anna felt her stare harden. "But I could bring him back—I *did* bring him back."

Jason sighed. "Made possible by this place...by Herodson."

Anna raised her chin, feeling an odd sense of defiance. "He's a strong leader."

"Are you kidding me?" Jason took hold of her shoulders and shook her so hard that her teeth clicked together. "He's a fucking dictator...a megalomaniac with god delusions. He *steals* people, Mom. He forced you to commit the single greatest act of genocide known to mankind. He even puts Hitler, fucking *Hitler*, to shame." He shook her again, even harder. "Don't you see? Even if it means wiping this place off the face of the earth, all the lives lost would be worth it if it rid the world of Herodson, too."

A wave of shame so powerful that it nauseated her washed over Anna, and she pressed her hands over her stomach. She knew all of this, knew it with every fiber of her being. She'd been telling herself all of these things for years. But somehow, hearing them in her son's voice finally made them sink in.

"Oh God," Anna whispered. Her knees felt weak, her head dizzy. "What have I done?" Had Jason not been standing there, already practically holding her up with his relentless grip on her arms, she would've collapsed onto the hardwood floor.

Clap. Clap. Clap. "Good show!"

Anna and Jason looked up the hall.

Cole continued his slow, taunting clap from the kitchen. "Oscar-worthy performances, both of you."

Anna and Jason exchanged a wary glance. How had he gotten in without them hearing? How much had he overheard? Did he know about the neutralizer? Anna blanched, concealing the syringe behind her back.

"Jason, Jason, Jason…you're not as sneaky as you think." Cole started down the hallway, Larissa and a youthful yellow-banded soldier flanking him. Anna thought she recognized the soldier, but she couldn't quite place him. "Our obedient hostess spotted you stealing away, Jason." Cole frowned, then squinted his eyes in mock concern. "Did I forget to tell you I ordered the Newmans to take turns keeping watch…just in case?"

Jason stepped in front of Anna as Cole drew near.

"How neglectful of me." Cole planted himself in front of Jason, staring at the younger man's face with reproach. "Have I waited too long to recharge your secondary commands? Is that how you slipped away from the house?"

"Yes," Jason said, his jaw clenching. Anna had the impression that he was speaking against his will.

"Hmmm…I thought as much." Cole reached out and grabbed Jason's wrist. "Might as well remedy that now." His eyes flicked beyond Jason to Anna and back. "What a convenient coincidence —you being *her* son." Again, he looked at Anna. "So is that where you and Sergeant Miller disappeared to all those years ago? Bodega Bay?" The corners of his mouth turned down, just a little.

"I'd always wondered. Mandy—Amanda Samuelson, you remember her, I'm sure—she idolized you for a while. Claimed you 'got out,' that you were brave enough to take back your freedom."

Anna sneered. "What you did to that poor girl was disgusting."

Cole barked a laugh. "I gave her true freedom. She was nothing, a sniveling worm, and I opened up the world to her, turned her into a goddess."

"You trapped her in hell," Anna snapped, "and she had no choice but to become a monster."

Cole tilted his head back and forth, like he was seriously considering Anna's words, weighing their merit. "She did grow a little full of herself at the end, if you know what I mean..." He squinted, studying first Anna, then Jason, then Anna again. "You know, I think I'll have your own dear son kill you, Anna. It'll be a poetic end, don't you think? The very person you destroyed the world for, destroying you in turn? At least you'll be able to look into your son's eyes as you die."

Fury raged within Anna. How dare this bastard threaten her, threaten to do something so awful to her son. Anna wasn't afraid of dying; she was afraid of what it would do to Jason if he were the one to kill her. She would do anything to keep that from happening. She'd take her own life first, if need be. Behind her back, she readjusted her grip on the syringe.

"Mom," Jason said through gritted teeth. "I can't stop myself... can't not do it..."

Surprising even herself, Anna lunged at Cole. She raised the syringe and, shrieking, shoved the needle into his eye. She compressed the plunger, injecting the neutralizer into his brain before Jason managed to tear her away from Cole, protecting the man against his will.

From her son's restricting hold, Anna watch Cole fall to his knees, his hands hovering around the syringe sticking out of his eye and his mouth opened in an endless, ear-splitting scream. For seconds that felt like minutes, she watched him suffer, listened to him scream, feared it might not be enough.

Until, in the blink of an eye, Cole's cry cut off, and his entire body relaxed. He fell to the side, his head hitting the edge of the bottom stair with a dull thwack. Thankfully, he didn't move again after that.

Larissa was the first to speak. "Is he..."

Jason knelt down beside Cole's body and pressed his fingers to the man's wrist. "He's dead."

Anna took a long, steadying breath as she attempted to process what had just happened. What she'd just done. Was it even possible?

A small, relieved smile parted her lips. Cole was dead. He was *dead*, and Anna had killed him. And now she and Jason and Peter could run away from this hell. She would finally be free.

"I..." The young soldier who'd been with Cole looked around the entryway, utterly lost. "I don't know what I'm doing here."

Without warning, Jason stood and took two steps toward the yellow-band, then knocked him out with a single strike to the jaw.

"Jason!" Anna shrieked.

"Can't have him running out and alerting anyone to what's been going on," he said, breathing harder than usual.

A moment later, Larissa rushed toward Jason and fell to her knees awkwardly, only partially avoiding the unconscious man's legs. "Forgive me!" She took hold of one of Jason's hands, but he pulled it out of her grip. Not to be put off, the desperate woman flung herself at his leg. "I didn't want to do any of it, I swear! I'm so sorry about what I did to your wife, but I did what I could to help her, I did." She looked up at Jason, eyes red and cheeks damp. "Cole wanted to kill her, but I convinced him to let her live, to let me practice my Ability on her instead."

Jason looked down at her, apathetic. "Why should I care?"

The woman sniffled. "Don't leave me here, please. Let me come with you?"

"Why?" The single word was harsh, but Jason's face was open, curious. "You could go anywhere, be anything without anyone being the wiser. Why do you want to come with us?"

"You've made a home," the woman said without hesitation. "You and your people, I—" She averted her eyes. "I saw them in your memories. I saw your home...on a farm...the happiness." She smiled wistfully. "It's like heaven. I think your memories of that place are the only things that have kept me sane over the past few weeks." After a several-second pause, the woman looked up at Jason and Anna. "I know you're planning on leaving. I can help you."

"How?" Jason asked.

"I can fly. A plane, I mean. I can fly us away from here."

Jason scoffed. "With what plane?"

The woman shifted her haunted stare to Anna, who cleared her throat and met Jason's doubtful glare. "We have several small jets and helicopters at the ready at all times, just in case our evacuation is in order. Especially since the uprising..."

Jason eyed Anna for a long moment, then nodded. "Alright, Larissa. Let's do this." He looked at Anna. "Where's Peter?"

"He's at home," Anna said, her heart sinking. "Gregory won't be leaving for the office for another hour or two. We'll have to wait."

"We don't have time to wait," Jason snapped.

"We won't have to." Collecting herself, Larissa stood and smoothed her hands down the front of her cargo pants. Slowly, she raised her eyes to look at Anna and smiled wickedly. "Let me take care of General Herodson, sugar. He won't even know we're there."

"No," Jason said. "He'll know we're there. He'll know *I'm* there." He looked at his mom, his blue eyes grayed and flat in the darkness. "He'll know who's killing him."

28

ZOE

LOCATION UNKNOWN

I awoke slowly. My mouth was dry. My tongue felt swollen. I could barely move. When I tried, it was like I could feel every single sinewy tendon, every weak muscle that seemed to be screaming, but I wasn't sure why. My mind was murky.

Opening my eyes, I let my surroundings settle into focus, and I tried to dust off the cobwebs of deep sleep. But I was so tired...

Shadows flickered above me, and I thought about the group campfires that had kept my friends and me safe and comfortable all those nights of traveling. All those nights...all those days of nonstop work and exhaustion, and none of it compared to this feeling.

Briefly, I thought I'd fallen asleep beside a fire, on an unfortunate mound of gravel and debris. But I wasn't warm; I was cold. I was in a bed and there was no sky above me, but a ceiling...and walls surrounded me. Walls I didn't recognize. At first.

It all started coming back to me—the strange house, the man who wanted my blood, the disfigured woman who was less than a shell of someone who had died a long time ago.

I gasped and sat up. This time my wrists weren't tied to the headboard, but still to each other, and I could feel a rope too tight and twisted around my ankles beneath the blanket that covered me. My head was pounding and heavy, and all I wanted to do was disappear and sleep.

But a faraway thought told me that I needed to get away. I needed to run.

Groggily, I focused on my bound wrists. *I need to run—*

"Don't even think about it," a gruff voice murmured beside me. Slowly, I looked to my right to find Carl sitting against the wall beneath the boarded-up window. He seemed to be a constant fixture in the room; he was always there, always drinking. The dancing light of a candle flame made his face appear more drawn and sickly than I remembered. His face was still gleaming with sweat, but his eyes were more sunken in, more hollow.

Knowing I didn't have the strength to fight, to move—to think, really—I fell back against the mattress and instantly regretted it. "Shit," I hissed, holding my forehead as I squeezed my eyes shut. The wound in my arm was a dull ache compared to the pounding in my head. "You drugged me." My voice was scratchy from disuse.

Lifting my bound hands once more, I touched the side of my face, where Randall's palm had collided with my jaw. It was still tender. When I opened my eyes again, I saw the marks. Shadows of what I imagined were newly formed bruises covered the inside of my arms. I wanted to cry as I thought about how much blood they'd taken. "How long have I been..." I whispered, mostly to myself.

Carl grunted. "I figured chloroform was better than what Randall had in store for you." He leaned his head back and took a swig from a pint bottle; the liquor was amber-colored this time, like whiskey or rum. He was trying to forget something—who he was and what he'd done, I assumed—and chase his demons away. *Good.* I hoped that meant he'd get sloppy.

But as much as I yearned and prayed to be free of this life-sucking place, I thought exhaustion might prove to be my greatest adversary. The thought of moving much at all made me feel sick to my stomach. I blinked a few times and then squeezed my eyes shut, willing the debilitating mist in my head, the heavy, invisible burden on my body, to expire. I needed to be stronger than this. I needed to think, to move. I needed to outsmart Carl, and I couldn't do that if I was unconscious.

"He doesn't like it when they talk," Carl said quietly and mostly to himself.

They... Although my senses were dull and sluggish, a shiver still seemed to shimmy its way up my spine as I recalled the list.

"You shouldn't talk to him. It only eggs him on."

I glowered the best I could in my weakness. "I wasn't egging him on," I said, my voice raspy when all I wanted was to scream. "This is my life I'm fighting for..."

I had the urge to close my eyes. *Stay awake.* Although I knew Carl wasn't my friend, it was clear that Randall—a poor man's General Herodson—was the one calling the shots.

I wasn't sure exactly what Randall had done to me, though I had a feeling that, given my weakness and the pain, he'd taken more blood than he should have. The bruising was already getting bad, and I thought it was probably better that I couldn't recall anything else, that I couldn't *see.* "I'm not sure if I should thank you, or—"

"Ha!" Carl blurted. I watched him from the corner of my eye as he guzzled from the bottle, closing his eyes and taking one long pull and then another, like they were his salvation for every sin.

My head fell to the right as I watched him. I tried not to feel sorry for the pathetic heap of shit he was.

When Carl opened his eyes again, he stared down at the bottle and rotated it in his hands. It was close to empty.

Unbidden, my mouth began to water and bile inched its way up my throat. Body fiery with pain, I leaned over the side of the bed.

There was already a bucket there, the bottom covered in bile and what looked like oatmeal, and I heaved over it, my body trying to expel anything left inside. But nothing came out. I hung over the bucket for a moment, panting before I spat the remnants of what I could from my mouth and laid back against the pillow. Sweating. Panting. Exhausted.

"Sorry," Carl said, almost indifferent. "I've noticed chloroform does that sometimes." All I could do was glare at him and wonder how sick I'd been earlier, once again grateful that I couldn't remember any of it.

"I need water," I said, hoping the hydration would help with some of the discomfort and maybe even clear my head a little. Automatically, I tried to sit up, but my head was reeling, and I lost my breath. I brought my hands to my forehead, like even tied together they would somehow stop the swirling room. I gasped and whimpered.

"Take it easy," Carl said, and suddenly he was next to me. He helped lower me back down and pulled the extra pillow out from beneath the bed again, using it to prop me up.

While the spinning slowed and eventually stopped, Carl still stood there, staring down at me. We were silent for a moment, me wondering what he was thinking in that drunken, cesspool mind of his, and him swaying a little where he stood. His eyes were expressive but he said nothing at all, and finally, like he suddenly remembered who I was and what was going on, he glanced to the side table and picked up a glass of orange juice. "Will you have some of this now?" His voice was gentle, almost, and I got the distinct impression that he was a little worried about me.

I nodded, not taking my eyes off of him as I studied the lines of his face, his eyes. I wanted to see what was left of his troubled soul, but there was nothing behind his shadowed, beady eyes; they were emotionless again.

Carl brought the glass to my lips, slowly, and I took a sip. The juice was room temperature, but it was still sweet and hydrating on my tongue. It was the best thing I'd ever tasted. I gulped it down until there was nothing left and my eyes fluttered shut. I heard Carl set the empty glass down and trudge back to his "spot" against the wall. When he sighed, I cracked my eyes open and watched him plop back down. Naturally, Carl picked up the bottle again and took a drink.

With a wince, I turned onto my side to face him and exhaled the pain.

"What?" he asked without looking at me. His attention was on the hardwood floor he was picking at with his broken, dirt-crusted fingernails.

I let my eyes close for a moment, then struggled to open them. It was strange how loud the sound of my own heartbeat seemed to be in our silence. It was methodical, almost soothing in my ears.

"Is—" I cleared my throat. It burned, raw from bile. "Is Randall your brother?"

Carl instantly shook his head, like the question was an insult. "My sister's husband."

"You don't agree with what he's doing to her, do you?" My heart broke a little bit for him as I began to understand.

Carl brought the bottle to his mouth again. He gulped once, then again, like it was water he needed to keep living. "Don't pretend you understand me," he grumbled. "You're fucking clueless."

"Maybe," I whispered, feeling like I knew Carl better than he knew himself. "You look for new Abilities that might help her," I said. Whatever Sandy was, she was an abomination. "Randall's gone mad, hasn't he?" I asked, but it wasn't really a question. "After all this time he thinks he can still help her."

Carl snorted. "He thinks your Ability will help her remember who she is—was."

My eyes flitted closed again, but with what little energy I had left, I pried them back open. I needed to know more. "Carl," I said quietly, "did you stay in here with all of them?" I wasn't sure why it mattered.

I was one of at least a dozen different mauled faces that flashed through his mind. I felt tears forming behind my eyes, despite my exhaustion. It was too hard to ignore what could be my same fate. "How many?" I whispered again. "More than were on the list?"

Carl finally looked at me, and his jaw clenched in disgust at all that he'd done. "Too many more to count. Now stop talking." He took a final, long pull from the bottle. When it was empty, he leaned his head back and let out a deep, despondent breath. Then another. With each breath, his breathing grew louder and slower.

I saw myself unconscious in bed, saw bruises forming on my arms and noticed my sweatpants were soiled. My skin was ashen, my lips dry and cracked. The bandage on my arm was bloodied and needed to be changed. Carl was staring down at me. Horrified. Sympathetic. Traumatized. Then I roused from unconsciousness and threw up all over his leg.

My brow furrowed as my eyes flitted open and I scoured his jeans. They were clean. Wearily, I gazed down at my T-shirt, realizing it was different from the one I'd had on before and that my sweatpants probably were too. He'd changed my clothes and taken care of me. He'd been mortified. *I* was mortified.

Slowly—gently—I buried my face in the crook of my arm and tried to withhold a scream. *Why—why is this happening?*

Then I realized something. In spite of my heavy, foggy brain, and the pain lacing my limbs, I could *see* inside Carl's mind. My Ability was coming back.

I lifted my arm slightly and glanced at Carl again. He was drifting to sleep. His mind was a nuclear dump putrefied by regrets, guilt, loss, and perpetual indecision between what he knew was right and what he wanted, which was to save his sister.

Whether it was Carl's drunken stupor or the fact that he was falling asleep, his nulling Ability was weakening more and more as the seconds passed, and though my Ability was weak as well, at least it was working.

Lying there, helpless, I silently screamed. I silently cried. I silently called for help and pleaded that someone would find me. Would help me.

I relived every moment I could remember since the car accident. I studied the people I'd seen, the bedrooms I'd passed and what few images still hung on the walls. I thought of the church, the blue house, and the maple tree. I projected every thought and feeling, every memory I could to anyone in the world that might be able to read minds in hopes that they would help me. I thought of Jake and Jason and my dad. I pictured Dani and Gabe, my mom and the Colony. I thought about everything I could that might be worth anything to someone trying to or willing to help me.

The more I thought about how little I knew and how weak I was—the more I realized I was utterly alone—the more I began to crack, and the silent tears broke free.

Carl stirred, and my Ability dimmed.

Rolling over, away from my captor, I sobbed once more into someone else's pillow and prayed that someone—anyone—would find me. I prayed that I would get out of this place before they drained me of all I had left. Before it was too late.

29

ANNA
DECEMBER 15, 1AE

THE COLONY, COLORADO

"You're sure you know how to fly this thing?" Anna said, hands on either side of the doorway as she leaned in to speak with Larissa. Anna had always hated seeing inside a cockpit, witnessing with her own two eyes all of the buttons and switches and dials and meters—all of the things that could be mishandled and lead to a crash. There was just so much in there that she didn't understand…that she couldn't control.

"I'm good." Larissa glanced back at Anna and flashed a quick smile. Amusement fading, she studied Anna with scrutinizing eyes. Her eyebrows drew together, and then her eyelids opened wide. "You have a flying phobia."

Anna swallowed, her mouth so dry it felt sticky. "Phobia is such a strong word…"

Larissa turned around as much as she could in her seat and reached for Anna's hand. "This is a Hawker 400XP, a twin-turbofan aircraft." She stared into Anna's eyes, so calm and certain. "I've flown planes just like this hundreds of times. Very rich, very important people trusted me with their lives on planes *just like this.* There's a reason I picked this one—trust me, sugar. I know what I'm doing." She gave Anna's hand a squeeze. "Alright?"

Closing her eyes, Anna drew in a deep breath and nodded.

"Your head says *yes*, but your face is saying *hell no…*" Larissa said with a weak laugh. "If you want, I can use my magic and make you think you're on a beach somewhere."

Anna felt herself blanch and shook her head vehemently. She wanted nothing more than for Larissa to be one hundred percent focused on flying the damn deathtrap.

Larissa released Anna's hand. "Why don't you grab yourself a seat. We'll be in the air before you know it." As Anna turned away, Larissa added, "Oh, and can you send Jason up here? I'll need his help to boost my illusion in a few minutes…unless you think you're up to it."

Feeling numb and more than a little shaken, Anna trudged down the aisle running between the single seats, hunched over so her head didn't rub against the cabin ceiling, to where Jason was sitting in the back left seat. Considering that there were only seven seats in the cabin, Anna didn't have to walk hunched over for very long.

She perched on the edge of the cushy seat opposite Jason's, making the leather creak. He didn't look away from the tiny, oval window, but Peter, sitting on the other side of the aisle, smiled at her.

"Jason?" Anna said quietly. When he still didn't acknowledge her presence, Anna reached out and touched his knee with her fingertips. "Jason, I know things didn't work out like you wanted, but—"

"Herodson should be dead right now." He looked at her, his gaze going from distant to sharp, focused, and scathing in an instant. "We should be finishing this, not running away."

"But Zoe needs us," Peter interjected.

Anna peered at her younger son, impressed by how well he was reacting to Jason's clear hatred for Gregory. Peter had never shared a strong bond with his father, and certainly a fair amount of apathy had formed on Peter's end since he'd gained access to Anna's memories, but the two had never really butted heads, either. Gregory was and would always be Peter's father; there was no denying that simple fact.

After a long, tense silence, Anna sighed. "Larissa is ready for you." When Jason didn't acknowledge Anna's words, she added, "Unless you need me to boost her..."

"No," Jason said, standing. He had to hunch over even more than Anna had. He paused in the aisle, facing away from Anna. "Just so you know, Zoe is the only reason I'm not hunting Herodson down right now." He stalked up the aisle to the cockpit, somehow moving in that graceful, deadly way of his despite his awkward posture. "Ready for me?"

Larissa responded softly, her words blocked by Jason's body.

Anna watched Jason move into the cockpit and settle in the seat to Larissa's right. He extended his arm across the space between the pilot and copilot seats and took hold of her shoulder. Jason's Ability was almost identical to Anna's, if a bit stronger, and like hers, the amount that he could amplify another's Ability was drastically increased with physical contact. Silently and repeatedly, Anna told herself that Jason boosting Larissa's illusion would not only keep their take-off hidden from everyone in the Colony, but make it so Larissa was diverting a minimal fraction of her concentration to creating the illusion and focusing as much attention as possible on flying the damn plane.

"Mom..." Peter's voice was gentle, the sound of cloth on leather, a soft hush.

Anna opened her eyes, only then realizing she'd closed them, and found Peter sitting across from her. He'd moved to Jason's vacated seat, and he was watching her with hopeful eyes and a reassuring smile.

"Did you bring anything that might help me sleep?" Peter

asked. His eyes flicked to her hastily packed duffel bag, filled with whatever remotely useful drugs, equipment, documents, and clothing had been lying around their house and was easy to gather —including, of all things, a stray lab coat. "Larissa said it should take about three hours to get to Sacramento—I'd rather use the time trying to figure out exactly where Zoe is, or maybe even find a way to let her know we're on our way."

Anna pressed her lips together firmly, staring at Peter and considering their options. She hated medicating him unnecessarily, especially after the many rounds of drugs and treatments he'd gone through both in his first life and in his second, Re-gen life. Finally, she sighed once more, nodded, and combed her fingers through her hair.

Hands on the armrests, she pushed herself up from her seat, retrieved a bottle of water from the cabinet near the front of the plane, and returned to Peter. She handed him the bottle of water before sitting to dig through her bag filled to capacity. Considering how hurried and disorganized her packing job had been, she was surprised by how quickly she found the bottle of diphenhydramine. She handed two of the bright pink pills to her son, then set her bag on the floor and relaxed back in her seat.

Until the plane's engines fired up, quickly building to a dull roar. Anna stiffened and clutched her armrests. Her nails dug deeply into the soft leather.

"Ready for takeoff," Larissa said over the intercom as the plane started to roll backward.

Anna squeezed her eyes shut, half-convinced that her heart was about to explode. Or that the engines were.

"Maybe you should take a couple of these, too, Mom," Peter said.

Anna's eyes snapped open. It wasn't a half-bad idea. Leaning forward, she fished around in her bag once more, but instead of pulling out the bottle of sleep aids, she found a small bottle of diazepam, her preferred antianxiety drug.

"Mom?"

"Hmmm?" With shaking hands, Anna tore the lid off the bottle and dumped a handful of the tiny blue pills onto her palm. Pausing, she glanced at Peter.

"Why do you think I have this weird connection with Zoe?"

Studying her son's youthful face, Anna frowned. "I'm not sure, sweetie." Not that she hadn't thought about it *a lot*, but she simply didn't understand it. Maybe, in time, she would. Maybe. "All I've been able to come up with is that it has something to do with the combination of your and Zoe's Abilities, mixed with your blood tie…" Shrugging, she shook her head. "But really, that's just me guessing." She might have been the one who'd engineered the form of gene therapy that enabled Abilities to manifest in a person, but even she was far from understanding everything about them—how they worked. *Why* they worked.

"Oh, okay." Peter turned his head to stare out the window.

"Sorry, sweetie, I know that wasn't much of an answer."

"S'okay." Peter closed his eyes. "I was just curious."

"That makes two of us," Anna said softly. She picked up two of the anxiety pills and popped them into her mouth, returned the rest to the bottle, then sat back and watched Peter while she waited for the drugs to kick in.

The plane started moving forward.

And Anna waited.

They were picking up speed, the engines' thrum increasing steadily.

And she waited.

The plane's nose lifted off the ground, closely followed by its back wheels.

And still, Anna waited.

The engines whirred and thrummed, the hours passed, and Anna relaxed in her seat, thoughts distant and slippery. She blinked lazily as she stared out the window at the cottony clouds, alight with late afternoon sunlight. She wanted to roll around in those clouds. She wanted to lose herself in those clouds.

With a harsh gasp, Peter awoke and leaned forward, almost falling out of his seat. His fingers clutched the armrests, and his eyes were opened wide and filled with fear. "Zoe..."

Anna reached across the several-foot gap separating her from her son and grasped his upper arms. "Are you alright?"

Peter didn't respond; he simply stared through Anna, seeing somewhere else...someone else.

"Peter!" Anna shook him. "What's going on?"

Peter blinked several times, and slowly his focus grew less distant. "She's desperate...losing hope," he said hollowly. "There's a woman—a vegetable—and they're trying to use Zoe's blood to reawaken her mind." Clearly dazed, Peter shook his head. "There're two men; one's taking care of her, sort of, and the other's ready to sacrifice her." He licked his dry lips ineffectively.

Finally, Peter's eyes focused entirely on Anna. "She's in bad shape, Mom. She's lost a lot of blood. If we don't get to her soon..."

Clenching her jaw repeatedly, Anna nodded. Her chest felt tight, her throat constricted. "Can you lead us to her?"

"I think so." Peter's eyes searched Anna's. "She's by a church and there's a maple tree outside the house...I think if you help me, I'll be able to sense exactly where she is." His eyes became glassy, and he pressed his quivering lips together. After a long moment, he added, "If we're not too late." A single tear streaked down his cheek.

Anna forced herself to stare up at the cabin's curved ceiling in an effort to stave off her own tears. Silently, she offered a prayer to anyone or anything that might be listening. *Please don't let us be too late. Please...*

"Mom?"

Anna started and tore her gaze away from the oval window to look up at Jason.

"We're about to start the descent." He lowered to one knee in the aisle and leaned his forearm on Anna's armrest. "Do you mind boosting Larissa's illusion while we land?" He glanced at Peter. "I'd like to hear whatever intelligence he's gathered, so we're ready for whatever we're walking into."

Anna nodded. "Of course," she said, stiffly pushing herself up and out of her seat. She started up the aisle but stopped when she felt Jason's hand latch onto her wrist. She looked back at him, eyebrow raised in question.

"We'll find her," Jason said with the utmost conviction. "This isn't how it ends for her." His familiar, sapphire-blue eyes hardened. "It isn't."

Again, Anna nodded, too choked up to utter a response. Carefully—she still felt a little out of it from the medication she'd taken a few hours ago—she made her way up the narrow aisle to the cockpit. It was a little awkward, but she managed to settle herself in the copilot's seat without too much hassle.

Larissa offered her a smile. "Welcome to my world," she said, her facial features relaxed and her eyes filled with contentment. It was clear that she belonged in the sky, that this was where she felt most at home. "The sun's just starting to set. It'll be a beautiful landing."

Anna felt a pang of pity that this was likely the last time Larissa would ever fly again.

"Yeah," Larissa said softly, nodding to herself. "I'm going to miss it more than a squirrel misses his nuts." She offered Anna another smile, apologetic this time. "Sorry, I don't mean to intrude, it's just that I've never been good at blocking out any of it."

"It's alright." Anna returned her smile with a weak one of her own. "I was married to someone like you, a long time ago."

"I know."

Anna laughed under her breath. "Of course you do."

"Seems like he was a really good man. You were a lucky woman."

Anna snorted. "Your definition of lucky must be different from mine."

Larissa was quiet for several minutes. When she finally spoke, her voice had taken on a sharp edge. "I was married before the Virus—*your* virus—changed everything. He was a great guy with a great job and big plans for our future...on his good days, at least." She met Anna's eyes briefly, then returned to staring out the expansive windshield. "He was bipolar, and he stopped taking his medication a few years after we got married. His good days were even better than before, but his bad days..." She laughed bitterly.

"I wanted to leave. I told him I would if he didn't restart his meds, but he refused." She cleared her throat. "He threatened to kill himself if I left, and no matter how hard I tried—no matter how many people told me I had to take care of myself, that I had to do what was best for me—I couldn't place my freedom above his life." Her voice was thick with emotion. "I just couldn't."

Anna reached over and took hold of Larissa's hand, feeling a strong kinship with the younger woman. "It's alright, Larissa. It's over now. You're *free* now."

Larissa swiped her hand over first one cheek, then the other before looking at Anna. "Because of you—your virus. You took the choice away from me, and I know the price was awful, but I'll be grateful to you for the rest of my life. *You* set me free."

"Well..." Anna cleared her throat and released Larissa's hand. "I don't know about that, but I do understand." She inhaled and exhaled deeply. "Better than most, I think."

"I know." When she spoke next, Larissa's voice took on a

wistful tone. "But now you'll get a second chance at happiness—with Tom and your kids, I mean."

Anna sighed. "I'm not going to get my hopes up." She doubted —severely—whether Tom, Jason, and Zoe could ever forgive her for all that she'd done. No, a long life and happy family weren't written in her stars. She'd accepted that long ago.

"Maybe," Larissa said, responding to Anna's personal thoughts. "But try not to sabotage your chances at happiness. Most people want to forgive, they're just waiting for a good enough reason to do it." She shrugged one shoulder. "You never know…"

Anna exhaled heavily. "Maybe, but I won't hold my breath."

Twenty minutes later, they were parked in an open hangar and gathering their things in preparation of exiting the plane. Jason and Larissa slipped out of the cabin and down the steps first, Larissa cloaking the plane and its four passengers in an illusion while Jason did a sweep of the hangar to make sure it was secure. Anna hung back inside the plane with Peter, waiting for the all clear.

Footsteps—boots on cement. There were too many. And there were voices; they were shouting. Anna held her breath, waiting for the ear-splitting sound of gunfire.

It never came.

Instead, she heard laughter. Familiar laughter.

She was dreaming. She'd fallen asleep, and they were still flying. This had to be a dream. It was the only explanation. And yet, she rose from her seat and made her way to the small plane's open door. In a daze, she descended the steps and walked toward the group of a half-dozen men and women laughing and embracing.

Standing in the middle of it all was Jason…and Tom.

Anna's heart fluttered, skipping beats erratically. She couldn't tear her eyes away from the man she'd given her heart to so many years ago. And Tom, by all appearances, was in an equal state of shock and awe.

When Anna reached the group on shaking legs, she and Tom

stood several feet apart and stared at each other. Their eyes roamed over familiar features, changed by over two decades but still so much the same. A spell wove around them, blocking out everyone else and encasing them in their own private world.

"Tom," Anna said breathily. "I—I—"

"Mom?" Anna felt Peter tug on the sleeve of her coat. "We need to hurry. I can feel Zoe's panic. Can you boost my Abilities now?"

Anna looked at her younger son, but it was Tom who spoke. "You can sense her?" He glanced at Gabe, who Anna had only just noticed was among the group, along with Becca and an unfamiliar man and woman. "Anything?" he asked, hope filling the single word.

Gabe shook his head. "Either she's still being nulled, or she's awake." He looked at the woman. "Sanchez? Anything?"

Rubbing her temple, the woman shook her head.

Tom took a step closer to Peter and rested a hand on his shoulder. "Can you tell us where she is, son? Can you help me find my little girl?"

Peter nodded and pointed toward the hangar's north wall. "She's that way."

30

DANI

DECEMBER 15, 1AE

THE FARM, CALIFORNIA

"Shhh...shhh, little one," came a rough whisper. It was Grayson, attempting to speak quietly, a thing he was renowned around the farm to be horrible at. Sure, he could use his voice to weave a captivating story that was so rich and detailed it was better than watching a movie, but he couldn't make his voice inconspicuous. It was too resonant, too enchanting. It was a voice that couldn't be ignored. No doubt it was Ability-related, however hard it was to pinpoint the actual Ability. Some were just like that.

I felt the warm bundle that was Everett being lifted from my arms. "No, no, I'm awake," I mumbled, eyes closed and mind groggy. "I got him. It's fi..." The fog of sleep drifted back in.

"Okay, come here, kiddo," Grayson not-whispered, pulling me back to consciousness once more.

I relaxed my hold, letting him take Everett without resistance, and dragged my eyes open. Golden light from the setting sun streamed in through the farmhouse's large living room window, bathing me in the last hints of warmth the day would offer.

Grayson smiled at me through his gray, bushy beard, his eyes twinkling. "A few days ago, you couldn't sleep no matter how hard you tried." He chuckled as he sank into the couch beside me. "Now you can't seem to stay awake."

I blinked sleepily, already wanting to close my eyes and float back to the land of dreams. Instead, I shifted on the couch, stretching and making several drawn-out, incoherent noises, then relaxed back into the couch. I felt minutely more awake. "I know." I offered Grayson a small smile. "I think it's Junior," I said, patting my tummy. "Must've inherited Jason's Ability to null. It's the only thing that makes sense."

"Remarkable," Grayson said, his voice—and eyes—filled with wonder. "And here we thought we were the evolved ones…the next evolution of man." He shook his head slowly, his gaze drifting down to the child sleeping in his arms. "But really, it's the next generation, those who follow us. Who knows what they'll be capable of achieving." He smiled, just a little. "What sort of a world they'll create…"

I splayed the fingers of both of my hands over my belly. "I just hope it's a safe world…a better one." I squinted into the last sliver of the sunlight through the picture window. "One that'll last."

Grayson patted my knee. "Nothing lasts forever."

I looked at him curiously, surprised by the unusually depressing statement. He was generally a reliable optimist.

He smiled, sadness—memories, I supposed—tainting the expression. "But let's hope they have a better go of it than we did." He laughed softly, the sadness fading from his eyes. "We sure mucked things up."

I rested my head against the top of the couch cushion. "Mmhmmm…" My eyelids drooped shut once more. "We sure did," I tried to say, but it sounded more like, "Weshhhummm…" Sleep claimed me once more.

I woke from my evening nap, part two, with much more energy. "Oh my God!" I screeched, jumping up off the couch and turning around in an indecisive circle. I was too excited, ecstatic even. I simply couldn't decide who to tell first.

A baby started crying in the dining-room-turned-office. I sensed Grayson in there with the twins. My telepathic radar told me that Carlos was outside in the shower, Annie was in the barn with Jack no doubt getting into some sort of trouble—relatively harmless trouble, I hoped—Camille and Mase were up in the room we kept reserved for them when they weren't staying at one of the Re-gen farms, and Chris was out in the stable with Vanessa.

"Everything alright, Danielle?" Grayson asked from the other room, a chorus of baby cries accompanying his question.

"Yeah, yes!" I called as I rushed to the mudroom. "They know where Zo is! They're going to rescue her right now! And Jason's with Gabe and the others! I'll be right back." I threw on my coat and boots, burst out through the back door, and ran toward the stable as fast as I could without tripping over my untied bootlaces or any other booby traps I couldn't see in the inky darkness.

"Chris!" I shouted. I slowed to a jog when I entered the stable. "Chris!"

"What?" Holding a lantern out, Chris poked her head through the stall doorway at the end of the aisle, blonde ponytail golden and swaying in the lantern light. Her shadowed expression changed from worried to curious when she caught sight of me speeding toward her. "What is it?" She stepped out of the stall, sliding the door shut behind her.

I walked the last few steps, breathing hard and flushed with excitement. "Gabe...I was napping...Jason...he's there!"

Chris's eyes lit up, and she grasped my shoulder. "Seriously?" She gave me an excited shake. "He's there? He's okay? He's with them?"

"Yes," I said, nodding even as she yanked me into a one-armed hug. "And yes and yes." The last two affirmatives were spoken against her down coat.

She pulled away and walked me to the bench opposite Vanessa's stall. "How? What happened? What else? Are Harper and Biggs there? What about Sanchez? And Zoe?"

I held up my hands in a useless defense against her barrage of questions. "They haven't found Zo yet, but they're close. They know where she is. Sanchez—"

"They're close? How—"

"Chris!" I said. "Holy crap…give me a chance to catch up!"

She raised her eyebrows in a clear, if silent, "Well then, go on…"

I took a deep breath. "Sanchez seems more or less okay, but still has one hell of a headache. Harper and Biggs should be close now—" I paused for a few seconds, focusing instead on my ever-present connection with Wings. Harper's mind was just a quick hop away. "Give me a sec," I told Chris. "I'm just finding out their ETA."

Less than a minute later, I refocused on Chris's eager blue eyes. "They're several hours away from Sacramento. They think they'll be there around midnight. And Gabe and the others know they're close to rescuing Zo, because Peter can sense her—I guess he shares some sort of a connection with her or something—and they're just closing in on the house where she's being held captive now."

"Peter?" Chris's eyebrows rose even higher. "As in…"

"Dr. Wesley and Herodson's kid, yeah," I finished for her. "She's there, too…Dr. Wesley, I mean. And Larissa, the woman who planted my fake memory…oh, but Cole's dead!" I waved my hands in the air excitedly. "Yay!" After taking a deep breath, I barreled on. "Thanks to Peter, they know that there's only two guys holding Zo prisoner, so they'll be pretty easy to take out. Finding her was the hard part, and now that they've done that…"

"Let's just hope they don't get overconfident," Chris said. "Situations like this can go sideways in a heartbeat."

I bit my lip, worry easing into my chest and souring my excitement.

"What kind of shape is Zoe in? What have these men been doing to her over the past three days? *Why* did they take her?" Chris asked. "Does Peter know anything about that?"

My worry quadrupled, and I frowned. "I—I don't know," I said, shaking my head. "Gabe didn't say anything about that." My frown deepened along with my concern. "In fact, he was really quick to pop in, pass along his message, and pop right back out of the dream." I felt my eyebrows draw together. "Do you think he was hiding something?"

"There's no way to know right now," Chris said, slapping her hands on her thighs and standing. "But all in all, it's a night for good news, I'd say." She strode across the aisle to the stall door, slid it open, and gestured for Vanessa to come out. "Hopefully we can keep this gravy train going. Come on, kiddo, let's finish your hair."

Cautiously, Vanessa moved toward the opening. The lantern light illuminated a long, half-formed French braid that was quickly slipping apart. She'd been so calm the previous evening that we'd managed to get her relatively clean. As it turned out, there really was an adorable teen girl under all of the grime and snarly hair.

"Sit right here," Chris said, directing Vanessa down onto the floor in front of the bench. Chris sat behind her and started running her fingers through the disintegrating braid. "We'll have to start over, but it'll go easier now that Dani and the baby are here to keep you calm, hmmm?"

Surprising me despite her genial behavior the past few nights, Vanessa glanced at me over her shoulder, smiling shyly.

Chris pulled a comb from her pocket and started running it through Vanessa's sleek black hair. "I thought braiding her hair might keep it from getting so bad this time."

"Makes sense," I said, nodding in agreement, but I was more than a little distracted as I tried to wrap my mind around how different Vanessa seemed over the past few days. She'd gone from a wild and all but frothing nightmare to a young, smiling woman so suddenly, part of me wondered if any of it was real. Part of me also wondered if having her out in the open, unrestrained, was really *that* good of an idea.

Chris had come to the split conclusion that something about either the baby's Ability or my pregnancy hormones was affecting Vanessa. Either way, it was impossible to ignore the fact that while my presence had exacerbated her condition before, it calmed her now.

Chris was nodding, slowly, thoughtfully. "Now isn't that interesting." Her combing stopped. "You know, this is the first time I've been able to actively sense the change your presence causes in her mind *as it happens.*"

I frowned. "What do you mean?"

Chris narrowed her eyes in concentration. "In her prefrontal cortex, there's one section that is usually a chaotic tangle of wild synapses—like an entire fireworks stand all going off at once—but when you came in here, it all settled down and, hmmm…it's almost like it's started thrumming in concert with portions of her temporal lobe." Her gaze grew distant. "Hmmm…" She pursed her lips. "It's this gap here, like it's been bridged by what I think is your pregnancy hormones. Unless it's the kiddo…hmmm…" Chris closed her eyes. "Regardless, when these two portions of her brain are linked up, everything seems to work properly."

I watched Vanessa's face. Her calm, almost serene expression. It was far from the face of a Crazy.

"But ten minutes ago, it wasn't like this," Chris said, continuing her mad scientist ramblings. "Those two areas weren't synchronized…there was nothing linking them, nothing allowing any kind of communication between them. I wonder if I increase this, it *might* strengthen the link a little more, and I think it might be able to sustain itself if…"

"Okay." I gave her forearm a squeeze. "Well, I think I'll just leave you to your—"

"Oh!" Chris pulled her hands from Vanessa's hair like she'd been burned. Her eyes were wide, her mouth open in a small "O."

Vanessa looked first at Chris, then at me, tears welling in her eyes. With a gut-wrenching wail, she threw herself back into her stall and onto her cot. Her sobs were so raw, so wretched, they made my heart hurt.

Chris raced into the stall and crouched on the floor beside Vanessa's bed. "Hon?" She reached for the girl, placing her hand on her arm. "Vanessa?"

"Don't touch me!" Vanessa shrieked, her voice thick with tears. Chris recoiled.

"Don't touch me…don't touch me…don't touch me…"

"Chris?" I stood and took a step toward the stall. "What's going on?" Because it looked like Vanessa's condition had just taken a major turn for the worse.

Chris looked at me, face ashen. "I think—" She swallowed roughly. "I think I just fixed her."

31

ZOE

DECEMBER 15, 1AE

LOCATION UNKNOWN

*G*lazed over and empty, her eyes are a promise of my own future—sucked dry of all that I am, frozen and scream- ing, unheard in hell. I can feel her dead soul. It's a stone in a sandstorm. Someone clings to her, to me. I can't see them, but I feel them and know they're there. Always there. Wait- ing. For me to die? *The thought is comforting.*

I peeled my eyes open. Sandy came in and out of focus, and then I saw *him.* He was there, again. I wanted to cry out for Carl to make him stop.

Carl's with me in the bedroom. He's staring through me again, but his touch is gentle. A rag is cool on my face. I know that acerbic taste, that paralyzed feeling. He's drugged me again. That, or it's just too much. Too much blood. Too much humiliation. We've been through too much, and I allow myself to believe I'm different than all the others. I'm his exception. I'm the only one he's cared for like this, the only one he's been willing to help. I wish he'd help me by making it all go away.

I woke to the scent and taste of vomit. On me. On my clothes. Carl was cursing at me, his hands shaking as he tugged my shirt off over my head, harshly like he was angry with me. I felt compelled to apologize. For throwing up? For existing? Even above my own stench, I could smell the booze; I could tell Carl was drunk. Remotely, I knew I'd been unbound and it was my only chance to fight, to flee and get away, but I could barely keep my eyes open.

Carl's eyes flicked to mine. When he saw that I was awake, his features softened. "Sorry," I thought he muttered.

"Zoe." I hear the voice again, this time it says my name and I feel a strange sense of peace. The voice has haunted me for weeks. It has followed me everywhere—my dreams over the years, these endless nights of hell—and it's now my only constant. "Zoe...you'll be okay." I want to smile. I'm happy the voice is back. I missed it when it was away.

I was jarred awake again, this time by the slamming of the bedroom door. My eyes flitted open, and I blearily scanned the room. I was alone. There was no Carl passed out against the wall, no Randall peering down at me.

"...not fucking working. She's the same, Randy. She's the fucking same!"

I heard heavy footsteps in the hallway, and their voices grew more distant. "Don't say that!" Randall shouted back. "Don't you dare say that. She's better, she looked at me. Actually *looked* at me."

"No, she didn't," Carl said, so quiet his voice was almost too muffled to hear.

"You don't know what you're talking about. You weren't there!" There were more footsteps and the slamming of drawers and cupboards. "I was right about this type of power. It's affecting her. I know she remembers me. I can feel it. Her seeing us together, really seeing me…it's *working*."

"Would you listen to yourself!" Carl shouted. "It's been a year. All the different powers you've been shooting into her are only making her worse. My sister's heart is beating, but she's fucking dead. Dead! I'm not going to keep doing this!"

"The fuck you aren't!" It was the angriest I'd ever heard either of them, but the menace in Randall's voice made me flinch. "If you'd stop drinking so damn much, you'd see that she's getting better. She's your sister, for Christ's sake," Randall growled. "How can you just give up?" More slamming. "You swore you'd do *whatever* it takes to fix her, Carl."

I held my breath, waiting for Carl's response. Hope bloomed inside me, and I wanted to cry. I was so desperate for him to let me go.

"What if you're wrong?" Carl finally said. "What if she's not getting better?"

"She is. And we're just wasting time." There were heavy foot-steps down the hall. "Prep the blood source. I'm drawing more as soon as I get back with more supplies. I think tonight might be the night. We'll do whatever it takes." The resolve in Randall's voice brought tears to my eyes, and I couldn't help the tremble in my chin. I wasn't sure how much more I could take of this. The days already bled together or were lost to unconsciousness. Had it even been days? Or had it been weeks? It felt like one long, endless nightmare.

Eventually I heard the front door slam. The house shook and then went silent.

I tried to compose myself, knowing Carl would be heading into my room any minute. He would try to wake me, to feed me, to make me drink something before giving me more drugs. I couldn't let that happen. For whatever reason, there weren't as many drugs in my system; my mind wasn't as heavy, though I still felt weak and achy.

I wiped a few falling tears from my eyes, then froze, staring at my hands. There were raw ligature marks around my wrists, but I wasn't bound.

Hearing footsteps coming up the hall, I shoved my arms back under the covers and shut my eyes, pretending I was asleep. Randall was gone. It was just Carl and me. I'd been untied. It didn't matter how hazy my mind was. I knew this was my one and only chance to get away.

The instant the door opened, my heart started to race and my mind buzzed back to life, but I forced my heaving chest to steady. Carl's footsteps were slow. They'd never been so condemning and encouraging at the same time.

What do I do? Carl was still nulling me, so I couldn't use my Ability in any way. I hadn't heard the door latch when he came in, and I hoped the shotgun was still outside in the hallway, though I had to come up with a backup plan in case it wasn't. I just needed to figure out how the hell I was going to get past him…overpower him…but the thought of that alone was enough to make it all seem hopeless.

Carl paused beside my bed for a moment. What was probably only seconds felt like minutes, suspended. Then, he turned and quickly left the room, and I heard the door latch this time.

I let out my breath, holding it again as I listened for his footsteps in the hallway. I waited for them to descend the stairs, but they didn't. It sounded like he had headed down the hall, into Sandy's room. When I heard what I thought was a chair scraping against the floor, I opened my eyes and slowly sat up.

It felt like my arms had been shredded, that my head had been filled with cotton, and my heart was racing so fast, echoing so loudly in my ears, it was all I could hear. I hoped Carl wasn't coming back up the hallway, because I wouldn't be able to hear him over the sound of my fear.

Ignoring my body's protests, I flung off the blanket and reached for the rope tying my ankles together. I fumbled with it, willing my fingers to work quickly and efficiently, though it seemed they'd forgotten how to do anything. But I didn't struggle for long. The rope came off more easily than I'd expected, as if Carl hadn't put much effort into binding me to begin with.

I didn't have time to wonder too much if it was because he'd been too drunk to tie the rope right, or if he'd been cautious of the sores the ropes had produced around my ankles. Or was there another reason entirely? I hung my legs over the side of the bed. Briefly, I tried to remember the last time I'd wiggled my toes or felt the floor beneath my feet.

I stood up as quietly as I could. The hardwood made no noise as I wobbled and had to brace myself on the mattress for balance. Had I any modesty left, I would've cared that I only wore a man's shirt. It was oversized, but it barely reached my upper thighs.

After a few deep, steadying breaths, I crept to the door, trying to stay upright and not make a sound. I was conscious of every foot placement, every muscle I forced to work despite the tingling numbness that began to spread throughout my body.

I listened intently for any movement outside the room before I reached for the doorknob. I turned it, ever so slightly, and cringed as the metal latch seemed to clank and echo throughout the entire house. I stared at the hinges and held my breath as I slowly pulled the door open.

Pausing mid-open, I listened again. There was still nothing. Adrenaline and fatigue made my body tremble. I opened the door a bit further and nearly sobbed in relief when I saw the shotgun leaning against the wall. I stuck my head through the doorway.

Blinking a few times to focus, I gazed around anxiously, half expecting to find Carl standing there, waiting for me. But he wasn't. I peered down the hall into Sandy's room and found him sitting in a chair beside her bed. His back was to me and his head was in his hands.

Closing my eyes, I ignored my weak, shaking body and bolstered my resolve to pick up the shotgun. *Pick it up! If you want to live, pick up the gun...* Carl would hear me the instant I did, I knew he would, there was no way around it. I just had to be able to aim and shoot him when the time came.

Not allowing myself to waste any more time, I stepped out of the room and grabbed the shotgun. It was much heavier than I expected, but I was determined to leave, to fight and kill and scream bloody murder if needed to get out of that house.

Shifting, I turned toward Sandy's room and lifted the shotgun, ready to aim for Carl barreling down the hallway toward me. But he hadn't moved.

I stepped closer and closer, my arms already tired and burning, but determination held the gun in place. I blinked once, twice, and took a few more steps. I didn't care about the details anymore, about the rooms I passed or what I could see out the windows. I could only focus on Carl and the fact that he wasn't moving. *Is this a trick?* Was he dead?

Finally, the floor creaked beneath my feet, and I froze, the shotgun's nozzle only a few feet from the back of Carl's head. "Do it," he murmured.

My heart stopped momentarily, and my resolve wavered.

He whipped around in his chair. "Do it!"

I knew he meant to frighten me, to coerce me. And I knew I should shoot him. He was right in front of me, and I had the gun. Freedom was a finger twitch away. Carl was giving me that, and yet he'd let Randall hurt me, let him shame me and turn me into an object, a blood bank, a thing to be used and discarded. But I couldn't do it. I couldn't pull the trigger. I couldn't kill him.

"Please," he whispered. His empty eyes were pleading.

My hands were sweating, my body trembling. *I can just walk away.*

Then my eyes met Sandy's. Those dead eyes, that curl of her lip, that drawn face that haunted my dreams. I needed to put her out of her misery. I needed to end it, all of it.

"Carl," I breathed, my attention transfixed in the depth of her pain.

I heard footsteps up the stairs and realized Randall hadn't really left, or he'd already returned, before I could decide what to do. My body took over, and I turned and lifted the gun, praying I could shoot him before he reached me.

Then I froze. Jake was standing in the doorway, his pistol aimed at me. My chest heaved and my eyes clouded with tears as I tried to convince myself that he was real. All I could do was stare at him. His familiar face drained of color and his eyes gleamed as they scoured every inch of me. I let out a whimper and dropped the shotgun, and it clanked and thudded to the ground. But Jake's pistol was still aimed at me.

I was confused. "Ja—Jake?"

But when I heard movement behind me, I realized Jake wasn't aiming at me, but at Carl. Weakly, I pivoted slightly to find him standing by Sandy's bed, his dark, stringy hair hanging in his face. He turned away from his sister to face me and Jake. Carl's features had softened, the tension around his eyes lessened. He almost looked relieved and then he closed his eyes.

"Don't fucking move," Jake growled, but Carl smiled, ignoring him as he reached behind his back.

There was one shot, then another.

I shouted, my hands flying to cover my mouth as I watched two crimson stains grow and spread over Carl's chest. He fell with a heavy thud to the floor. His fingers twitched around the pint of vodka he'd pulled from his back pocket, and his eyes fixed on Sandy as they dulled and began to dim. I shook my head and took a few awkward steps toward him. A disturbing mixture of relief and sadness flooded me, and I fought to grasp just one.

Carl gasped for air, and I could see his life, see him unfolding in my mind as my Ability jump-started again. I could feel his regret, could taste the blood staining his teeth. I saw me. I felt his love for his twin sister, turned Crazy, turned monster. I felt the ease with which he took his final breath before his life was extinguished and he was gone.

And then I fell to my knees and silently cried. For him. For me. For Sandy.

"Zoe," Jake whispered, and he crouched beside me. He tentatively reached for me, and I shut my eyes, hating that he saw me like this, that the people whose hurried footsteps carried them into the room saw me like this. But I didn't care enough to move.

I could feel Jake's unhinged concern and anger. He was afraid to touch me. "There's another one," I said, but I didn't open my eyes. I knew the moment I did, I would see the expression on Jake's face and crumble.

"He's already dead," Sanchez said quietly from the doorway.

Randall's dead? And though I didn't think it was possible given the fact that Jake was already here, with me, I felt even better. It was over.

I could feel other minds in the house—near the room, downstairs—but I ignored them.

Finally, I opened my eyes and stared down at myself. I needed a bath, needed clothes... I shifted my gaze to meet Jake's. He was distressed, questioning. His jaw clenched and unclenched, and I could see the truth of things in his amber eyes. I was a mess with my purple and green arms, my bandaged bicep and bloody wrists and ankles, my ashen skin... I knew that some of the others were injured—Tavis was dead. And there was something else looming around him, something big, but I didn't want to feel any of it. I didn't think I could bear it. So I let out a groan and pushed his mind and everyone else's away.

"I'm disgusting," I whined, hoping to put a smile on Jake's face, but it was barely audible.

His eyes were gleaming, but he tried to smile. "Let's get you out of here," he said.

I nodded, and Jake gathered me precariously into his arms. "I won't break," I said automatically, but the worry and pain in his eyes told me it looked otherwise.

Jake held me tight against his chest as I gripped onto his shirt, to that smell so acute and perfectly him that I swore to myself it was my new favorite shirt and, despite its dirty, tattered appearance, I would never let him wash it again. The tighter I gripped him, the easier it was to push the impending sobs away.

As Jake rose to his feet, I remembered Sandy. When I looked over my shoulder at her, she was staring up at the ceiling, oblivious to our presence. "We have to help her," I said, begged him with my eyes. "We can't leave her like this."

Jake considered my words for a moment, his eyes fixed on the half-dead woman, before nodding at me and then at Sanchez.

I looked at her, relief flooding me as I realized my no-nonsense sparring partner, my friend, was still alive, though her face was a bit swollen and bruises colored her cheeks. She offered me a pursed-lip nod of her own as Jake carried me toward the doorway. I glanced one last time at Carl's body, a heap on the floor. My exhaustion outweighed any satisfaction or remorse I might've felt had I been in a different state of mind.

I wound my arms around Jake's neck, relieved to see that at least he and Sanchez were okay, and as we exited the room, I noticed others lined up in the hallway. Becca was there first, her eyes filled with relief as she draped a white coat over me.

I flashed her a weak but grateful smile and noticed Gabe standing beside her. He looked distraught, but offered me a nod as I passed. Then I locked eyes with my dad, and I couldn't stop the instant sobs I'd been trying to lock away.

"Oh, sweetheart," he croaked, and Jake slowed long enough for my dad to lean in to kiss my forehead, tears of his own filling his eyes. "I was so afraid…"

But before I could say anything, I saw a large form that was all too distinguishable through my blurred vision. "Jason," I said and brusquely wiped the tears from my eyes. It was him, standing there with his aggravatingly expressionless face, like always. He was alive. He was there. They'd found him. It had all been worth it.

"Hey, Zoe," he said, but I was scrambling out of Jake's arms, nearly stumbling, too ecstatic to care because my brother was alive. I wasn't sure whose arms were around who first, his trying to help me up or mine clinging to him.

"I started to think you were dead, but then the dream…" I trailed off because it didn't matter. None of that did anymore. My dream, Becca's vision that I'd gleaned, had never come to pass. We could go home, all of us. Jason held me more tightly, and I let out a happy, choked sob.

But when I opened my eyes, I gasped, stunned and confused. A teenage boy was standing next to me with dark, disheveled hair, proffering the white lab coat that had been draped around me. "You should probably put this on," he said. He looked sickly, but his eyes were illuminated with curiosity and kindness.

Tentatively, I took the coat from him and carefully shrugged it on, wondering why he seemed so familiar to me. When I saw my mom at the top of the landing, watching with tears in her eyes, I knew.

Feeling light-headed all over again, I glanced between them. My mom was here…away from the Colony. With my dad and Jason and…

I looked at Jason, confused, then my eyes landed back on the boy. It all started to make sense. I *knew* him. "Peter?"

"Hey, Zoe," he said, and I knew his voice instantly.

I blinked. "You…you were in my head."

32

DANI

THE FARM, CALIFORNIA

"*T hank you so much, Pretty Girl,*" I said to Wings, showering her with as much affection and gratitude as I could pour through our telepathic bond. Really, with her and Jack, our connection went beyond telepathic. We were a part of each other.

I placed my hand on the sweaty fabric of my tank top, just over the itty bitty swell I may or may not have been imagining on my abdomen. *And now she's a part of our secret little circle, too.*

Eyes widening, I stared down at my hand, at my belly, at the lemon-sized life growing within. *She?* Had I really just thought of it—*her*, I felt certain—as a girl? I shook my head. *Now, how could I possibly know that?* But I did. I knew she was a girl. I *knew*.

Is it her? Is she communicating with me? I sat up straighter and looked around the cottage's living room, lips parted in a combination of shock and awe. *Am I passing information about me to her as well?* I already suspected she had some intuitive form of Jason's Ability, so why not some form of mine as well?

Chris came bustling in through the front door, shut it, and

paused with hands on hips to glare at me. "Sorry I'm late—oh my Jesus God...damn it, Dani!" She swept across the room. "You're sweating like a pig! It's the middle of the night; you should be resting!"

Hot flashes were my latest unfavorable pregnancy symptom. Of course, I would take nonstop sweating over vomiting any day of the week. I shrugged. "I *am* resting...while I talk to Zo and Jason and the others." I flicked my eyes toward the hallway and Annie's door, hidden just out of sight. "And keep your voice down. She's drifting."

Chris snorted and crossed her arms, then rolled her eyes and crouched before the hearth. Almost without thought, it seemed, she began to tend to the dying fire. "How is everyone? Are they on their way back? Is—"

"Chris..."

Chris looked at me, eyebrows raised.

I met her eyebrow raise with one of my own. "I'm limiting you to two questions at a time. Kapeesh?"

Chris pursed her lips, but at least she held her tongue.

I smiled minutely, settling back into my recliner.

"They found Zo—she's alright," I said, before Chris could badger me. I felt constantly on the verge of crying, I was so relieved. "Not in great shape—she's a little beat up from the accident, and the men who kidnapped her drugged her and took a lot of blood..." I frowned, recollecting my composure as my chin trembled and my eyes stung with unshed tears. Every time I imagined what she'd been through...

I cleared my throat. "Zo was pretty tired when I spoke to her, so we didn't talk for long, and Jason and the others are focused on getting back here, so all of my convos were pretty brief." Letting out an agitated, exhausted breath, I leaned my head back. "Jason and I are going to talk more when they get on the plane."

I stared at the embers glowing beneath the new pieces of firewood Chris had placed above them. Even though I'd heard his mental voice, part of me wouldn't believe Jason was really safe, was really coming back to me, until I saw him with my own two eyes. Part of me expected the worst. It was almost like that part of me was waiting for something else to happen to him...like hope had been cauterized out of that part of me.

"And Harper and Biggs?" Chris asked.

I nodded slowly, still staring into the blossoming fire. "They met up with the others about fifteen minutes ago. That was how I found them."

"Wait," Chris said, "back up. Did you say 'plane' a second ago?"

Blinking lazily, almost like I was waking up, I focused on Chris. "Yeah. They're flying back down here...on a plane. A real, live airplane. Can you believe it?"

"Honestly?" Chris said, shaking her head and sitting back on her heels. "There's not much I won't believe these days." A moment later, she added, "But a plane—*that's* definitely unexpected."

Chewing on my lip, I nodded my agreement. Unexpected, indeed. "They're going to land at the Petaluma Airport. We should saddle some horses for them." I returned to staring at the fire. "And get a cart ready—in Zo's condition, it'll be better if she doesn't have to ride."

Chris stood and took a step away from the fireplace, but froze and looked at me, eyes narrowed. "What about Wings and the other horses? How big of a plane are we talking about here?"

I smiled. "They're already on their way back...on the ground." My smile widened to a grin. Wings's giddiness at being able to run free with her small herd, unburdened and unrushed, was spilling into me. Pulling at me. She wanted me to join her. *I* wanted to join her. But I had a telepathic date with my husband, something that went beyond the hurried "Hey, glad you're alive, can't wait to see you!" we'd been limited to just a few moments earlier.

I shook my head, then pushed myself up out of the comfortable chair. "Let's get those horses ready."

Chris led the way to the door, tossing my coat to me before heading outside. She paused in the doorway and pointed to the rubber goulashes on the floor by the door. "Boots, too, hon. You're not going to be one of those barefoot mamas, not on my watch."

I sighed heavily even as I pulled one boot, then the other onto my bare feet. It would've been much more comfortable with socks, but we were in a bit of a time crunch. Larissa had told me they'd be landing in a half hour to forty-five minutes, assuming they managed to get into the air relatively quickly.

"Not with how easy it is for a cut to get infected these days," Chris went on. "Not to mention what a blood infection could do to a pregnant woman..."

"Chris, seriously, you can stop." I straightened and crossed my arms over my chest. "The damn boots are on my damn feet, okay?"

Chris sniffed. "You should be wearing socks, too."

I rolled my eyes and wiggled my toes inside their rubber confines. "Don't I know it..."

"Well, good." Chris met my eyes, expression stern. A moment later, her lips spread into a broad grin, and she pulled me into a tight hug, which I returned readily. "They're coming home," she said, her voice barely above a whisper. "Our family's coming home."

33

ANNA

SACRAMENTO, CALIFORNIA

From her vantage point in one of the two back seats of the small but luxurious charter jet, Anna catalogued her companions, studying—assessing—each one to the soundtrack of hushed conversations and roaring engines. At first sight, they seemed such an odd band of people, such a curious grouping. The meek young woman, the hardened soldier, the confident scientist, the silent watcher, the sickly boy…some had been military in the old world, some had been lost souls, but all of them, like Anna, had been trying their hardest just to survive from day to day.

"Something amusing?" Gabriel said from the seat on the other side of the aisle. His voice was dry, devoid of humor.

Anna shook her head. She felt like a lifetime had passed since they'd parted ways so many months ago. It seemed a lifetime *had* passed for Gabriel, as he was clearly a different person now. He, like his childhood friend sitting on the floor of the plane up near the seat where Zoe dozed, had been one of the lost souls, before. Anna caught her eldest son's eye over the top of the seat separating them, and a second later, he looked away, a minute, wistful smile on his face and a thousand-yard stare filling his eyes. He, too, had been a lost soul, but not anymore. That much was clear as he carried on a silent conversation with his wife, some eighty miles away.

Anna didn't know much about the woman seated across the aisle from Jason—Sanchez, she'd introduced herself as—or Biggs, the man in the seat facing Sanchez's, other than that both had clearly been in the military. It was evident in the way they carried themselves and in the way they interacted with each other that they'd been part of the same company, or had at least known each other for quite some time.

Movement drew Anna's attention to the cockpit. Tom stood in the opening, hunched over as he murmured inaudible words to the group's medical doctor, Harper, who'd been hovering back and forth between Zoe and Sanchez since he joined them less than an hour ago. Harper turned sideways, allowing Tom to squeeze past.

Sanchez seemed to be doing alright despite the cuts and intense bruising on the left side of her face. Anna was far more worried about Zoe—not only had her wounds from the accident not been tended to properly, but it had been clear when they'd found her that she was dehydrated and severely anemic. Her pulse was still too weak, her skin sallow from the loss of too much blood. Anna didn't think it was possible to feel more thankful or relieved than she'd felt the moment Tom had put an arrow through Randall's head just outside the house. They'd been incredibly lucky that the two kidnappers had been separated when Anna and the others had launched their rescue. Killing Randall had been almost too easy, and the other—Carl—had all but killed himself.

Tom clapped Harper on the shoulder as he squeezed past, giving the younger man what looked like a grateful nod. His eyes met Anna's for the briefest moment before he paused to crouch down beside Zoe's seat. Gazing up at her, he took her hand in his. Though Anna couldn't hear the words exchanged between them, she recognized the look on Tom's face—filled with love, affection, and so much worry. He'd looked at Anna like that before, too, more times than she could count. But now, as she watched the tender father–daughter moment, she felt like an intruder, a voyeur…one who couldn't look away.

Until Tom glanced at Anna, once more.

Her heart pounded, her lungs constricting. She and Tom had yet to speak beyond a stilted greeting and brief words in passing, and she wasn't sure she was ready to *really* talk. Not there, in the middle of the night on a cramped plane filled with nearly a dozen others. She had no idea what to say, let alone what *he* might say. Awful things, she imagined. Terrible, painful, heartbreaking things.

"Wes?" Gabriel was leaning across the aisle. He reached for her arm and gave it a squeeze. "Wes?" He shook her gently. "You alright?"

Anna couldn't breathe. Her head was suddenly throbbing, and she could feel sweat beading on her forehead, her neck, all over her body. She clutched the front of her jacket, looking around wildly as the cabin closed in around her.

"Wes?"

Gabriel was halfway out of his seat when Anna burst up from hers. She lurched into the compact lavatory in the very back of the plane, shut the door, and barely had the toilet seat raised when the first dry heave struck. Followed by another, and another, and another. Luckily, she hadn't had the chance to eat or drink much of anything all day, not with all of the escaping and flying and rescuing.

Sighing, Anna pressed her back against the wall and sank down to the floor. There was barely enough room for her to sit with her knees pulled up against her chest, but it would do. It had to. She lifted her hands, watching them tremble. With how severely she was shaking, she doubted her legs were strong enough to carry her back to her seat yet.

Anna took a deep breath. She needed to pull herself together, she *had* to. She wasn't caged in with some random band of survivors—it was her husband, son, and daughter, the very family she'd abandoned to protect...the family she'd *ruined civilization* to protect. And she truly did feel like an intruder, like she didn't belong in their world.

Minutes passed, ten, maybe twenty, and Anna figured they must be close to touching down. She'd felt them enter their descent shortly after locking herself in the lavatory. They had to be almost there. Closing her eyes, she took a deep breath and straightened her spine. She couldn't hide forever. She wouldn't.

Anna wiped the back of her hand over her mouth as she pushed herself up off the floor. Clearing her throat, she pulled the lavatory door inward. It folded open eagerly, revealing Tom's wiry form. He stood with his hands braced on either side of the doorway.

Eyes wide, Anna took a step back and fell onto the toilet. She barely managed to slow her descent with a hand on the miniscule counter.

"Anna..." Tom's eyes held oceans of secrets...judgements... resentment. But the pity was the worst of all.

"I'm fine," Anna said hoarsely, gripping the edge of the toilet seat so hard it hurt her fingers.

Tom inhaled deeply, the succeeding exhale holding years of irritation. Without taking his eyes from her, he held out a palm to the side, signaling one of the other passengers to leave them be. Was it Peter or Jason, Anna wondered, or maybe Gabriel?

Tom crouched down, much as he'd done beside Zoe's seat, planting one knee on the floor and resting an elbow on his other. "Anna, we need to talk about—"

"How did you find us?" Anna blurted. When Tom responded with a quizzical tilt of his head, she clarified, "When we landed in Sacramento."

"Ah..." Tom rubbed his hand over his short, salt-and-pepper beard. Anna had never seen him so unkempt, but she didn't find the vagabond look overly unappealing on him, either. "Well, it's sort of hard not to notice a plane landing these days…"

"But the illusion," Anna said, wanting to draw out this topic until the plane's wheels were on the ground and it was time to get out of the damn metal cage. "You shouldn't have been able to see us."

Tom shook his head, smiling ruefully.

Anna's breath caught in her throat.

"Illusions don't work on me anymore," Tom said, blue eyes sparkling. He nodded up the aisle, toward the cockpit. "Even illusions created by one as strong as Larissa, it seems, and it was easy enough to sense who was on the plane." Reaching across the short distance separating them, Tom took one of Anna's hands in his. "Listen, Anna…"

Anna's heart rate escalated, her breaths coming quicker.

Tom paused and eyed her. His brow furrowed, and she thought she saw a flicker of pain or maybe sorrow shadow his gaze. Sighing heavily, Tom released her hand. "Later, then. We're about to land, anyway." Groaning, he climbed to his feet. "Come on. You should get back to your seat and buckle up before we touch down." He extended his hand toward her. "I know how much you hate flying."

Anna looked at his hand, then up at his face, then back down at his hand. Clenching her jaw, she forced herself to reach out to him, to accept his help up. Because that's all it was, a helpful hand up.

Tom's hand remained wrapped around Anna's until she was halfway into her seat.

It was just a helpful hand, she reminded herself.

It was nothing.

It was *nothing*.

But in her heart, it had sure as hell felt like something.

34

ZOE

DECEMBER 16, 1AE

PETALUMA, CALIFORNIA

Four days was all it had taken to reduce me to the weakened, pathetic heap I'd become. The growing strength of my Ability over the past year, my advancing weapon skills, and my seemingly endless self-defense training had done me absolutely no good in protecting me against the twisted minds of Carl and Randall. I couldn't help but upbraid myself for that as I sat on the tailgate of an abandoned service truck on the lone landing strip at the Petaluma Airport, chagrinned.

At least, thanks to Becca, I finally had real clothes on, my tore up, holey ones that I'd been wearing the night of the accident; she'd had the presence of mind to grab them from the top of the dresser back in the room that had been my prison. I didn't care that there were rips in my jeans and that my long-sleeve shirt was tearing at the sleeve seams, they were mine. And even more fortunately, someone had thought to salvage my leather jacket from the wreck, so I was fairly warm in the wee, cold hours of the morning. Someone else's socks covered my bare feet and I had no shoes, but that was fine; it wasn't like I'd be walking very far, anyway. All of us were waiting for the horse cavalry to arrive and take us home.

I rubbed the back of my neck, wrought with tension and feeling a little bruised. In spite of the unknown amounts of blood that had been drained from my body and the residual nausea and fogginess from what remained of the drugs in my system, I was feeling better—relieved, if a little anxious. Not only was I alive and going home, but my family was here, living—breathing—all of them. I was still trying to wrap my mind around that and the fact that Tavis wouldn't be joining us.

Closing my eyes, I let the brisk, clarifying air of predawn fill my nose and stir my senses. The flight from Sacramento had been short, if a little crowded and bumpy, and I'd dozed in and out of consciousness. Larissa was a good pilot and seemed to be a trust-worthy addition to our group; both the remorse of what she'd been forced to do to Jason and Dani and her growing appreciation for our group were palpable. Her self-loathing and abhorrence of all that she'd been a part of made her real, made her human, someone I knew we could trust.

But even with the increased number of our group in such a small, confined space, everyone had been mostly quiet on the flight home. Exhaustion. Trepidation. Indecision. There were many emotions that had hung in our silence, amplified by my Ability after days of suffocation, and it was more difficult for me to turn off than I was used to. And the auras were back; everyone had them now, except for the Re-gens. The glowing colors were constant and strong now, beautiful even, and impossible to ignore.

I closed my eyes and took another deep, rejuvenating breath, trying to exhale the knot forming in my mostly empty stomach. Having everyone together could be bad...or it could be good. Regardless, I felt tension, thick as the ropes that had been bound around my wrists, following my mom everywhere she went. She was uncertain—everyone was uncertain about her.

"I think it's a good thing."

My eyes popped open, and I felt my face pale a little. I was still getting used to Peter's presence, both in my mind and physically as he stood beside me. His dull, stone-gray eyes were haunting and curious all at once. And as peculiar as he was, he intrigued me. Since first laying eyes on him, I hadn't been able to keep my mind from wandering to his or my eyes from seeking him out.

"And why do you think that?" I asked, shelving my indecision. I wasn't sure how I felt about Peter yet—if I trusted him. His Ability was a sponge, and I wasn't sure I liked the idea of one person being able to do a little bit of everything that we could, no matter how unassuming he seemed. And then there was the lingering imprint of his mind in mine—the one that had been a part of me for so long it was now uncannily familiar.

Peter shrugged and sat down beside me on the rusted tailgate. He stared at the members of our group as they milled around and engaged in stilted conversations. His gaze landed on our mom and Gabe, who were speaking under the cover of one of the jet's narrow, cream-colored wings.

"There are so many of you with strong Abilities," Peter said. "So we'll be safe." Peter thought about his answer a moment longer. "And my mom can do anything if she has the proper motivation. So, like I said, it's a good thing we're all together."

I scoffed. "All of these people suffered because of our mom and her *proper motivation*," I reminded him, my gaze landing on my dad. He was lost in his own world. I could feel his reeling thoughts. And his eyes seemed to continuously float to my mom. "Her presence affects everyone here."

Peter was silent, like he was considering my words, measuring and processing them, for the first time. The familiar hoot of an owl echoed off in the distance before he spoke again. "Maybe she can help make things better." I could feel his eyes on me before he turned his attention back to the group. "I've seen her memories," he continued quietly. "She's suffered more than you know for us...*all* of us. No matter what you think."

Wondering if Peter really and truly realized the severity of her decisions, I turned to him. "That's what happens when you create a deadly pandemic, Peter." It wasn't bitterness that harshened my tone anymore, but honesty. "You don't get to do something like that and live without any repercussions."

Peter stared at me. I wasn't sure if it was offense or confusion I saw in his narrowed, moonlit eyes. "She's given up everything for the three of us. I think she deserves to be happy, if possible."

Part of me agreed with Peter. That same part of me that still yearned for the mom I never had. Having my family together was a dream come true, but the implications of having my mom back were etched on everyone's faces: the way Sanchez and Harper cast sidelong glances, and how Jake's and Biggs's shoulders tensed when she walked by them... My dad's eyes softened, and he was distracted again, which worried me the most. If she left him again —left us—my dad would be far more than broken, no matter how noble she believed her reason to be this time.

And as for Jason, it was hard to tell. His eyes constantly flicked up the strip, toward the airport entrance as we waited for Chris and the horses to arrive. He was antsy, ready to get back to the farm, back to Dani, that much was obvious. I withheld a smile as I imagined what his response would be when Dani told him she was pregnant. Although I knew they'd been speaking telepathically almost constantly since Dani had been able to lock onto our minds, I also knew, with absolute certainty, that news of the baby was something Dani would want to deliver in person.

"Are there many people who have had babies?" Peter asked, and I let out a despondent breath. *So this is how it feels to have someone lurking around in your head.* I wrapped my arms across my chest, too fatigued to care too much, and leaned back in the bed of the truck, every one of my muscles screaming at me. Though I'd tried to stay out of people's minds, or at least had kept my observations to myself, apparently I was an open book for Peter to peruse.

"How long?" I asked him. "How long have you been in my

head, following me?" I tried to think back to the first time I'd felt something *off* inside my mind, tried to pinpoint the moments I'd felt the most unsettled. But it seemed a frequent feeling that had rarely relented over the years. A couple weeks ago, I'd thought the dreams, at least initially, were a result of my dad withholding some majorly scarring memories. But now? I recalled feeling a strange presence when I went to sleep sometimes when I was younger, and even now it sometimes happened, feeling unnatural and uninvited but surprisingly comfortable.

The steady echo of hooves resounded in the distance, along with what sounded like wagon wheels clanking and bouncing over uneven asphalt. Within the next few minutes I knew excitement and chatter would ensue, so I braced myself for the hubbub of a long-awaited homecoming.

I sat up, my legs dangling from the tailgate. "So? Why were you in my mind?" I prompted again.

Peter shook his head and smiled a little. "You were in mine."

I chuckled, baffled and almost entertained by the revelation. "Of course I was," I mumbled. "I don't get it," I said and brushed off a piece of crusted mud from my jacket. "I've been having strange dreams about my mom for a long time," I thought aloud. "A featureless woman, calling for me, scaring the shit out of me, even though I knew—*wanted* it to be her. And now"—I looked at Peter—"I wonder how much of it had to do with you."

Peter's eyes narrowed. "If my dreams were anything like they are now, I can't always shut you out of them, sort of like our minds, or maybe our Abilities, were always linked in some way. I can find your mind now too, even when I'm not sleeping. That's how I knew where to find you." His voice was distant. "I called you the sad girl...you were always so scared in your dreams, at least that's what I've gathered from Mom's memories. I don't actually remember much of it myself because, you know..." Peter shrugged. He was a Re-gen, so I knew his memories were limited at best.

Briefly, I wondered if I'd gotten things mixed up in my head, that it wasn't really the faceless woman reaching for me, but Peter's mind instead. We were both quiet a moment, trying to put the pieces of our childhood nightmares together. Finally, I gave up, at least for now, and lifted a shoulder. "It's got to have something to do with Mom. My Ability blocker, maybe? Gabe or Mom might be able to figure it out." Peter's head bobbed in agreeance.

As the sound of the wagon drew closer, Jason, my dad, and a few of the others started gathering up what few things we had with us. Just as I decided I should probably climb off the truck and help, I thought of something. "Hey, Peter?" I said, turning to face him again. "Why did you start trying to talk to me after all these years? I mean, I've never heard your voice in my head before, at least, not that I can remember. Why are things so different now?"

Peter licked his lips and his eyes skirted to our mom, who was talking to Harper, and my gaze followed. "Mom's been worried about me a lot lately. We've been doing some tests, a *lot* of them. I'm different now. I can do things like that, I guess."

I tried not to let the sympathy I felt show. "Do you feel better?"

Peter picked at the chipping white paint on the tailgate. Pursing his lips, he nodded. "But I'm not sure how long it will last." He glanced at our mom and said in a lower voice, "I haven't said anything to my mom, because it makes her sad."

His longing for a sense of normalcy was obvious. "At least you're here now," I said, suddenly earnest to give him hope. I'd seen the desperation and disappointment on too many Re-gen faces back at the farm when they thought they couldn't be saved from degeneration. "We don't have laboratories and electro machines, but we have a lot of strong Abilities, like you said, and a settlement full of Re-gens who have gotten better—who can help *you* get better."

"Thanks," Peter said, though I wasn't sure he believed me. "I'm just happy we're away from that place—that my mom's here now, with you all." Peter straightened, and I almost thought I could sense anger radiating from him. "You don't know the things my da—*he* made her do, Zoe. The things she's had to go through."

Seeing a flash of his memories—of the atrocities Peter had gleaned from my mom's memories—I looked away, focusing on the shadowed outline of horses and the cart that came into view instead.

Harper walked over to us. His aura was bright yellow, and his eyes surveyed me. "How are you feeling, Baby Girl?" Fingers under my chin, he tilted my face up to examine me.

"I'm better," I said, though I was still a little weak. "But if you pull out your penlight, I might lose it."

Chuckling, he winked at me. "I want you to eat another one of these," he said and pulled a granola bar out of his back pocket. "You're still too shaky for my liking."

"I'll be fine," I promised and unwrapped the granola bar. "Really, I'm feeling better." I took a bite. It was salty and sweet, and tasted surprisingly good given how stale it was and the expiration date.

"When we get back to the farm, after you get cleaned up, I'd like you to come to the infirmary," Harper said, his eyes shifting to Peter, then back to me. "Both of you."

Glancing at Peter, I answered for both of us. "We will, H. I promise." Peter gave Harper a slight nod, but said nothing.

In true Harper fashion, he leaned forward and kissed my forehead. His concern and relief and exhaustion were unignorable. "As soon as we're ready to go, we'll get you settled in the cart."

As Harper strode away, Chris brought the cart to a stop a couple dozen yards away, and she was all smiles and tears in the moonlight. Shadow, Cookie, Jason's unnamed horse, Brutus, Poppy, and a couple of the other horses came to an anxious stop behind her. I couldn't help but smile, happy she was finally here, though my heart dropped a little at not seeing Dani sitting beside her, even though I'd known she wouldn't be coming. Becca's prophecy had shackled Dani to the farm regardless of her desire to leave, at least until the baby was born.

Shadow's head bobbed and white puffs of breath filled the air around the horses as they snorted and pawed, catching their breath. I grinned, happy to see Shadow. I wondered if he'd even noticed that I'd been gone. I couldn't ask him like Dani could, but that was okay. My connectedness to Peter, my bond with a boy—my brother—whom I'd never met before tonight, seemed strangely similar to what I imagined Dani's bond might be with Wings and Jack. It was a connection I couldn't turn off, at least not yet. Peter and I were like two tin cans attached by an unsnippable string.

I was about to climb off the tailgate when I noticed my mom coming over to us. She passed Jake, who carried a duffel bag filled with all of our surviving weapons and belongings from the accident, and they exchanged a long, drawn-out gaze. I could feel his anger toward her and knew he was just barely holding back all he wished he could say to her, even though he wasn't sure exactly what it was or what he hoped to accomplish. And my mom knew it.

She continued toward Peter and me, Jake's eyes following her retreating form. I watched his jaw clench in the gray-blue night.

My mom scanned me briefly, head to toe, then looked at Peter. "Sweetheart," she said, "it's time to gather your things." She ran her fingers through his dark, longish hair.

My insides twisted a bit at the endearment in her voice, at her motherly touch. I tried not to let it sadden me. *"I called you the sad girl..."* Peter's words resonated more deeply than I'd realized.

Peter jumped off the tailgate with ease and, after my mom gave me a small, timid smile, they walked back toward the plane.

Finally tearing my gaze from her, I noticed Jake walking over to me, a juice box in his hand. I chuckled softly, though it was a tad frail-sounding. I hated feeling so pathetic. "This sucks."

"Just drink it," he said, amusement in his tone. "Doctor's orders."

"Like I told Harper—I feel better." The drugs were leaving my system. If anything, I was still in a little bit of a shock from all that had happened in the last few hours. "What I really need is a shower." I took a sip from the juice box. "Yum, apple juice," I said dryly, though it did taste good despite my general dislike for it.

"That's Grade-A," Jake teased. "Not even expired yet."

"Oh?" I smiled. "You sure know how to win a girl over."

With a heart-stopping smile, Jake sat on the tailgate beside me and tucked some of my dirty hair behind my ears.

I leaned my face into the palm of his hand, my eyes closing of their own accord against his bone-thawing heat. I'd missed him, his touch, the sound of his voice.

"Zoe," he said, and I knew what question was coming; I could see it in his mind. "Did—"

"No," I said fervently, "they only took my blood. That was the only thing they cared about."

Jake's shoulders sagged as some of the tension left his body, and his eyes shifted to the green sleeves of my jacket, to the bruises hidden beneath the leather.

"That's all they cared about," I quietly repeated. And it was true. I hadn't been a person to Randall, only a blood bank.

I vaguely heard Chris talking to the others as Jake's thumb brushed the side of my face, giving me solace. "You're with me now," he said, reassuring us both.

I thought about the first time I'd awoken to find Carl standing with me in an unfamiliar room, and suddenly the whole experience started to feel more real. My vision blurred and my chest tightened. I pictured Tavis's bloodless face. "I thought you were all dead." I could hear the fear in my voice, and I shut my eyes. Jake pulled me against him. "I thought that was how things were going to end. After everything...I was so angry..."

"But they didn't," he said, his voice assertive and low. "And thanks to your mom and Peter, we found you. And we have Jason back."

Gently, I pulled away from him and wiped the tears from my eyes. "I know this is hard for you," I said. "Her, being here. I wish things weren't so complicated." I exhaled. "I wish you could meet my parents under normal circumstances." I tried to laugh, but it was riddled with unease and exhaustion.

Jake offered me a weak smile. "The truth is, Zoe, I don't know how I feel about all of this, but none of it matters."

I frowned. The breeze picked up, and I wrapped my arms around myself.

"Of course it's not easy." He glanced over at Becca, talking to Peter and my mom. "Re-gens, Crazies, Clara...all of it's because of her." Jake looked down at the asphalt a moment before his eyes met mine again. I could feel his thoughts churning around inside his head as he tried to make sense of them all. "But it's because of her that I've been able to save you, that I even met you in the first place. I'm not sure I would've otherwise." He let out a ragged breath.

I'd never thought about his regeneration, and what seemed like our destiny, in that way before.

"So," he continued, "I guess it's not as easy as I thought it would be to hate her." Jake took both of my hands in his, not knowing how happy it made me to hear him say that. "And if it weren't for Peter this time—" His voice broke. "Yeah," he exhaled and rubbed his forehead. "It's a lot to process."

I wrapped my arms around his neck, pulling him to me. I wanted him close, needed him closer.

"Bizarre doesn't quite cut it anymore," he muttered, and I smiled against his neck, choking back a relieved, hopeful sob.

"Thank you," I whispered, my grip tightening around him. "For not hating her. For not giving up on Jason—for not giving up on me..." I tried and failed not to picture where I would be now, had Jake and everyone not shown up.

"It looked like you had things under control," Jake said lightly, though I knew it would take him a long time to move past the utter fear and borderline panic the last few days had burrowed inside him.

"I hesitated," I said, angry with myself. "I felt bad for him." I cleared my throat. "Besides, I'm not sure how far I would've made it before Randall found me and brought me back." I felt my eyes clouding with tears again, recalling how reluctant I'd been.

Jake pulled away, pinning me with his piercingly determined eyes that had saved me in more ways than he would or *could* ever know. "You're alive, that's all that matters. You're with me and your family. You're going home, and you'll get to see Dani and Sam and..." Once Jake realized the implications of his words, he brushed a stray tear from my cheek. "Harper said Sam's doing okay. You don't have to worry about him."

Jake's gaze was suddenly vacant as he peered past me, his mind elsewhere. "We buried him," he said, almost like a confession. I saw images of Tavis's lifeless body and a freshly covered grave at the base of a giant oak tree. Its branches were naked and sleeping, though I knew they would be green and protective in the months to come.

I nodded, though I felt like weeping.

"We're ready for you," Jason said, coming up to us. His lips pursed and his eyes fixed on me, but he said nothing else.

I wiped the remaining dampness from my eyes and slid off the tailgate with Jake's help.

"I'll load up our things," Jake said, leaving me and Jason to walk toward the cart and horses.

"Are you sure you don't want a transfusion when we get back?" Jason asked. He took my hand in his so I could use him for some added balance as we walked toward Chris, who was making out with Harper at the cart.

"No," I said, shaking my head. "I'll be fine. If I was trying to run a marathon or something, maybe, but I think I just need some good ol' rest. And real food." I groaned, thinking about food. "Maybe Chris will make me one of her apple pies." I grinned, trying to reassure him, but it was lost upon him. Jason was distracted, and I knew his thoughts were probably of Dani. "So... are you excited to finally get home?" I asked him, unable to prevent a small, knowing smile at what was to come.

"Yeah," he said, but there was concern in his voice.

I ignored the fact that his aura—a dull blue—was only faint as I studied him, hoping, for once, his expression would give a little bit more away. "What is it?"

"We've been talking, but..." Jason gave me a sidelong glance, then asked, "How's she doing? I mean *really* doing? I feel like she's holding something back."

I smiled inwardly. "Dani's okay, Jason." I squeezed his arm. "At least better than when she thought you were dead—when we *all* thought you were dead. She was a mess, but now that she knows you're alive and on your way home...she's better. And from the sound of it, a lot has happened since we've been gone. So, tonight's dinner conversation should be fairly interesting." We both looked at our dad as he helped Peter and then our mom into the cart.

"Yeah," Jason grumbled, "Interesting." We stopped beside one of the cart's wheels. Chris's eyes were gleaming as she wrapped Jason in her arms, seeing him alive and real for the first time in weeks.

When she was finished fussing over him, she turned her attention to me, until finally Harper stepped in and interrupted. "If we don't get these two home," he said, motioning to Jason and me, "Dani's going to have a conniption."

Chris let out a belly laugh. "Isn't that the truth." She motioned to the cart, but just as I was about to climb up, I noticed Shadow standing off to the right, his ears perked up and alert. "Sorry, just one more sec," I said and took a few wobbly steps over to him.

Shadow gnawed at his bit, and his nostrils flared as he took a step toward me.

"Hey, boy." I trailed the tip of my finger down his silken

muzzle and stepped closer. "It feels like I haven't seen you in forever." Kissing the side of his face, I inhaled his scent and thought of the farm. *I'm finally going home.*

"Who's riding you tonight?" I asked, not expecting a reply.

"I think that would be me," Biggs said. He stepped over and patted Shadow's rump. "If you don't mind, of course. My horse is still en route back to the farm from Sacramento."

"Of course you can ride him," I practically chirped. I was still so happy Biggs had come back he was welcome to ride Shadow as much as he wanted. And then I realized Everett and Ellie would be at home, waiting for us too.

"Come on, Baby Girl. I wasn't joking when I said Dani's going to throw a fit. Let's get you home."

Biggs grinned at me, and I felt myself smile, *really* smile, for the first time in what felt like forever.

"How are you feeling?" My mom asked from her seat across from me in the back of the cart. Her eyes, even her tone, were soft… soft, but guarded.

"I'm okay," I said. "It feels good to be outside, in the fresh air, even though it's a tad chilly." I glanced at Peter who sat cross-legged beside her, swaying with each bump in the road. His gaze scoured the landscape of rolling green hills, live oaks, and the wooden fence lines that followed us along the frontage road home. I could sense his curiosity and wonder at all he was experiencing for the first time.

"Your friend, Harper, seems like a good man to have around," my mom said. "He takes good care of you."

I nodded. "Yes, he does. Always. But then, we all take good care of each other. That's what families do." I hadn't meant it to be snide, though I felt it'd come out that way.

331

Eyes fixed on mine, my mom said, "I can see that. I'm happy you and your brother have such good people in your group."

If that was her underhanded way of telling me Jason and I didn't need her, I wasn't biting. I looked at Peter. "It seems like you'd be a good guy to have around, too," I said. "If it weren't for you, I don't know when they would've found me."

Hearing Jake's baritone, I looked over at him as he spoke to Jason as they rode side by side behind the cart.

"Becca told me about her prophecy—the one about you two," my mom said, ruminating.

I ran my fingers through my hair and sighed. I hadn't thought about it in a while. *"She'll die because of you... The woman with the long black hair and teal eyes...you'll save her, but she'll die because of you."* I took a much-needed breath. "Yeah, it's a lot to wrap your mind around. I've sort of stopped trying." I shook my head, thinking about the poisoning... I *had* died, and Jake had saved me. "I wouldn't be sitting here right now if I'd never met him."

She eyed Jake a moment, then said, "He loves you."

I laughed awkwardly. "Yeah, I know."

Peter's focus shifted between Jake and me, like he'd never paid attention before.

My mom's eyes flicked to Jake again. The way she studied him made me feel sad, though I wasn't sure why.

I was still having a difficult time feeling her mind, given the fact that the neutralizer hadn't faded completely yet. But then her gaze slid from Jake to my dad, who was talking and riding along-side Biggs behind them, and I knew.

"Have you two talked yet?" I asked, knowing *that* would be an intense conversation.

"Not really, no." She cleared her throat and met my gaze. "Why, has your father said anything to you?"

I shook my head. "But you've got to talk to him," I said, almost pleading. "I'm worried he'll—" I steadied my breath, trying not to let my resentment for the last twenty years of our lives harden my voice. "You don't know what it was like for him. If you're staying, you have to fix things."

She was silent for a moment, considering something. "There are many relationships that need repairing." And given the fact that I barely knew my mother, having only really met her under singular circumstances—in a faded memory, under the influence of Clara, and one other time in a dream—I wasn't sure how she planned on doing that.

"Are you going to try?" I asked, a little too hopeful.

"Does that mean we're staying with them, at the farm?" Peter asked, and the loving mother she was, she grabbed his hand and held it in her lap.

"I'm not sure yet, sweetheart." Her gaze shifted to my dad again. "I'm not sure."

I wasn't expecting that answer, and my heartbeat quickened. "Where else would you go?" I knew Peter had a better chance with all of us than he did anywhere else outside the Colony. I didn't say that though, not with him sitting there, hopeful, like me.

"Can you possibly go any slower, Zo?" Dani's voice was sharp with unbridled anticipation. *"I've been waiting for you to get back here for* hours... *"*

"We're almost there—"

The sound of barking dogs stole my attention.

"You're here!"

I peered around Chris and Sanchez in the cart's driver seat to see the outline of the farm, still shed in darkness, come into view. Chris steered us through the gate, where we were greeted by Jack and Cooper bounding our way...and Dani and Annie. They stopped at the driveway as Grayson and Carlos strode out from the farmhouse, cradling babies in their arms and Sam following slowly behind them. Dani looked close to bouncing in place, biting her lip as she impatiently waited for our approach.

"We're home," I breathed and smiled at Peter, but when my

333

eyes met my mom's, my smile faltered. She looked petrified. "Everything will be fine," I said, a little louder than a whisper so she could hear me.

She met my gaze and gave me a single, curt nod before she swallowed and looked around at the homestead we'd created for ourselves. I could imagine she'd never seen anything like it before, not without holding cells and concrete rooms where people were experimented on and tortured.

"I promise." I smiled, trying my best to reassure her.

The cart came to a halt in front of the barn, and everyone began to move in a rush. My gaze went instantly to Dani. She rocked back on her heels, her hands in her pockets and her eyes gleaming as her gaze met Jason's. He was off his unnamed horse in an instant and striding toward her. Dani met him in the middle and was in his arms before Grayson could even help me out of the cart. There was an orchestra of greetings and hugs, tears and laughter as the dream of being home became real.

But my growing smile faltered when I saw Sam. His eyes were shimmering, his chin quivering as he surveyed the group. It was like he'd hoped it wasn't true, that he would find Tavis among those of us returning home. When his pale eyes met mine, the saddest I'd ever seen them, I lost what was left of my strength.

"Sam," I rasped, barely able to take a few steps before I nearly fell to my knees in front of him. "I'm so sorry," I said, wishing I could rewind everything and make Tavis stay behind—that I hadn't promised Sam I'd bring Tavis back to him, safe and sound.

Sam didn't say anything, his eyes fixed on me until he ran into my arms.

"I'm so sorry," I repeated, yearning for him to feel my words, to believe them as he sobbed, inconsolable, in my arms.

"I know." He hiccupped and gripped me tighter.

35

DANI

DECEMBER 16, 1AE

THE FARM, CALIFORNIA

For the first time in weeks, I felt whole. Complete. The empty places in my heart that could be filled, were. More so, even; they were full to bursting. I choked back a joyful sob and gripped the back of Jason's jacket more tightly. It was the same one he'd been wearing the last time I'd seen him. I inhaled deeply, breathing him in. He smelled the same, too —like *him*.

And as I clung to him in the wee hours of the morning, pale moonlight and all of our family and friends surrounding us, I realized that part of me had expected him to come back different, after all he'd been through...but he hadn't. He was the same Jason. *My* Jason.

"Red..." One of his arms was wrapped all the way around the back of me, his hand clutching my side like he was trying to fuse us together. His other hand was buried in my hair, and he pressed his lips against the top of my head. "God, I missed you." His breath heated my scalp, and the yearning in his voice warmed my heart. "Red...God..."

I made a squeaking noise and nodded against his chest, neither of us ready or willing to put any physical distance between us just yet. "For a while there, I really thought you were dead," I said, my voice thick with emotion. I was coming to understand that while being happy was a lovely feeling, happiness that piggybacked extreme fear and sadness was the greatest feeling in all the world. And I hoped to never, ever feel this kind of happiness again. The up and down—it was too much.

Jason's arms shook as he tightened his hold on me. "I know." He inhaled and exhaled heavily. "I wish...I just wish it hadn't been so—so..." He paused, struggling for the right words. "I don't know—so hard, I guess."

I squeezed my eyes shut. Jason wasn't vociferous, but he always knew what to say, at least when something needed to be said. He always had a snappy comeback or a sharp retort. It was so strange to hear him struggling to voice his thoughts. Me, on the other hand, I struggled plenty. Which was why, once again, the only response I could manage was a nod and a muffled "I love you so much."

Jason's fingers tangled in my hair, pulling a bit, but I hardly cared. "God, if anything happened to you...if you'd pulled the trigger when Cole made you put the gun—" His whole body was shaking now. "He was so close to killing you...to making you—"

"But I'm okay," I said, forcing myself to pull away enough that I could look up at him. "Somehow, amazingly, despite *everything*, we're both here. We're both home. We're both okay." I beamed up at him. I'd been wrong; it was possible to feel even happier. I knew it, because I felt an unbelievable surge of joy as I drew in the breath to tell him, "We're better than okay, Jason." I cleared my throat, my lips shaking and eyes stinging. "I—I'm pregnant."

For the briefest moment, Jason's eyes lit up, but the light—the anticipation and excitement and joy—faded so quickly, I almost doubted I'd seen it at all. He searched my eyes. "The documents from the Colony," he said slowly, carefully, "they said...none of the babies lived...and some of the mothers died, too."

I was shaking my head before he could finish. "They're different," I explained. "None of them are like us—or like *you*, I suppose. I've been over this a dozen times with Harper and Gabe. Your cells are already genetically stable, remember? And Becca said the baby would be safe so long as I stayed on the farm, so..." I shrugged. "Becca's never wrong."

Jason's eyes narrowed.

I rolled my eyes. "If it'll make you feel better, we can ask your mom about it later. She's the expert on all of this, so—oh!" I squeaked.

Jason released me and captured my hand, wasting no time in leading me toward the cart, where Dr. Wesley was standing with Gabe and a teenage boy who could only be her youngest child, Peter. Both mother and son looked more than a little lost, though Gabe appeared to be trying to acclimate them to life on the farm with words and enthusiastic hand gestures alone.

"Dani's pregnant," Jason said as we closed the distance to the trio. And he didn't speak quietly. Around us, excited voices quieted and eyes turned our way. I caught Chris's, and glanced at the stable. No telepathy necessary; she picked up on my silent request for privacy and quickly rounded up the humans and horses and herded them toward the stable door to start getting the animals settled in for the night, or rather, for the morning.

By the time I looked at Dr. Wesley, her attention was entirely on me. "Congratulations are in order, then." She bowed her head, her sleek, gray-streaked black bob swaying.

I indicated Jason, hovering beside me, with a flick of my eyes. "He's, er, concerned about it...because of the results of Project Eden."

"Ah," Dr. Wesley said, nodding sagely. "Those results don't apply to you." She scanned the rest of our companions, who were halfway to the stable. "Your friends, yes, they'll have fertility troubles for a while yet, but you two, you should be fine." She frowned. "Of course, there are the normal childbearing issues to worry about, but..." She shook her head and focused on Jason. "With Gabriel and Harper here to look out for Danielle, she should be fine."

"And you," I said, eyeing her quizzically. When she didn't respond, I quickly changed the subject before the elephant in the driveway could become too obtrusive. "So you see," I said, looking at Jason. "I told you. I'll be fine." I placed my hand on my belly. *"We'll* be fine."

And as wonder slowly transformed Jason's scarred face, a high-pitched squeal sped our way.

"Sorry!" Chris called from the stable door. "Couldn't hold her back."

I laughed as Annie flung herself at Jason. She practically climbed up his body, clinging to his neck and waist like a spider monkey as Jason wrapped his arms around her. "Imissedyou-ImissedyouImissedyouImissedyouI—"

"Missed you, too, munchkin," Jason said, closing his eyes and smiling. He extended one of his hands toward me and pulled me against his side. "So much."

◈

"You shouldn't be out here doing this, Zo," I said, taking the armful of bridles from her with minimal resistance and walking them to the extra hooks we'd drilled into the wall of the tack room months ago. I hung the leather and metal contraptions up one by one.

"Well, neither should you," Zoe said, somewhat grumpily. Barely fifteen minutes had passed since she and the others had returned, and she already looked like the walking dead, she was so beat.

I glanced over my shoulder in time to see her plop onto one of the extra hay bales we'd stacked in here for the winter. They looked like they were made of shimmering gold in the dim lantern light.

Zoe caught my eye and cringed, just a little. "Sorry," she said, sighing. "I know I'm in shitty shape right now, but you know I hate feeling useless." She rubbed her eyes and laid her head back against the edge of a second-level hay bale. "I hate that everyone's exhausted and unpacking anyway at four in the fucking morning, and it's all because of me and my apparent need to be a goddamn damsel in distress all the time."

I could hear the frustration in her voice, threatening tears. Closing my eyes, I hung my head briefly, hating hearing Zoe sound so weak. She was the stronger of the two of us, the one with a backbone of steel and a razor-sharp tongue. She was the one who pushed me to keep going, who could convince me to want to keep fighting, who would find a way, who would make things work, no matter what. It was her courage, her strength that inspired me. And when she was like this, deflated and defeated and somehow lost, *I* felt lost, too.

With a deep breath, I hung the last bridle on an iron hook and turned around. "Oh, Zo..." I sat beside her, which was a minor feat in and of itself, considering how poky some of the renegade straws of hay were, and hooked my arm around her waist. "It's okay. You're home now. Everyone's home and safe and it's all okay. *We're* all okay."

She rested her head on my shoulder just in time for me to feel the first jerky convulsion as she lost her battle against tears. "I—I'm so so—sorry," she said miserably.

"Zo..." I raised my other hand to stroke her unusually tangled and grimy hair, not caring one bit that she was far from clean. "None of what happened was your fault."

She hiccupped. "But—"

"I'm sorry," I interrupted. "But did you slap a fake memory

onto my mind or kidnap Jason? Did you lay the trap that caused the car crash?" I laughed bitterly. "Did you tell Tavis to drag you away from the accident or pull the trigger or ask those assholes to abduct you and tie you up and steal your blood? Did you—"

"Alright, D," Zoe said, sniffing and laughing morosely. "I get it. You can stop bludgeoning me with sarcasm."

I smiled, just a little, and looked up at the ceiling, eyes stinging *again*. Damn my stupid pregnancy hormones for making me constantly on the verge of crying.

Zoe laughed once more, and there was actually some amusement in the sound this time. Pulling away, she wiped her eyes while looking at me sidelong. "Please, D, like you wouldn't be about to cry right now otherwise. Sure...blame the poor, defenseless unborn baby."

I barked a laugh and felt a sudden, rush of relief. It always amazed me how laughter could wash misery away like a wave smoothing out footprints in sand. Smiling at Zoe, I fished a handkerchief out of my pocket and handed it to her. "You've got some wayward snot..."

Her eyes went wide, and then she smacked my arm. "Smartass!" But she did take the hanky.

I pursed my lips, suppressing a grin. "Go to bed, Zo. You look like crap."

She glared at me, but her Caribbean-blue eyes sparkled with laughter. "I feel like crap." She stood shakily, almost falling back onto the bale of hay. "But I have to stop by the infirmary first—H's orders."

I jumped up and supported her with an arm around her waist. "You're not collapsing on my watch. Let's get you into the house."

Zoe started to run her fingers through her hair and paused mid-action, her eyes fixed on the raw marks around her wrist, before she pulled a strand of hair out and stared at it. She sighed. "I think I need to wash up first," she said and wrinkled her nose.

"Well, I wasn't going to mention it, but…"

"Hey!" She feigned offense and nudged my shoulder.

I laughed, a good, loud belly laugh. "Why don't I hand you off to Jake?" I said, pointing toward the solemn man in question with my chin as he entered the stable carrying a saddle. "I love you, Zo, but I'm sure he'd appreciate seeing you all naked and soapy much more than I would."

Zoe rolled her eyes as I transferred her into Jake's much more capable hands, trading him for the saddle. As I carried it back to the tack room, I heard Zoe call out, "Jason! Go rescue your wife! She's carrying heavy things in the stable!"

Shaking my head, I grinned. I was almost to the tack room when I heard the rush of footsteps as Jason jogged toward me. "Red…"

"Jason," I said, drawing out his name and continuing on my way. With a faint grunt, I hoisted the saddle onto its stand and turned to face my towering husband. He stood a few yards away, arms crossed over his broad chest. "What?" I mirrored his pose, leather creaking as I leaned back against the saddle.

For seconds, we stood on either side of the small tack room, staring at each other. Slowly, Jason reached behind himself and shut the door, never taking his eyes off me.

"Jason…" I drawled again.

He started across the room, closing the distance between us slowly, like a predator stalking prey.

My heartbeat thudded in my chest, my pulse suddenly racing. "We're in the stable," I said, swallowing roughly.

"I don't care."

"Anyone could walk in." My mind wasn't focused on much beyond Jason, but I managed a fleeting thought of gratitude that Carlos had moved Vanessa up into his room while we'd waited for the others to return.

"They'll understand."

Suddenly, Jason's lips were on mine, his hips pressed against mine, and I no longer cared where we were or who walked in or what someone might see. I only cared about getting closer to him. In that moment, I only cared about loving him.

36

ZOE

DECEMBER 16, 1AE

THE FARM, CALIFORNIA

What had only been a handful of hours since we left Sacramento felt like a never-ending, muddled day of obscure conversations and a rainstorm of emotions. The cool water of the outside shower was exactly what I needed to resuscitate my mind and body, despite the breezy, dusky morning. Complete exhaustion was one thing, but fuzzy senses were unsettling.

Tugging on the water cord, I let the brisk waterfall run down my face, over my back, and down my legs, rinsing away what remained of that room, of that bed…of that not-so-distant nightmare. The fact that things could've been worse wasn't lost upon me, but it still left me feeling uneasy in my own skin. Somehow the crisp water made me feel better, for once, and helped keep my emotions in check, despite my intermittent shivering.

The sound of someone at the entrance to the shower startled me. "Christ!" I shrieked and attempted to cover the most private parts of my exposed body.

"Just me," Jake said. He took in my alarmed expression as he stepped inside, a towel draped over each shoulder. "Sorry," he said with a barely there smirk. "You snuck out of the house pretty quickly. I thought you might need one of these"—he hung the towels over the fence—"and maybe some help." His partial smile hardened and his eyes narrowed on my arms and wrists, then moved up my neck to the right side of my face...then the left.

I knew exactly what he was staring at; I could feel Randall's handprints, still tender on my cheeks and jaw. I'd seen myself through Jake's eyes—through everyone's—enough to know the bruising looked pretty bad.

"Thanks for the towel," I said, trying to dissolve his quiet concern. "That will definitely come in handy."

Jake dipped his chin, his eyes fixed on mine, thoughtful. "Why didn't you let Chris draw you a warm bath?"

I lifted an indifferent shoulder and refocused on my shower. "It's too crowded in the house right now," I said. "I needed some space." I pulled the handle again so I could splash water on my face and ran my fingers through my wet hair. I fought my teeth from chattering, but I was feeling more and more normal by the minute.

Realizing Jake was still standing there, expectant, I glanced at him. The fixedness of his gaze had thawed and he lifted his eyebrow. "Mind if I join you?" He held up the body wash I'd forgotten, and a washcloth. "I'll make it worth your while." He offered me a small grin.

I couldn't refuse that smile, and I didn't want to. Jake's calm, steady demeanor was a welcome respite from the ebb and flow of overstimulated emotions in the house. "Worth my while? In that case," I said with a soft chuckle. "Of course you can join me. But it's freezing, just so ya know."

"Exactly why I wondered why you were out here." Jake pulled his T-shirt off over his head, removed his shorts, and stepped toward the water. Briefly, I remembered our first semi-naked encounter in the locker room at Fort Knox.

"Why are you smiling?" he asked, one eyebrow arched in question.

My smile broadened. "No reason." I splashed more water on my face and stepped aside so he could rinse off. Unlike Sanchez, my dad, Gabe, and Becca, who all had scrapes and some bruising, Jake's body was unmarred. The only remnant of him being injured at all was the dried dirt and blood that caked certain areas of his skin. He set the body wash on the ground. "Feeling a little over-whelmed?" he asked, wiping water from his face.

All the talking and questions and emotions had definitely been that—overwhelming—after days of mostly silence and solitude. My feelings and those of everyone else felt intensified, especially now that we were *all* together. "You could say that," I said. I eyed the faintly pulsing aura around him.

Leaning into the water, Jake scrubbed the top of his head. I watched as chills broke out over his skin, and when he noticed me watching him, he stopped mid-scrub. "What is it?"

I shrugged. "You're just glowing a tad," I said, half-jokingly. Though I wasn't sure *glowing* was the right word. "That's all."

His eyes widened a smidge before narrowing on me again. "You never really did explain that to me." Which was true; he'd been gone so much after Jason's disappearance I had to wonder what other developments he might've missed, though nothing in particular came to mind.

I crouched for the shampoo I'd actually remembered to bring, but Jake grabbed it before I could and shook his head. He stepped aside, guiding me back under the streaming water. "There's not much to tell, really," I began. He squirted some of the shampoo into his hand, and I tilted my head slightly back out of habit and shut my eyes. "I thought I saw it around you once, but now it seems pretty constant. I'm not sure how to turn it off yet." I nearly groaned as Jake's fingers massaged my head, and I wanted to melt.

When I opened my eyes, he was listening intently. "Everyone has a color, except for Dani." I smirked. "She has two. Becca doesn't have one either, none of the Re-gens do."

"An aura, huh?" He maneuvered me back under the water and helped me rinse my hair.

I shrugged again, meeting his gaze as he peered down at me. "That's sort of what Gabe and I talked about. He thinks it has something to do with my Ability seeing emotions, not just feeling them. But it's all theory at this point."

"What's my color?" he asked, and his eyes sparkled. "Pink?"

I couldn't help the incredulous scrunch of my face as I shook my head. "No. Not pink," I said. "Though that would be funny."

"Not really," he said and furrowed his brow as he imagined it.

My growing smile widened as I studied his aura for a moment. It was a slightly effervescent mixture of burnt orange and scarlet red. "Yours is sort of crimson," I said, chewing my lip in contemplation.

Jake opened the body wash to squirt some into the washcloth in his hand. "That's got to be weird, seeing people glowing all the time."

"I'm definitely still getting used to it," I admitted. "But if it's anything like emotions and memories, I can probably turn it off, eventually." The moment his sudsy hands began to lather soap on my shoulders, back, and arms, my eyes closed again of their own accord, and I felt the tension in my muscles disperse. "That feels… so…good…" I groaned.

Jake chuckled. "Good." His hands were strong but gentle, and soft despite the roughness of his fingertips. And like the cleansing, frigid water that cascaded down my skin, his touch was soothing.

"I'm surprised you're not shrieking and wiggling around," he said with a hint of laughter. I knew he was thinking about when he'd dunked me in the Arkansas River back in Colorado. I didn't have to see him to know he was smiling.

"Why? Because the water's cool and you wish you could taunt

me some more?" I said dryly. "Not this time. This is just what I needed."

We were quiet for a moment, the sound of the water rushing over my ears and the feeling of Jake's hands on my body keeping me distracted and my mind still. "How's Sam?" I finally asked. "Is he doing any better?" I'd left him alone in his room per his request.

"I'm sure he'll be okay, Zoe," Jake said. "It helps that he has all of us. He knows he's not alone."

Jake's gentle, attentive, methodical scrubbing on my back stopped, and he picked up my hand to scrub my arm. He studied the angry, red wound on my bicep. I hadn't re-bandaged it since Harper had examined it, wanting to clean it off before I covered it back up.

"What did Harper say?" Jake asked, eyeing the pink, irritated skin around it. It was difficult for him to see wounds on me, on any of us, really, because it was so easy for him to heal.

"He said I'll be fine. It's a deep cut, something in the van—when it rolled—but I'm okay. I promise." I squeezed his hand. "I'm not going to break. It's not infected. I'm fine."

Jake squirted more body wash onto the washcloth and slowly began to massage my hand, then the skin around my raw wrists and up my eggplant-colored arm. "I don't think this is a good color for me," I teased, but Jake ignored me.

"Are you sure you don't want a transfusion?"

I shook my head. "Not unless there's something really wrong with me. You're not a damn blood machine."

He didn't look away from my arm as he gently cleaned around the cut.

"I'm sorry," I said, knowing it bothered him that he couldn't help me, only because I wouldn't let him. "But you know how I feel about this. I just spent the last four days hooked up to machines that were sucking the life right out of me. Why would I want to do that to you, especially when it's not necessary?"

"You know it's not the same," he said, his voice flat. He was frustrated with me, and I couldn't blame him. If our roles were reversed, I'd want to help him, too, but I just wanted to heal on my own.

I scoured his body, knowing I wouldn't find a bullet wound, but wondering where he'd been shot all the same.

"The chest," he said, eyeing me sideways. "I'm fine."

"I know," I said. I couldn't help but worry, no matter how perfect he looked.

"Like I said," he grumbled. "It's not the same."

"If my cut gets worse," I said, "or I don't start feeling better soon, I'll let you know, okay? I promise."

Jake's eyes cut to mine, then he pulled the shower lever. "It's your choice."

With a final, shivering rinse, I pivoted around, needing to break the tension between us. "Your turn," I said, eyebrows dancing. "You know you want me to scrub your baaack," I sang. "And fast, because I'm starting to freeze, I think."

Jake conceded. His mouth quirked in a sultry smile, and he quickly turned around. I lathered up a handful of body wash on the washcloth.

"Apricot, my favorite," he drawled, and I couldn't help but laugh.

Rising on tiptoes, I gripped his shoulders and kissed the side of his face. "What's wrong, you don't like smelling fruity?"

"Oh, I love it." He dropped his head so I could scrub around his neck and down his back. "I didn't see any soap in your stash," he said, "so Dani lent that to me before she and Jason shut themselves up in the cottage. Don't use it all, it might be her favorite one or something."

I barked a laugh. "It's not, and even if it was, she and Jason will probably never emerge from their little haven again anyway. She won't miss it." Remembering Jason's expression when Dani told him about the baby—the pure joy and excitement that lit up his face—I wasn't sure he would ever let her out of his sight again.

"I wonder what they're going to name her," I thought aloud. I guided Jake back a couple steps into the falling water.

"Her?"

"Yeah, Dani says it's a girl." I washed the suds from his back. "Do you think she'll name her after Grams, or maybe Callie?"

"Who's Callie?" Jake asked, but I waved his question away, too busy wondering.

"Her old roommate. Maybe she'll name her after her mom, Ceara."

"Maybe," Jake said. He shook out the water from his hair and scooted over so I could rinse off one final time. The water stopped just as I finished. "Or," Jake continued, "maybe they'll want to start a family without being tied to painful memories of the past. Maybe they'll pick a new name."

I nodded. "It's possible. That's what I would do."

I wrung the excess water from my hair, still thinking, when blurred images of children—*our* children—flooded my mind. My eyes widened, and I looked at Jake.

He handed me my towel, but I was frozen. He frowned. "Why do you keep looking at me like that?"

"You—" I pointed at him. "You want to have kids." I'm not sure why, but I was shocked. There was always a chance it could happen, but we were careful; I guess I assumed it was for a reason.

Jake's expression softened. "Of course I do," he said, catching me a little off guard. We hadn't talked about kids, ever. In fact, we never really talked about us and our future, let alone a family. We just sort of…were. His expression tensed again. "Don't you?"

I let out a nervous laugh. "I don't know. I mean, I like kids, other people's kids…"

Jake was confused. Images of me and the twins and Annie and Sam flashing in his mind, of his plea for us to settle down and start a new life here. He was revisiting memories of me, like he was making sure he hadn't missed something—a conversation or a look, a sign, anything.

Though Jake's expression was calm and thoughtful, I felt a spike of nervousness in him, too. It was the most surprisingly endearing thing I'd ever experienced before. He really wanted a family...with me. And suddenly I felt a little nervous and even a tad giddy.

Wrapping my towel around me, I stepped into him. I studied his face, his shrewd copper-colored eyes and how they searched mine. "I didn't realize a family was so important to you. I mean, I should have. I think you'd be a wonderful father." His eyes held mine, still unsure what to think. "I've just been living so much in the present I sort of forgot that we get to have a future together, too."

The small furrow in his brow lessened.

Brushing a light kiss against his lips, I said, "Just because I haven't really thought about it, that doesn't mean I don't want to, Jake. It's just—"

Everett, I thought it was by the sound of his hiccupped wails, began crying inside the farmhouse. I squeezed my eyes shut, forgetting the "perks" to having baby twins around, plus Dani's baby girl on the way.

"It's just," I said, starting again, "that there's a lot going on right now, and I think we have enough babies in the house for the time being, don't you?"

Jake let out a steadying breath, wincing a bit as Everett's crying grew louder. "Yes," he said. "Staggering them a bit would be good."

We both laughed, and Jake wrapped his arms around me, pressing a long, gentle kiss against my lips before he let go.

"Hey," I said, as he was about to step away. "I'm serious. You and me"—I peered down at my nonexistent watch like I often did—"a year or two from now." I pointed up to our bedroom window and lifted my eyebrows playfully.

Jake smiled and kissed me again before we began to dress in our clean clothes.

"I can see it now," I said. "Me waddling around with a giant white belly." I tugged my sweatpants on, suppressing a groan at the comfort of having my own clothes, soft and clean against my skin.

"That'll be a sight to behold," Jake joked, and I playfully smacked his arm.

"That's right. And you better learn how to make ice cream... and pickles."

37

DANI

DECEMBER 16, 1AE

THE FARM, CALIFORNIA

We slept late into the afternoon, having finally crawled into bed sometime after four in the morning, and I woke feeling like I'd been asleep for weeks. I lay in bed, snuggled against Jason and warm and cozy under Grams's quilt, utterly content. Sharing my bed with Jason was something I'd doubted I would ever experience again. But there he was, right where he belonged.

I could feel him playing with my hair, winding this or that curl through and around his fingers. I exhaled contentedly. I loved how much he enjoyed playing with my hair. It was soothing beyond belief, and on this particularly lazy afternoon, it threatened to lull me back to sleep.

A low, deep chuckle vibrated in Jason's chest. "I thought you'd never wake up."

I stuck out my lower lip and craned my neck to look at his face, resting my chin on his chest. "Awww…were you getting bored?"

He pressed his lips together in an obvious attempt to avoid

smiling and sighed dramatically. "So bored." His eyes shone with mischief. "Until you started talking in your sleep..."

I groaned and buried my face in the crevice between his arm and his torso.

"Careful, Red, you're verging on armpit territory..."

I snorted into the fleshy void. "What did I say this time? Anything remotely coherent?"

"Let's see...there was something about a snake in the bathroom and the sun going out in the ocean..." He paused for a moment, and I lifted my head to watch his expression as he made fun of me. Over our months on the farm, this had become another of his favorite things to do when we lay in bed, working up the nerve to actually rise and shine and join the others. "Oh, and you sounded pretty upset about losing your library card." He laughed. "You said you wouldn't be able to find the animals without it."

"Ah..." I flopped onto my back, laughing. "I knew my library card was still good for something." Jason started to sit up, and I touched my fingertips to his arm. "Where are you going?"

He looked at me, his eyes eager. "Nowhere," he said, drawing the covers down to my hips and scooting around so he could rest his head on my abdomen. "I want to see if I can hear it."

"Her," I said, lifting my head to smile down at him and combing my fingers through his short, dark hair. I was trying my hardest to ignore the fact that I needed to pee.

Jason's eyes widened. "You think it's a girl?"

My smile grew into a grin, and I laid my head back on the pillow. "I don't think; I know. We have a connection, she and I... it's got to be something to do with our Abilities. It's something I want to ask your mom about, but so far, it's become pretty apparent that she's going to have a combination of our Abilities. She's been nulling me while I sleep—so I *can* sleep. That started several days ago, and I couldn't be more grateful to her."

Jason pressed his lips to my belly. "It's amazing." His whiskers tickled my sensitive skin, and I squirmed. He turned his head to the side, once again resting his ear on my abdomen. "*She's* amazing."

I nodded, grinning like an idiot as some of his awe poured into me. "She is. Our amazing little girl." Sensing two familiar minds heading our way, I glanced at the door. "Speaking of…"

The doorknob turned, and the door inched inward. Like they were part of a bi-species comedy duo, Annie and Jack stuck their heads through the opening, one right on top of the other.

"Hey sweetie…Sweet Boy," I said, waving for them to join us.

They didn't waste any time. The bed dipped and shook as the small girl and larger dog quite literally jumped up and quickly found the best, most obtrusive ways to join the snuggle-fest. Jack claimed the still-warm space Jason had abandoned moments earlier and settled in, resting his chin on my shoulder. His black nose was about a millimeter from my jaw.

"Don't do it," I said, trying not to laugh when his dark little doggy eyebrows rose and he emitted the most pathetic whimper. "Jack…"

My dog whined again, his tail thumping a despondently slow rhythm against the mattress.

I rolled my eyes. "Fine, but just one."

Jack's tail picked up pace, thumping in triple time, and he licked the entire side of my face.

Annie squealed her approval and delight, I cringed and wiped my cheek on the pillow case, and Jason laughed. It started as a low chuckle, but it quickly gained strength until it became a whirlwind of amusement, of happiness, that I couldn't avoid. The three of us laughed for what felt like hours, and when we'd finally quieted, we let out a collective, contented sigh.

"We should get up," Jason said, reluctance dangling from each word. "There's work to do. The farm won't run itself."

Boy was he right. Much as we'd tried to maintain the place, too many tasks had gone undone since his abduction. We'd put so much effort and manpower into searching for him that it had been impossible not to neglect some of our duties around the farm.

I nodded and planted a smacking kiss on the top of Annie's head. "Alright, troops. Up and at 'em."

The sun was just sinking behind the hills to the west of the farm when the four of us walked into the farmhouse through the mudroom door and were smacked in the face with delicious smells. There were, by almost anyone's count, too many cooks in the kitchen with Becca, Chris, Biggs, Sanchez, Camille, and Grayson hustling about.

Annie and Jack ran ahead, the tiny wild child all but attacking Zoe, who was reclining on the couch in the living room, Cooper snuggled in beside her. Jason and I paused in the mudroom doorway, basking in the controlled chaos filling the home's living space.

Multiple pairs of quick footsteps pounded down the stairs, and a few seconds later, Jake and Gabe entered the kitchen. They headed straight for us, Jake passing by with a nod of hello for both Jason and me, and Gabe flashing a grin and offering a quick "About time you joined the party."

Confused, I watched him follow Jake into the mudroom and join his old friend in hunting through the jackets cluttering the coat hooks on the wall.

"Let us know when the oven's hot enough!" Chris called after them right before the back door swung shut. She caught my eye and winked. "We're having pies tonight to celebrate the *grand homecoming*."

"So much for getting back to work," Jason said. He leaned down and planted a soft kiss on my cheek, then made his way toward Zoe, who was now buried under two dogs and a small-ish child.

Smiling and shaking my head, I went the other direction, stopping at the kitchen island, just opposite Chris. I watched her stir a batter of some sort in one of the enormous wooden bowls Tom had crafted months ago, using one of the wooden spoons he'd made around the same time. "Cornbread?" I guessed, based on the batter's yellow color. My stomach grumbled eagerly. My appetite hadn't just returned, it had reawakened with a vengeance.

I'd directed my question at Chris, but it was Becca who answered despite being elbow-deep in a mass of spinach and other veggies in a giant wooden bowl of her own. "Yes, and there's pot roast cooking in the hearth, and some acorn squash and potatoes roasting, too." She grinned, clearly taking pride in her work as our head cook. Sarah had taught her well.

"Sounds like a feast," I said, my stomach voicing its excitement in a full-on growl this time. I glanced around the room once more, noting several significant absences, and I couldn't hold back my curiosity. "Tom and Dr. Wesley...?"

"Tom's out in his shop," Chris said, still mixing. "And Anna's upstairs, resting with Peter in our room."

"Oh." *Bummer.* I'd been hoping to talk to her about what to expect when expecting a baby with Abilities. "So, what can I do to help?"

"The usual," Chris said, glancing to the large farm table nearby. "Set the table and fill up water glasses?"

I shrugged. "Okeydokey." I wasn't as bad at cooking as I used to be, but the only meal I was usually allowed to help actually prepare was breakfast...when breakfast was oatmeal or grits or some other generally gruel-like concoction. It was hard to screw up gruel.

As I made my way around the kitchen island toward the end cupboard that held the glasses and dishes, I caught movement out of the corner of my eye. I glanced at the mouth of the hallway, then froze and did a double take when I saw who was standing there—Vanessa and Carlos.

I hadn't known we were doing this tonight. Wasn't it too soon? Didn't Vanessa need more time? She'd been so distraught, literally inconsolable since she'd been, well, *cured*.

Apparently not, because Vanessa stood in the doorway, seemingly unfazed by all of the eyes on her. She looked pretty in the periwinkle wool sweater I'd given to Carlos for her. Her hair was wavy and so long that it almost reached her waist, and it was so dark that it appeared black except for where the candlelight filling the room hit it just right, making it shimmer a dark, almost red-brown, like it was sprinkled with crushed garnets.

Carlos stood behind his older sister, hands on her shoulders. His eyes were opened wide—nerves, I thought—but his jaw was set.

"Well, shit, Carlos," Chris said, setting down her oversized spoon and wiping her hands on the front of her apron. "I wish you'd told me you two were planning to do this right now. I would've prepared everyone first." She looked around the room and shrugged. "Just so you all know, Dani and I accidentally cured Vanessa…"

The mudroom door opened and shut, and two pairs of heavy footsteps sounded on the hardwood floor, then stopped, I assumed because Jake and Gabe realized what they'd just walked into. In the shadowy hallway behind Carlos and Vanessa, I could see Mase, watching with interest.

Carlos shook his head. "It wasn't like that. I didn't know she was going to—"

"I'm sorry," Vanessa said, back straight and head high. "It's my fault. I just…now that everyone's here, I wanted to apologize for, well"—she lifted her shoulders, then let them drop—"for everything." After that, her words tumbled out in a rush. "I mean, I know I was a huge pain in the ass and you were all afraid of me and what I might do if I got loose, and I just couldn't sit up in Carlos's room a second longer knowing that any of you still thought of me like that crazy animal person I was."

She looked around the room, examining each of our faces. Her gaze lingered on Annie, cuddled up with Zoe and the dogs, then settled on me. "I know I won't ever be able to say I'm sorry enough, but I really am. You can't know what it was like—what *they* were like, always whispering and nagging and pushing and pushing and *pushing* and never shutting up." She shook her head, eyes shining. "It's like they were the worst, most paranoid parts of me walking around, dressed up like people I loved. The things they would say…"

"It's alright, hon," Chris said, starting to make her way around the island.

"No." Vanessa held her hand up. "I want to finish. I need to finish." She took a deep breath, eyes scanning us all once again. This time her focus settled on Zoe. "You can see what people think, their most hidden, ugly thoughts, right?"

"Well, I…" Zoe exchanged a look with her brother. "I don't really…yeah, I can."

Vanessa's eyes widened. "Doesn't everyone have those crazy thoughts that they can't control? You know, like when you're riding in a car and you're like, 'I could totally open the door right now and just roll out,' stuff like that." Her eyes lowered to the floor. "Or like when someone says or does something that totally pisses you off and they're standing so close that you could, like, scratch them or bite them or stab them really easily and they wouldn't be able to stop you because who expects somebody to do something crazy like that. People think stuff like that…right?"

For seconds, there was nothing but the chorus of our breaths. Until, thankfully, Zoe broke the tense silence. "You're right, Vanessa, everyone thinks like that sometimes, and if they tell you otherwise, they're lying."

Vanessa started blinking rapidly, and when she spoke, her voice was pitched just a bit higher. "Yeah, well, that's what they were like. My, um"—she raised her hands and made air quotes—"*friends.*"

Carlos cleared his throat. "But she's better now."

"How do we know for sure?" Sanchez asked, adding, "No offense," as an afterthought.

"Because she has an aura now," Zoe said, eyes narrowed and head tilted to the side. "When we left for Colorado, she didn't have one, but now she does." She smiled faintly. "It matches her sweater."

38

ANNA
DECEMBER 17, 1AE

THE FARM, CALIFORNIA

"I just can't believe you actually did it," Anna said, shaking her head. That wasn't completely true; she could believe it. She would believe almost anything, given enough evidence. And when Gabe had told her about Vanessa's enormous announcement the previous night, her jaw had almost unhinged. "I tried for so long to fix the faulty deletion in the P-strand, and sometimes I'd think I was close, but every single time, the solution evaded me. I might've been successful had I had someone with an Ability like yours on my team, but I hadn't even thought of it."

Chris's brow furrowed, and the corners of her mouth turned down. "I wish I knew how to describe what I did in scientific terms, but in all reality, it just sort of happened. It was easy—scarily easy, but it would've been impossible without Dani's help. Or, rather, without the help of the hormones she's throwing off because of her pregnancy."

"So you're certain it was her hormones and not the child itself?"

Chris shrugged. "Honestly, I'm still not sure."

The two women stood on either side of the island, chopping the final batch of root vegetables for the evening meal—a stew of some sort—which Becca was busy tending at the fireplace-turned-hearth. The way these people had adapted to life without the amenities of modern civilization astounded Anna. She'd been outside of the Colony for barely two days now, and she felt like she would never adapt. She was a foreigner in her own land. But her children gave her hope. If they could adapt to this new way of living, not to mention Gabriel, then maybe, just maybe, she could, too.

Anna's eyes narrowed as she considered Chris's words. She herself might not be able to bottle Chris's "cure," but maybe Chris could teach others with similar Abilities to learn the procedure. "Do you think you could replicate what you did? Could you achieve the same results in another of the tainted?"

"I don't see why not," Chris said. "That is, assuming it's the hormones and not something specific to Dani's kid, with enough time and a pregnant sidekick..." She snorted and leaned her elbows on the dark green- and gold-flecked countertop. "Hell, or I could just get knocked up and be a one-woman show, traveling around the world, curing Crazies at every stop."

Which reminded Anna—she owed Chris a debt, one that could never be repaid. Not ever. But the least Anna could do was acknowledge what she'd done and express her sorrow for the catastrophic loss Chris had endured.

Anna licked her lips, then cleared her throat and placed her palms on the counter, one on either side of her cutting board. "Listen, Chris..." She could hear her voice quaking, could feel moisture forming between her palms and the granite, but she refused to drop her gaze from Chris's honest blue eyes. "Last spring, when Danielle was in the Colony, she mentioned that the Virus...that you lost your sons, and—"

"Stop." Chris's voice was quiet, thick with emotion. Her eyes had strayed from Anna's, and she now stared out the bay window in the breakfast nook. "I understand why you did what you did, and I understand that if you hadn't done it, that bastard would've found someone else who could." She looked at Anna, stared through her eyes and into her soul. "You were a tool, a weapon. You were used, that's all."

Anna opened her mouth, but realized she had no idea how to respond, so she closed it again.

Chris reached across the island and covered one of Anna's hands with hers. "As far as I'm concerned, any mother who claims she wouldn't watch the world burn to protect her kids is either lying or a crap mom. Either way, she's nobody I want to know."

Anna's throat tightened, and she gritted her teeth together to prevent her chin from quivering. "But I didn't just watch the world burn." She swallowed roughly. "I set it on fire."

"Like I said..." Chris gave Anna's hand a squeeze, then withdrew. "You were just the match. It was Herodson who started the fire."

A masculine throat-clearing came from the doorway to the dining room. Both women turned their heads to find Tom leaning against the doorframe.

Anna felt her eyes open wide. How much of their conversation had he heard? What would he think of her if he'd seen her giving in to weakness, almost breaking down in tears? What conclusions might he draw, and how could he use them to toy with her in the future?

Except...this was Tom, not Gregory. Tom wouldn't study her weaknesses, wouldn't file them away to use against her later. Tom wouldn't try to manipulate her. At least, the old Tom, the Tom she'd loved so long ago—still loved, if she was willing to be honest with herself—would never do any of those things. But she didn't know *this* Tom, not anymore.

"Sorry to interrupt," Tom said, his voice gentle. He looked at Chris first, but his attention quickly switched to Anna. "I'd like to talk."

"Uh…" Anna looked from Tom to Chris and back, feeling utterly at a loss for words. "We're sort of, um…"

"No, no," Chris said with a quick wave of the hand. "It's fine." She started toward the mudroom. "I need to track down Harper for, um, this thing we're working on anyway." Seconds later, the back door opened, then closed, and Chris was gone.

Tom took a step into the kitchen, just one, small step. Immediately, Anna could feel her heart rate pick up speed, could feel her chest constrict and her head begin to throb with the beginnings of a panic attack. She couldn't do this, not now.

"Anna, I just want to talk," Tom said quietly, and he took another step into the room. Toward her.

She wasn't ready for this; she couldn't handle it, not right now. He had every right to hate her, but she couldn't bear to hear him say it.

Tom's eyes scoured her face, and she knew exactly what he was doing.

"Please," she whispered, "stay out of my mind. I—"

He shook his head, his eyes soft and beseeching. "Honey, why are you panicking?"

Anna's chest rose and fell too quickly, and beads of sweat sprang to life on her forehead and the back of her neck. "Tom," she said hoarsely. "Please…I can't breathe."

"I'm not going to hurt you, Anna." Another step. "I just—"

She slapped her hands on the countertop, making her palms sting. "But you are hurting me," she wailed. Anna was shaking uncontrollably, her whole body coated in a clammy sheen of sweat. "Just being in the same room with you hurts me!"

Tom froze, still several steps away, his face stricken.

Needing to move, Anna turned away from him and stalked around the island to the other side, where she began to pace. "I know what you must think of me—how you must feel about me. And I don't blame you. I get it, I really do. After everything I've done…after everything with Gregory." She ran both of her hands through her hair, tugging when she reached the ends. "But still, every time you're near me, all I can think about is how much you must despise me, and it's like I'm being gutted." She turned away from him, covering her face with her hands as she tried to calm herself, to breathe.

"But I don't despise you," Tom said so quietly that Anna was certain she'd misheard him.

"What—" She peered at him over her shoulder. "What did you just say?"

Tom returned her stare, so earnest, so sturdy, so sure. He stole her breath when he looked at her like that. "I don't despise you, Anna."

All she could do was continue to stare at him, owllike with all of her stunned blinking and standing still.

Slowly, like a cautious birder stalking his quarry, Tom made his way around the island. "I've hated the circumstances that made you leave, and I've hated the situation you were forced into, but never, not once in all the years since you left, have I *ever* thought badly of you." He stopped within arm's reach of her, his lips curving into a quiet, gentle smile. "I loved the woman I married thirty years ago, and I'm sure that if you give me the chance to get to know the woman standing right here in front of me, I'll love her just as much."

Anna's chest no longer felt constricted, but rather too full. She no longer felt the need to flee, but worried she might float away. She'd loved Tom since the day she first met him, had hated the day she'd first left him, thought she'd die of a broken heart when she saw him again years later, and now he was standing in front of her, in this place where they might actually have a chance to be together, and she thought her heart might burst with joy. Silent tears turned to quiet sobs.

Tom moved closer and cupped the side of her face. She didn't flinch from fear his touch would turn painful, didn't have to pretend she enjoyed it. She choked a small laugh and shut her eyes, allowing the feeling of his hand against her cheek to sear into her memory. "So," Tom said timidly, "what do you say?"

"I—I don't—"

"C'mon, Doc," Tom said, resurrecting his nickname for her from long ago. He winked at her, shedding decades of physical and emotional wear and tear in a millisecond. "Let me buy you dinner?"

Anna laughed, wiping the tears from her cheeks with shaking hands. She felt so giddy, the noise simply burst out of her. "I think it's free."

Tom grinned, wide and proud. "A few months working the farm'll convince you otherwise."

Which meant he wanted her to stay. Anna couldn't help but smile up at him. Because now, more than anything, she wanted to stay, too.

"So, that's pretty much it," Anna said. "Children born of parents with Abilities usually have some combination of their parents' Abilities, though the rule's not universal." She sent a fond glance to Peter, sitting beside her at the large kitchen table everyone had gathered around for her second dinner on the farm. "And Abilities can start to show up in odd ways throughout the pregnancy, almost making it seem as though the mother has additional Abilities for a while, but it doesn't always happen in noticeable ways." She shrugged, meeting Dani's attentive eyes on the far side of the table. "Again, there's no universal rule, and it's not like there have been that many cases to study. Just myself and a few others…"

She took one final bite of stew, then set her spoon down in her bowl and sat back with a contented sigh, feeling overwhelmingly satisfied. She'd had a second helping of the delicious venison stew, and she *never* had seconds. But there was just something about fresh food—freshly caught, freshly gathered, freshly grown—that made it taste better than anything she'd eaten inside the Colony.

"Is everyone finished?" Becca asked from her spot opposite Anna, squished between Mase and Camille. Anna could hardly believe they could all fit, regardless of how large of a farm table it was. But somehow, they managed.

Murmurs of assent filled the room, accompanied by nods and a few grunts.

"Well, then," Becca said, the dusk light streaming in through the windows adding golden highlights to her brunette hair. "There's something I need to share with you all."

Silence descended, sucking the comfort and good spirits out of the room.

Becca looked around the table, scanning the faces of her companions. Finally, she cleared her throat. "My visions are complicated." A small frown line appeared between her eyebrows. "And they're not always certain or clear." She sat up straighter, commanding the room. "But there is one I have known for some time now. One I have been waiting for, and...dreading." She nodded, as though assuring herself that this was the right time, the right place, the right *way* to share her vision.

Anna noticed Dani and Mase sharing a meaningful glance across the table.

Becca took a deep breath. "Everything we've done has been leading up to this, and I know you won't be happy with me for not sharing this vision earlier, but I swear, if I had, all would have been lost. Everything that's happened *needed* to happen. I'm certain of it."

Anna didn't dare breathe. She doubted anyone did.

Except for Becca. Taking another deep breath, the serene young woman closed her eyes. "General Herodson...he's coming for us. He'll be here soon, and he won't be alone."

39

ZOE

DECEMBER 17, 1AE

THE FARM, CALIFORNIA

"General Herodson…he's coming for us. He'll be here soon, and he won't be alone."

A collective inhale followed Becca's announcement, and the group roused—tensing, straightening, standing—then raised fretful voices that filled the dining room.

"What the hell, Becca?"

"Shit!"

"You knew the whole time?"

"This isn't fucking happening…"

"How the hell could you keep this from us?"

"How soon is *soon*?"

"Saw that coming a mile away."

My own heart rate jolted into panic mode, but it was the reality that this was going to happen that jump-started my fear, not that his coming was a surprise. Jake squeezed my knee beneath the table.

I stared at my mom and Peter, who were next to me for a moment, then glanced at my dad and Jason. While Jason's jaw flexed, he said nothing. I wasn't the only one unsurprised by

Becca's revelation. It would only have been a matter of time before Herodson reappeared, harassing and threatening our family again. This time, I knew, would be different. One way or another, I felt certain that this time would be the last.

Becca's gaze darted around like she was second-guessing herself. "It had to be this way," she said, almost too quietly to hear.

Mase stood up, stoic and protective. "Listen," he said flatly, his voice commanding the room. Sanchez's hand was on her hip as she stood at her seat, the other rubbing her temple. Grayson and Chris were having a quiet but animated conversation with Harper at their end of the table, while Biggs's eyes flicked frantically toward the sleeping twins in the living room. Gabe pushed his plate away from himself and rested his elbows on the table, all the while Larissa sat silent and observant, and Annie and Sam simply stared at the adults, eyes wide as they played with the remaining broth in their bowls.

"I told you, all of you, that you would need us. This is why," Becca said with more certainty.

Harper stood in silent distress, his chair scraping against the floor as he pushed it out behind him. Everyone looked at him. The look on his face summoned hot chills down my arms and up my neck, and then I saw it—still images of his vision. A mass of hostile, unfamiliar faces flashed in his mind, then a wash of crimson blood, and I felt Harper's growing fear.

"Becca's right," he said, his gaze scanning us all with a furrowed brow. "We need them. I've seen the soldiers in my dreams." When his gaze landed and stayed on Becca, he nodded. "The Re-gens are our only hope."

Sanchez scoffed, her eyes darting between Becca and Harper. "But you could've said *something* so we at least knew to start preparing for a goddamn war."

"We have children to think about now," Biggs added. "And New Bodega might be in danger, as well."

I glanced at Dani, wrapped in Jason's protective arms, both of them watching the intensity rise in the room. I wondered what churned in my brother's mind. Strangely, from Dani's mind, I didn't sense surprise, but more like a sense of understanding.

"If I had told you sooner, you would've changed the path, but not the inevitable future," Becca retorted. She pointed in the direction of the Re-gen farms a couple hills to the west. "The Re-gens wouldn't be here to help you if we'd changed course. Jason might never have been found—he might even be dead." She looked at Gabe and then at my mom. "We wouldn't have Dr. Wesley to help us, either."

My mom's eyes widened, and she took a deep breath and stood. "Becca's right. I'm the only one who might be able to stop him."

"Mom—" Peter said, but she spoke over him.

"I'll go to him. I'll leave right now." My mom looked around the room, at all the expectant faces. "I'm the one he wants, I can change his mind."

"No," Peter said, jumping out of his seat. "You can't go back there." Tears filled his eyes. "He'll kill you."

Our mom wrapped her arm around his shoulders, trying to calm him. "No he won't, sweetheart. Your father needs me. He won't hurt me, I promise." But Peter and I both knew her promise was an empty one. With the General, there were no certainties.

"What makes you think that after leaving the Colony with Jason *and* Peter, Herodson will show you any sympathy?" I asked bitterly, unwilling to consider her leaving as an option. "He knows you weren't under his mind spell, that you're immune to him. He knows he can no longer control you. Going back is suicide. It's pointless. We could use you here; you know how he thinks."

My mom's eyes shifted from me to Peter. "Sweetheart, I have to try to—"

"Wes is right," Gabe said, exhaling as he gazed around at the distraught faces staring at him. "She's the only one who stands a chance against him. He has too many men at his disposal, too many Abilities. Our best option is that she gets him to stand down."

I knew how difficult it was for Gabe to say those words, how acerbic they were on his tongue. But I couldn't allow it. "You can't send her back there," I said, standing. "You of all people know what he's capable of. She doesn't stand a chance, especially not alone. You don't even want her to go."

Gabe's fists met the tabletop and the dishes shook and clinked. "Of course I don't want her to go back there, but what other options do we have? To fight? We don't stand a chance against an army!"

"We'll think of something!" I shouted back at him. I met my dad's absent stare but looked away just as quickly. I couldn't worry about the tumultuous thoughts tumbling around in his mind when I had enough of my own to deal with. "Becca," I said, looking at her. "How much time do we have?"

Her eyes darted around the table. "I'm not sure," she said quietly. "But in my vision, Gabe and Sanchez are still a little scraped up from the accident." We all looked at them, as if their faces somehow held the answers we needed.

"We don't know if sending my mom anywhere would even help," I said, glancing around the table. "Unless Herodson has enough planes to transport his army, their caravan has already left Colorado and could be here by tomorrow."

"Let's hope to God that he's not," Chris said, and she tossed her napkin onto the table as she stood. "We need to prepare for him to be on our doorstep at any moment."

Becca cleared her throat. But with all the noise, no one heard her begin to speak.

"Quiet!" Mase shouted, and again, everyone froze.

Clearing her throat again, Becca said, "You forget that his numbers are smaller and his loyalties are divided. Although I do not know how many still follow him, I know they are few in comparison to before. We have the Re-gens now. We have Dr.

Wesley. We have strong Abilities and the advantage of him being *here*, where he's not as familiar with the layout of the land."

"Where *is* here, Becca? The farm?" my dad asked, his voice calm and steady. "Will it happen in New Bodega?"

"You will encounter him on the road in the farmlands, the one lined with eucalyptus—"

"Lakeville," Jason said. "It's here in Petaluma; the trees start a few miles off the freeway."

"It's the quickest route to us," Jake added, being all too familiar with the roads from his weeks of searching for Jason.

Becca nodded. "It will be morning when he comes." Both Jake and Jason scooted their chairs backward and stood.

"Chris, Sanchez. Let's get an inventory of our ammo," Jason said, falling back into his normal role as our fearless leader. "Dad, I'll need you and Gabe to set up a trip into town. Dani, maybe you can help them make contact. We're going to need all the help we can get."

I grabbed Jake's arm. "I think it's time for that transfusion now," I said.

Jake nodded. "Tell Harper to get everything ready."

I lay bleary-eyed in my bed, recovering. Jake, exhausted and regenerating, slept beside me. The fact that Jake was asleep, knowing the General and his armed forces could be here in the morning, was a testament to how much of a toll the transfusions took on him, no matter how little blood he needed to give. I brushed my fingertips over the tanned skin of his hand splayed out on my stomach. I was beginning to understand that while blood was vital and kept us all alive, it was more than that to Jake—it was his life force. I could *feel* its energy and animation as it cycled throughout my body, refueling me. It was like I'd been running on fumes, and now I felt full and sated. The sensation was

371

only a glimpse of his raw vitality and strength, and it felt other-worldly.

I peered up at the ceiling. The room was darkening as the final rays of sun slinked behind the hills, and the candlelight cast flickering shadows all around. I knew I should try to get some rest too, though it seemed impossible. According to the animals, the General wasn't close—at least not yet—but that didn't matter. He was coming, and that was enough to scare the exhaustion from every cell in my body.

There was a gentle rap on the bedroom door, and it slowly creaked open. My mom poked her head in. When she saw Jake lying beside me, she straightened. "I didn't mean to bother you," she whispered. "Since the door was open a smidge, I thought I'd check on you."

"He's dead to the world," I said quietly, nodding to Jake. "You can come in if you want."

Tentatively, my mom stepped inside with a steaming mug in her hand, and I sat up against the pillows.

"Gabe showed me the herb garden, and I saw the chamomile. I figured you could use some." She set the mug on my nightstand. "It's what Peter likes to drink on his bad nights, when he can't sleep. Danielle said you preferred coffee, but I didn't think that was—"

"Tea's perfect," I said, cutting in. "Thanks, Mom."

Her eyes widened infinitesimally, and she lowered herself to the edge of the bed.

I frowned. "Should I not call you that?" I asked, feeling a returning tightness in my chest. "I won't if—"

She shook her head, her dark hair swooshing against her face. My hair was still longer than hers, at least in the front where it touched my collarbone, and I wondered if she'd ever let her bob grow past her jaw, down past her shoulders like the picture I'd seen of her from so long ago.

She peered down at her hands clasped in her lap. "Of course

you can call me Mom," she said, finally looking at me. "I'm just surprised you want to, after everything."

The last time I'd seen her she'd ripped my heart out and refused to be a part of our family. But so much had happened since then, and all of that changed...

Tears, once again, could not be kept at bay, though I tried to blink them away. I worked to steady my breath before I spoke. "Having you back," I started and took another deep breath. "That's all I've ever wanted...a mom. *My* mom." I stared down at my fingernails, longer than usual, as I picked restlessly at them. I sniffed and wiped away a stray tear. *Pull your shit together, Zoe.* But I couldn't. I was only just grasping the fact that the biggest battle of my life so far was finally over, and my mom was sitting right in front of me, tears in her eyes, too. More tears came, and I covered my face with my hands. "I'm sorry. I'm a mess."

"Oh, Zoe," she said, and her warm arms wrapped around me. "I'm so sorry," she whispered as she stroked the back of my hair. "I didn't want to leave you. It was the hardest thing I've ever done, you have no idea—I'm so sorry." She rocked me back and forth, and I could feel her chest heaving against mine as she held me, *consoled* me, like the mother I'd always needed. "I'm so sorry," she repeated, and I tightened my hold on her. "Shhh, I'm here now," she whispered, and soon my tears began to cease. My mom was there in front of me, holding me.

I let out a small laugh, barely able to believe the turn of events, and pulled away. I reached for the box of tissue on the nightstand. "Dani says I get wayward snot," I said, half-jokingly. I plucked a tissue, then handed my mom the box. "Apparently it runs in the family."

My mom choked out an emotional laugh and took a tissue. "I should let you rest."

"It's no use," I said and blew my nose. "There's too much going on to sleep. Too many things that need to get done and plans to make. And I'm already feeling better."

"You need to rest."

"No, I need to help."

My mom's eyes narrowed, and she leaned forward. "Don't make me get your brother," she threatened. "Or Danielle."

I gaped at her. "You wouldn't."

She nodded. "If you want me here, you'll have to get used to the phrase 'Mother knows best,' just like Peter's had to do." She smiled.

"Wow, you fit in already," I said and leaned back against my pillow. "There's no need to tell, I'll stay here until Jake wakes up at least."

My mom's smile widened in victory, then faltered, and her teal eyes were cast in worry. "I know all of this is my fault, but I promise you, Zoe, I won't let Gregory hurt you, or your brothers. I've—"

"I don't blame you," I said. "Not for this. I sort of expected it, actually. You getting away from him that easily..." I shook my head, wishing I'd been wrong. "He's been in the shadows my whole life. I'm just glad I'm old enough to fight back with you this time. All of us can, as a family." I glanced at Jake, his back to us now as he snored softly. "I know it's selfish, and I hate that this is happening, that there's absolutely no guarantee any of us are going to survive the next couple days, but I'm glad you left him and that place. I'm glad you brought Peter here, and I'm glad that you and Dad are talking again, that we're all together. It's worth it to me." I shut my eyes as my head started pounding.

"Here," my mom said. I opened my eyes when she scooted closer and reached for the tea mug. "Have some of this. It's cool enough now."

I leaned forward and she brought the oversized mug to my lips. I sipped the hot liquid, loving the way it coated my throat and insides. After another sip, I leaned back again.

"Now *rest*," my mom reiterated, brushing a stray strand of hair from my eyes. Her gaze drifted over my face, and she held the ends of my hair between her fingertips. She smiled. "I always wondered about the woman you'd grow up to be," she said, though her mind seemed far away. She dropped her hand and straightened. "You and Jason are so beautiful and strong. I couldn't be prouder of you both."

She rose from the bed and smoothed her tan cardigan, glancing at Jake, then back at me. "Try to get some sleep. It's going to be a long couple of days," she said and turned to leave.

"Mom?"

She turned around. I held up the tea mug with a small smile. "Thank you," I said, though the tea wasn't all I was grateful for.

40

ANNA
DECEMBER 17, 1AE

THE FARM, CALIFORNIA

Anna stared out the nearest window in the dining room, the waning moonlight teaming up with her exhaustion and mounting nerves to trick her into seeing trespassers—attackers—where there were none. At least, not yet.

Zoe was still upstairs, resting with Jake, and the children had gone to bed in another of the upstairs bedrooms hours ago, guarded by the watchful canine duo of Jack and Cooper. Camille and Mase had made the short trip up valley to the Re-gen farms to rally the proverbial troops, leaving behind Becca as the Re-gen representative during the tiring late-night planning session.

The only others missing from the "war room" table were Danielle and Jason. The pair had slipped away to the living room to sneak in a quick power nap; Jason had insisted, and considering how exhausting Danielle's telepathy could be and how much they would depend on her for coordinating their efforts over the coming days, everyone had agreed that snatching up rest whenever possible was wise. After all, she would be their only telepathic connection to the farm while the others were away. They couldn't risk burnout, not where her invaluable Ability was concerned.

"You know him best, Anna," Sanchez said, dragging her back into a conversation she'd effectively been zoned out from for minutes. "What do you think?"

Anna rubbed her temple and glanced around at the faces surrounding the table. "I'm sorry." She smiled apologetically and shook her head. "My mind was elsewhere. What did you want to know?"

Sanchez made a visible effort to contain her frustration, taking a deep breath and just barely rolling her eyes. She was so very military it was almost comical to Anna. "Is everything we're doing pointless? Isn't Herodson going to be prepared for *us* being prepared for him, and have tactics and strategies in place to counter anything we might do?"

Again, Anna shook her head. "He'll assume that I'll be expecting him to come after me at some point—I did betray him, after all—but nothing more specific than that." Her eyebrows drew together. "I'm not sure I follow your thinking."

Sanchez gestured, with more than a little hostility, toward Becca. "We've got his favorite crystal ball, so doesn't that mean he knows that we know he's coming *now*?"

"Ah…" Anna smiled broadly, and Sanchez blinked in confusion. "I see where you're mistaken. No, he won't know, at least not because of Becca's presence here. He thinks she's dead," Anna said, and a quick scan of her companions' surprised faces told her that nobody had considered that possibility. Even Becca wore the telltale raised eyebrows, wide eyes, and parted lips. "After Danielle escaped, I stumbled upon one of Herodson's creatures, Clara—I believe some of you are familiar with her—attempting to kill Zoe. It was Clara who ended up dead instead, and wanting to sever as many ties as possible between your group and Gregory, *and* seeing that Clara was roughly the same size and build as Becca, I burned her body until it was unrecognizable, then showed it to Gregory, claiming the body belonged to Becca."

"And he just took your word for it?" Sanchez asked.

Anna arched one brow. Quite the skeptic, that Sanchez. "Why wouldn't he? He believed he had a double hold on me, one on my mind and one on my heart. Of course, I also offered to do a DNA test to verify the body's identity." She smiled primly. "The results were quite conclusive, as I'm sure you can imagine."

At the end of the table, Gabe started chuckling. "Did you show him my charred remains, too, Wes?"

"I think—" Daniel began.

"That would've been pushing it," Anna said, shaking her head yet again. "I decided that I'd rather he think you were with my children than Becca. I couldn't have him start doubting my claims; it would've been too risky." She met Gabe's clever blue eyes. "He knew that you, Camille, and Mase left with Danielle—assumed you'd been the one to help them escape—but I gambled that even the three of you together wouldn't be enough to rouse his vindictive side, not like the urge to seek retribution from Becca would've been, had he believed her to still be breathing." Anna felt a sudden chill as she thought aloud, "Gregory is a man who acts on need, not on anger. Gabe's betrayal angered him, but Becca's would've been, well…"

Everyone eyed Anna, including Becca herself, clearly expecting more.

She sighed. "Becca is—*was*—one of the first successful Regens. She was with him the longest, a testament to his moving one step closer to achieving his ultimate goal—the Great Transformation." Anna swallowed thickly. "Gregory doesn't like to lose assets, especially when the loss threatens his grand plans. And you, Gabriel, while clearly a valuable ally, weren't the only person Gregory had under his thumb who could enter dreams. His plans were achievable enough without you." Anna could only imagine how Gregory had reacted when he finally realized that she'd left him—that, in his eyes, she'd betrayed him yet again.

"Clever, as usual," Gabe said with a bow of his head.

"Necessary," Anna countered. "On top of Becca's importance to him, the night Becca helped you and Danielle escape was undeniable proof that Gregory has weaknesses, that he could be beaten. Or, at least, that he isn't all-powerful, and that fighting against him isn't always a death sentence. He wouldn't have been able to let such an extreme betrayal stand; he would've had no choice but to come after her—after all of you. It's not in his nature to let something like that go, not when it weakens his very position."

"Might it be wise to—" Daniel said, trying to interject again.

"Just like he's doing with you," Chris said, leaning back in her chair on the opposite side of the table. She stretched, then crossed her arms over her chest. "Which you knew he would do. It's why you stayed with him for so long. It wasn't just for Peter; it was for Tom and Zoe and Jason, too, wasn't it—you knew it would lead to this."

Under the table, Tom's hand found Anna's. As he laced his fingers with hers, she felt some of her anxiety and tension abate.

"You've been struck by an arrow," Daniel said. It was his third attempt to enter the conversation, and though he hadn't spoken noticeably louder, his voice reverberated throughout the room, demanding everyone's attention. Larissa, Carlos, and Vanessa actually glanced down at their own bodies, looking for Daniel's ghostly arrow. "Imagine that, despite Harper's wishes to remove the arrow and treat the wound immediately, you keep pushing him away, demanding to know who shot it and why. Did the shooter poison the arrow, too? What kind of poison might he have used?" Daniel looked at Harper. "What would you tell that patient?"

Harper looked around the room, shifting in his chair and laughing under his breath. "Um...to shut up and let me work?"

Titters and laughter filled the dining room. Daniel joined good-naturedly, but his hawklike focus switched to Anna. "And why might it be wise for you, the patient, to listen to the good doctor?"

Anna took a deep breath, not only recognizing the proverb and understanding his meaning, but silently thanking him for his much-needed lesson in what truly mattered. They needed to stop focusing on unnecessary whys and hows of the events leading up to their current predicament and put their collective mental fortitude into the whens and wheres and hows of the upcoming struggle. *That* was what mattered, far more than what used to be. "Because I'd likely die otherwise," Anna said in answer to the question.

"Ah, yes…" Daniel sat back in his seat, interlocking his fingers and resting his hands on the table. "Interesting, that." Slowly, he nodded to himself. "Very interesting…"

Chris snorted. "Alright, wise one," she said with affectionate sarcasm. "We'll get back on task."

Standing, Sanchez clapped her hands together and rubbed them back and forth. "Alright, let's get an action plan going." She moved to stand in front of the whiteboard that took up nearly half of the room's interior wall and picked up a dry-erase marker. "Start throwing out tasks, people; we'll assign and prioritize as we go."

There was a long, drawn-out moment where everyone looked around the table at each other awkwardly. Finally, and somewhat surprisingly, Tom chimed in with, "I think it's safe to say that Abilities will be a main element of Herodson's battle strategy." He looked at Anna. "Is it possible to make neutralizer for all of us?" He raised a shoulder, then let it fall. "It would be nice to know we're at least protected from mind control and the like." He frowned. "Unless you and Jason would be able to protect us by nulling?"

Brow furrowed, Anna shook her head. "We can only create a sort of nulling field for those nearest to us—within a several-yard radius. But, as for the neutralizer…" She turned her attention to Gabriel. "Have you managed to collect any of the equipment I listed in the instructions I included with my letters?"

"Just a centrifuge and a couple of microscopes."

Anna frowned and nodded at the same time. "There used to be a couple of labs in Petaluma that would've had the other things I'd need, but they might not be around anymore. I'll need a telephone book—not just for Petaluma, but the whole Sonoma Valley. Santa Rosa is even more likely to have what I need."

Sanchez was already writing "SCAVENGING TRIP TO PET/SR – NEUTRALIZER" on the board. Finishing, she pointed at Gabriel and Anna with the end of the marker. "You two should go, and you'll need some muscle." Her eyes landed on Biggs.

The soldier-turned-father shook his head. "I think I'd be better utilized spearheading the trip into New Bodega. They know me. They trust me. If it's me who asks for help, they're more likely to give it."

Sanchez wrote "DIPLO TRIP TO NB – REQUEST AID" and added Biggs's name underneath, then added her own name to Anna's and Gabriel's. "I'll go with the scientists, then." She added Jason's name as well. "He's not here, so he doesn't get a say."

Chris snickered. "We'll see about that..."

"We'll do a quick run for ammo and weapons in Santa Rosa, too," she said, ignoring Chris and adding "– ARMS" to the first task on the board. "We should be able to find plenty, since the New Bodega scavenging teams have only cleaned out the western half of the city."

"I'll go with Biggs," Daniel said quietly.

"You can use your silver tongue to sweet-talk Bethany into helping us," Chris teased.

Daniel blushed and cleared his throat. "Well, I don't know about that..."

The room filled with tension-relieving laughter, which seemed to unseal everyone's lips and open the floodgates for ideas. It wasn't long until the board was filled—Sanchez had been forced to tape several laminated maps up on the wall, using their backs for additional note-taking space.

After nearly an hour, Sanchez set her dry erase marker on the table. "Alright, should we break up and let the stragglers know what their responsibilities are going to be?"

"And then get some rest," Harper added. "Sleep deprivation might gain us more prep time, but we'll be fuzzy-brained and ineffective. Everyone gets a full night's sleep tonight. Doctor's orders." He shot a quick glance in Becca's direction. "Assuming you're certain we're not under threat of imminent attack first thing in the morning…"

Becca shook her head. "Sanchez and Gabe were more healed in my vision. Besides, the animals will warn us, I've seen that much, and since we've heard nothing from them yet, and since morning is fast approaching, I think it's safe to say they won't be coming *this* morning. We have some time to rest and prepare."

"So we need to keep Dani on alert," Chris commented.

"Not Dani," Becca said. "It is Annie who will warn us of Fath —General Herodson's impending arrival. I've seen it."

Quizzical looks were exchanged around the table until, for the first time since dinner, Vanessa spoke. "The Tahoe pack— Snowflake and the other wolves—that's who'll tell Annie, isn't it?"

Becca shrugged.

"It makes sense," Carlos said. "She still talks to them every day. At least, that's what Dani told me. Her link to them is really strong."

"Right, so…" Harper scooted his chair backward and stood. "Let's spread the word about duties and hit the hay."

Sanchez rubbed her hands together once more. "Yeah…that's not going to happen. I'm way too amped up to sleep."

Harper settled a stern look on her. "Try, or we'll have Gabe here put you to sleep for a few hours."

Sanchez opened her mouth, but before saying anything, she closed it again, shoulders slumping. It seemed she realized there was no way around it. One way or another, Harper would see to it that everyone rested while they could.

Chris joined Harper, curling her arm around his back and resting her head on his shoulder. "We'll pop in to check on Zoe and Jake and pass on their duties and such," she said, finishing with a yawn.

"And Jason and Dani...?" Sanchez prompted.

Chair legs scratched on the hardwood floor, throats cleared, eye contact was avoided. It was obvious that disturbing Jason—or, rather, disturbing Danielle while she rested under Jason's watchful eye—wasn't something anyone was eager to do.

Sighing, Anna raised her hand partway. "I'll do it," she said with a sniff.

But when she reached the doorway into the living room and laid her eyes on the expectant couple, sound asleep on the couch, Danielle nestled against Jason, Anna couldn't bring herself to actually step into the room. Not because she was afraid of Jason's irritation; she didn't know when her son and daughter-in-law would have another chance to steal such a peaceful, intimate slumber together. She wanted to preserve this moment for them. She wished she could make it last forever.

"Let them be," Tom said from behind Anna, his voice barely above a whisper but making Anna suck in a startled breath nonetheless. "There's nothing they could do tonight that can't be saved for the morning."

Anna nodded, in absolute agreement with Tom, but she was also faced with a bit of a conundrum—where to sleep? The couch had been her bed until now. "I suppose Peter and I could sleep in their cottage," she said, thinking aloud.

"Nonsense." Tom rested his hands on her shoulders.

Anna held her breath. Was he going to ask her to stay with him tonight?

"Peter's already upstairs in Mase and Camille's room," Tom said. "There's plenty of room for both of you there."

Anna exhaled, both relieved and disappointed.

Tom's strong, callused hands started massaging her shoulders, and Anna had a hard time holding in a groan. Her head lolled forward, her eyelids drooping.

"Or," Tom whispered, "you could stay with me."

41

DANI
DECEMBER 18, 1AE

THE FARM, CALIFORNIA

"I wish I could come with you guys," I said, my face smooshed against the front of Jason's damp raincoat. It was a chilly morning, and the half-risen sun didn't seem to be making much of an impact on the clouds or drizzle.

"I know, Red." Jason's arms tightened around me, and he pressed his lips against the top of my head in a prolonged kiss. "But," he said as he pulled away just enough to not choke on my hair while he spoke, "Jack'll be with us, so you'll be there in spirit."

He had no idea how true his words were. I mean, he sort of knew, but nobody really knew...except for Annie...and other drifters...and maybe Peter, now, if he'd absorbed my Ability like he seemed to do with everyone else's. It was just one of those things a person had to experience to understand.

Not that I told Jason that. Instead, I nodded against his chest and sighed. Jack would be going with Jason on the scavenging trip up to Petaluma and Santa Rosa, along with Jason's mom and Gabe to head up the search for scientific do-dads. Sanchez, Jake, and

Larissa would also be joining them for added protection. With Jack accompanying them, I'd be remotely aware of where they were and what they were doing through our passive, ever-active bond. And through Cooper, who'd already left with Zoe, Tom, Grayson, and Biggs for New Bodega, I'd be able to drop in every now and again to check on their status without actually interrupting their progress. I would be, for the day, a glorified phone operator.

Jason inhaled and exhaled, deep and slow. "I hate leaving you, even just for the day." He kissed the top of my head once more. "Damn prophecies..."

I laughed bitterly and pulled away enough that I could peer up at him. "Tell me about it." Sure, many of us owed our lives to Becca's prophecies, but still. I bared my teeth in an attempted smile. "I know leaving the farm before the baby comes might kill me, but staying here for another four months is definitely going to drive me batty."

Jason's dimple appeared as he suppressed a smile. "Well, lucky for you, Vanessa's stall just opened up..."

"Don't even!" I said, laughing and swatting his arm. "You're such a turd sometimes."

"Ah," Jason said, finally flashing a smile. "But I'm your turd."

I rolled my eyes, my chest shaking with barely contained amusement. "You are ridiculous...like, the biggest dork in the world." I shook my head, chuckling. "Why am I the only one who seems to see that?"

Jason's smile broadened to a grin. "Because you're the only one I *let* see it." His eyes softened, heated, melted me. "Because you're the only one I love."

And I was suddenly a puddle.

I reached up and interlocked my fingers behind his neck so I could pull his face down to my level. I pressed—no, smashed—his lips against mine, kissing him more fiercely than I'd done in ages. "I love you, too, you big turd," I said against his lips. "So be careful out there and come back to me." I kissed him again, hard. "Or. Else."

Jason made a noise that was part laugh, part groan, and utterly hoarse. He pulled away, and I watched his eyes search mine, trace over the lines of my face, memorize me. Finally, he smiled, just a little. "Yes, ma'am."

And as he walked toward his horse, Nameless, as he rode out after the others, who were already almost to the end of the driveway, gravel crunching under hooves and the wheels of their cart, all I could think was, *Come back to me...come back to me...come back to me...*

I was Jack.

I trotted along beside Mother's mate, looking around, listening, guarding my pack-mates, who had ventured into another large two-leg cave.

The sad woman, who I knew from Mother was her mate's own mother, emerged from the two-leg cave. "No luck here, either," she said, and because of Mother's presence, I understood her meaning. Sort of. She shook her head and made one of those sharp two-leg noises that was like she was tired or sad. "I'm not sure how far we'd have to travel to find a thermocycler or a spectrophotometer..."

"It was a long shot anyway," Mother's mate said. "We'll focus on weapons and ammo from here on out."

I barked my agreement, wagging my tail. Or perhaps it was Mother's agreement. It was so hard to tell where she ended and I began when she was running with me. I wagged my tail harder. I loved when she was running with me.

I felt her start to pull away, start to separate herself from me. I felt her sadness, her hesitancy. She didn't want to leave. She never did.

But still, leave she did.

I inhaled deeply and opened my eyes, then leaned back in surprise. "What the—" Annie's pixie face with those serene, too-wise baby blues was mere inches from mine. I clutched my chest and worked on slowing my suddenly rapid breathing. "Sweetie, we talked about you doing that—specifically, you *not* doing it, remember?"

Nodding, Annie crawled into my lap, snaking her arms around my neck and nuzzling the crook of my shoulder. She was such a little creature sometimes. A nice, usually gentle creature, but a not-quite-human creature, nonetheless.

I sighed and wrapped my arms around her, holding her close. I couldn't be irritated with her when she was being so sweet and cuddly. "Any word from Snowflake's pack?" I asked, referring to the Tahoe pack's alpha, the wolf I'd spoken with last spring when I'd stumbled across Annie in the woods by Lake Tahoe and had promised to raise her as my own.

Annie shook her head, her wild blonde curls tickling the side of my face. I smoothed them down before they could reach my nose and trigger a sneezing fit. "Snowflake let the other packs know," she said, yawning. One glance at the sky, at the sun just barely glowing through the cloud cover, told me it was past time for my wild child's afternoon nap—or rather, what accounted for a nap with a little girl who only drifted, never dreamed. I could've used a nap as well, but my mind wouldn't allow rest, not while Jason and Zoe were away and our immediate future was so uncertain.

"Did you tell her not to interfere?" I asked, biting my lip. The last thing I wanted was for such beautiful, noble hunters to fall casualty in a war that had nothing to do with them. "Her pack-mates just need to keep a watchful eye and let us know when they see more people. We don't want them to get hurt."

Annie nodded and yawned once more. "Snowflake knows," she said, rubbing her face against my shoulder sleepily.

I took a deep breath and started the awkward process of standing up with a not-so-small child latched to my front. "Alright, monster, let's get you settled in your nest so you can drift away."

"Can I go with Jack?" She knew to ask whenever she wanted to drift with Jack or Wings, just as I did whenever I planned on slipping into one of her favorite animals. We'd developed a drifter's code of conduct, if you will. It sounded silly, but it was especially important in moments like this, because Annie drifting with Jack would effectively cut me off from him.

"Not today, sweetie," I told her as I carried her down the porch stairs. I couldn't afford to be out of communication with either of my canine emissaries today. "You can choose anyone but Jack or Coop."

She made a very doglike whining noise, and I pulled away and craned my neck so I could see her face. Her bottom lip protruded in an adorable, if dramatic, pout.

I gave her "the look"—my version of Grams's go-to don't-push-me expression.

Annie, strange child that she was, pouted for a moment longer, then flashed me a brilliant grin. "'Kay. I'll go with Snowflake."

"What a good idea," I said, leaning in to press a kiss to her forehead. We reached the cottage's front door a moment later, and it wasn't long until Annie was peacefully drifting in her nest of pillows and blankets and I was heading back out into the patchy afternoon sunshine to check on our farm-based preparations.

I followed the sounds of grunts and shouts to the eastern pasture, just on the other side of the pond and its wall of willows and tall, leafy trees. My eyes widened as I took in the veritable army of Re-gens scattered in twos and threes throughout the overgrown hayfield, having made the short trek down valley to our farm to learn from our relative combat experts. I'd known there were nearly a hundred Re-gens, plus there were several dozen of the Tahoe folks thrown in the mix today, but I hadn't seen the Re-gens all together since they first arrived, a shambling, muddy horde, so many months ago.

We'd all wondered what Becca's eerily recited words had meant the day she'd led them to our doorstep: *"We need your help, and one day soon, you will need ours."* Now we knew, and I was happy as hell to have them with us, fighting for a mutual cause— our lives. With Dr. Wesley's insider knowledge that the General had *maybe* a couple hundred even remotely battle-worthy people at his disposal, and that he was too cautious not to leave the bare minimum required to guard the Colony behind in Colorado—at least sixty of his soldiers and guards—it was looking like we'd at least have a chance.

I spotted Chris several dozen yards away, her blonde ponytail swaying and bobbing as she demonstrated a dodge-and-lunge evasion move for a handful of captivated Re-gens. While Becca had been trained in self-defense back at the Colony, similar training hadn't been a part of standard Re-gen "programing." Being Herodson's favorite, she'd received special, additional training alongside a few others. If the rest of the Re-gens wanted to stand and fight against their previous captor—and the massive turnout to Chris's voluntary combat training session pointed over-whelmingly to a "hell yeah"—then they needed to learn, and fast. Luckily, being quick learners was one of the Re-gens' most wide-spread, dependable characteristics.

My galoshes squished and squelched in the mud beneath the grass as I picked my way across the field toward Chris, nodding hello to people as I passed.

"Dani!" Mase called, his gravelly voice deep and booming.

I turned halfway, barely catching my balance before I ended up on my butt in the mud.

"Careful," Mase said, jogging my way. "It's slick out here."

I dug the heel of my rubber boot into the soft, slippery earth. "At least it's a good cushion for all of the inevitable falls."

Mase nodded. "The hay, too. That's why we chose this spot."

A crease appeared on his dark, stony face, just between his eyebrows. "You shouldn't be out here. It's too cold, and it might rain, and—"

"Jason?" I asked, eyebrows raised. I folded my arms over my chest. "He told you to keep an eye on me, didn't he?"

Mase smiled, but the friendly expression did little to soften the stubborn glint in his murky gray eyes. "He *asked* me to look after you while he was away." Mase placed his hand on my arm, his fingers engulfing my relatively weak limb easily.

I opened my mouth to argue, but Mase cut me off before I could even get started. "We've got two groups out on missions today, and you're the telepathic communication hub. They're depending on you being ready and able to communicate with them if necessary. You need to be at full strength."

He had a point, so I didn't complain when he started leading me back toward the pasture fence. "Why don't you hang out with Carlos and Cami in the house?"

I shook my head. "Carlos kicked me out."

Mase gave me a sidelong glance, eyebrows raised.

"He doesn't like having non-Re-gens around when he's doing electrotherapy." I shrugged. "Especially not when there are others administering it, too." He and the other sparklers had taken over the living room midmorning as their electrotherapy headquarters while they carried out a massive effort to provide a daily electrotherapy session with each Re-gen until the General arrived. Carlos couldn't do it, risking overexerting his Ability and burning out for who knew how long, because of his part of our defensive strategy to take Herodson's vehicles out of play with an electromagnetic pulse. He had, however, insisted on coordinating the effort.

Mase nodded thoughtfully. "I forget sometimes that electrotherapy affects you normals differently."

I snorted. Differently was an understatement; I knew firsthand, and thanks to Mase, I'd survived. "How are the Re-gens doing?

Are they nervous? Or afraid?" I asked as we headed past the farm-house and toward my little cottage.

"They're nervous—we all are," Mase said. "And I suppose you could say they're afraid, but not of getting hurt or dying."

"Oh?" Curious, I watched him as we made our way along the stone path.

"What they fear more than anything is being enslaved again," he said. "So many of us have regained so much out here, so much more than just our freedom and the right to think for ourselves, or even than our better health." He shook his head, his eyes lighting up. "Since we left the Colony, it's like we've all regained pieces of ourselves—our *old* selves. We're not the same as we were in our past lives—we know we'll never be that—but we're somewhere in between, now. We all remember more, feel more, can live more… it's not something any of us are willing to give up. We'd rather die fighting."

"Well, um…that's great." I just hoped it wouldn't come to that. After everything, the Re-gens deserved a second chance at life. We all did.

I sat in the recliner in front of the cottage's hearth, staring into the flames while my mind was elsewhere. Not drifting elsewhere, just focused. I'd spent the past few hours rallying the animal troops, so to speak, conversing with nearby coyotes, foxes, and cougars to gauge how willing or able they'd be to assist in our defenses. I was planning on reaching out to the hawks next, then the ravens and crows, the bats, the porcupines…I had a list. It was a long list.

But for the moment, I was taking a break to check in on my two-legged friends. I searched the familiar sparks of life surrounding Cooper until I found Zoe's mind. They were still within New Bodega's walls, but they were no longer stationary, as they'd been for hours during the afternoon. A quick peek through

Cooper's eyes had told me Zoe and the others were on horseback, making their way toward the gate.

"Hey, Zo."

"Hey, D," Zoe said, her mind-voice distracted.

"Am I interrupting?"

"No, no, it's just..." Zoe sighed mentally. *"I'd hoped for more. We all did."*

I bit my lip to hide a frown. *"So, not good news? I popped in a few times, but all I caught through Cooper was a lot of arguing."*

Zoe laughed bitterly. *"Arguing...tell me about it. They want to help, but they can't afford to give much aid—just a handful of volunteers and enough weapons and ammo to arm them to the teeth."* She paused, and I could practically feel her frustration. *"They're scared. They say they can't risk giving up too many of their guardsmen, especially not with the possibility of being attacked."*

"But they won't be attacked if we stop the General..."

"Trust me, we tried that argument, but our logic fell on deaf ears."

I closed my eyes and rested my head back against the cushy chair. *"Well, we can't blame them for looking out for their own."*

"But that's just it, D," Zoe said, and I could almost hear the threat of tears in her mind-voice. *"We are their own."*

42

ZOE

DECEMBER 21, 1AE

PETALUMA VALLEY, CALIFORNIA

"Feel anything yet?" Harper asked for the seventh time. He was referring to any other human minds—Crazy, Ability-altered, or other.

"No," I said, playing with Shadow's fringy mane between my fingers. He was just that in the darkness of early morning, a shadow. I leaned against him, exhaling what felt like a week's worth of anxiety. "Nothing."

Harper, Mase, my mom, and I were holed up in a barn with our four horses, hiding and waiting and growing more edgy with each passing minute.

"And nothing from Sanchez at her post," my mom stated quietly and mostly to herself. She peered out the broken door of our hideaway, alongside Lakeville Highway. It was one of our group's many hiding spots littered along the road—the route we knew Herodson would be along at any moment. Dani had checked in with a warning from our Tahoe animal friends hours ago. We'd been mostly ready then, and now we were just anxiously—and very impatiently—waiting.

The air inside the barn was musty, but the space was relatively clean and empty, a fortune not all of our scattered groups up and down the road were lucky enough to share. We were in the heart of the eucalyptus-lined portion of the road Becca had seen in her vision, though there were about seven miles between our two furthest posts. Most disturbing was that we were also only about ten miles away from the farm—our home, where Dani along with Peter, Grayson, Camille, Vanessa, Larissa, and the kids were holding down the fort. And a ways beyond that were the frightened citizens of New Bodega. But unlike them, we weren't willing to hide behind the walls, waiting. Stopping Herodson here was our greatest priority.

"*And*," I added, "no alarming communication from Dani back at the farm." I was trying to reassure them and myself. "That's a good thing."

Mase cleared his throat, and I couldn't resist the question I knew rested on all three of our tongues. "Where are the Re-gens, Mase?" I asked. They'd left hours before us, and they still hadn't arrived. All I could think about were the flashes of Harper's vision in my mind. It was times like these that I wished Harper's Ability had been more developed, easier to manipulate, so we knew what more to expect. Our numbers were pathetic without the Re-gens, and we wouldn't stand a chance if they didn't arrive soon.

Mase shrugged. "They'll be here," he said in his gravelly voice, his eyes settling on each of us a moment. He didn't speak much, but when he did it was impossible not to pay attention.

Harper grunted and leaned back against the wall. Although none of us had actually said anything aloud, we were all starting to wonder if Becca's vision might've been wrong, that the location we were supposed to head him off at might've been different. Or maybe what she'd seen had only been one of many possible futures. *What if Harper's vision is how it all ends?* Blood—a mass of soldiers... Regardless, it didn't seem likely that Herodson would take so long to get to us. Not when we had Peter, his only son, and my mom. And it definitely didn't seem like Becca to change the plans and not show up at all.

I folded my arms and leaned my head down on Shadow's back. Something didn't feel right, but there was nothing any of us could do but wait.

"I could've found what I needed for the neutralizer by now," my mom muttered, and she began to pace. She glanced up at me and paused. Shutting her eyes, she rubbed her temple. "Sorry, I know it doesn't help to dwell on what can't be changed." She looked outside again, no doubt wishing the answers would simply materialize and all our problems would go away. "I just wish we knew what the hell was going on." She was beginning to worry that the General knew our plan of attack. But I shuddered to think it, because if he did know what we had planned, we wouldn't stand a chance against him, and we would all die.

We'd scouted the surrounding area over the past thirty-two hours on foot, Dani through the animals, and me with my mind a few times. There was nothing; no one but the five other small groups of us stationed around the turnoffs and highway exits in the area, just in case Herodson decided to take a detour. With the Regens' apparent absence, I resented the New Bodega council even more for not sending proper reinforcements with us. We were too spread out like this without more help; we'd be ineffective.

I opened my mind to Biggs and the New Bodega volunteers stationed with him at the Frates Road exit about five miles up the road. There was no distressing mind chatter amongst that group yet, nothing that their one-way telepath felt necessary to report, anyway. I felt only tension and restlessness.

My focus shifted to Chris, Gabe, Carlos, and another volunteer, who were waiting in the farmhouse on the opposite side of the road. They were just as impatient as we were. Gabe was pissed off, like my mom, that they hadn't spent the time making the neutralizer, especially when our advantages were so few.

But Chris and Carlos were anxious for a completely different reason—Carlos's possibility of burnout after using his electromagnetic pulse to shut down all the vehicles within a half-mile radius of us. Although it had seemed like our greatest advantage in the beginning, I worried our plan would leave us trapped with an army of our enemies, our numbers too few.

Come on, Becca. We need you...

I peered out at the horizon. It was glowing with the promise of daybreak, and the tractors, trucks, and trailers—leftovers from the world before—began to take form in the lifting darkness. Lucky for us, we had plenty to hide behind and use for cover.

With a huff, I stepped over to my discarded crossbow and quiver. My hand found the gun strapped to my thigh, ensuring it was still there as I crouched down and pressed my fingertip against the point of one of my arrows. It was cool and sharp. Jake had made a bunch of them for my birthday in September, and I almost smiled as I mentally compared my birthday arrows to the clothes, chocolates, flowers, and drunken pub crawls that had marked my birthdays in the past. I wasn't sure birthdays mattered much anymore, but it was still the thought that counted. I slid the arrow back into my quiver, feeling strangely content with the new me.

Checking the clip in my pistol, I tried to focus on our array of Abilities, our training—our limited training. I silently groaned. Fighting in a battle? A war? We were a hodgepodge of soldiers, scientists, and displaced Ability wielders who had only *some* training at best. The thought of it made my armpits damp and my palms sweaty in spite of the cool morning.

I glanced over at Mase, who was rifling through his own bag of ammo and weapons. I was grateful he was there. The only reason he was with us instead of with Becca and the other Re-gens was because we'd needed his strength to construct the contingency barricade a half-mile past us, should any of the General's vehicles be unaffected by Carlos's electromagnetic pulse. To Mase, a few rusted vehicles, rebar, tractor wheels, and a couple dozen rotting fence posts might as well have been a stack of firewood for as easily as he'd moved them into place.

When I stared out at the pastures again, the soft hues of sunrise stretched beyond the horizon, making the overgrown, undulating grasses look to be on fire. I wondered what Dani and the others back at the farm were doing now. Were they anxiously watching the sunrise, too? Was Dani having any luck locating the Re-gens' murky minds? Or were they too far away for her to sense, like me? Despite our current shortage of Re-gens, I hoped she at least had a group of them with her. It helped give me peace of mind that the animals at the farm would protect them, too.

"Where do you think she is?" I whispered, referring to Becca. "I mean, it's been almost two days. Do you think they're okay?"

"I'm not sure," my mom said, glancing up at me. "But you know Becca as well as anyone. She's resourceful, and she's always got her eye on the endgame. If she's not here, there's a reason."

I nodded and returned my attention to the road and surrounding minds, listening, feeling. Waiting.

"Still nothing, Baby Girl?" Harper asked again.

"Do you have a hot date, Harper?" my mom joked, and I wondered if it was the fact that he'd come along to help us fight, in spite of some of us telling him he should stay back, that was bothering him. He was the closest thing we had to a medical doctor, after all, and if anything happened to him, we'd be screwed. But he'd wanted to fight; he was a soldier, first and foremost. It was what he'd said he needed to do.

But when I really looked at Harper, I saw something in his eyes and noticed the shakiness of his hands. There was something else, a fear beyond the General and his men. His anxiety felt different from ours. As soon as I opened my mind to him, I understood. He'd had another, different vision.

"What did you see?" I couldn't help the high pitch of my voice. "Is it Becca? Or—or us?"

"No, no. Nothing alarming." He snorted. "Well, not that affects the rest of you, anyway."

I glared at him through the shadows. "What does that mean?" He was hesitant to say, and I couldn't help it; I searched deeper, needing to know. It had something to do with Chris, but she was—

A wave of minds seemed to swoosh into mine, and I nearly lost my balance. "They're coming," I breathed. They were moving closer, a lot of them all around us.

"He's coming!" Sanchez shouted in our heads, closely followed by Dani's, *"Shit! Guys! A couple of the hawks just spotted movement on the road. They must've been using some kind of an illusion or something, but it's down now. Get ready, and for God's sake, be careful!"*

I sobered, my heart racing.

"There are two Humvees and two trucks headed north," Sanchez added. *"That doesn't seem like enough."*

Although smaller numbers were better odds for us, that wasn't even close to the size of the group my mom had anticipated him bringing.

"Once they're far enough past us, we'll ride toward you. Carlos, get ready. At the speed they're going, the lead vehicle will be in position in about three minutes."

"Shit," Harper grumbled and snatched up the duffel with extra ammo and first aid supplies. "That can't be all of them. There were more in my dream…and he wouldn't come with only a dozen men, not when he knows the Abilities we—"

We heard gunfire beyond us, coming from the Frates exit area.

"Biggs!" I shouted.

"They're here! Dozens of them! There are too many; we need backup!" It was the one-way telepath from New Bodega.

I could feel dozens of new minds; all of them were trained and programmed to kill. But they were fuzzy, and I assumed they were operating under the General's ingrained mind commands.

"There are too many for Biggs's team to take on alone," I rasped. "We have to help them!"

"No," Harper said, reaching for my arm. "We stick to the plan, Zoe. The people with Biggs are armed, they can handle themselves. They have to." But I heard the doubt in his words. I felt it, too. "We can't let Herodson get away from us. We have to stick to the plan and take him out, or this will never be over," he said slowly, and my mom agreed.

I nodded, but I was distracted. The sound of gunfire filled the once-still morning, each shot a roulette game, some of the pulsing minds in my head dimming, others extinguishing completely.

"As soon as Carlos immobilizes those vehicles, I need you to get into Herodson's head, Baby Girl. I need to know what he's planning—where they all are and if there are more of them. That's the only chance we have." But he forgot we didn't have the Re-gens to help us.

"I'll help Biggs and the others," Mase said, already striding toward his horse, Ghost, his ammo bag slung over his shoulder. I took a step toward him.

"The Re-gens will come," my mom said, tugging me toward the door. "They will." I let her guide me outside, needing to push the chaos away and focus. *Find the General. Kill the General. Find the General. Kill the General.* Only then would it all be over—the soldiers would stop fighting, and innocent people would stop dying.

We sprinted away from the barn, in the direction of the convoy that was still out of sight but rapidly heading our way. We ducked and weaved around tree trunks and a small pump house, following the route we'd gone over and over during our preparations. *Just stick to the plan...*

Jogging a few more yards, we hid inside the small pump house, our temporary hideaway while we geared ourselves up for what was to come, but it barely fit the three of us. Old tractors and plowing equipment were scattered around it and the giant barn in front of us, perfect for added concealment when the firing began.

My eyes shot to my mom. "I can sense the rest of us," I said through panting breaths. Some of our people were racing on horse-back and others were getting into position, ready and waiting for a full-fledged battle. I searched for the General or any new minds that might be in the truck. "I can sense the minds in the trucks—of the soldiers by Biggs—but I can't sense the minds in one of the Humvees."

Harper's eyes flashed to mine as he readied his gun, ensuring it was locked and loaded. "Can you?" Harper asked my mom.

"No, but he's clearly in there. But I can't null their minds if I can't feel them," she said. I heard the tremor in her voice as she turned to watch the vehicles approaching in the distance. "They have to be protected by someone, something bigger and stronger than nulling—a shield of some sort," she said, frowning.

"Then what about the EMP?" I nearly screeched. "Will it still work?"

"Fuck," Harper spat and peered out at the road.

My mom stared at me, thinking. "Let's just hope that Gregory was so worried about protecting his mind—his control over every-thing—that he didn't consider anything—"

And then it happened. My body hummed and the gunfire to the north of us faded as the sound of fast-approaching, rumbling engines sputtered to nothing. The three of us stared out the cracked door, watching the two Humvees rounding the bend in front of us roll to a stop, the rest of the caravan still further down the road. All of them stopped.

Within seconds there was another wave of gunfire across the street, followed by another down the road. There was shouting and the sound of metal on metal, and I wasn't sure what else. I found Jake and Sanchez's minds, but still nothing of Jason or my dad, which I assumed meant Jason was nulling all other Abilities around them and they were safe.

I strained to see out through the opening. The two Humvees nearest us were still closed up and untouched. The shield the General was using obviously hadn't protected the function of the vehicles, since they'd been stopped by Carlos, but the people inside at least one of them were still safe from us.

Gunfire. Blaring, incessant gunfire was exchanged at the farm across the street.

"Let's go," Harper said, tossing me my crossbow. He turned to my mom. "Anna, stay in the shed. You'll be safe in here for now."

She balked and glanced at me before she took a step forward. "What? No. I'm not staying in here. I'm—"

"Going to get killed," he said brusquely. My mom paled, but he continued. "Without Re-gen backup, our plans are shot to shit. You didn't risk everything—all of us and the lives of your kids—so you could run out there and get yourself killed in the first five minutes by a stray bullet to the head."

"Right," she said. "Just like I didn't do all of this to hide in here while my children get shot at and maybe killed!"

Harper's tone hardened. "Do you want to end this, once and for all? Our Abilities are worthless on them, we have no backup; all we have left is the element of surprise. At this point, you might be our only weapon against Herodson." Harper was angry, worried, struggling. But so was my mom. "Fine," he finally said. "Go around the left side of the barn." He pointed at what stood a dozen yards in front of the pump house and bent down. Harper unzipped the duffel with all the ammo and a few spare weapons, pulling out a handgun. He handed it to her. "I'm assuming that at some point in your twenty years at the Colony you learned how to use one of these?"

My mom nodded and accepted the gun. I could tell she didn't like the feel of it in her hands any more than I did. "Take cover behind that dually." He nodded in the direction of the truck a dozen or so yards to the left of the large, hay-filled barn. "Except for the Frates exit, the rest of the gunfire is south. So if you see anyone who's not one of us coming up from the left, shoot to kill. We'll be close; we'll hear the shots. We need you to be our eyes."

It was a shoddy plan, sending her to the opposite side of the barn alone, but there was little we could do about that amid the ringing of gunshots to the right and left of us. I knew Harper was just trying to keep her alive. I gave my mom a tight-lipped smile.

Harper tossed her two extra clips. "Watch your ass out there." He nodded at her, then looked at me. "Okay, let's move it," he said, and the three of us ran out of the pump house, heading toward the front of the barn—toward the road—and the junk piles south-side just in front of the road. "You see anyone, kill them!" Harper said to us, just loud enough to hear over the gunfire. "If they aren't our people—they're dangerous." I wholeheartedly agreed.

My mom nodded to us as we drew closer to the back of the barn, and we parted ways—my mom heading around the north while we went south. I watched as she disappeared around the side of the building, headed toward the dually, and I hoped—prayed— she would be okay.

After a few more pounding heartbeats and a couple missteps, Harper and I noticed the back door of the second Humvee was open.

"Shit," I heard Harper say, and we stopped behind the barn to regroup. "They're mobile," he said, his voice low, and I could tell the wheels in his mind were turning—recalibrating our plan.

My ears were ringing, though the gunshots seemed fewer than before. "I'm not sure where they are. I still can't feel their minds."

Harper opened his mouth, but however he was intending to respond, he was cut short by a saccharine voice, shouting above the gunfire.

"I can feel your mind, handsome!" It was a woman.

What the hell? We both straightened, readying our weapons.

"I heard voices, so I know you're not alone. Why don't you bring your friend on out here?" The voice was getting closer, growing louder. How she wasn't afraid of getting shot at, I couldn't fathom.

Without warning, Harper nudged me past the barn. "Go," he commanded.

But I dug my heels into the ground and glared at him. "Go? What are—"

Harper's rifle was aimed at my forehead.

43

DANI

THE FARM, CALIFORNIA

"*Shit! Guys!*" The telepathic curse was out of my mouth before I could think. I hadn't meant to shout at the many human minds I was connected to between the farm and the eucalyptus grove. I took a deep breath, focusing on what was important. "*A couple of the hawks just spotted movement on the road,*" I told our scattered troops. "*They must've been using some kind of an illusion or something, but it's down now. Get ready, and for God's sake, be careful!*"

"*Get into the cottage, Red,*" Jason said, his response drowning out the others. "*You've done everything you can for us. Now you need to protect yourself and the farm.*"

"*Okay,*" I said, biting my lip. I took two steps toward the front door of the cottage, but hesitated before entering and joining the others who'd stayed behind and placed both hands over my barely there baby bump. I bowed my head and closed my eyes. "*I love you,*" I said to Jason right before I slipped through the front door into Peter's nulling field, severing our telepathic connection. In that single action, I severed all of my connections, human and animal alike. And therein lay the problem, so far as I was concerned.

I'd recruited hundreds, maybe thousands of creatures to help us defend ourselves and our valley, but what none of the others currently out in the battlefield seemed to understand was how useless the animals' desire to assist us would be without me there to direct them. It was their active connection to me that helped them decide where to go, who the "good guys" were, and who wasn't. It was the animals' connection to me that made it possible for them to even recognize the enemy. And right now, encased as I was in Peter's nulling field—which protected me from having my mind influenced by another Ability, let alone detected by one—I had zero connection with the animals.

I hurried over to the kitchen table, where Grayson, Larissa, Camille, Vanessa, Peter, Sam, and Annie were seated, Ellie and Everett in their carriers on the floor nearby and the dogs and our resident cat family lounging nearer to the hearth. "Alright," I said, pacing alongside the table. "Herodson's here—or there, or whatever." I waved one hand frantically, then scanned the faces of my companions. "We're all in agreement—I'm heading out to direct the animal troops, right? This is what's best, no matter what happens?" The seven of us had come up with an extension of the plan to defend our home after the others had departed, one that they—specifically Jason—couldn't argue against, since *they* weren't here.

Grayson nodded. "It's the best way I see to keep our people safe." He glanced at the twins. "The only way."

Larissa, Camille, Vanessa, and Peter nodded. Only Sam and Annie abstained.

"Guys? Any objections?" I focused on Annie and Sam, the youngest two members of our impromptu council, sitting side by side, eyes opened wide and unblinking.

Finally, Sam nodded, too. "You should go. I'll listen, and if they get too close to us…" He held up his bow and looked to the guns lying on the tabletop.

"We'll hold them off for as long as we can," Peter added, meeting Sam's gaze with a reassuring nod. "We'll do whatever it takes."

I halted my pacing and smiled at them, touched by how immersed they'd become in protecting our family.

A moment later, Annie slid off her chair and padded over to me. "I'll go with you." She looked up at me with her big blue eyes. "Mama."

My heart all but convulsed. "No, honey." I dropped to my knees and shook my head emphatically. "You'll be safer in the cottage. You have to stay here. I can communicate with the animals on my own. It'll be safer this way."

Scowling, Annie shook her head. "No it won't!"

"Annie—"

She stomped one furry booted foot. "Snowflake and the others are on their way, and they want me to help them know who to fight."

"They—*what*?" It was the first I'd heard of the Tahoe pack planning on joining the fight, and although their potential presence was a big plus, I highly doubted they'd arrive in time to be of any real help.

Annie nodded, her eyes serious. "Snowflake sent a bunch of the wolves ahead days ago."

"Oh my God," I whispered. Wolves were stealthy. They were incredibly fast and lethal. Having them as soldiers on our side could be invaluable. And I knew, without a doubt, that having Annie speak with them would be far more effective than me, because she'd lived with them for months—she shared a connection with these wolves akin to my connection with Jack and Wings. "I—"

I looked at the others seated at the table, my eyes tearing up. How could I bring Annie out there? Here, she was safe, protected, *hidden.* Out there, she would be in danger...exposed. But even with all of the foxes and coyotes and birds and other animals I'd managed to call in, the Tahoe wolves might very well make all the difference. For all of us.

Distant gunfire shattered our collective indecision, and my heart rate hop-skipped to double time. *Jason,* I thought. *Zo...*

"I'll come with you," Larissa said. "An illusion hiding this whole place might not be as good as a nulling field, but at least it's something."

I looked at Larissa, then back at Annie, then at Grayson. More gunfire broke the tense silence, a ticking time bomb.

"We'll snuff out all the candles and lanterns," he said. "We'll douse the fire. Nobody'll have any reason to suspect that we're here."

My focus returned to Annie. I crouched and placed my hands on either side of her face. "Are you sure, Annie?"

She nodded, her eyes ancient.

I swallowed roughly, then cleared my throat, certain I was about to make the biggest mistake of my life. Afraid that if I didn't, I would live to regret it until I took my final, dying breath. Afraid that if I didn't, breath would whoosh from my lungs all too soon—that death would come for us all on this day. "Alright," I said, spurred by the now incessant rat-tat-tat-tat rat-tat-tat-tat and crack crack crack of gunshots miles away. I met Larissa's eyes and took a deep breath. "Alright. Let's do it."

Mere seconds later, Annie's hand in mine and Jack, Cooper, and Larissa trailing behind me, I marched out through the front door. The animals' minds sprang to life within my telepathic radar almost as soon as we were out of the house, heading toward the hill behind the farmhouse that led up to our little cemetery, homemade crosses and etched headstones scattered throughout.

When I'd considered where to base my clandestine operations, I'd thought it best to stick to higher ground, picking the best vantage point on the farm's land. Plus, it seemed somehow fitting to be near my closest fallen friends while I fought to protect the lives of the living. Though Larissa and Annie had joined me, I didn't see any reason to change my plans now. Anyone who came to the farm looking for people would look in the stable and barn, or the farmhouse first, being the most central. The cottage would be last. But in the cemetery, hidden among the tombstones—why would anybody think to look for us there?

Unless they sense us...

But we'll be fine, I repeated to myself over and over. Doubt was unhelpful. And even if the General's forces made it to the farm and *did* sense us, they'd have a barrier of irate horses, cows, and goats to battle through to get to us—not to mention the myriad of wild animals gathered throughout Hope Valley, prepared to fight with us tooth and nail.

"Biggs," I said as we hiked up the muddy hill, reaching out to the leader of the group surrounded by the most enemy minds, according to all the blips on my mental radar. Jason's group seemed fine for now, as did Zoe's and Chris's. *"Do you need reinforcements?"*

"Dani? What are you—yes! There's too many of—" He cut off, and I couldn't help but wonder if some of the echoing gunfire belonged to him. *"There's too damn many of 'em. Any kind of backup would help. A goddamn squirrel would help."*

"You got it," I said, sending not squirrels, but a throng of raccoons, along with the foxes and coyotes nearest them—nearly forty in all—and a mismatched band of several hundred owls and hawks prepared to drop stones on the enemy from high above like primitive bomber planes. *"I sent in the—"*

"Oh my God..." I could sense maybe sixty or seventy unfamiliar, dangerously focused and hostile human minds not quite a mile away, west of the valley and moving toward us slowly enough that I thought they might be on foot, but fast enough that I'd have wagered they were running. They hadn't made it through the barricade, they'd *gone around* it, and they were heading straight for the farm. For us.

And regardless of their speed, there were too many of them.

"This is good enough," I said breathily, laying down amongst the soggy tall grasses covering the hillside and pulling Annie down with me. We were barely halfway up the hill, but the grass and shrubs were taller where we were than at the top, and since I now had more than myself and my unborn little girl to think of, I figured maximum cover was best. I scratched Jack's furry neck, and reached out to rub Cooper behind his ear as a quick thank you and reassurance of what was to come.

Larissa eased down onto her stomach beside us and turned her face to me as she closed her eyes. "Don't talk to me," she said softly. "I need to concentrate on making the strongest illusion of an empty hillside possible. With luck, they'll never even know we're here."

Taking her instruction seriously, I nodded but didn't actually respond. Miles away, I sensed one of the human minds in Biggs's group wink out, closely followed by another, along with a smattering of animal minds. A few of the enemy had fallen as well, but the reinforcements I sent to them—it wasn't enough.

"You doing okay?" I asked Annie, brushing her wild curls out of her face.

"Yeah." When her eyes met mine, her focus was distant. She was partially melded with the wolves.

"They're not close enough to help us here," I said, noting with surprise that the lupine battalion consisted of well over thirty wolves. It was notably more beasts than had been in Snowflake's pack this last spring. *"Who's the alpha?"* Not Snowflake, since I didn't sense her mind and, as Annie had said, she'd sent a group of wolves ahead to aid us.

"Rain Dancer," Annie told me before pointing out his mind to me. *"He's this one. Smart. Tough. Wise. He is a good wolf. A strong wolf."*

"Okay, sweetie, listen carefully..." And keeping a close mental eye on the approaching wave of enemy troops, I said, *"Merge with Rain Dancer. I'll watch over you while you drift with him, I promise, but I need you to take him to Biggs—you know who I'm talking about, right?"*

"Yeah..."

"And you can feel where he is, right?"

"Mmhmmm..."

"Okay, good." I inhaled deeply, then held my breath, hoping, once again, that I wasn't making an enormous, irrevocable mistake. *"When you're drifting with Rain Dancer, guide the wolves toward Biggs. He needs the wolves' help. They all do. And make sure the wolves move like ghosts. If they don't, they will be ghosts,"* I told her, threading my words with primal meaning I knew she'd be able to understand and pass on to the wolves.

"Okay." Annie's eyes closed, and her mind went dormant. Because she wasn't really there anymore; she was in Rain Dancer.

And then, as I focused all of my attention on another mass of people approaching from the opposite direction, I felt panic start to set in. There really were simply too damn many of them. Even with the horses and cows and goats clustered around the farm, waiting to stampede if necessary, I didn't see how we would fend our attackers off if they sensed us.

"I'm so sorry," I said to the newly formed soul cuddled within my womb. She'd never had a chance to live, and while I dared to hope that our efforts to assist the others had paid off and that most of our friends would live, corrosive doubts sunk in as to whether my farm-bound companions could look forward to such a hopeful future...or to any future at all.

"Please," I said, calling out to the uncommitted minds all around us, to the crows and ravens and deer and bats, to the creatures who'd yet to decide whether we were worth fighting for or if we were better off left for dead. *"Please—we need you. If you help us, I swear to you, you and your kind will forever be safe on our*

411

land. Please! Help us!" And as I spoke en masse telepathically, I pictured the approaching swarm of the General's troops as seen from one of the raven's eyes, camouflaged and sneaking over the opposite side of the very hill Annie, Larissa, and I were huddled on. *"Protect us from these people, and we'll protect you in the future!"*

From the raven, I felt something click—an agreement of sorts. A moment later, I felt something similar from the crows, then from the bats. From the deer, I felt nothing but radio silence. So be it.

As I sensed the air-bound minds approaching, a hum filled the air. It was almost electrically charged. I looked to the west, to the place where a multilayered blanket of blackness darkened the morning sky. The crows and ravens and bats were on their way.

I reached down to my thigh and drew my pistol, praying that we, feathered, fanged, and armed, would be enough.

I took a deep breath, then another and another as the sky darkened overhead and the minds of the enemy neared the crest of the hill. And then I blinked, a huge, new mass appearing on my radar just to the south of us. A strange-feeling mass, filled with muddled, complex minds—minds I hadn't been able to sense until they were practically right on top of me. A mass led by the one and only Becca Vaughn.

I grinned as nearly half of the Re-gens drew nearer to our position and relief flooded me, driving away the dread and acceptance of what I'd felt was sure to come. With a slightly lighter heart, I closed my eyes and concentrated. Speaking telepathically with Re-gens was always more difficult than any other type of mind I communicated with.

"Becca," I called out with my Ability. *"Can you hear me? Where have you been? Do you know what's happening?"*

Choppy, half-formed images appeared in my mind.

Re-gens hiding in a large building, in an area I didn't recognize.

. . .

Re-gens sneaking along the trees lining the east edge of the farm, up the driveway, around the farmhouse and cottage, surrounding our home, protecting it, and climbing up the hillside toward the cemetery.

The General's people cresting the hill, attacking.

Re-gens and dark, winged creatures fighting, falling.

Me, firing my gun, even as I was hiding amongst tall grasses on the hillside.

Grayson and me, standing side by side in the sunlight with the twins in our arms and Annie and Sam standing in front of us, holding handfuls of flowers.

"They're close, Dani..." Larissa's whispered voice was strained, and for good reason. I could see our foes' shadowed silhouettes against the horizon as they approached. "We have to run!" Her voice was too loud. She was going to get us killed if she didn't shut up. "We—"

"*No.*" I looked at her, my focus unyielding. *"We stay here,"* I said in her mind. Reaching out, I latched a hand around her arm and held her fast to the ground. *"Stay down!"*

Though her eyes were wide with fear and darting around frantically, Larissa conceded, and as we settled back down, a fast-moving wave of shadows slithered over us as the bats and ravens

413

and crows closed in. Near the base of the hill, I could sense the clouded Re-gen minds, creeping closer.

When the first round of gunfire exploded, closely followed by shouting and another round of gunfire, I threw myself over Annie's body and squeezed my eyes shut. And as chaos erupted around us, I whispered telepathically, *"I'm so sorry. I should have made you stay behind."* I couldn't fathom the risk of losing both Annie and the baby girl inside me, should something happen to me.

From Rain Dancer's mind, Annie's response was, *"I would've snuck out to join you anyway."*

With a whimper, I held her a little closer and kissed her forehead. She was so brave. Too damn brave. I could be brave, too.

So I boosted myself up on my elbows, sighted the nearest of the General's soldiers, and pulled the trigger. As the enemy body dropped, the Re-gens drew closer and the cloud of dark-sheathed bodies descended from the sky, cawing and biting and screeching and clawing. Through the veil of chaos, I sighted another enemy, and I pulled the trigger once more. I'd be damned if I wasn't going to do everything possible to keep my girls safe.

44

ZOE

DECEMBER 21, 1AE

PETALUMA VALLEY, CALIFORNIA

"H," I said shakily, frozen in place and staring down the barrel of his rifle. "What the fuck?" It was a rough, confused whisper. The morning sunlight illuminated the battle warring behind his eyes as he glanced around, scanning the area like he was searching for answers.

"Disarm your friends and bring them to me," the woman demanded, sounding irritated. "Now."

Harper focused on me, and only me. When his gaze hardened, I knew this wasn't going to end well for me.

"H, this isn't you," I said, frantic. "Whatever it is, fight it. You *have* to fight it."

Conviction radiating off of him, Harper stripped me of my pistol and crossbow and tore the quiver off my back. "You heard the lady," he growled and tossed my things out, beyond the protection of the building.

"What the fuck are you doing, H? Don't listen to her, she's poisoning your mind!" I shouted. Dying in the crossfire or at the will of Herodson was something I'd almost expected, but not a shot to the head from Harper.

But without hesitation, the cool barrel of his rifle pressed against my temple, and he motioned for me to step into view. "Move it," he said coldly, and I knew my friend was gone, locked away in his own mind somewhere.

Fighting back tears, I stepped out from behind the barn and into the open. I focused on a curvaceous Latina who had her hair pulled up in a ponytail and a pleased smile parting her full lips. It almost looked like she was wearing lipstick. Though she looked out of place surrounded by rusted metal and farm equipment, she seemed strangely familiar.

"Well, well, well. What do we have here?" She looked intrigued as she eyed me. She was a tad out of breath, like she'd run here from the safety of the Humvee for some reason. And how she'd spotted us, I had no idea.

She giggled, her eyes shifting from my gun, crossbow, and arrows to me. "And you were going to use a bow and arrow to kill me? Really? I'm bored already," she deadpanned.

"I guess you wouldn't mind if I grabbed them then," I said, wishing her dead for mind-controlling my friend.

She sneered and looked at Harper, licking her lips, like she was really seeing him for the first time. "And you," she said, taking a step toward him.

Harper looked at her, but his glare returned to me, pinning me in place like he only had one single objective: control and kill if necessary.

"You look good enough to eat," she purred as her bronze hand reached out for Harper's bicep. "I think you and I—"

My stomach churned. "Get away from him, psycho," I growled, unable to control my tongue.

I could tell she didn't like that very much; her eyes narrowed on me, though her smile was wide. "Why? Seems to me he's not your friend anymore." She smiled broadly. "He's mine. So I wouldn't worry too much about it." She glanced to Harper. "Bring her to the Humvee," she said and nodded toward the road. "We'll see what the General wants to do with her."

I realized then that the air was still and the morning was mostly quiet, save for a few errant gunshots.

Harper gripped my arm tightly and prompted me to move.

I nearly tripped over a hunk of metal as I stared at him, refusing to break eye contact. "H, look at me, H," I pleaded. "It's me, Zoe. It's Baby Girl. You *don't* want to do this." He shoved me ahead of him. "Harper—"

"*Zoe?*" psycho asked, an all-too-amused pitch in her tone. Dread filled me as her brown eyes scoured me from head to toe. "*You're* Zoe, as in Jason's sister?"

And then it hit me. I'd seen this woman in Dani's memories. I'd heard horror stories and wanted to rip her face off, even before now. "And you're the bitch I'd hoped was dead," I spat.

I took a step forward, wanting to put a bullet between Cece's eyes for being such a horrid person, for what she'd done to Dani and my brother almost a year ago, and what she was doing to Harper now. But Harper jabbed his gun into my back and gripped my arm tighter.

Cece tsked and took another step closer, her gaze glued to my face. "All I need to do is even *think* the magic words and you're dead. And let's be honest, I've known you a minute, and I already can't stand you."

"The feeling's mutual," I snapped. Becca's warning for Dani to stay at the farm if she wanted the baby safe was finally starting to make sense.

Cece laughed. "You really are your brother's sister...such a conundrum." She shook her head, the wayward brown tendrils from her ponytail blowing in the breeze around her face. "I never could understand what he saw in that twit Dani. And you have a gun pointed at you, and you think you're being cute. Idiocy must run in the family." She winked at Harper. "That's okay, I know the perfect remedy."

"It must piss you off then," I blurted, desperate to postpone the inevitable. I knew Jason was her weak spot, I could feel the angsty yearning she still had for him—the unattainable one that got away —thanks to the weakening shield around her. Which meant that the shield-maker was inside the Humvee.

"What do you mean?" she asked, taking the bait.

I tried to withhold my satisfaction in watching her wheels turn. "They're married now," I said.

Cece's stare bored into me, and her lips formed a thin, pursed line. It'd pushed her beyond her limits; I could see the gleam of satisfaction in her eyes. "Watching you die is going to be fun. Well," she amended quickly, putting up her palm, "not as fun as killing Dani will be, but then, I've been waiting all year to do that. It makes me sad that I won't actually be there to hear her screaming and see the terror on her face when our troops arrive."

Horror must have filled my eyes, because Cece's sneer turned into a grin. "Oh, you didn't think this little convoy was all of us, did you? We split up. The others took a different route." She shook her head, and I could feel her gratification. "I'll tell you a little secret," she whispered and leaned a bit closer to me, though not enough that I could reach her if I tried. "We have seven trucks headed to your quaint little farm right now—big trucks, filled with lots of guns and angry men, most under my control. They'll be all over that place before Dani even knows they're there."

The fact that there were more of them—a lot more, from the sounds of it—heading to the farm was enough to let the weight of defeat pummel my stomach, making it roil. "They won't make it," I said evenly, trying to knock her down a peg. This wasn't over; we hadn't lost, not yet. "There's no way. If you think we left Dani there defenseless, then you're an idiot. We have an entire *town* on our side," I lied, though Dani did have an animal battalion of sorts, and I hoped to God that they stood a chance. "You only have a small army." *Say something, Dani! Contact me!* I couldn't warn her, not if she didn't reach out telepathically first.

I watched as Cece's eyes clouded with doubt and her grip tightened on her pistol. "You're lying."

"There you are," said an eerily steady, approaching voice. "What are you doing, Cecilia?"

Cece spun around, and we both straightened when we saw Herodson walking up. I hadn't noticed him in my battle of wits with Cece.

The General had two men flanking him on each side, guns aimed at me—at Harper too? I wasn't sure. Herodson was pure menace, and no matter how many times I'd been warned about him, had seen him in memories, seeing him in person made my skin crawl with pure terror.

"I saw these two trying to escape the fight," Cece lied. "But don't worry, I stopped them."

Herodson studied her. "Really?" His gaze shifted to Harper, dressed in his military clothes, and then his eyes rested on me before they returned to Cece. "That seems unlikely. Are you sure this gentleman is not the reason you jumped out of the Humvee so quickly? As helpful as you are at manipulating the male mind, I have to say, Cecilia, your little distractions grow bothersome after a time."

When Herodson looked at me, really looked at me and narrowed his eyes, assessing me, my mouth went instantly dry, and I wondered if death would be better than anything he had in store for me. I could almost feel his arms around me as a child, those vengeful eyes boring into me...

He turned to face Cece. "If I have to remind you again, Cecilia," he said, his voice flat, "that you do what *I* say, not what your pathetic hormonal tendencies tell you to do, I'll kill you. Do we have an understanding?" He clasped his hands behind his back.

Herodson continued scolding her, but my attention was drawn behind him to the Humvee, where I noticed more movement. There was a mangled-looking man—a Re-gen, perhaps—standing dumbly by the open rear door of the second Humvee, where I assumed the General had been sitting. The Re-gen seemed disoriented, like he didn't understand his surroundings.

Unbidden, my mind opened to him. He had no aura, and his head was mush, as if one too many experiments had fried his brain. Whatever he was, his Ability was amped up and strong, but it was fading, fast.

Then I felt the pain and suffering of the friendly minds in the near vicinity. I felt dimming minds and blank ones; there were fewer, and that realization frightened me. I tried to pinpoint Jake or Sanchez, my dad and my mom, to make sure any of them were still safe. But then I realized Herodson was staring at me again, and I lost all train of thought.

"But—" Cece pleaded. With my mind open, I could see the light brown glow of her aura and her gaping mouth and fearful gaze as she took a step toward the General. The shield was fading, I was sure of it. Mind-meddling was all I could do at this point.

"Your one saving grace, my dear," he said over his shoulder to her, "is that with your help, most of the men have *decided* they want to join the winning side—the *right* side—and I have most of the rebels contained and in the custody of my men, all of which puts me in a slightly better mood.

"Now," he said, smiling at me. "Sorry about that, Zoe." He eyed me another moment before speaking. "It's been a while since I saw you last." He reached out and touched the strands of hair hanging around my face.

I felt the color drain from my cheeks as the realization hit me: he wasn't glowing, not even a little bit, as the shield protecting him began to fade, allowing me to glimpse the auras of the men flanking him. A black fringy shadow was all that surrounded the General, and even though it was faint and partially hidden, it didn't feel like the others.

Bile rose in the back of my throat. Herodson wasn't…human,

not completely. I tried not to quiver or offend him as all my fears and questions coalesced and I fought to stay focused. I had no quips or snide comments. I just stood there, Harper's gun still trained at my head, his grip still tight around my arm, and a demon from hell staring right into my soul.

"You look just like your mother," Herodson said. "Your eyes..." He stared at me, like he was lost inside them. I knew he could control my mind, that he could manipulate me if he wanted to, but he hadn't. I wasn't sure why. Unable to stand staring into his cold, gray eyes, my gaze shifted to the Re-gen at the Humvee again.

When the General noticed, his grin returned. "Ah, I see you've spotted my new toy."

"What did you do to him?" I asked, feeling my brow furrow at my own curiosity.

With a contented exhale, like he was taking in a work of art, Herodson pivoted so he could see the Re-gen slowly coming toward us. "This is an old friend I decided had better use. He gestured to the Re-gen-ish man. "FM-01 is a small side project I started when I got wind that Cole was in the area again." He tapped his head for effect. "I couldn't risk my old foe getting in here, nor could I allow any of his accomplices' Abilities to affect me. So, I found a solution, as always. FM-01 is my very own Ability force field, if you will."

When the General realized I was less than fascinated, he cracked his neck and gestured toward his Humvee. "Come. The middle of a junk-cluttered field hardly seems an appropriate place to catch up, given that we haven't seen each other in over twenty years."

I shook my head and took a step backward. There was no way in hell I was going anywhere with him. I'd rather be dead. But I realized my mistake too late, and as his anger flared, I thought for sure I *would* be dead. The General gritted his teeth. Before I even knew what was going on, the back of his hand met with my face.

Stunned, my eyes shifted to Harper, who stood by, oblivious, and to Cece, who appeared to be enthralled.

Reluctantly, my eyes refocused on the General, my own anger flaring as I brought my palm up to my stinging face. I felt around in his mind, a deflated mess of partial memories and walls he'd constructed over time. All I could see were images of death and a hunger for power. And my mom's face.

He didn't love her. This went beyond love. He was haunted by her, obsessed.

Both his jaw and his hands clenched. "Until I find your mother, you will stay with me, Zoe. And if she left, thinking she could protect you that way, I'll find plenty of uses for you, mark my words."

Knowing that Jake, at least, wasn't dead—perhaps captured, but definitely not dead—I knew he wouldn't want me to give in. And my mom hadn't given up her life and risked Peter's so I could be imprisoned by the General.

"I would rather die," I ground out. "You *ruined* my family. You took her away from me. You—"

"I'm sorry to hear you say that, Zoe. Truly I am." General Herodson's eyes narrowed on me, and he scratched the side of his face. "You want to come with me," he said, his words resonating throughout my mind, and I knew that now, more than ever, I needed my mom to null him, to stop him if she was ever going to.

"Mom!" I shouted. And just as my mind started to feel a little fuzzy and detached, I heard her voice.

"Gregory, please. Wait!"

45

ANNA
DECEMBER 21, 1AE

PETALUMA VALLEY, CALIFORNIA

"Gregory, please. Wait!" Anna blurted, stumbling around the corner of the barn and toward the cluster of people threatening her daughter's life dozens of yards away… threatening her daughter's mind. When she'd registered that there was no gunfire coming from their post, she'd assumed the worst and come running, only to find Gregory approaching. She'd hid behind one of the tractors, watching while she kept her own mind veiled from any who might sense her, but once she'd heard Zoe's desperate cry, she'd known she couldn't hide anymore.

"Don't, please. I—" She tripped over a stone sticking up out of the ground, barely catching herself before continuing on toward her demented "husband" and endangered daughter.

Anna avoided looking at Cecelia, one of a half-dozen of Gregory's favorite tools, his Controllers. And somehow, she kept herself from looking at Zoe, from seeing the way fear was undoubtedly transforming her. Instead, Anna focused on Gregory, just like he'd always wanted.

"I thought I'd never see you again," she practically sobbed. She had to play to her strengths…to his weaknesses. Now, with Zoe's free will on the line and Anna out in the open, it was the only way.

Gregory bristled, standing straighter and folding his arms over his chest. He tilted his head back, just a little, and eyed her. "I was under the impression that not seeing me again was exactly what you wanted, *my dear.*"

"No!" Anna continued stumbling onward, moving slowly so as not to startle Gregory into doing something in haste. He'd already struck Zoe once; she couldn't bear to watch him hurt her again. She allowed herself to trip once more, this time over nothing. Better she appear weak, unsteady, out of sorts. Better Gregory and his pet Controller think she wasn't a threat.

"I didn't have a choice, Gregory. *Jason*"—Anna spat her eldest son's name—"brought a woman like Tom, but stronger, and she made me believe horrible things." Anna shook her head frantically, willing tears to pool in her eyes, forcing her voice to quaver. "They threatened Peter…they threatened *our son.*" Anna took a shaky breath, reminding herself not to rush her plea. Gregory didn't like things like this to be rushed. "If I didn't come with them…they've got him locked up now, Gregory!"

The great General Herodson arched his neck to the side in a long, drawn-out stretch. It was a tell of his. Anna should know; she'd spent over two decades learning how to read him, how to deceive him. The neck stretch meant he was listening, considering. It was a good sign. Probably.

Anna glanced at FM-01, surprised to see him alive, however warped, and walking somewhat unsteadily toward Gregory. The Re-gen had been far from functional when she'd escaped from the Colony, and she couldn't imagine how Gregory had managed to get him up and running. But that didn't matter right now.

Anna refocused on Gregory. "Now that you've broken Larissa's hold on my mind, I can see everything so clearly." She'd almost reached Zoe. Almost reached Gregory. Almost reached freedom…victory. "Let's go get Peter," she said as she passed Zoe, passed Harper and the pet Controller, and headed straight toward Gregory, all the while picturing Tom. She let all of the love and hope and respect and adoration she felt for Tom show on her face while she looked into Gregory's open, eager, hopeful gray eyes. "Let's go home."

And once more, Anna stubbed the toe of her boot on the earth, purposefully and hard this time. She tripped, stumbling past Gregory and directly into FM-01.

The Re-gen yelped. Their legs tangled. Arms flailed.

But not Anna's arms.

She grabbed onto the front of FM-01's jacket, while reaching down for the small hunting knife Tom had tucked away inside a special sheath he'd sewn into her right boot. She jerked the knife free and jammed it into the side of the Re-gen's groin and, if she was lucky, shredded his femoral artery. If bleeding out didn't break his concentration and shatter his shield, nothing would.

Anna and FM-01 hit the ground, and so many things happened all at once. Too many things.

FM-01 howled, kicking and flailing until Anna was thrown to the side.

Anna felt the shield fall and the minds of Gregory's people burst into existence around her, most notably Gregory himself and his pet Controller.

Gregory shouted, "YOU—WHAT DID YOU DO?" and strode toward Anna, taking hold of the front of her coat and lifting her off the ground.

Anna grinned. And nulled Cece and Gregory and every damn one of his people.

Eyes wide and feverish, Gregory roared and shook Anna. Hard. "How could you, Anna? You were mine—you were with *me*. I loved you."

"I didn't love you," she said.

As Gregory's veneer cracked, his grip on her coat slipped, and Anna stumbled backward. She tripped over FM-01's body, and fell heavily. Fireworks filled her eyes as the back of her head exploded with pain, and piercing, fiery agony followed. Her back burned, the feeling of searing torn flesh.

Remotely, she heard a single, muffled noise. A gunshot, she thought.

And then she heard nothing. She saw nothing. She thought nothing.

She was nothing.

46

ZOE

DECEMBER 21, 1AE

Clip. Clop. Clip. Clop. Clip. Clop.

Shadow's hoof steps were steady and predictable, like the sound of my heart beating, dull and even in my ears. I felt like I was in a wasteland of nothingness. The lulling sound and movement of Shadow's body was my only comfort—I clung to it. The mourning silence around me was deafening, a screaming, ear-piercing void that followed our procession home.

It was like it hadn't happened, any of it, and yet like it would be ingrained in my mind for the rest of my life. Until now, there hadn't been a single moment to process, to think. Not about the men dropping their guns behind Cece and the disorientation that had registered on her face as she realized her mind control was no longer working on any of them. She had no idea it was because of my mom.

The instant Harper's rifle fell from my head, I crouched on one knee to snatch my pistol from my discarded holster. My fingers moved more swiftly than I expected, the training and adrenaline kicking my responses into overdrive. Pivoting on one knee, I aimed the handgun at Cece's chest and pulled the trigger.

The cracking sound of the bullet had gone unheard at the time, but as I replayed the way Cece's eyes had widened in shock and surprise, the sound was too loud to ignore. She'd looked at me, and her eyes had narrowed as she stumbled backward. The memory would've brought a grim smile to my face, were I still capable of smiling.

Cece only wavered on her feet, so I pulled the trigger again, aiming for her forehead, where no bulletproof vest could deflect the nine-millimeter bullet I wanted to end her vile existence.

Pensive and ready to pull the trigger again if I had to, I watched Cece's body finally go limp and collapse to the ground. There was no gasping for air or struggling. There was nothing but a blank mind, and I couldn't help the satisfaction I felt in seeing her lifeless body lose its aura, once and for all.

"Zoe?"

Twisting around, I aimed the gun at the encroaching person to my left. It was Harper.

He took a step toward me, his green eyes wide as they flicked from the pistol aimed at his chest to my face. "Are you okay, Baby Girl?" he whispered. He was in apparent shock, though his hands were up in surrender. Quickly and full of concern, Harper's eyes scanned me, making sure I wasn't injured—that he hadn't injured me. "I'm so sorry, Baby Girl, I—"

The emotion in his voice melted away my hardened intent. "I know, H," I said, lowering my weapon. "It's okay." I shut my eyes and let out a deep, relieved breath. "I know what Cece was capable of." When I opened my eyes again, Harper's were wide and fearful, but they weren't focused on me anymore. They were glued to some fear-provoking sight beyond me.

Feeling a rising panic, I tracked him as he jogged over to where the General crouched and murmured... over my mom's motionless body.

I stopped breathing, the General fading from existence and all adrenaline and satisfaction snuffed away by panic.

"Move," Harper snapped, and he pushed Herodson aside.

I slowly rose to my feet, unable to look away, unable to find my breath. I hadn't dared to move, should a single shift in the air tip the scale, risking my mom's life.

"I said get out of the way!" Harper shouted, shoving the General away from her body. Herodson stumbled backward, not giving Harper's boldness a single thought as he stared down at my mom, shocked and frozen.

She's only unconscious, *I told myself, knowing my mom was nulling Herodson and the rest of his people, breaking his hold on them and making them vulnerable.* Right? *As I stood there, trying to convince myself that she would wake up and we would finish this and go home, everything around me seemed to happen in a slur of unfocused actions and words.*

Harper's eyes were on me, I was able to feel his sorrow. Then my dad and Jason, Jake, and Sanchez were there, their guns drawn and aimed at Herodson and the four men that were still standing behind him.

I took a step toward my mom, toward my dad and the General as they hovered over her, Harper standing aside, his eyes pinned in my direction. He was saying something to Jason, but I couldn't hear him. My heartbeat was too loud, the only sound the blood in my veins and my rapid breaths.

"...loved you!" Herodson shouted. "All I've ever wanted is you! How could you?" I recognized the crack of desperation and grief in his voice, though it sounded distant and false.

"Mom?" I said, my voice only an echo. She still didn't move.

429

Someone sniffled, bringing my gaze up to the cart a few horses in front of me, filled with at least a dozen bodies, both injured and lifeless, Larissa in the driver seat. So much death…

My dad leaned over my mom's body and pushed the General away. "Get away from her, you crazy son of a bitch!" Then his fist met Herodson's face. Smash. My dad shouted and hit him again and again, his fist and twenty-five years of anguish packed behind every punch. After that, a swirl of cursing and yelling and crunching and blood had been all I could process. "…piece of shit!" Smash. Smash. Smash.

Herodson started mumbling something, trying to regain his bearings, but my dad's fist was unrelenting. Smash. Smash. Smash.

I'd never seen my dad so enraged, his façade so cracked. It frightened me. I could only think of one reason why my dad might risk his life and everything he had left to assault the General.

That's when I finally realized how bad it was. The woman who had just been brought back to me, who had spent her entire life as a chameleon to protect her children and lived in a labyrinth of lies, might just have been taken away from me. All I could do was call for her, will her to answer me.

My feet started moving, carrying me toward her, but strong arms wrapped around me, pulling me into something hard and unyielding.

"No, Zoe," my brother's voice was commanding. "It's not safe."

I struggled against him, unable to take my eyes off of her lifeless body, only partially visible through the chaos of the beating my dad was unleashing on the General.

"She's dying, Jason," I cried, denial clouding my mind and offering me hope. "Jake can save her. She needs us! We have to help her! H, you have to do something, please! Jake!"

Jason's arms only tightened around me. "She's already gone,

Zoe," he whispered. "There's nothing we can do." The frailty of his voice gave me pause.

That's when I had the nerve to really see. I stared past my dad pointing a gun at Herodson, for the first time seeing the blood on my mom's face—on her body. And a moment later, I'd noticed the prongs of the tractor plow she was draped over.

My knees gave out, and I fell, Jason doing what he could to catch me. Turning into his chest, I clung on and screamed and cried. It wasn't fair. None of it was fair. Everything was too hard. I just wanted it to be over, to be alright. I wanted to have my family just a little bit longer. Knowing I never could—never would—I cried harder.

Hearing my dad say, "You will never hurt anyone in my family again," I opened my eyes, and through tear-blurred vision, I watched as Herodson wobbled on his knees, trying to stay upright. His cold eyes were swollen and red, his nose and lips bleeding.

Whether it was his physical state or his broken mind in the wake of my mom's death, Herodson made no protests when my dad pulled the trigger—once, twice, three times—until the General's chest was splattered with crimson and he toppled over. His eyes remained open, staring blankly at me and Jason as he took his final breath.

Chest heaving, my dad stood there, staring down at Herodson's mangled body before gaining the wherewithal to take a few shaky steps back, over to my mom, falling to his knees. I watched the sharp edges of rage fall and soften in his features. I watched him lean down, pulling my mom into his arms. And I watched him weep, soaking the front of her shirt as he tightened his hold around her.

As much as I wanted to run to my dad, I knew to let him be, to let him grieve. Like me and Jason, he'd only had her back for a few short days, and now she was gone again, only this time it truly would be forever.

I wrapped my arms around my brother's neck, hoping to

console us both. Although I thought I felt Jason's breathing hitch and his arms tighten around me, it had been hard to tell while I cried. I mostly cried for my mom, realizing that she would never know the world without the General, that she would never know of his death or that we didn't have to fear him anymore.

I swiped the tears from under my eyes when I heard the rapid clip-clop of hoof beats on the road. Mase rode up to the Humvees on Ghost. He peered around at the bodies of dead soldiers littered along either side of the road before they trotted over to us. He was splattered with blood and his face swollen.

Mase brought Ghost to a halt and threw his leg over to dismount. He froze when he saw my mom's limp body in my dad's arms. He seemed shocked, but the expression disappeared when he glanced to the right, where Jake and Sanchez held the four scared, disarmed men at gunpoint. I knew they weren't dangerous anymore, not without the General or Cece's hold on them, but I didn't care about their well-being enough to say anything.

"Half of the Re-gens showed up," Mase explained, looking to me and Jason. "Animals came, too. But there have been lives lost, and those who are well enough are helping the injured and gathering the dead."

The dead...

Clip clip clop.

Shadow took a clumsy step, bringing me back to the road, to the horse walking in front of me with my mom's body draped over the saddle.

My heart squeezed and ached, and my chest tightened. I shut my eyes. *Did Becca know this was going to happen?*

And then I cried.

47

DANI

DECEMBER 21, 1AE

THE FARM, CALIFORNIA

Grayson and I stood side by side in front of the stable, each holding one of the twins in our arms, and waited. Vanessa and Larissa stood a few yards away, talking softly, while Becca, Peter, and Camille sat on the bench beside the stable. "It's over," I overheard Becca say to the other Re-gens at one point. "It's finally over…"

For a long time, Grayson and I stood together in somber silence, rocking from foot to foot to keep Ellie and Everett dozing. For a long time, I couldn't think of a single thing to say. For a long time, the minutes passed feeling like seconds, and like hours. Timeless…inconsequential.

We breathed, we blinked, and we rocked. Forever and for what felt like no time at all.

"Maybe we should've left the twins inside," Grayson thought aloud. "There's still time to get them settled in the crib. They'll probably fall right back asleep."

I looked at him, then returned my stare to the end of the driveway, where gravel met pavement. "Biggs will want to see them," I said simply.

There really was no reason for us all to be out there, waiting for the victors to return from battle...for the funeral procession to arrive.

I could sense them approaching, fewer in number than they'd been hours earlier. Our home troops were fewer, too. Seven Regens had lost their lives in the battle of the farm, along with three wolves, four coyotes, a fox, and over a dozen birds and another dozen farm animals.

But Grayson and the others and I remained out in the driveway to wait anyway. We didn't know what else to do. It was over. Herodson was gone. Dead. Finally...

But so was Dr. Wesley—Anna Cartwright. Zoe's mom. Jason's mom. Peter's mom. Tom's wife.

Out of the corner of my eye, I spotted movement as Annie and Sam walked around the edge of the stable. Both held handfuls of milkmaids, the small white blossoms spilling out of their hands. I watched them approach, their faces uncertain.

Annie stopped in front of me and held out the flowers, showing me her bounty.

"You picked flowers," I said, stating the obvious. It was the only thing I could come up with. How she was standing before me rather than cowering under her nest of pillows was beyond me. Regardless of how quickly the gunfire and killing had stopped after both Cece and the General had fallen, I would have been a quivering, scaredy mess at her age.

Annie stared up at me, her big, blue eyes unblinking, unafraid. She was made of iron, this wild child of mine. "They're for Jason and Zoe and Tom."

"That's very nice," I said, readjusting my hold on Everett to free up a hand so I could comb my fingers through Annie's silky hair.

Sam skimmed the gravel with the toe of his right boot, and

Annie hopped in place, just once. "I was talking to Snowflake, and she said that whenever she misses one of her pack-mates that have gone away to the not-here, she runs through a field of flowers and watches the petals fly all around her because it helps her see that even when the flower is gone, the roots are still there." Annie blinked once, and gave her bouquet a shake. "The plant is still there."

Sam shrugged, his eyes fixed on the ground. "We thought that maybe thinking about it that way might help Zoe and them," he added quietly. "It helped me."

My eyes stung as I fought back the urge to cry.

Annie reclaimed my attention by reaching out and placing her small hand over my barely protruding belly, just under Everett's bottom. She looked up at me and smiled the tiniest possible smile. "The baby is part of the plant, just like Anna was, and she's only just beginning."

"Oh, well, that's just—just—" I stared down at my wild child, chin trembling and eyes overflowing with tears. How was it possible that this five-year-old was wiser than every adult I'd ever met in my entire life?

"We already gave some of the flowers to Peter," Annie told me, eyes serious. "He said thank you."

"Where's Peter now?" Grayson asked when it became apparent that I wouldn't be able to speak for a while yet.

It was Sam's turn to smile that tiny, sad smile. "Sitting in the field where we got these flowers."

A single, choking sob escaped from my throat. A moment later, I heard hooves crunching on gravel, and I looked out toward the road to see a column of horses and riders pouring onto the drive-way, Jason, Zoe, and Tom in the lead. And right along with them came a fourth horse, a lifeless rider draped over the saddle.

Taking a deep breath, I wiped under my eyes, one after the other, cleared my throat, and held my head high. This was no time for either my best friend or my husband to see me blubbering.

They would need me to be strong…or, at least, to appear strong. It was time for me to pay them back for all the strength they'd lent me over the years.

Jason was the first to dismount, and as he strode straight for me, Grayson leaned in and said, "Might need free hands for this welcome home, Danielle."

Numbly, I nodded and handed him Everett, who he accepted a bit awkwardly.

Seconds later, Jason dropped to his knees before me and pressed his face against my belly. His body jerked with the strength of his sudden, uncontainable sobs.

"Shhh…shhh…I'm here," I said, running my fingers through his hair and leaning into him. "*We're* here," I amended, and his fingers dug into my lower back, holding me tighter, bringing me closer, refusing to let go. "We're both here. With you…always."

48

MASE
DECEMBER 31, 1AE

THE FARM, CALIFORNIA

Mase lay on his back in bed, bathing in the morning light filtering through the lacy curtains and basking in the feel of Camille's soft body draped partially over his. The house was quiet, most of the others still asleep, and he was happily left with his thoughts.

Mase gazed down at Camille, suppressing a grin. She always slept like that, an arm and a leg thrown over him, like she was trying to keep him from leaving her alone in their bed.

Their bed. Like leaving her, even for a minute, was even possible.

He inhaled deeply, savoring her sweet, slightly floral scent, and exhaled a contented sigh.

Camille stirred, stretching out all four of her limbs with shaking intensity, then arched her neck to look up at him. Her lips curved into a sleepy smile, her eyes barely showing any hint of gray mixed with the rich hazel anymore. Her eyes contained secrets, knowledge, a true awareness of their shared past...of their lives *before*.

Sure, Mase's memories were still trickling in here and there, and Camille shared what she could with him—or maybe just what she wanted to share—by writing her own thoughts and memories out in her constant companion, her journal, but Mase doubted he would ever possess as much of his former self as Camille currently did.

He glanced at the small leather-bound book resting on the nightstand on her side of the bed. It was actually her fourth journal; the others were lined up neatly in the bookcase nestled between the room's two east-facing windows, also on Camille's side of the bed. If Mase were given the chance to trade his ability to speak for a full return of his memories, like Camille had, however unintentionally, he wasn't sure he would take the deal. He liked who he was, now…where he was in life and who he was spending his life with. He wouldn't risk losing that, not for anything.

There was a light tap-tap-tap on the bedroom door, and a moment later, it creaked partway open and Dani poked her head into the room. "Oh good, you're up!" She opened the door further and had taken several steps into the room before she gave pause and stared at Mase and Camille, eyes opened wide and expression sheepish. "Sorry, forgot to ask if I could come in. Do you mind? I had an idea that I thought would be a kinda neat addition to what the Re-gens have planned for New Year's. I mean, I thought it would be cool—like, sort of a sad cool, but still cool—and I wanted to see what you guys thought." She smiled, looking uncomfortable. "And I also wanted to see if you'd help…" Her uncomfortable smile widened to an awkward grin.

Mase chuckled and waved Dani in, and as she shut the door and crossed the room to sit on the edge of the bed, Mase and Camille shifted around so they were propped up and waiting attentively.

Dani turned to face them and pulled her legs up on the bed, curling them under herself. "Okay, so I know Jason and Zoe and Tom and Peter aren't really in the ring-in-the-new-year-with-a-bash kind of mood," she said in a rush, clearly excited, "but I think we could turn this shindig into something that's bigger than that, something that means more…a remembrance of the past and everything and *everyone* who's gone now with a special tribute kind of thing, something that'll last." Dani sucked in a breath, which Mase thought was, impossibly, her first since she'd started talking about her mysterious idea.

Crossing his arms and nodding, Mase looked at Camille. She was staring at Dani, mouth quirked to the side in an intrigued smile. A secret smile. Which only confused Mase. Frowning, he returned his attention to Dani. "Sounds interesting." He glanced at Camille, then back at Dani, feeling like he was missing something. "What would you want us to do?"

Dani's focus shifted to Camille. "It's really you, Camille, who'd make this whole thing work." She took a deep breath and rushed onward, "I know you don't use your Ability much anymore, and I totally get it—I'd be scared of having another seizure-stroke thing, too, if I were you. I mean, I've burned out enough times to know how dangerous it can be to overexert our Abilities, but I also know how much harder it is to do that—like almost impossible, so far as I can tell—if you have someone boosting your Ability." She hiked her shoulders up until they were practically touching her ears. "So, I'd totally understand if you didn't want to do this and I wouldn't be mad at all, but would you maybe consider using your Ability to help with this if we were super careful and we had someone to boost it?" She scrunched up her face and cringed. "Maybe?"

Camille reached for her journal and pen, opened the leather book to the spot marked by the journal's royal blue ribbon, and quickly scrawled her response. *"I'd love to—but who will boost me? Jason?"* Without being asked, Mase gave voice to Camille's words.

Dani shook her head. "Peter, actually." She bit her lip, one lonely shoulder hitching higher. "He and Becca found me a little bit ago when I was milking the goats. Peter said he overheard my thoughts, and then Becca had a vision about it, so both offered to help." She smiled to herself. "Peter, um—" Dani cleared her throat and lowered her gaze to the comforter. "He said his mom would've loved it. I guess she'd been trying to get Herodson to do some sort of a memorial or monument back in the Colony, but the bastard kept putting it off."

"So, what are you thinking of doing for this monument?" Mase asked. "Something metal, obviously," he added, nodding toward Camille.

Dani perked up a bit, straightening her spine and leaning forward. "This brings us to Becca's vision, actually. She's the one who suggested I come to you guys for help." Dani shrugged and, clearly excited, rubbed her hands together, looking from Camille, to Mase, and back. "All my ideas were lame, but Becca claimed you'd have a great one. Said all I needed to do was get you guys out to the barn, and the four of you would take it from there." Dani leaned forward and clamped her hands around Mase's foot, which was poking up under the blankets. She shook the foot excitedly. "Becca promised to help you plan it out and make it *amazing*."

Mase flashed Dani a quizzical smile, then looked at Camille, eyebrows raised in question. He wasn't surprised to find Camille grinning from ear to ear, and he knew from just looking at her that she already had a plan. He also knew, without a doubt, that it would be amazing.

With a grunt, Mase tossed his twenty-third armful of scrap metal onto the heaping pile he'd already hauled out to their little grave-yard on the hill. Arms finally unburdened, he wiped his brow. He had, for the first time in a long time, actually broken a sweat.

"That's good, Mase," Becca said from beside Camille, who was perched on the stool-sized boulder between Ky's and Ben's gravestone markers. Peter stood behind both young women. "We've got plenty to work with now."

Camille closed her journal and held her hand out to Mase, beckoning him to approach. When he reached her, she pulled him down and planted a tender kiss on his lips. A thank-you clearer than words could ever be.

Mase still wasn't sure what was about to happen, but he was anxious to find out. He was also anxious about what the strain of using her Ability so much would do to Camille—regardless of her and Peter's and Becca's assurances that she'd be fine—and about whether or not they'd be able to finish up before anyone else on the farm caught on to what they were doing.

Dani had remained back at the farmhouse to rouse the others for a big, communal New Year's Eve breakfast, a breakfast she'd hoped would keep everyone busy in the farmhouse long enough for the Re-gens to complete their work.

"Are you sure you're up for this?" Mase asked Camille, his eyes searching hers. When she nodded, no hint of uncertainty on her face, he straightened and looked at Peter. "And you? You're sure you're up for this, too?"

Smiling sadly, Peter nodded. "I'm healthier than I've been in years. It's all my mom ever wanted for me."

"Good." Mase reached over Camille and grasped Peter's shoulder. "At least in that regard, we can know that she died with peace in her heart. In the end, it's all any of us can ask for."

Swallowing roughly, Peter nodded and shifted his focus beyond Mase, to the heaping mound of junk metal staining the tranquil hilltop graveyard. "Shall we begin?"

Camille craned her neck to look up at Peter, and Mase caught half of her smile. She nodded once before her focus shifted to the mountain of metal as well. And as Peter rested his hands on both of her shoulders to boost her Ability to manipulate metal, Mase moved to the side.

"You guys might want to sit down for this," Peter said. When

Mase looked at him, his eyes were closed, his face locked in concentration.

Becca settled on the overgrown grass gracefully, folding her legs and resting her hands in her lap. For a moment, all Mase did was stare at Peter and Camille curiously. Until, that is, he had no choice but to take a knee, because the earth started groaning and shaking, and it all seemed to be coming from the pile of metal.

When Mase looked at the pile once more, he couldn't believe his eyes. It was almost like it was melting, sinking into the earth. He shook his head. Not *almost*; the scrap metal *was* sinking into the earth, being swallowed up by the hillside.

And as he watched, as he gaped at what the woman he loved was doing with her mind, something incredible happened.

It started out as a tiny, fragile sticklike thing. A sapling, Mase thought to himself, somewhere in the back of his awestruck mind. But it grew quickly, gaining height and thickness, sprouting more fragile sticklike things. *Branches,* the coherent part of Mase's mind whispered oh so quietly. Dozens, maybe hundreds of branches.

Because as Mase knelt on the ground in that small graveyard on a hill with the brand-new sun hovering mere inches over the hillside, a tree of pure metal grew out of the ground just a few dozen yards away. Its branches shimmered in the morning sunlight, reaching high and wide, sheltering the four Re-gens from the bright glare. It truly was beautiful. And impossible. And amazing.

Stunned, Mase tore his eyes from the tree of pure metal and stared, mesmerized, at Camille. At beautiful, impossible, amazing Camille.

He couldn't imagine ever loving anyone more.

49

JAKE
DECEMBER 31, 1AE

THE FARM, CALIFORNIA

J ake stood behind the farmhouse, his attention fixed on the hilltop, on what looked like metal rising up from the ground up on the hill. "What the hell..." He took a step just as the back door swung open and shut again.

"Jake?" He heard the patter of footsteps down the porch steps. "Jake, you—"

After a moment's pause, he tore his gaze away from the growing *thing*. Dani stood behind him, her curls wild and blowing in the breeze and her cheeks flushed. Her green eyes were opened wide, but for some reason, she didn't seem as taken aback by the object on the hill as he had been.

"You weren't supposed to see it yet," she said, her eyes locked beyond him. "It's supposed to be a surprise."

"Zoe asked me to find Peter," Jake said, and he looked back at the metal branches slowly extending away from what appeared to be a glinting tree trunk. "You knew about this?" When Dani didn't say anything, he looked back at her, waiting. She shook her head, unable to pull her gaze away from the metal tree growing up on the hill.

Dani snapped her eyes shut quickly and shook her head again. "I mean, yes, but no. I didn't know what they were going to make exactly, I just knew they were going to create *something*." She moved forward to stand beside Jake. "That's a big something."

"You could say that," he said and let out an amused, quiet grunt.

"We thought it would be a nice addition to tonight," Dani said. "A way to commemorate everyone."

Everyone who was gone was implied, and Jake nodded. "It's actually kind of perfect." He crossed his arms over his chest as he watched the four Re-gens atop the hill gradually cast in the forming limbs' shadows.

"Really?" Dani asked, peering up at him. "How's that?"

Jake scratched the side of his face and nodded up toward the hill, toward the graveyard. "Since Zoe has been spending so much time up there, I was going to save one of the benches I've built for the bonfire tonight and put it up there."

Dani's knowing eyes widened and her smile reached from ear to ear. "That's a great idea! Do you have one ready? Maybe Mase can put it underneath the tree, you know, before everyone sees it."

Jake nodded. "But there are a couple finishing touches I'd like to make first."

◈

Other than the chirping conversation among a family of blackbirds exploring the cool metal branches beneath their feet, there was silence. Everyone—all nineteen members of the remaining group —stood around the fabricated tree, gaping in awe.

Earlier, when Jake had seen it being created, literally coming out of the ground, he'd watched it grow into this monstrously beautiful *thing*. But seeing it up close was different. The tree was a work of art, a masterpiece. And there it was, in the center of grave hill, sprawling, captivating. Chills rushed over his skin as he took in the branches that twisted and turned, almost protective in the way they reached out over the group, like they were trying to shelter everyone beneath them.

Tom and some of the others had moved to the trunk of the tree, touching and admiring the details of the bark and the intricate leaves growing out of the metal branches. But Jake's focus was on Zoe, standing a few feet from him. Her hands covered her mouth as she stared up at the monument in amazement.

"I can't believe it," she murmured into her hands. "It's beautiful." Then, she noticed the bench. Her eyes narrowed, and hesitantly, she took a step closer. Closer, until she crouched down in front of it. Her fingertips traced the image Jake had carved on the backboard, while the fingers of her other hand moved to her hip, to where the Celtic knot tattoo was hiding beneath her clothes.

"It's not perfect," Jake said, realizing he should've asked Jason or Tom to help him with the carving. But knowing how much the symbol meant to Dani and Zoe, that it represented their unbreakable bond, it seemed appropriate, necessary even.

Zoe studied him for a moment, then shifted her gaze back to the bench. Had it been too soon to inscribe the names of the fallen into the wood; were the memories still too fresh? Jake began to wonder if he should've waited.

When Jason joined them, crouching beside Zoe, he reached out, touching one of the names that were etched among the two-by-fours. Jake had tried to capture memories of all their friends and loved ones, those who helped them fight from the beginning, like Dave and Sammy, Sarah, Ky and Ben, and those more recently lost, like those who helped to fight the General's soldiers, and Tavis, and Anna, of course.

Both Jason and Zoe seemed dumbfounded as they stood and took a step back together, assessing the entirety of the sight in front of them. While the memorial was meant as a tribute for all to appreciate, it was obvious it held special meaning to the Cartwrights. After all, every name carved on that bench was one of Zoe or Jason's friends, their family.

Zoe walked slowly over to Camille, wrapping her arms around the smaller woman's neck. There were muffled words murmured, followed by a silent, desperate squeeze before Zoe took a step back, wiped the tears from her eyes, and turned to face Mase.

His mouth quirked into a smile, and he shrugged. "It was mostly Cami—"

Zoe's arms were around his neck before he could formulate a complete, nonchalant response. She moved on to Becca next, then Peter. Tom and Jason also thanked the Re-gens, grateful for such a memorable and meaningful gift.

"It's beautiful," Tom said to Camille, and then everyone was chatting and laughing and asking questions that Camille could only smile and deflect to Mase to answer.

Tom stopped in front of Peter, and they seemed to exchange a sort of quiet conversation with their eyes. Until, finally, Tom pulled Peter against his side, his arm wrapped around the young man's shoulders. "Your mom would love it," Tom said, his voice strained.

Jake looked away, not wanting to intrude on such a private moment.

"Can you believe this thing?" Jason said, walking up to him. He pointed over his shoulder at the tree. "Who knew?"

Jake chuckled as he thought about the strangeness of watching a metal tree grow out of the ground before his very eyes. "It'll be nice to see how creative some of us can get now that everyone's Abilities aren't solely focused on defense tactics and precautionary measures." Jake grinned inwardly, remembering his conversation with Harper about his visions the night before as they sat out on the porch, having an after-dinner drink.

"Thank you…for the bench," Jason said, and he extended his hand.

Jake accepted it, noting that Jason's grip was tighter and his grasp lasted longer than necessary.

"I know it's mostly for Zoe, but…thank you," Jason said again.

Jake gave him a curt nod. "It's for everyone," he said. "We all spend enough time up here, I figured it wouldn't hurt. Besides, it's not like it's finished. I need you to fix it up for me. It's looking a little rough."

"Nah man, you did good." Jason patted Jake on the shoulder and gave one final nod of appreciation, then stepped away to reclaim Dani's hand from where she stood in a herd of people.

To Jake's surprise, Dani glanced back with a smile aimed right at him. She winked, and Jake smiled back. He turned away, but stopped short. Zoe stood in his path, her jewel-colored eyes illuminated as she stared at him. Jake almost lost himself in their vivid, hypnotic depths.

"You knew about this," she said, then her eyes widened. "That's what you were doing when you never came back to breakfast this morning."

Jake brought his palms up and shook his head. "I *saw* it, and only accidentally. I didn't know about it before that."

"Yet you still had time to make a bench to put under it?" She placed her hands on her hips and lifted one of her eyebrows. "Seems fishy." She looked back at the tree.

"There's no conspiracy, I promise," he said. "It was already something I'd been working on, a bench I'd put together for the bonfire, actually. I guess you could say I knew it had a higher purpose." He folded his arms over his chest and flashed Zoe a smirk. "It's not like I could keep a secret from you, anyway." Which was another reason he'd kept his distance from her all morning.

"You better not keep secrets," she chided and didn't hesitate as she jumped into his arms, nearly knocking him over as she wrapped her legs around his waist. She snickered, though her eyes were still a tad damp, with happiness, he hoped. "I love you," she said and placed a kiss against his lips. "Thank you, all the time, for everything."

Jake laughed. "For everything?" His grip around her tightened. "Even when you say I nag you about your clothes, or when I tell you you've been snoring?"

Zoe rolled her eyes. "No, but for everything else—and I don't snore." She playful batted at him before settling back into his hold. "Thank you for waking me up early to watch the sunrise and for making sure I get the last cup of coffee. That sort of thing."

A deep laugh rumbled from his chest. "Yeah, well, that's more about self-preservation."

"I can respect that," Zoe said and her smile grew. "So, does this mean we're short a bench for tonight's festivities?" She glanced at those few who still lingered around the tree, everyone else already heading back down the hill.

"I'm sure we'll figure something out."

Zoe's mouth quirked up at the corner, and her eyes filled with mischief as she leaned her forehead against his. "Who needs a seat when there are always dark corners to hide in?" Her eyebrows danced merrily, making Jake chuckle again.

"This is true," he agreed.

Zoe kissed him once more, but this time her lips lingered on his and her eyes remained shut. "One of these days..." She breathed out slowly. "We'll have a place of our own, a quaint little house up on the next hill, still close but not *that* close. And we can do whatever we want, *wherever* we want."

Jake's blood rushed faster, felt warmer. "That sounds nice," he groaned. "Soon the farmhouse won't fit us all, anyway."

Zoe pulled away and tilted her head to the side. "Are you alluding to *our* family, Mr. Vaughn, or to someone else's?"

Tucking a stray lock of hair behind her ear, Jake shrugged. "Our family, Dani's family, Biggs and Harper's families..."

Zoe straightened, her mouth hanging open. "What? Chris is

pregnant? And she didn't say anything?" He could hear her appre-hension and excitement. "I didn't sense it?"

"Calm down," Jake laughed. "I don't think so, at least not yet."

"Buuut…" Zoe prompted.

"But Harper's had two, very similar visions these past couple weeks, and it seems likely she will be at some point. He's obvi-ously happy, but also afraid." Harper knew how dangerous preg-nancy was for her, not just because of the lingering effects of the Virus, but childbirth in general.

"So *that's* what's been distracting him."

"Yes, but don't say anything, Zoe. I'm not sure he's told Chris yet." Harper had been worried how she would respond, given the fact that she'd already lost her two boys.

"H would be a wonderful dad—and Chris with her own child in her arms—they'd be a beautiful family."

Zoe jumped down, out of Jake's arms, and laced her fingers with his. "Either way, you're right, we *definitely* need a place of our own. Our kids are getting their own room, because Mama's gonna need her beauty sleep." Zoe peered at him, a knowing grin on her face as they made their way back down the hill.

Jake couldn't wait to start their family—to have a sense of purpose and normalcy…even if he did still need a bit more finesse when it came to the whole taking-care-of-the-kids part of it.

Zoe laughed and squeezed his hand. "Don't worry, you'll have plenty of time for practice," she told him, clearly mind-lurking.

Jake shook his head. "You just couldn't help it, could you?"

She laughed. "I'm only kidding. You'll be a great father," she said, and she ran ahead of him as he reached for her, evading him. She smirked. "There have to be some perks to this Ability, right?" She flashed him a smile that made him unbelievably happy.

Jake followed after her, thinking those teal eyes he'd been destined to save had become his whole world. He'd never felt more whole and at home than he did with Zoe, and he couldn't wait to start his new life with her by his side.

50

ZOE

DECEMBER 31, 1AE

THE FARM, CALIFORNIA

Dani and I sat on our knees on the perfectly placed bench, each of us wrapped in our respective blankets as we etched our initials into the trunk of the metal tree. Although it was a dark night, with only a sliver of moonlight, and there was a bit of wind, being outside with only the dogs for us to worry about and our companionable silence was a nice reprieve from all the commotion down at the farm. It was New Year's, which meant we'd had a late dinner and there would be celebration and bonfires long into the night.

"It's hard to believe it's been over a year since everything changed," Dani said quietly. "I mean, time's gone by really fast, and I guess, really slow."

I nodded, thinking the same thing. "And all the people we've lost. It's hard to believe that, too." I was still trying to accept the fact that despite my family's role in their deaths, it had all seemed inevitable from the beginning. Fate had a funny way of taking choice away from you, no matter how in control of your life you thought you were.

"Hey, Zo?"

"Yeah, D?"

Dani paused from etching her and Jason's initials in the tree. "Do you think it's true what people used to say, that those that die are up there, looking down on us right now?" She pointed to the sky.

I couldn't help but smile. "I've thought about that so many times. You have no idea."

"And? What have you decided?" Dani readjusted the blanket around her and faced me.

Looking at her, her eyes sparkling in the moonlight, I nodded. "I think that life isn't what we thought it was. Everything seems predetermined, and everyone has a destiny." I thought about it for a minute.

"Maybe your mom and Sarah and Grams are sitting around a campfire," she said, and I wondered if Alice and Tavis might be together, too. "And they're listening to Ky and Ben retelling stories of their mischievous childhoods." Dani laughed. "I can picture it perfectly."

I laughed softly, and then we fell silent again, Cooper and Jack still scouring the hillside, following the scents of critters burrowed underground for the night.

"And we're here, home on our little farm, spending New Year's Eve celebrating their lives and all that's happened," Dani said, and she unfurled herself and scooted off the bench down onto the grass. Lying on her back, she stared up at the stars through the metal branches above her.

Needing no invitation, I joined her, wiggling close for warmth as we stared up at the bright, silvery pinpricks in the sky. "Yes, we are." I felt an unexpected sense of happiness. Tonight was bigger than celebrating the closing and start of a new year. It was still hard to fathom all that we'd lost leading up to the General's death. And I wasn't just thinking about my mom. Everything that had happened, our friends who had died, had all been in the name of

451

freedom…it had all been about fighting for the right to survive, to live. And we'd done it. Things would be different for all of us now.

"So, does that mean it really does feel like home to you now, Zo—and not in a bad way?" Dani peered over at me, her fire-red curls fanning out around her porcelain-white face. "Like *home*-home?"

"Yeah, D," I said, deciding that for as much as she'd changed, Dani was still Dani. That it would always be us, and that's all I needed. "It feels like *home*-home." I stared up at the twinkling stars, trying to remember any of the constellations I used to know. "I think that's Ursa Major," I said, pointing as if Dani could see which star out of the millions I meant.

"Yep, it sure is. And that's Orion's—"

A thin, glowing white comet trail shot through the sky, and we both squealed, "A shooting star!"

After a few giggles and the novelty had worn off, I thought about the last time we'd gone stargazing. It must've been four or five years ago, whenever I was last home before she'd moved to Washington. Then I thought about all the close calls and how many times we almost lost each other, almost never had this moment. "But here we are," I whispered.

"What's that, Zo?"

I rolled onto my side to face her. "I was just thinking about how long we've been friends, almost our entire lives."

"And we have another eighty years with each other, too," Dani sang happily.

I snorted. "Wow, we're going to be really old."

"That's right, so you better not get tired of me too soon, other-wise you're screwed."

I stared at my best friend, newly sister-in-law, as she rested her open hand on her slightly protruding belly. "Never, D."

"Oh, hey!" Dani chirped and rolled toward me. "Did Chris tell you about her and Vanessa's new project?" Dani waved her hand. "Well, it's not like they've started anything, but—"

I laughed. "What it is, D?"

She grinned from ear to ear. "They want to figure out a way to help other Crazies."

"Really?"

"Yep. They're still working out the specifics, but these Abilities of ours have gotta be good for something, right?"

I nodded, having thought the same thing many times. "Yeah. That's great—"

"You ladies planning on joining us?" Sanchez's voice echoed in my mind. *"Daniel says it's almost time."* Dani and I exchanged fretful glances.

"I guess we should head back," I said, climbing to my feet, then helping Dani up. I tightened the blanket around her.

"How long have we been up here, anyway?" she asked, but I wasn't sure.

I shrugged. "All I know is we don't want to miss Grayson's fireside speech." Wanting to join the others before the sun rose, we clomped our way down the hill, back toward the farm.

"Come on, boys," Dani said, calling to the dogs who bounded past us.

Dani and I trudged across the farm, headed toward the flames that danced by the pond. The closer we drew, the louder the chattering voices became. On special occasions like this, it wasn't just our group that huddled around a bonfire—or bon*fires,* tonight—but dozens of Re-gens had come to join us, as well— those who wanted to celebrate their new lives free from Herodson. Those who had hope for a second chance at life, an actual future.

When we finally reached the group, Dani and Jason shared a silent exchange, and Jake offered me a full, heart-stopping smile, one that I hoped was a promise of unspeakable things to come before we resurfaced from bed tomorrow. His eyes were gleaming, and I wondered how much he'd had to drink. I couldn't resist returning his smile, and I leaned down for a kiss.

"Yum," I said, licking my lips. "Spicy. Sweet. Rum?" I asked, glancing down at his empty glass.

"Harper's concoction," he nearly purred, and I kissed him again. "Oh boy, we're in trouble." I shed my blanket, already getting warm so near to the fire's blaze. "I'll grab a drink and get you a refill," I offered and took his glass before I headed over to the cart we'd set up as a mobile bar. Grayson was studying the liquor bottles lined up along the edge of the cart, his reading glasses on the tip of his nose. "Need some help, Mr. G?"

He startled and looked over his shoulder at me. "Well, actually, yes." I knew he was nervous about the speech. Not the act of speaking, but its importance tonight.

"Here, let me help," I said and looked at his empty glass. "What do you like to drink?"

"I generally prefer something smooth, but I'm not too picky."

Opening a bottle of Scotch, I motioned for him to hold his glass out. "A few sips of this should do the trick." I winked at him, knowing he wasn't a big drinker.

Grayson held his glass out and nodded in thanks, then he headed back to his seat near the fire.

"Uh-oh! The bartender's back!" Dani called as she wiggled into the seat beside Jason.

I presented a mock bow to the onlookers. "That's right, *Mrs.* Cartwright," I said. "And what can I get for *you* this fine celebratory evening? I can make the best cocktails in all the land." I gestured to the plethora of options lined up behind me. "Something refreshing? Something sweet? Something that fizzes and pops?"

"How about something nonalcoholic," Jason grumbled, his gaze cutting to Dani's stomach.

I glared at him. "Thanks for stating the obvious, Jason."

Dani squinted, pursing her lips as she thought. "How about something warm?"

"You got it," I said, and I nodded to Harper, who sat closest to the kettle. "H, a hot toddy for the pretty lady, please. Hold the rum." I glanced around at the faces around me. "Any other takers?"

Peter and Sam were leaning back in their chairs, chatting between themselves and paying not an iota of attention to me. Carlos met my eyes and shook his head, Annie curled up in his lap as she stared into the flames, her eyes heavy with sleep, and Vanessa, who was wrapped in a blanket in the chair beside him, was content to stare into the fire, too.

Chris sat up and stuck her mug out for Harper to refill. "Rum in mine though, please," she said.

Harper stared at her mug.

"What?" Chris said. "What's wrong with you? Pour," she demanded. I tried not to react as Harper considered his options.

Finally, he said, "Are you sure? Have you been feeling alright?"

Chris's brow furrowed, and she shoved her drink at him. "Of course, I feel fine. Fill 'er up," she insisted. As Harper slowly poured what looked like only a drop into her drink, Chris reached out and tipped the butt of the bottle up a tad more. "Keep going," she said. "It's been a long week." Finally, she put her palm out for him to stop, and Harper looked more than relieved.

I glanced at Dani. Her eyes were fixed on me, questioning.

"What's the smile for?" she asked me silently.

I smiled again and turned around so no one would see it— though Jake caught my eye, and I shied away. *"I'm not supposed to say anything,"* I admitted, but I couldn't help it. I told Dani my secret—Harper's secret. *"Harper saw a vision...of Chris pregnant."*

"Whaaaaaaat!" Dani squealed in my head, but when I looked back at her, her face was still, save for the small twitch at the corner of her mouth.

"Not now, but sometime in the future, and he's freaking out. He's not sure how she's going to react. And you know how he is about the dangers of pregnancies as it is."

"Understandable." She glanced at Harper. *"And you know this how? Did he tell you?"* Dani asked, her face a perfect mask of indifference.

"Jake told me," I explained, *"but Harper confided in him, so don't say anything, D. But can you believe it! Harper, a dad? Chris, another baby?"*

"No, I can't. But I'm so happy if it's true!"

"There's going to be a lot more drinking if there's going to be a lot more babies," I silently mumbled, making Dani laugh.

After pouring myself some of Harper's tincture and refilling Jake's glass with the same, I turned around, winked at Dani, and headed back over to Jake; his eyes were on me, unmoving, like he could hear the conversation Dani and I were having. I flashed him a bright smile of reassurance and nestled in beside him.

It was soon after that when I watched Grayson down what was left of his Scotch and wipe his whiskered mouth with the back of his hand. He cleared his throat. "Attention, everyone!" he called from beside the cart. "I'd like to share a few thoughts with you, before dawn."

I peered out at the mass of people and bonfires stretching along the edge of the pond. Heads, young and old, "normal" and Re-gen alike, turned in Grayson's direction. Conversations quieted.

Out amidst the shadows, I noticed three figures moving toward us. Becca, Mase, and Camille. The three of them sat in the grass nearby. Becca smiled at her brother, then at me before she turned her full attention to our orator.

My old history teacher stepped up to the cart, poured himself another gulp of Scotch, and righted himself before taking a deep breath. "Now," he started, "for those of you who don't know me, my name is Daniel Grayson. I've lived in this area all my life, taught history and told stories to Jason, Zoe, and Danielle since they were wee ones." He smiled in our direction, then took a swig of his Scotch. He coughed. "Boy," he said, "that's strong stuff." There were quiet chuckles in the crowd.

Grayson cleared his throat dramatically. "The people of New Bodega know me for my storytelling, because when you get to be my age, you have a *lot* of stories to tell. So, I guess that's why I was elected to speak tonight. But I'm not here to tell you a story." He paused for a moment, and I saw images of his life flash through his mind. "I've seen a lot throughout my life; I've lost loved ones and had my share of struggles. But nothing remotely close to what the last year has brought us.

"We've been stripped of everything we once had and who we once were. We've been thrust into a world we're only just beginning to understand. We've done things against our will and made decisions we wish we could unmake. We've had to pull ourselves up by the bootstraps and adapt and change to everything that's been thrown our way. We have new Abilities to embrace and explore and, with them, new dangers to look out for. We've lost friends and have made new ones, but we've also made enemies. We've experienced raw, unfathomable heartache, loneliness, and desperation. And we've lost hope a time or two." He held up his index finger. "But..." He let the word trail off as he assessed us all.

"*But*, we've overcome all of it. Sitting here, tonight, together— this is a testament to our strength." Grayson's eyes skirted over to the horizon, and I noticed the purples and blues of dawn beginning to break beyond the hillside. "Tonight—no, today," he continued, "is about celebrating a year of survival and newfound hope. It's about being with our friends and loved ones and remembering those that are no longer with us—their sacrifices and their footprints left in our lives. Today is about taking time to appreciate life, which, as you all know far too well, is unpredictable and can be far too fleeting. So please," Grayson continued, holding up his Scotch, "raise your glasses to a year past and a new year to come. I wouldn't want to be stuck here with anyone else."

Collectively, we all raised our glasses, the sound of sniffles and crackling fire all I could hear. "Happy New Year, everyone," Grayson said, and there was an encore of cheers and Happy New

Year wishes as the sky came to life, radiating a promise of hope and life and new beginnings. We toasted to our pasts and celebrated our futures.

I took a drink, then another, before I looked to Jake. His eyes were shimmering, just as I knew mine were, and he wrapped his arms around me, pulling me against him. "Happy New Year, Zoe," he whispered.

"Happy New Year," I whispered back. I kissed him, letting the promise it held linger a moment before I rose to my feet. Becca was standing beside us, her eyes bleary, which made my chest tighten. I gave her a hug while Jake shook Mase's hand. "Happy New Year, Becca," I said, squeezing her tightly as I remembered who she'd been when she'd first joined us in Colorado.

"Happy New Year, Zoe," she rasped.

We all moved around the campfire, hugging each other and sniffling, wishing each other a prosperous new year, minus the drama and danger of the year past. I gave Sam and Annie each a giant hug, and Annie jumped up into Jake's arm, flirting with him like she did with all the boys. Sanchez and Biggs, each holding a sleeping twin in their arms, gave us awkward hugs. And I laughed as Harper nearly lifted me off the ground, his hug all Harper-enthusiasm. I couldn't imagine a hug from him being any other way. My dad and Peter were standing beside Grayson, the men laughing about something, old times maybe, though my dad's smile didn't reach his eyes.

I leaned in and gave Peter a big squeeze. "I'm happy you decided to stay with us," I said, meaning every word of it.

Peter stepped away from me and shrugged. "You're all the family I have left now," he said, but despite the ache I still felt in his heart, I knew he was happy to be with us.

"Hey, sweetheart," my dad said, coming up to me. He wrapped his arms around me, his hold solid and comforting. I hugged him back, more than happy we were together, that I had my dad, my brothers, Dani, and Jake to start the next chapter of my life with.

But when I reached Jason and Dani, I couldn't will the tears back any longer.

Dani's arms were around me so fast I nearly lost my balance. "Love you, Zo," she cried into my shoulder.

I squeezed her tighter, laughing and sobbing at the same time. "Love you, too, D. Happy New Year."

When I tried to pull away, her embrace tightened. "I'm not ready to let go," she sniveled.

"That's okay, D. Me neither," I halfheartedly joked, then something occurred to me. "Next year, this time, you'll have a little one in your arms, D. Can you believe it?"

That made her step back, and she beamed at me. "No, not really." Laughing under her breath, she shook her head.

I nudged her. "You know we'll need to plan a girl's night every now and again, right? Make time for your old friend Zoe." I winked at her.

Dani laughed. "I wouldn't have it any other way."

I kissed her cheek. "To next year, then," I said. "To families and babies and copious amounts of drinking."

"To next year," Dani laughed, and her arms tightened around me again. "Happy New Year, Zo."

The End

Thank you for reading The Ending Series, we hope you enjoyed Dani and Zoe's adventures. For more Ending Series fun, check out:

The Beginnings: Origin Stories
&
World Before: A Collection of Stories

MORE BOOKS BY THE LINDSEYS

ALSO BY LINDSEY SPARKS

ECHO WORLD

ECHO TRILOGY
Echo in Time
Resonance
Time Anomaly
Dissonance
Ricochet Through Time

KAT DUBOIS CHRONICLES
Ink Witch
Outcast
Underground
Soul Eater
Judgement
Afterlife

FATELESS TRILOGY
Song of Scarabs and Fallen Stars
Darkness Between the Stars

THE NIK CHRONICLES
(Patreon exclusive serial)

LEGACIES OF OLYMPUS

ATLANTIS LEGACY
Sacrifice of the Sinners
Legacy of the Lost
Fate of the Fallen
Dreams of the Damned
Song of the Soulless
Blood of the Broken
Rise of the Revenants

ALLWORLD ONLINE
AO: Pride & Prejudice
AO: The Wonderful Wizard of Oz
Vertigo
AO: LOOKING GLASS
(Patreon exclusive serial)

**THE LAST
VAMPIRE QUEEN**
(Patreon exclusive serial)
Season 1: Awakened

ABOUT LINDSEY POGUE

Lindsey Pogue is a genre-bending fiction author, best known for her soul-stirring, post-apocalyptic survival series, Savage North Chronicles and Forgotten Lands. As an avid romance reader with a master's in history and culture, Lindsey's adventures cross genres and push boundaries, weaving  together facts, fantasy, and timeless love stories of epic proportions. When Lindsey's not chatting with readers, plotting her next storyline, or dreaming up new, brooding characters, she's generally wrapped in blankets watching her favorite action flicks with her own leading man. They live in Northern California with their rescue cats, Beast and little girl Blue.

Access VIP Vault Exclusive stories, audiobooks, and more!
www.lindseypogue.com/newsletter

PATREON: https://www.patreon.com/lindseypogue
LINKTREE: https://linktr.ee/authorlindseypogue

MAIN SOCIAL MEDIA

FB Reader Group: Lindsey Pogue Reader Group
TikTok: @authorlindseypogue
Instagram: @authorlindseypogue
YouTube: Lindsey Pogue

OTHER SOCIAL MEDIA

Facebook: @authorlindseypogue
Pinterest: @authorlindseypogue

ABOUT LINDSEY SPARKS

Lindsey Sparks lives her life with one foot in a book—so long as that book transports her to a magical world or bends the rules of science. Her novels, from Post-apocalyptic (writing as Lindsey Fairleigh) to Time Travel Romance, always offer up a hearty dose of unreality, along with plenty of history, intrigue, adventure, and romance.

When she's not working on her next novel, Lindsey spends her time hanging out with her two little boys, working in her garden, or playing board games with her husband. She lives in the Pacific Northwest with her family and their small pack of cats and dogs. www.authorlindseysparks.com

PATREON: https://www.patreon.com/lindseysparks

MAIN SOCIAL MEDIA
FB Reader Group: Lindsey's Lovely Readers
Instagram: @authorlindseysparks
YouTube: Author Lindsey Sparks
Discord: discord.gg/smTeDHQBhT

OTHER SOCIAL MEDIA

Facebook: @authorlindseysparks
TikTok: @authorlindseysparks
Pinterest: @authorlindseysparks

www.authorlindseysparks.com/join-newsletter

CPSIA information can be obtained
at www.ICGtesting.com
Printed in the USA
BVHW072251100123
655899BV00005B/681

9 781949 485042